Behind the Scenes With Burt

OTHER BOOKS

Breaking Cat News

Elvis Puffs Out

Lupin Leaps In

Take It Away, Tommy!

Behind the Scenes with Burt

GEORGIA DUNN

 A **BREAKING CAT NEWS** ADVENTURE

Andrews McMeel
PUBLISHING®

FOR MY SON,

LUKE FAILLACE.

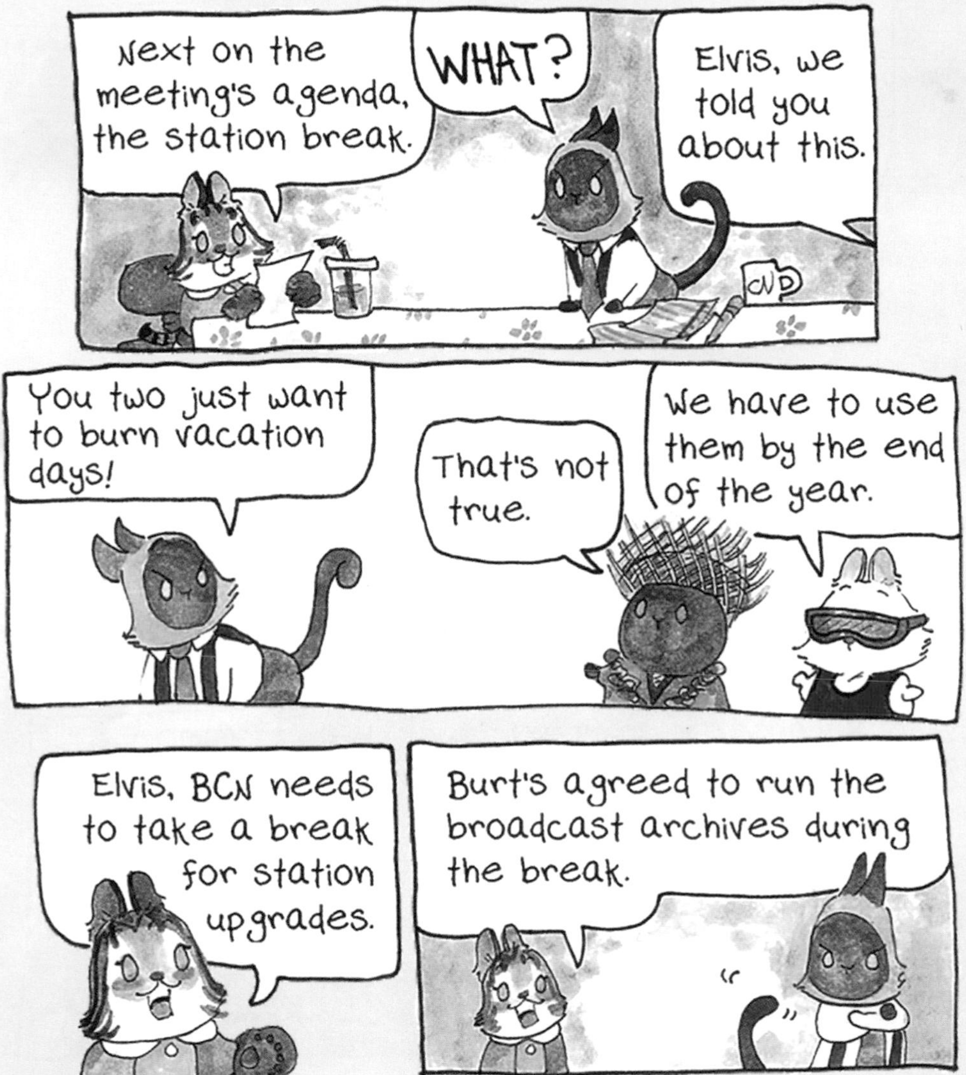
Next on the meeting's agenda, the station break.
WHAT?
Elvis, we told you about this.
You two just want to burn vacation days!
That's not true.
We have to use them by the end of the year.
Elvis, BCN needs to take a break for station upgrades.
Burt's agreed to run the broadcast archives during the break.

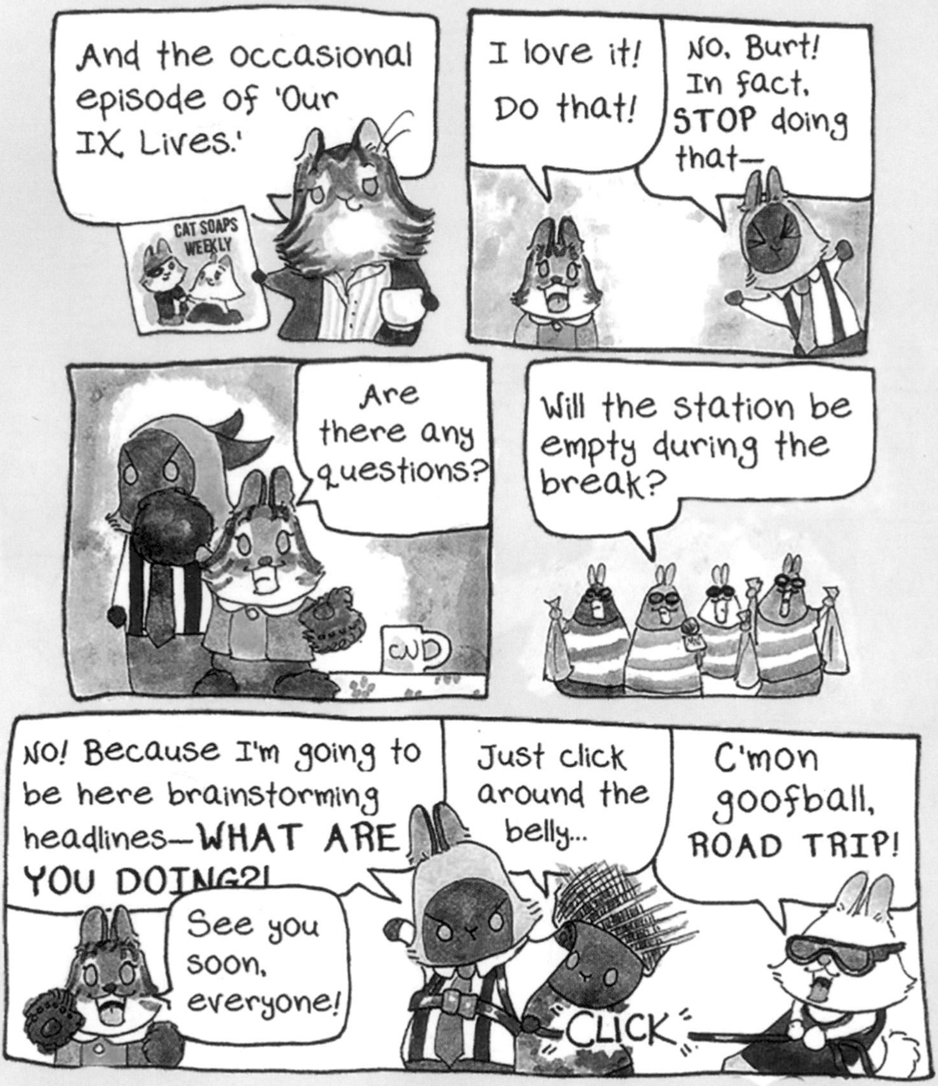
And the occasional episode of 'Our IX Lives.'
CAT SOAPS WEEKLY
I love it! Do that!
NO, Burt! In fact, STOP doing that—
Are there any questions?
CWD
Will the station be empty during the break?
NO! Because I'm going to be here brainstorming headlines—WHAT ARE YOU DOING?!
See you soon, everyone!
Just click around the belly...
CLICK
C'mon goofball, ROAD TRIP!

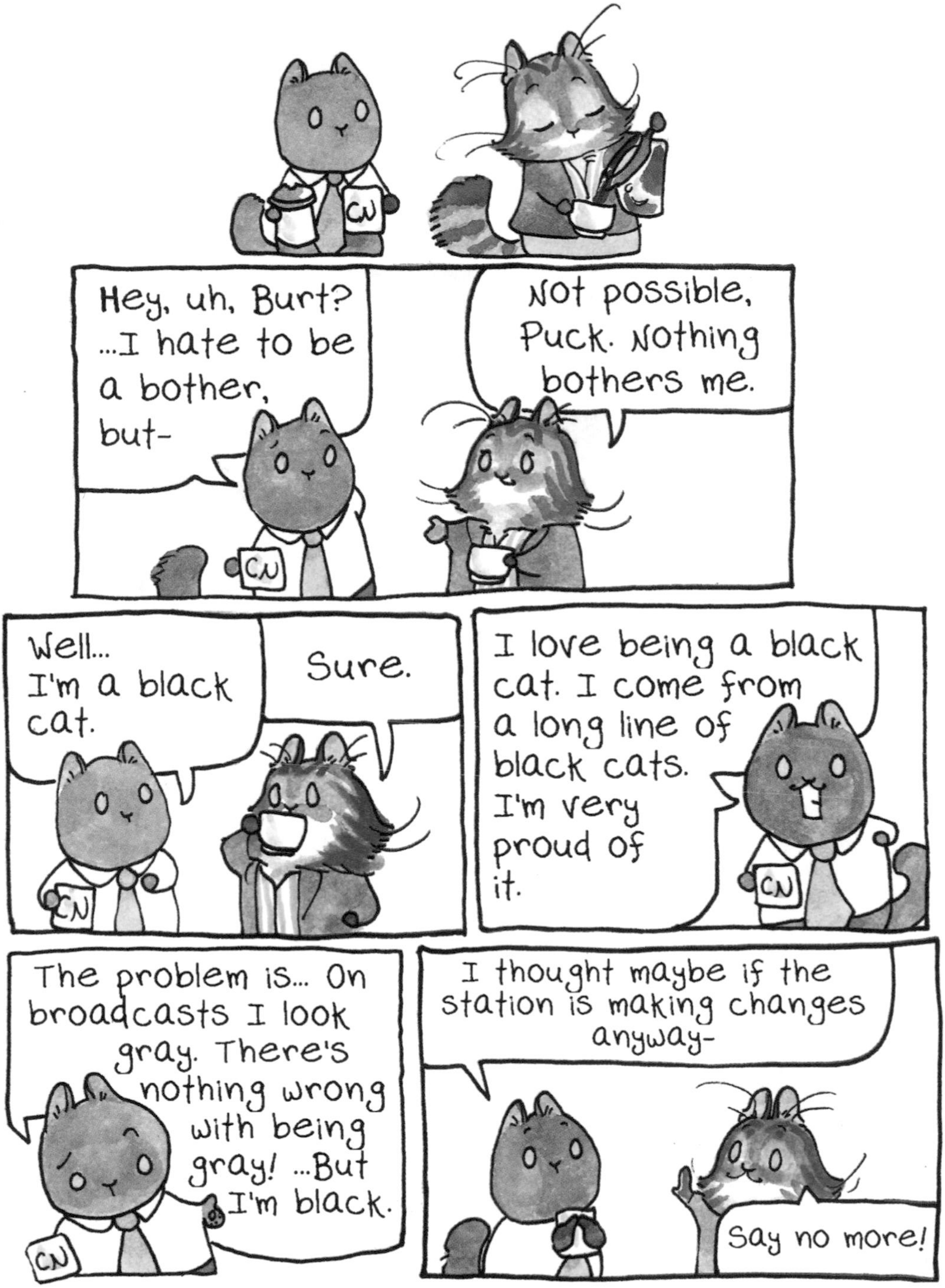
Hey, uh, Burt? ...I hate to be a bother, but-
Not possible, Puck. Nothing bothers me.
Well... I'm a black cat.
Sure.
I love being a black cat. I come from a long line of black cats. I'm very proud of it.
The problem is... On broadcasts I look gray. There's nothing wrong with being gray! ...But I'm black.
I thought maybe if the station is making changes anyway-
Say no more!

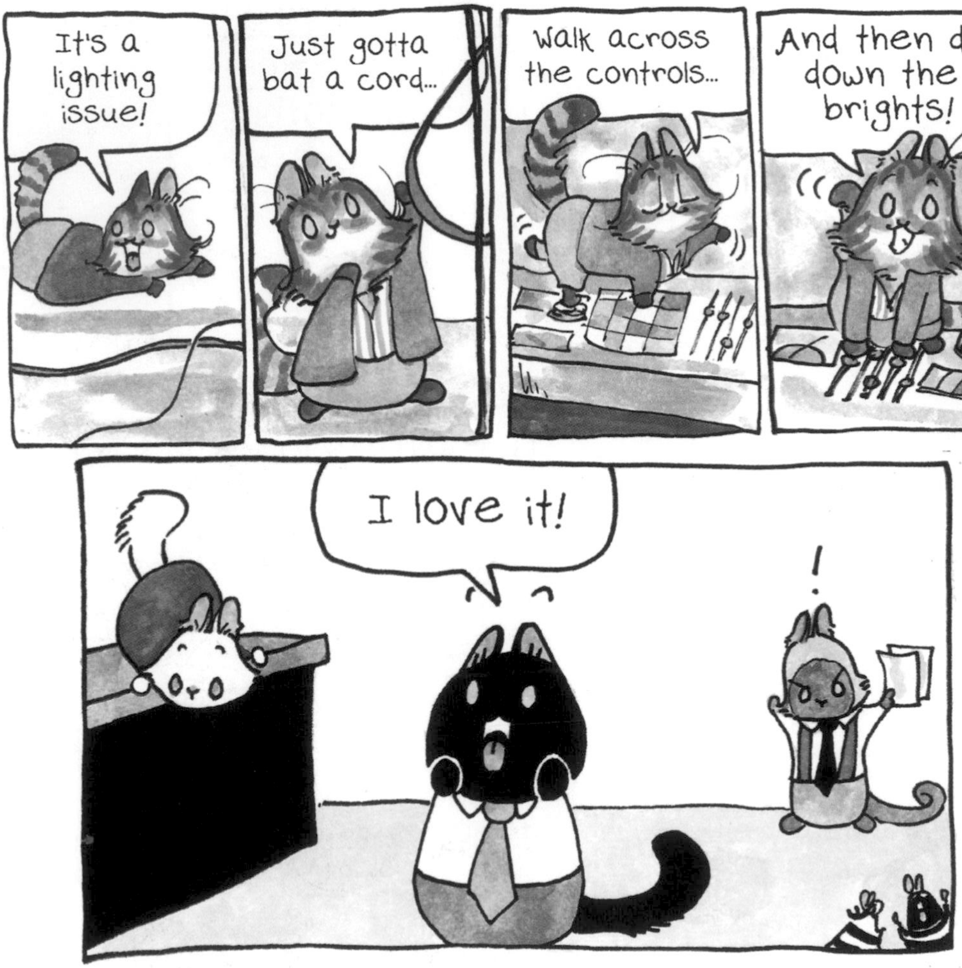
It's a lighting issue!
Just gotta bat a cord...
Walk across the controls...
And then dial down the brights!
I love it!
!

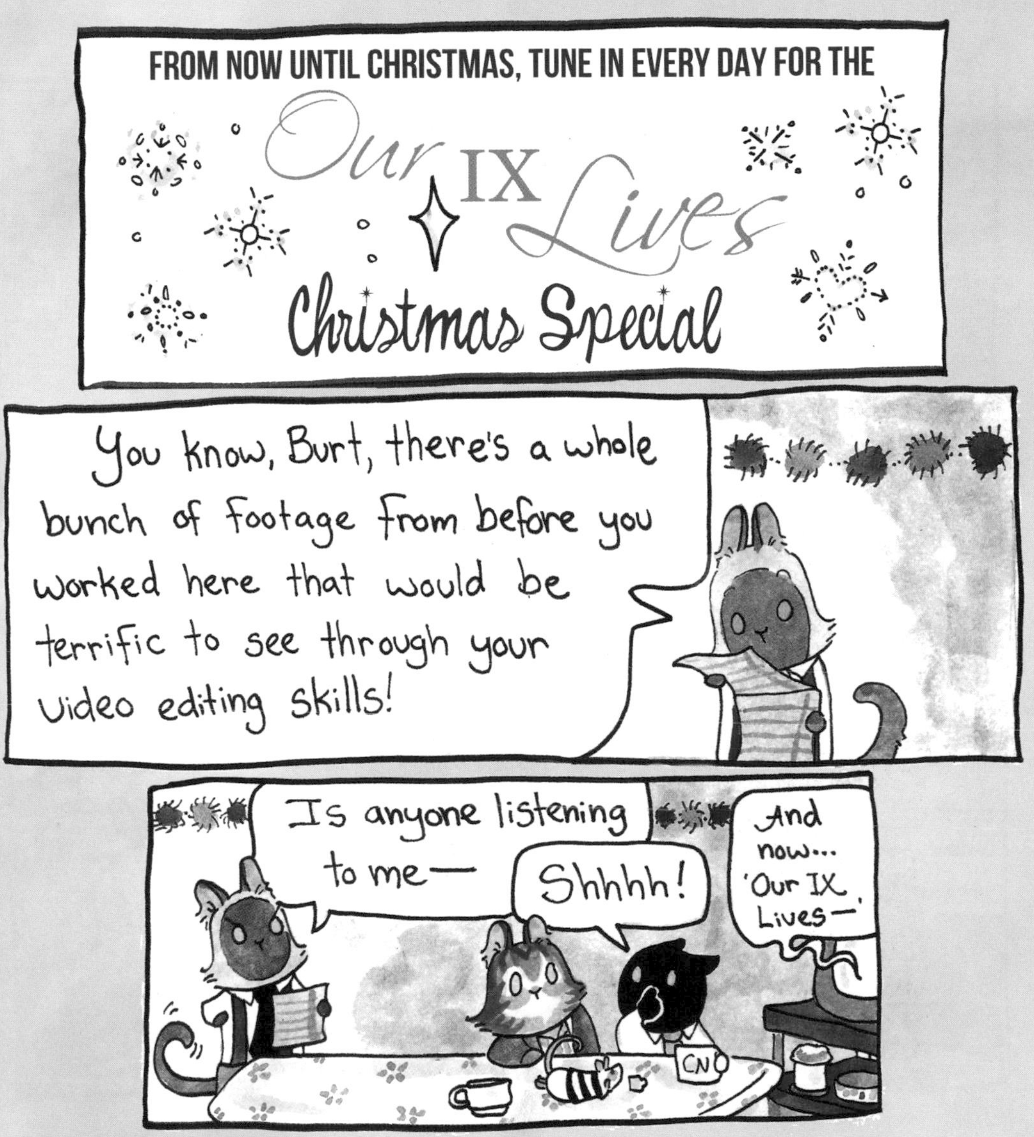
FROM NOW UNTIL CHRISTMAS, TUNE IN EVERY DAY FOR THE
Our IX Lives
Christmas Special
You know, Burt, there's a whole bunch of footage from before you worked here that would be terrific to see through your video editing skills!
Is anyone listening to me—
Shhhh!
And now... 'Our IX Lives—'
CN

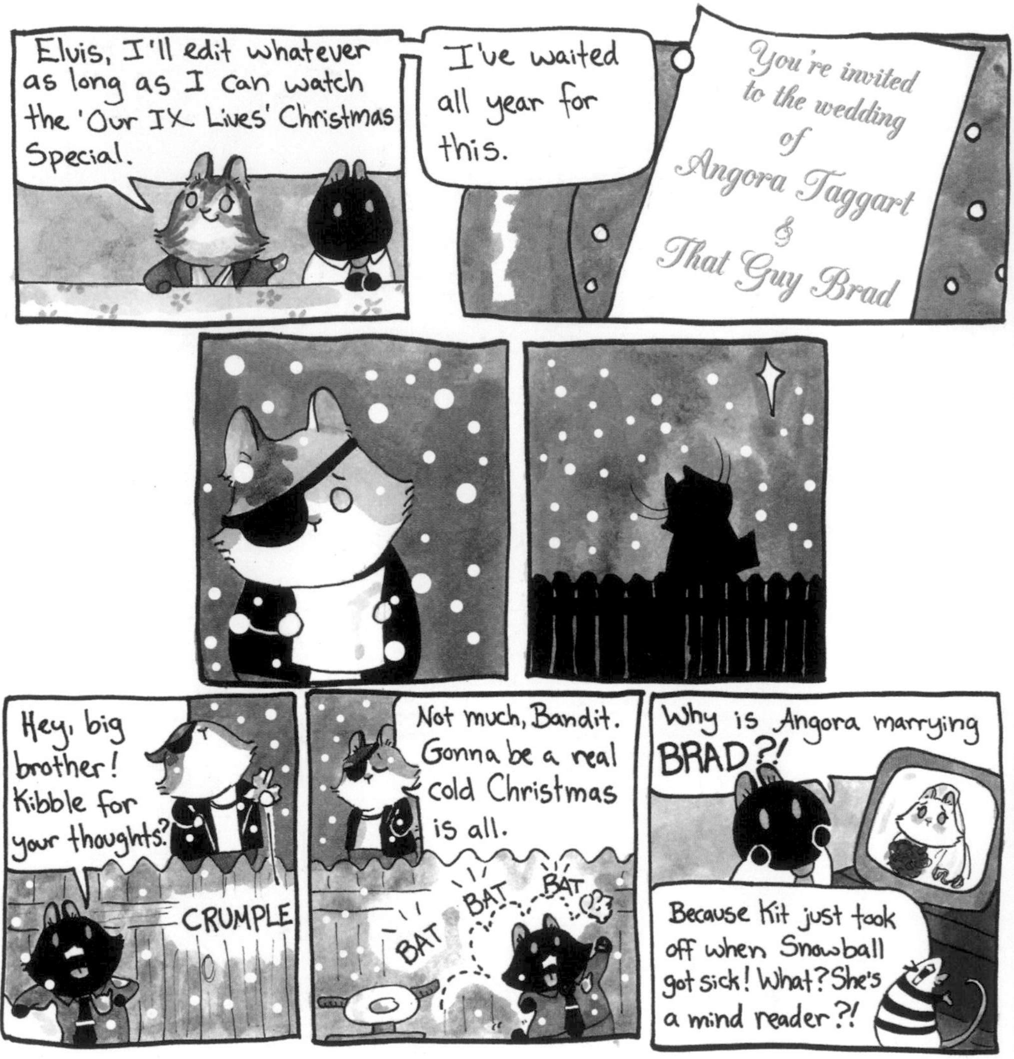

Elvis, I'll edit whatever as long as I can watch the 'Our IX Lives' Christmas Special.
I've waited all year for this.
You're invited to the wedding of Angora Taggart & That Guy Brad
Hey, big brother! Kibble for your thoughts?
CRUMPLE
Not much, Bandit. Gonna be a real cold Christmas is all.
BAT
BAT
BAT
Why is Angora marrying BRAD?!
Because Kit just took off when Snowball got sick! What? She's a mind reader?!

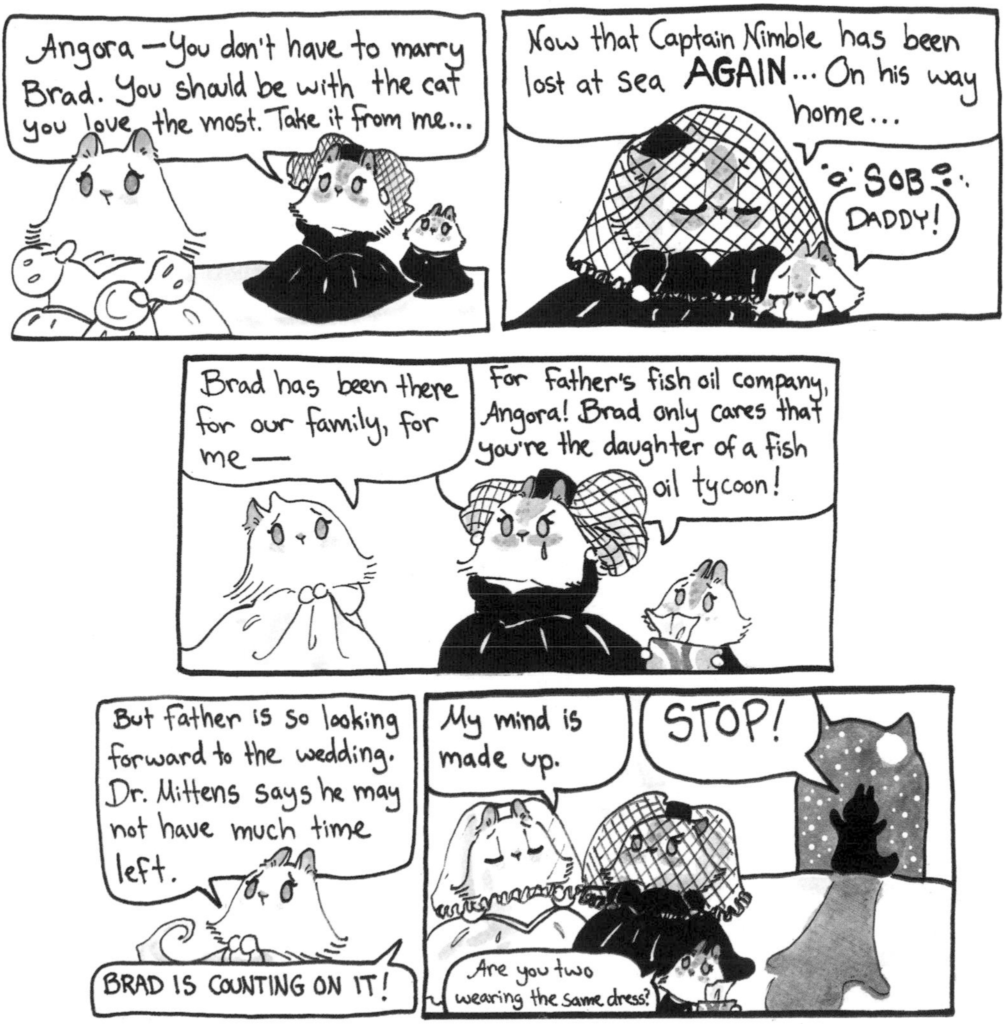

Angora — You don't have to marry Brad. You should be with the cat you love the most. Take it from me...
Now that Captain Nimble has been lost at sea AGAIN... On his way home...
SOB
DADDY!
Brad has been there for our family, for me —
For father's fish oil company, Angora! Brad only cares that you're the daughter of a fish oil tycoon!
But father is so looking forward to the wedding. Dr. Mittens says he may not have much time left.
BRAD IS COUNTING ON IT!
My mind is made up.
STOP!
Are you two wearing the same dress?

This wedding must not take place!

If it proceeds, I foresee only BETRAYAL, COOL HIGH SPEED CHASES, AND GREAT DANGER.

AUNT PAISLEY!

It's Paisley, Captain Nimble's PSYCHIC TWIN SISTER!

No one has seen her since she helped Bandit escape from jail!

That was before Bandit had a spiritual experience while trapped in a mine shaft and joined the police force.

OH, THAT PAISLEY.

Our IX Lives

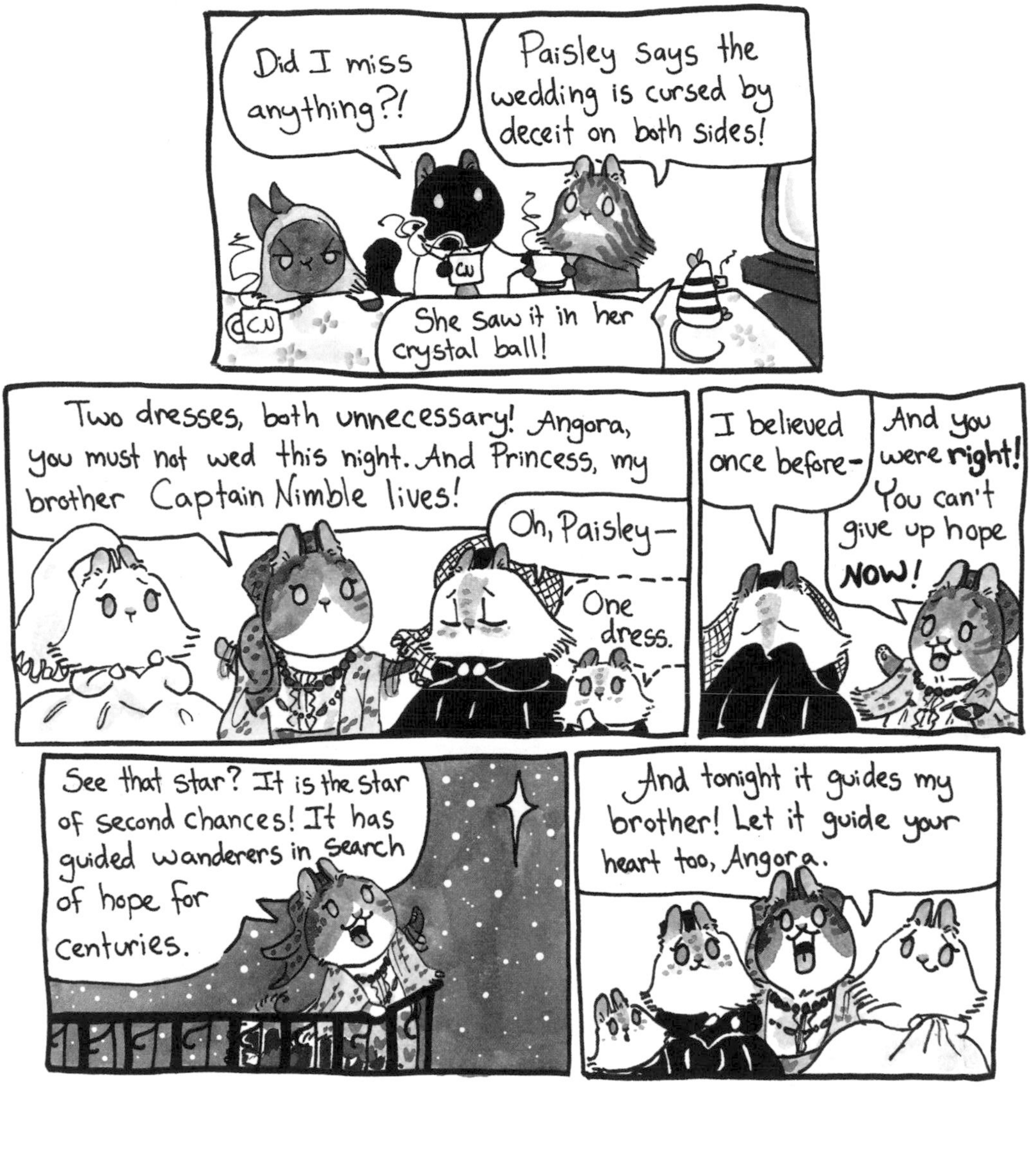
Did I miss anything?!
Paisley says the wedding is cursed by deceit on both sides!
She saw it in her crystal ball!
CU
CU
Two dresses, both unnecessary! Angora, you must not wed this night. And Princess, my brother Captain Nimble lives!
Oh, Paisley—
One dress.
I believed once before-
And you were **right**! You can't give up hope **NOW**!
See that star? It is the star of second chances! It has guided wanderers in search of hope for centuries.
And tonight it guides my brother! Let it guide your heart too, Angora.

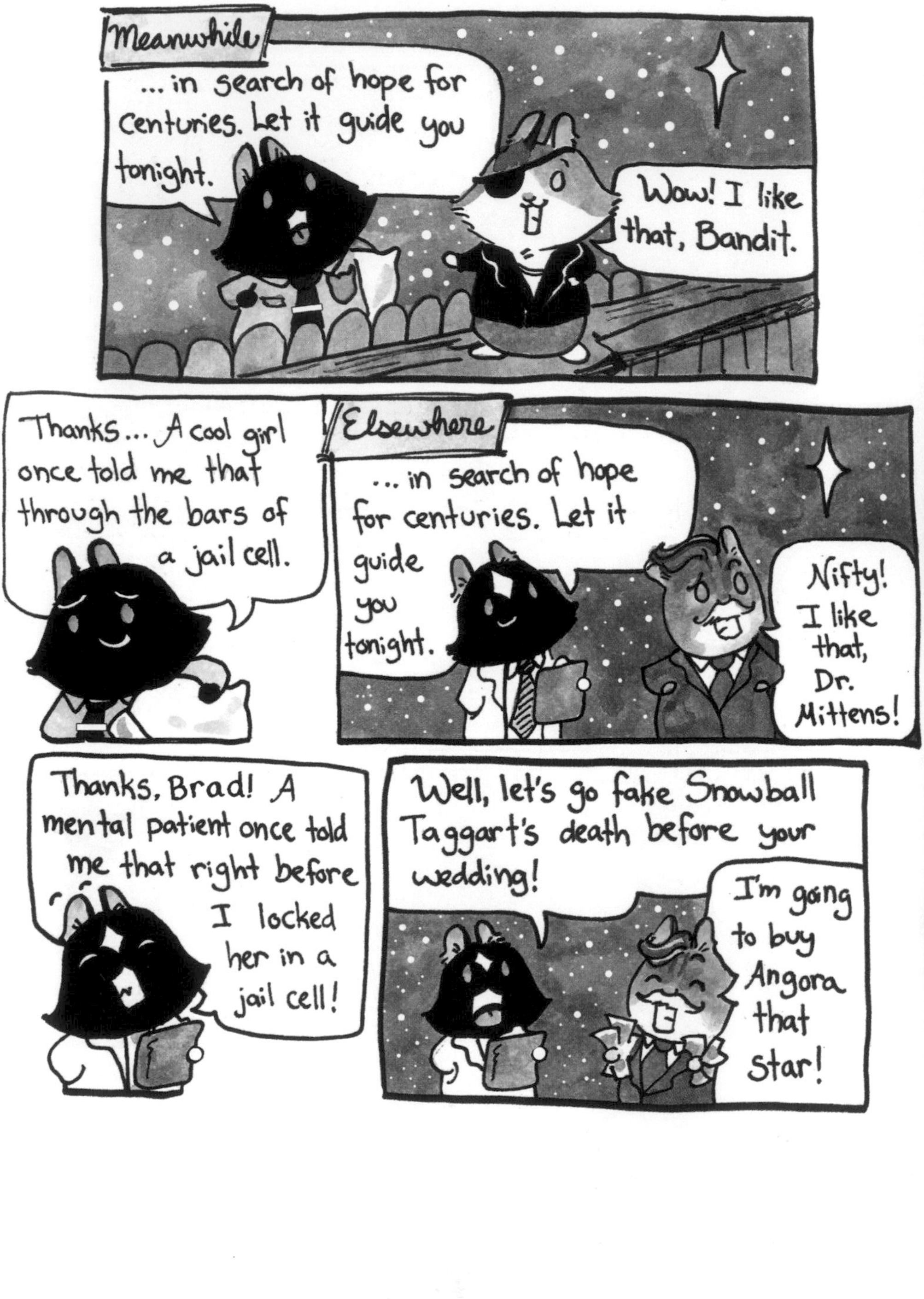
Meanwhile
...in search of hope for centuries. Let it guide you tonight.
Wow! I like that, Bandit.
Thanks... A cool girl once told me that through the bars of a jail cell.
Elsewhere
...in search of hope for centuries. Let it guide you tonight.
Nifty! I like that, Dr. Mittens!
Thanks, Brad! A mental patient once told me that right before I locked her in a jail cell!
Well, let's go fake Snowball Taggart's death before your wedding!
I'm going to buy Angora that star!

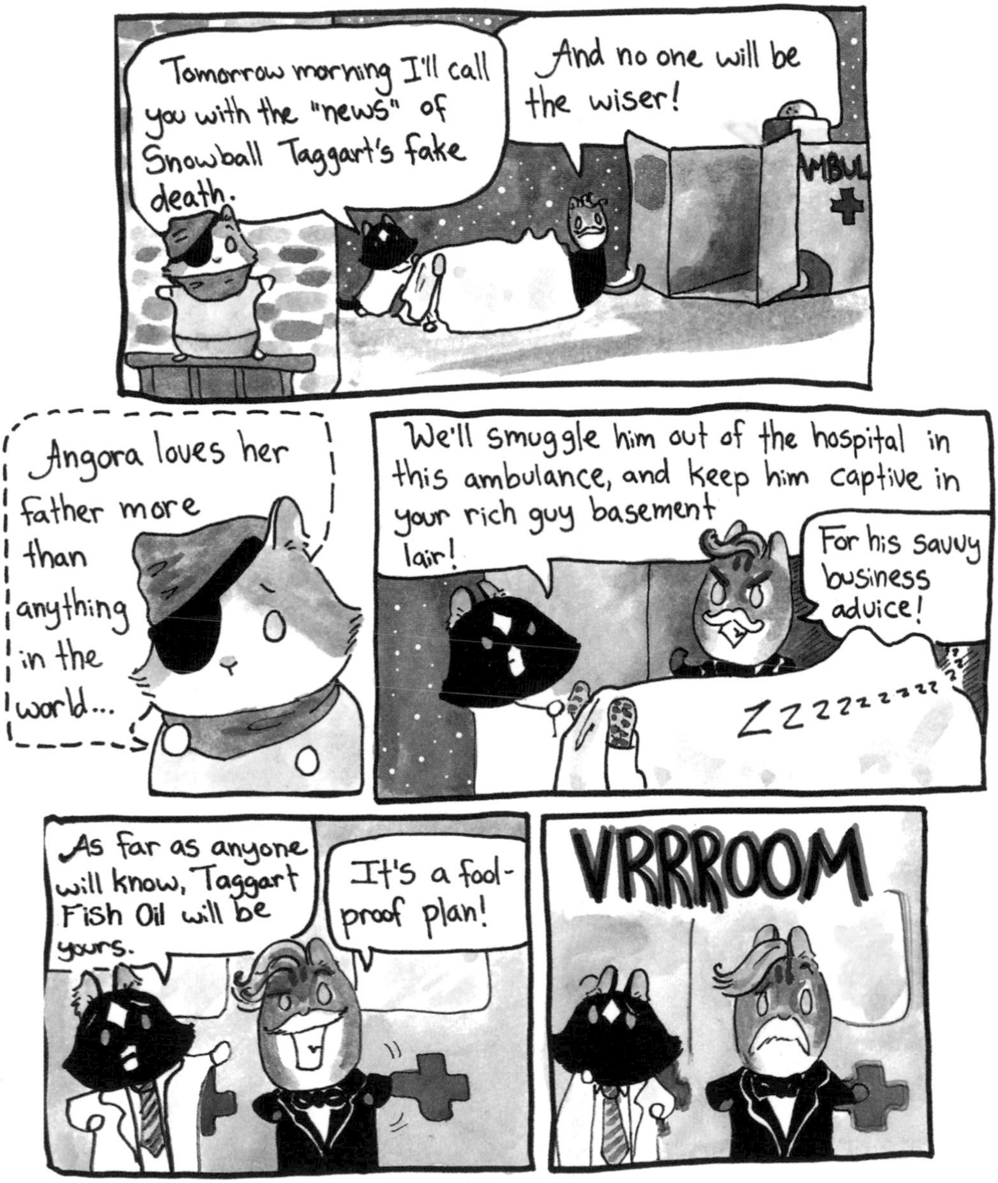
Tomorrow morning I'll call you with the "news" of Snowball Taggart's fake death.
And no one will be the wiser!
AMBUL
Angora loves her father more than anything in the world...
We'll smuggle him out of the hospital in this ambulance, and keep him captive in your rich guy basement lair!
For his savvy business advice!
ZZZZZZZZZ
As far as anyone will know, Taggart Fish Oil will be yours.
It's a fool-proof plan!
VRRROOM

Mmm?

What...?
What is
happening?

Stay calm,
Mr. T!

I'm going to get you
somewhere safe!

No, no, **no** —

I'd rather be harmed by
the **rich** than saved
by the **poor**!

I'm not
doing this
for you.

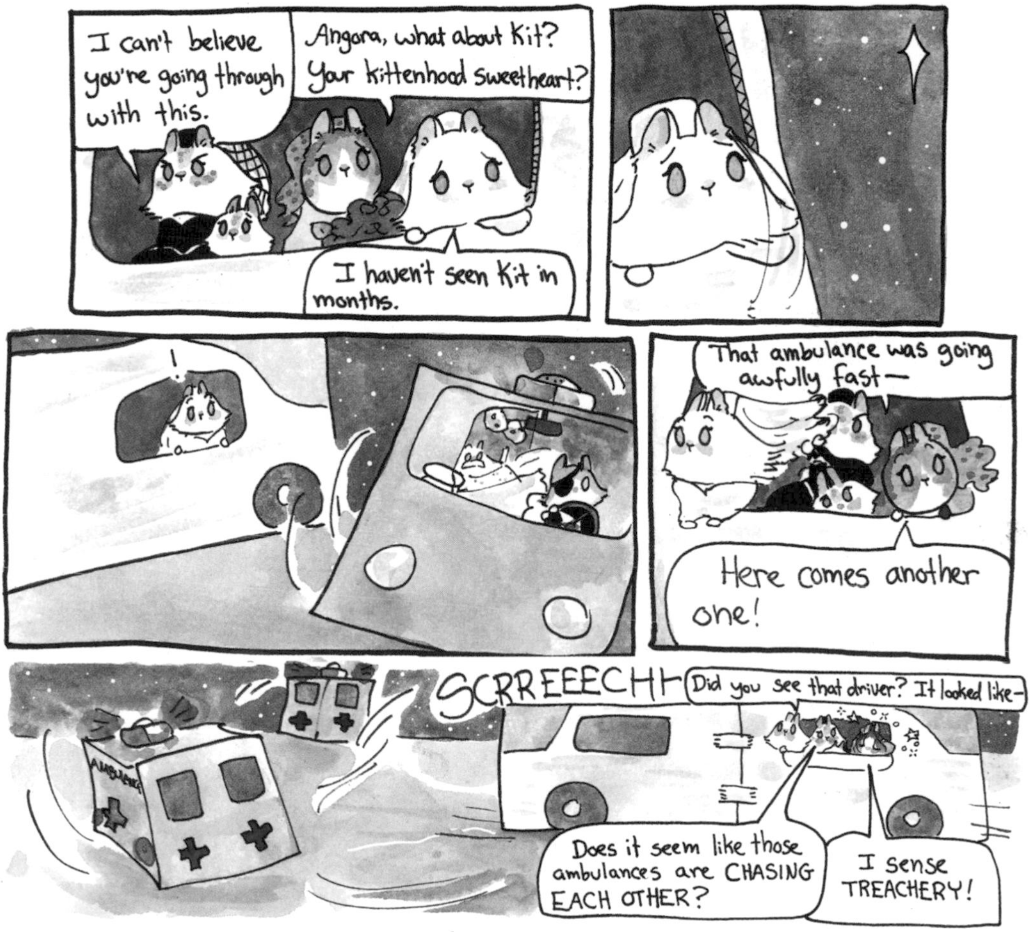
I can't believe you're going through with this.
Angora, what about Kit? Your kittenhood sweetheart?
I haven't seen Kit in months.
!
That ambulance was going awfully fast—
Here comes another one!
AMBULANCE
SCRREEECH!
Did you see that driver? It looked like—
Does it seem like those ambulances are CHASING EACH OTHER?
I sense TREACHERY!

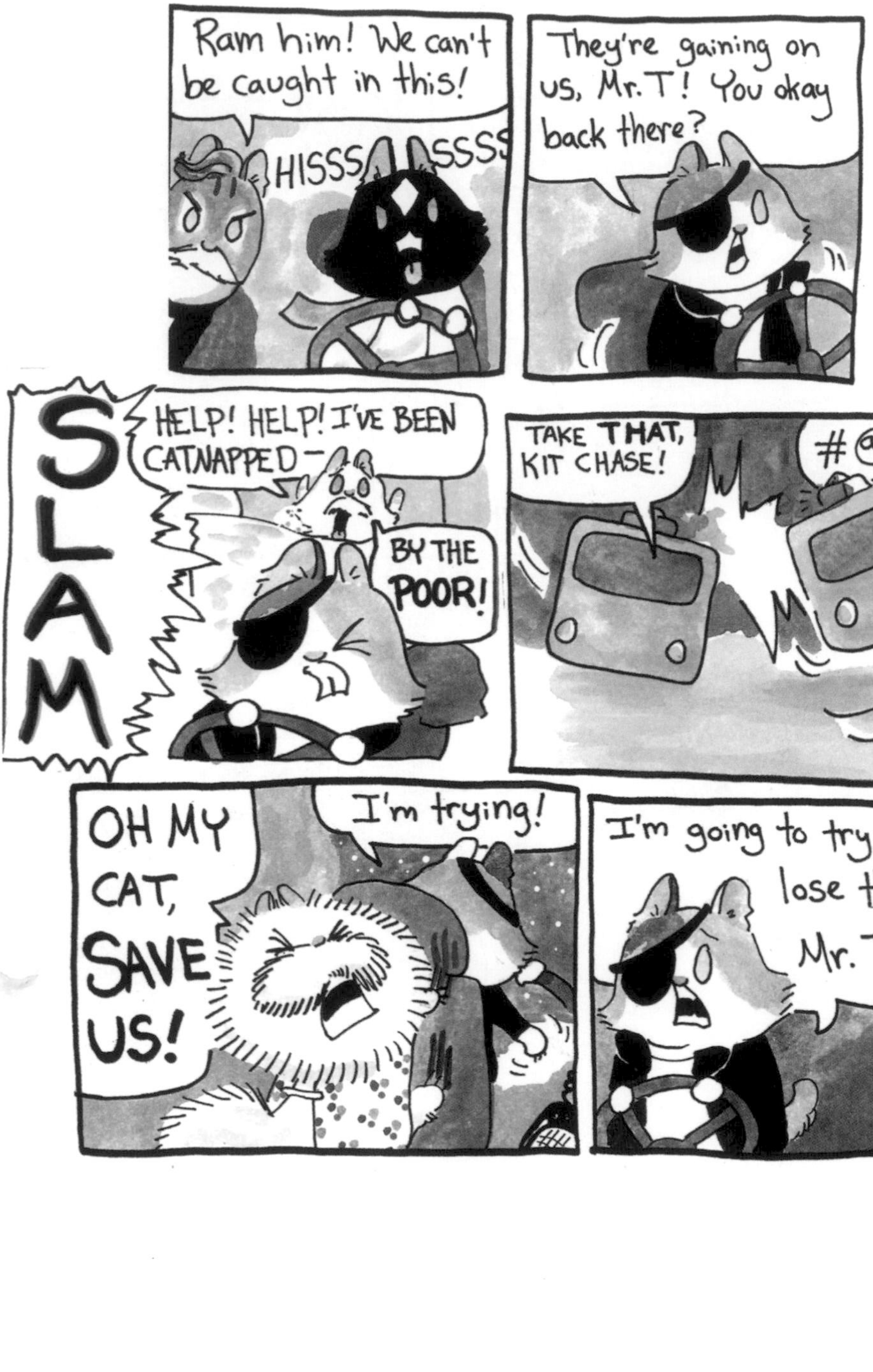

Ram him! We can't be caught in this!
HISSSSSSS
They're gaining on us, Mr. T! You okay back there?
SLAM
HELP! HELP! I'VE BEEN CATNAPPED—
BY THE POOR!
TAKE THAT, KIT CHASE!
#@☆!!
OH MY CAT, SAVE US!
I'm trying!
I'm going to try to lose them, Mr. T!

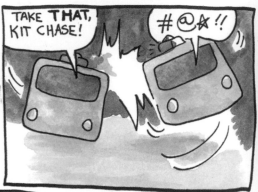

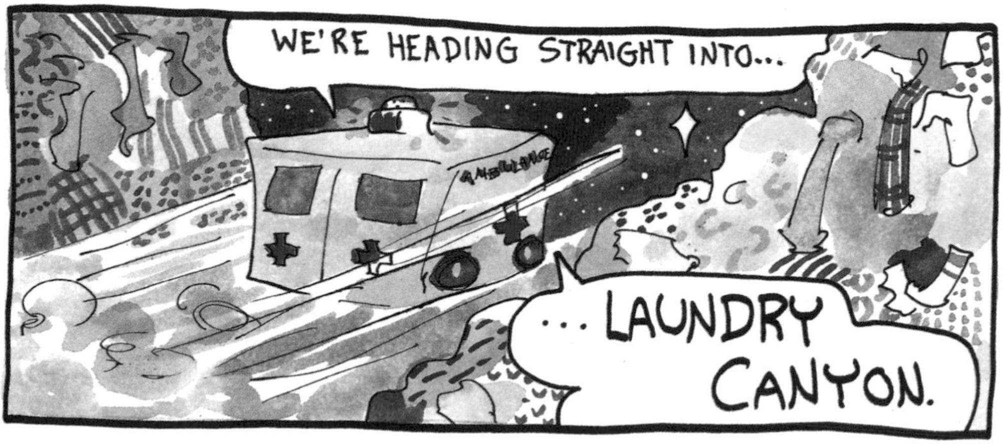
WE'RE HEADING STRAIGHT INTO...
...LAUNDRY CANYON.

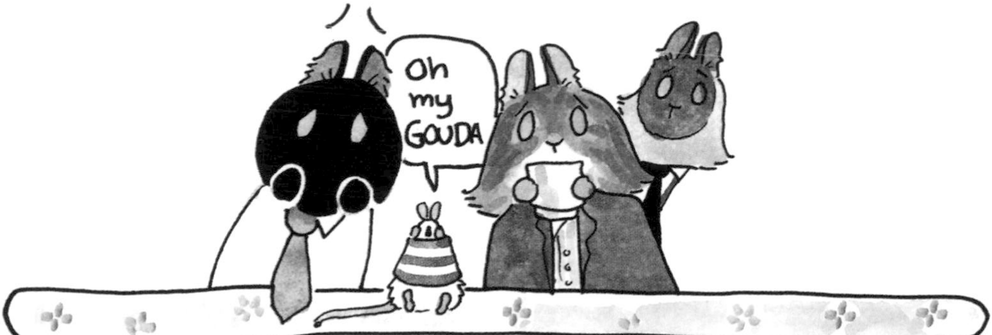
Oh my GOUDA

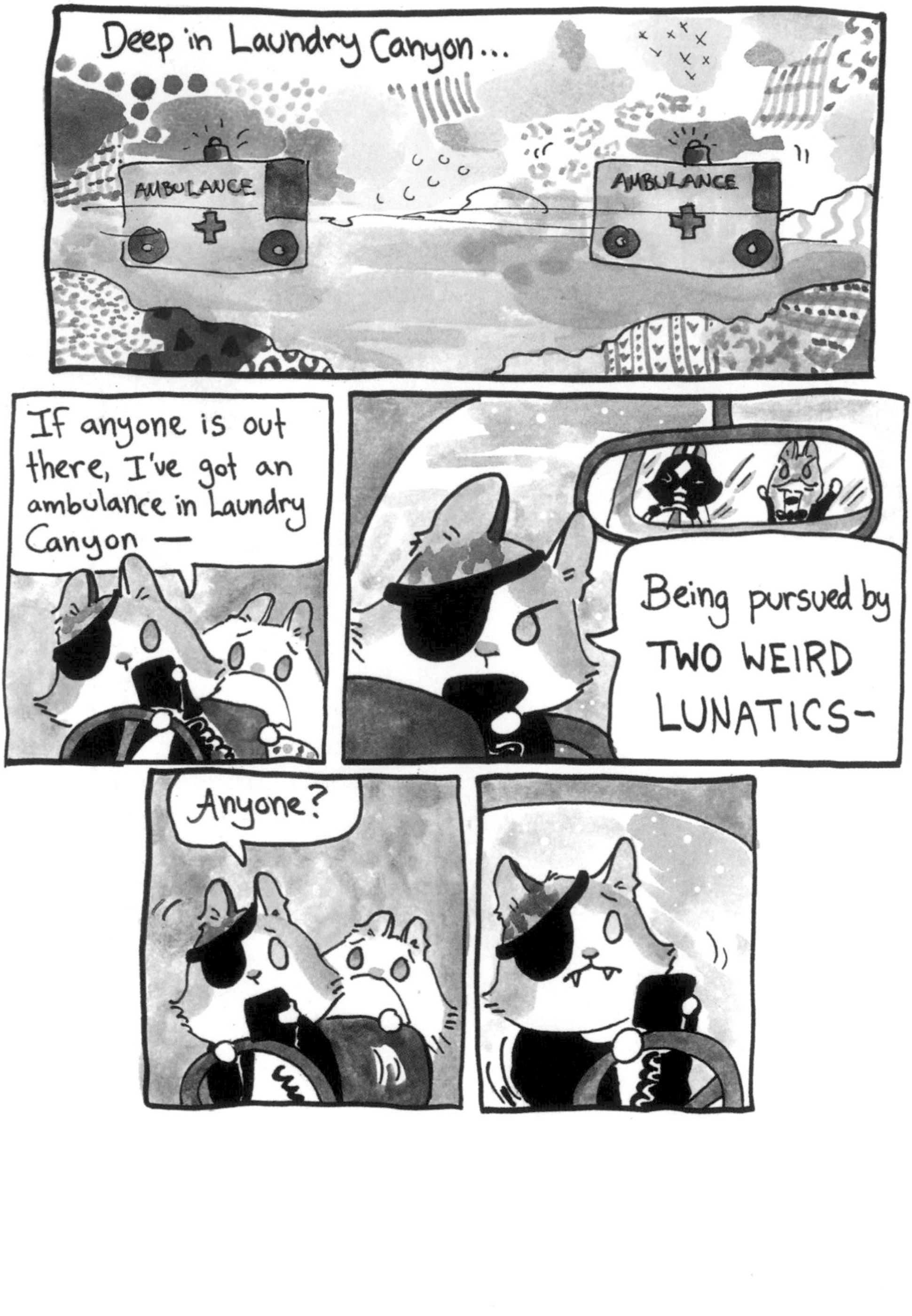
Deep in Laundry Canyon...
AMBULANCE
AMBULANCE
If anyone is out there, I've got an ambulance in Laundry Canyon —
Being pursued by TWO WEIRD LUNATICS-
Anyone?

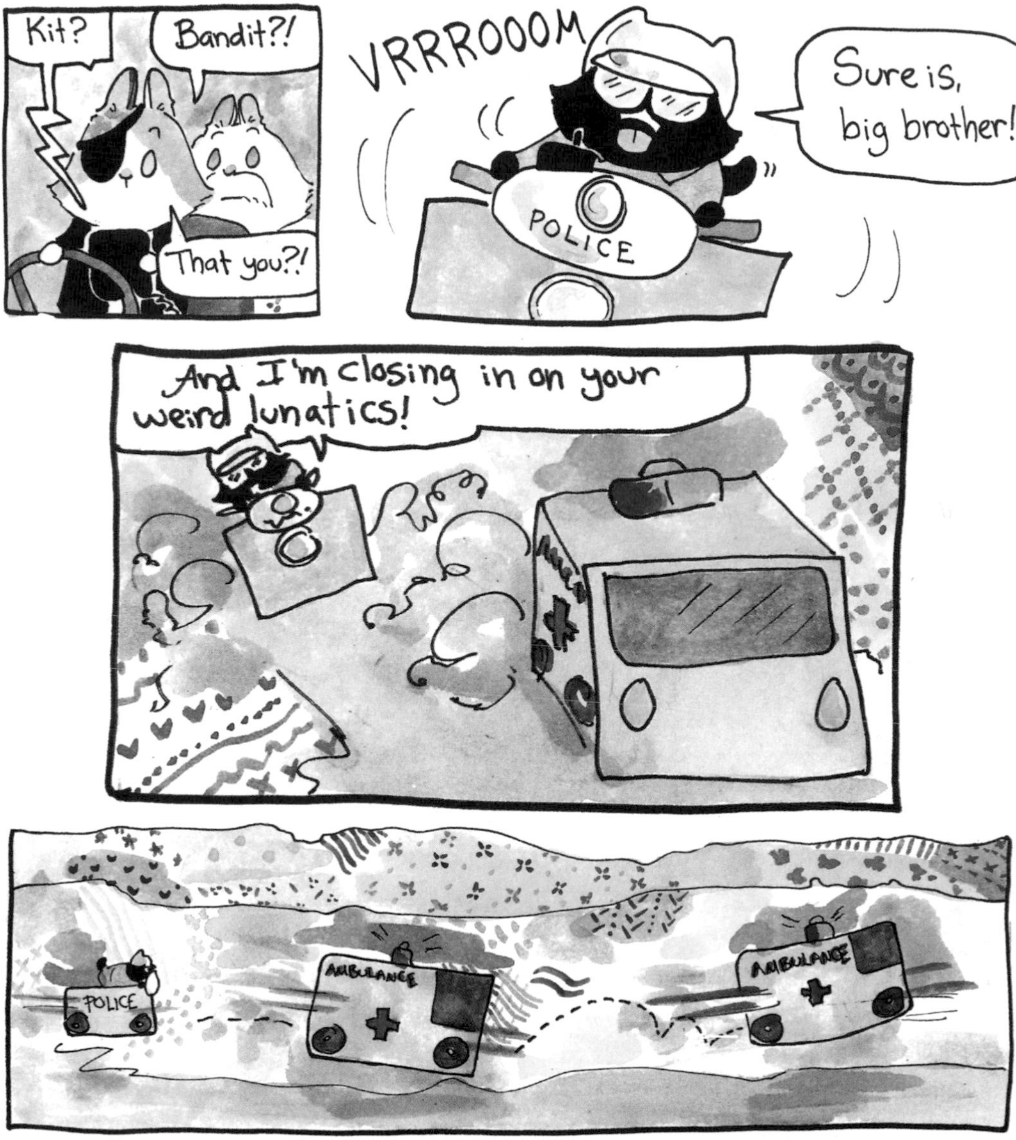
Kit?
Bandit?!
That you?!
VRRROOOM
POLICE
Sure is, big brother!
And I'm closing in on your weird lunatics!
POLICE
AMBULANCE
AMBULANCE

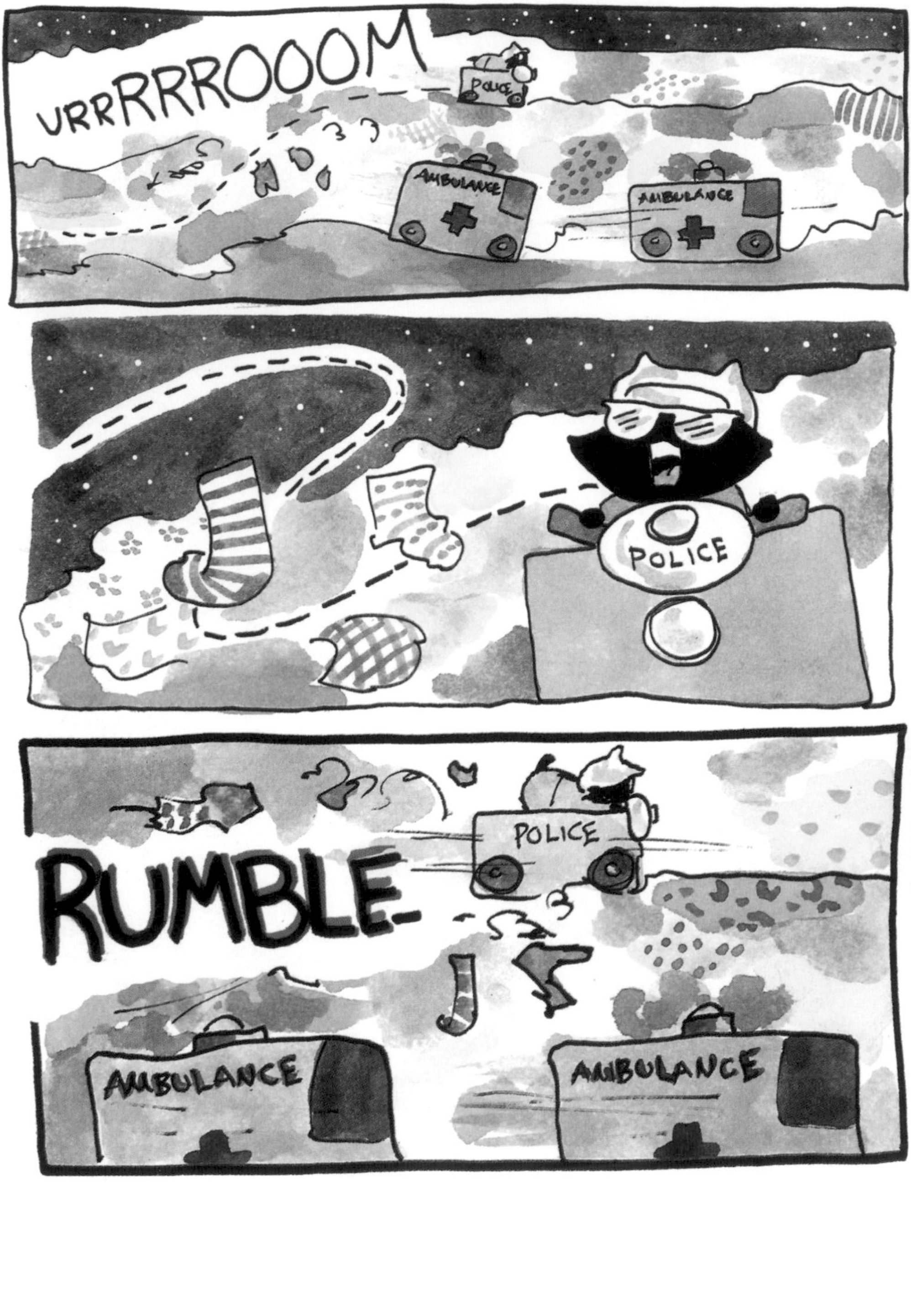
URRRRROOOM
POLICE
AMBULANCE
AMBULANCE
POLICE
RUMBLE
POLICE
AMBULANCE
AMBULANCE

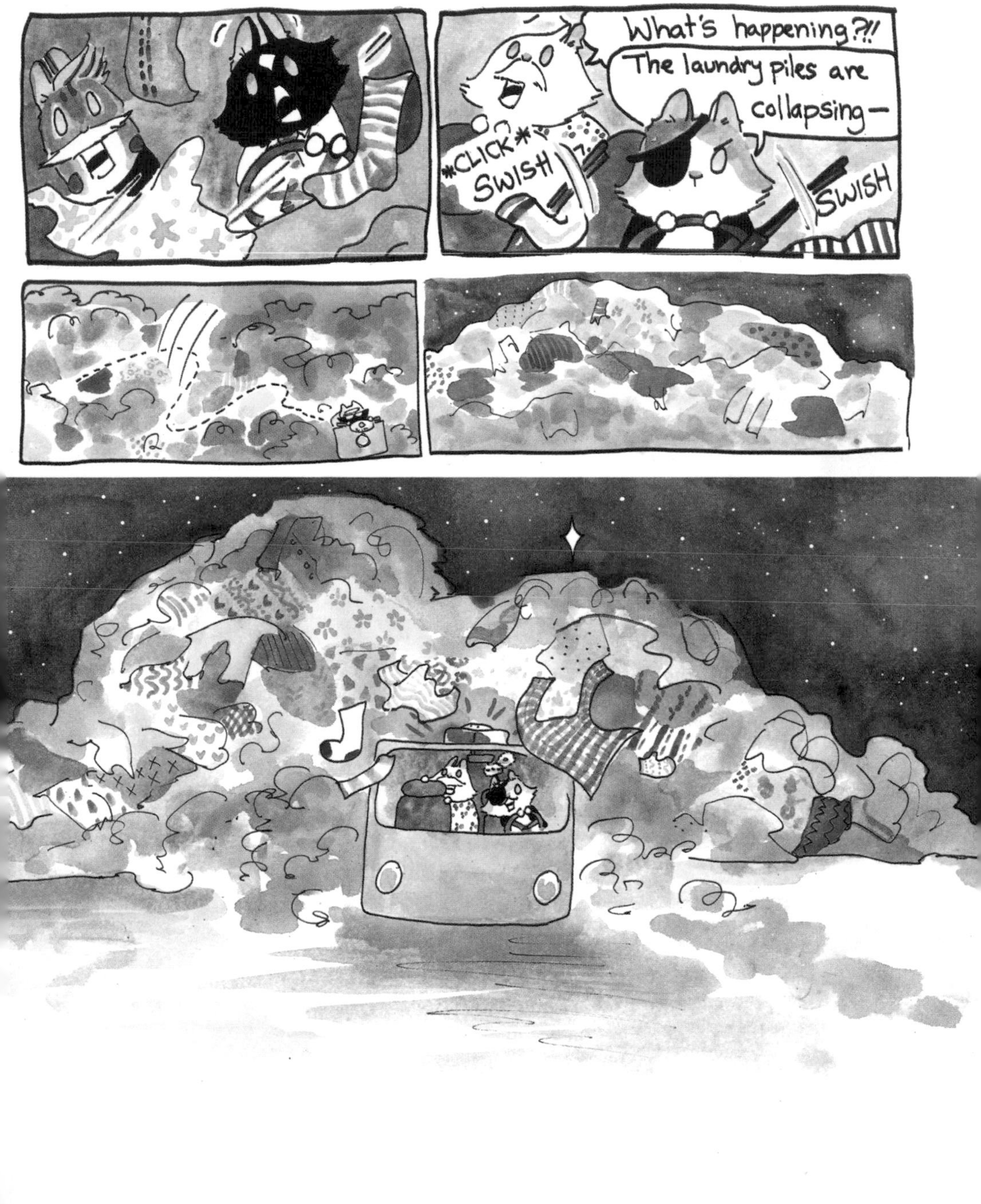
What's happening?!!
The laundry piles are collapsing—
CLICK
SWISH
SWISH

OMC! You should see E. He is GLUED to the screen right now!
I dug the ambulance out. What now?
We'll never catch up to Kit!
We don't need Snowball. Marry Angora now, deal with Snowball later!
I knew Elvis would like it if he gave it a chance!
Who do you think Angora will marry? Brad or Kit?
We only have to catch up to Angora!
Well, she can't marry Kit.
Because **I'M** marrying Kit, **OBVIOUSLY.**

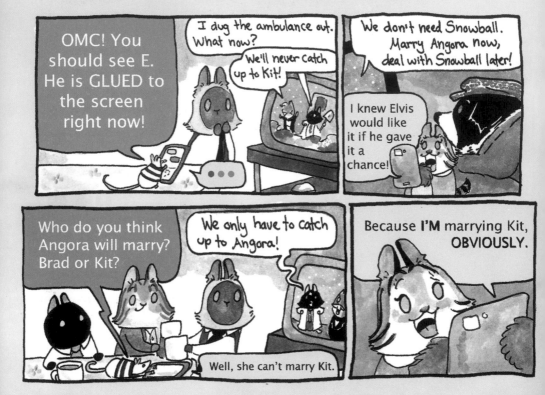

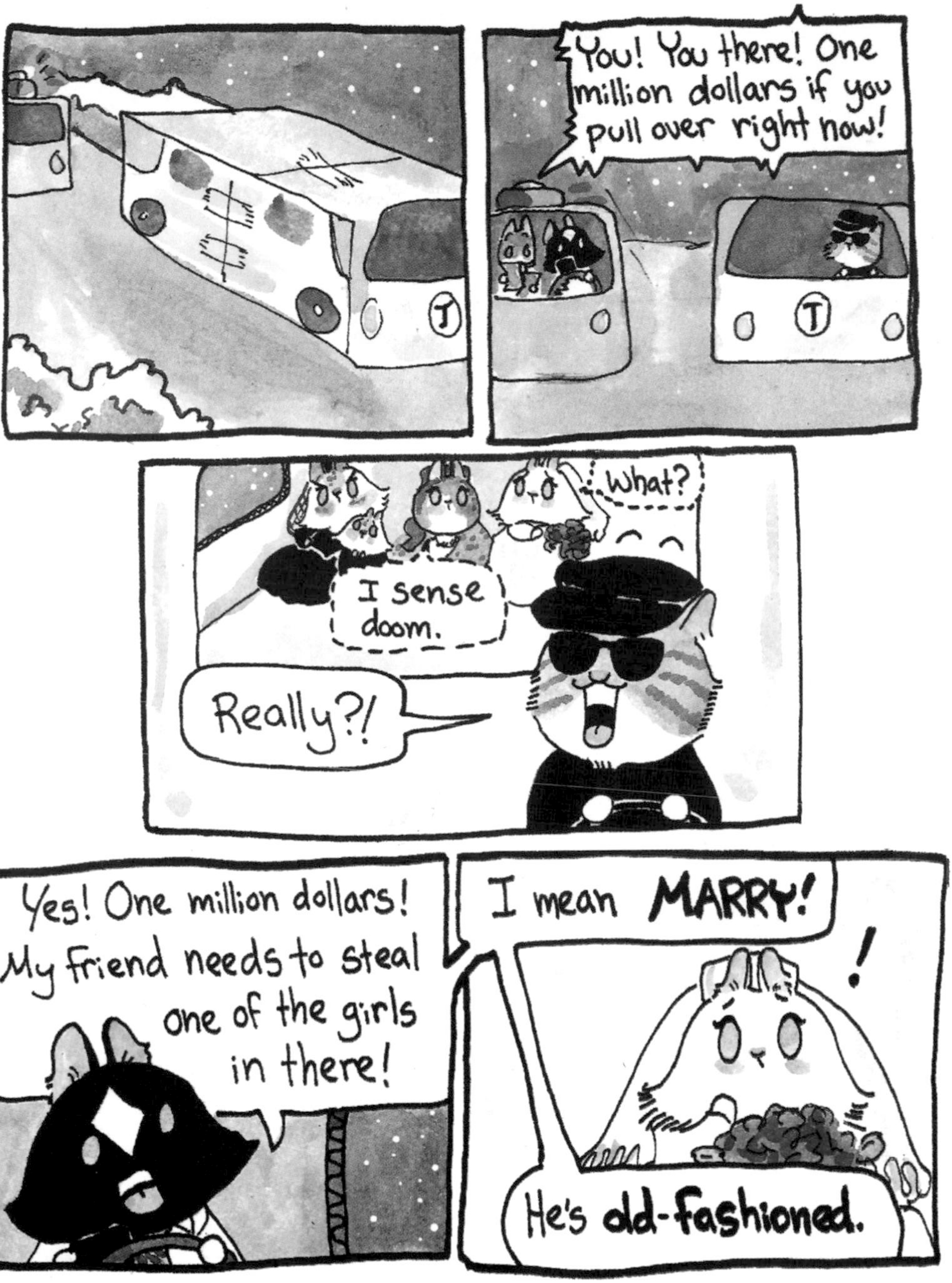
You! You there! One million dollars if you pull over right now!
What?
I sense doom.
Really?!
Yes! One million dollars! My friend needs to steal one of the girls in there!
I mean MARRY!
!
He's old-fashioned.

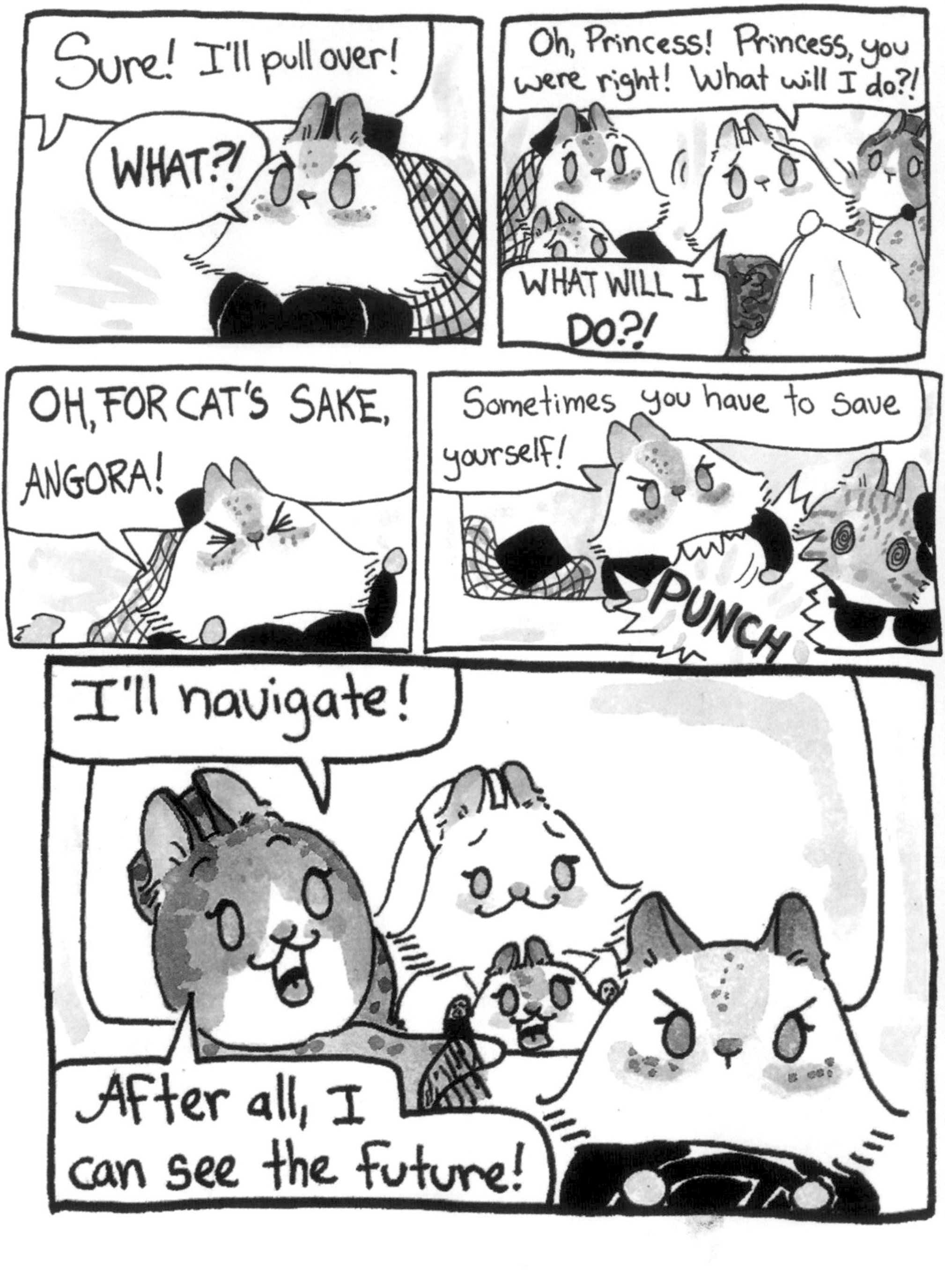
Sure! I'll pull over!
WHAT?!
Oh, Princess! Princess, you were right! What will I do?!
WHAT WILL I DO?!
OH, FOR CAT'S SAKE, ANGORA!
Sometimes you have to save yourself!
PUNCH
I'll navigate!
After all, I can see the future!

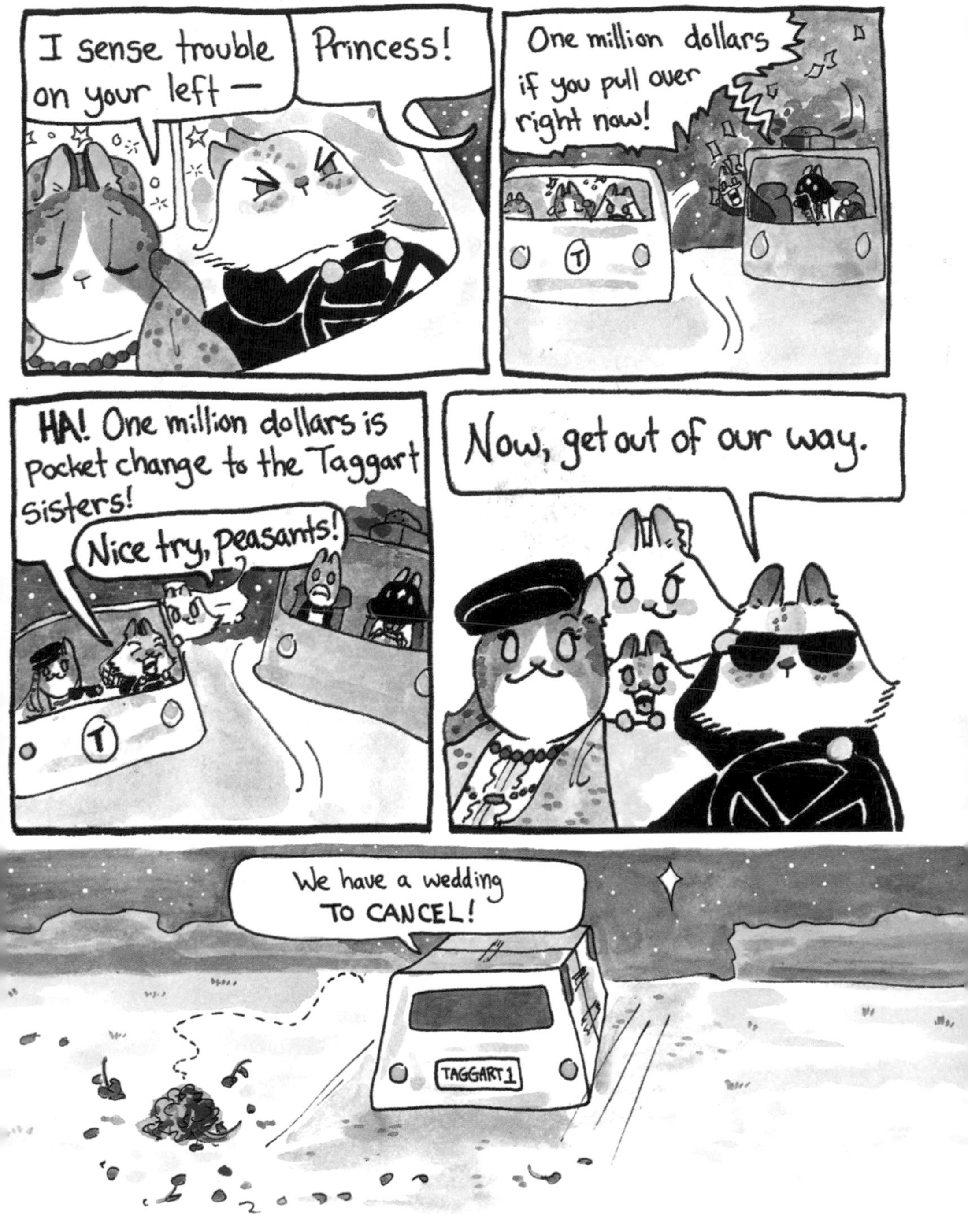
I sense trouble on your left —
Princess!
One million dollars if you pull over right now!
HA! One million dollars is pocket change to the Taggart sisters!
Nice try, peasants!
Now, get out of our way.
We have a wedding TO CANCEL!
TAGGART 1

For Cat's Sake

Who's that?

Father O'Kittery. He's been trying to save the Chase brothers for years.

He ran their reform school. Practically raised them! Bandit's gone good, but he still worries about Kit.

...Kit seems like a pretty good guy.

RIGHT?

Father O'Kittery! I need your help!

! GASP

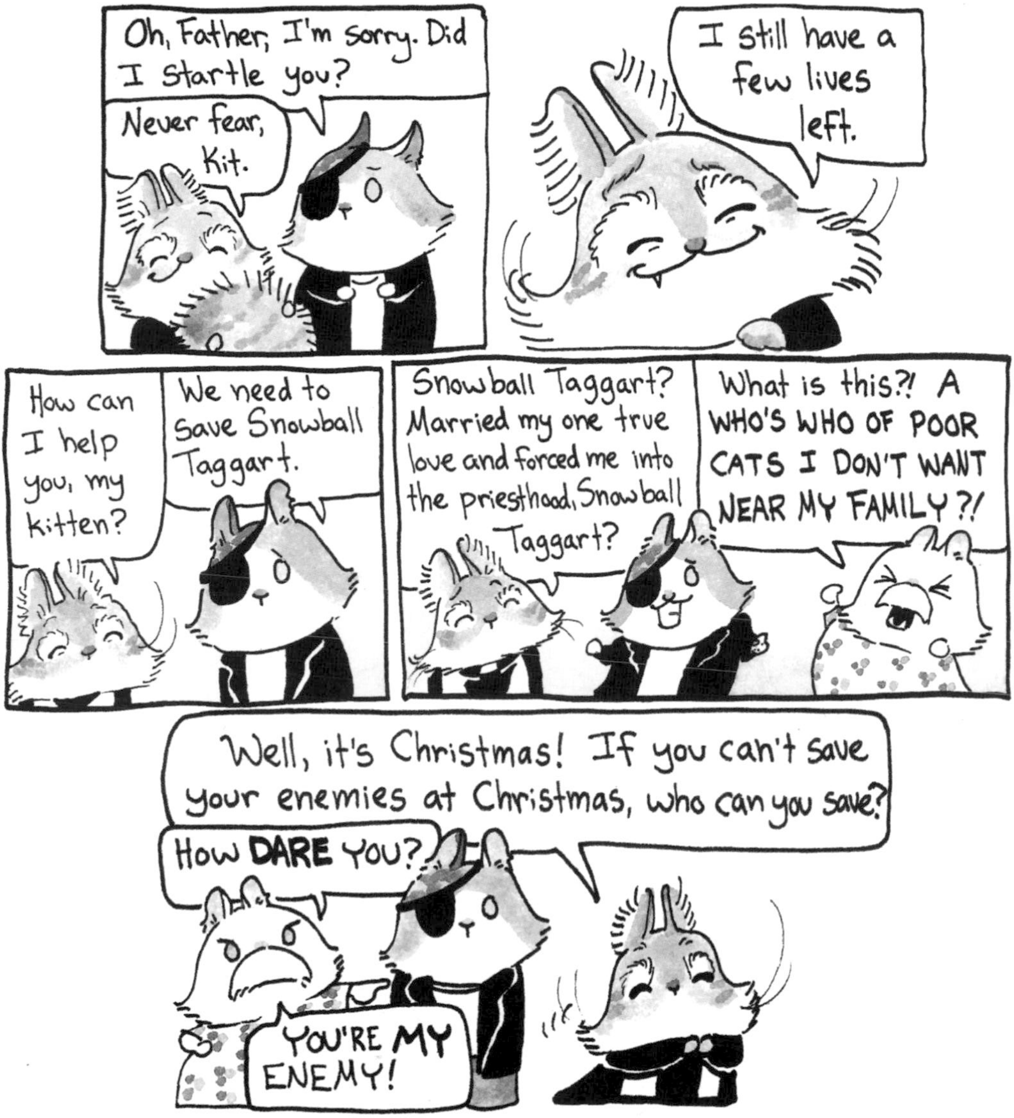

Oh, Father, I'm sorry. Did I startle you?
Never fear, Kit.
I still have a few lives left.
How can I help you, my kitten?
We need to save Snowball Taggart.
Snowball Taggart? Married my one true love and forced me into the priesthood, Snowball Taggart?
What is this?! A WHO'S WHO OF POOR CATS I DON'T WANT NEAR MY FAMILY?!
Well, it's Christmas! If you can't save your enemies at Christmas, who can you save?
How **DARE** YOU?
YOU'RE **MY** ENEMY!

Father O'Kittery!
Why, Princess, my girl, what's wrong?
My sister needs to cancel her wedding.
Father, can you Forgive me?
No need to cancel the cake, right?
I mean, it's already here-
There, there, Angora Taggart. Cat has done well to guide you here-
He certainly HAS!
C'mon, man-
Father?!

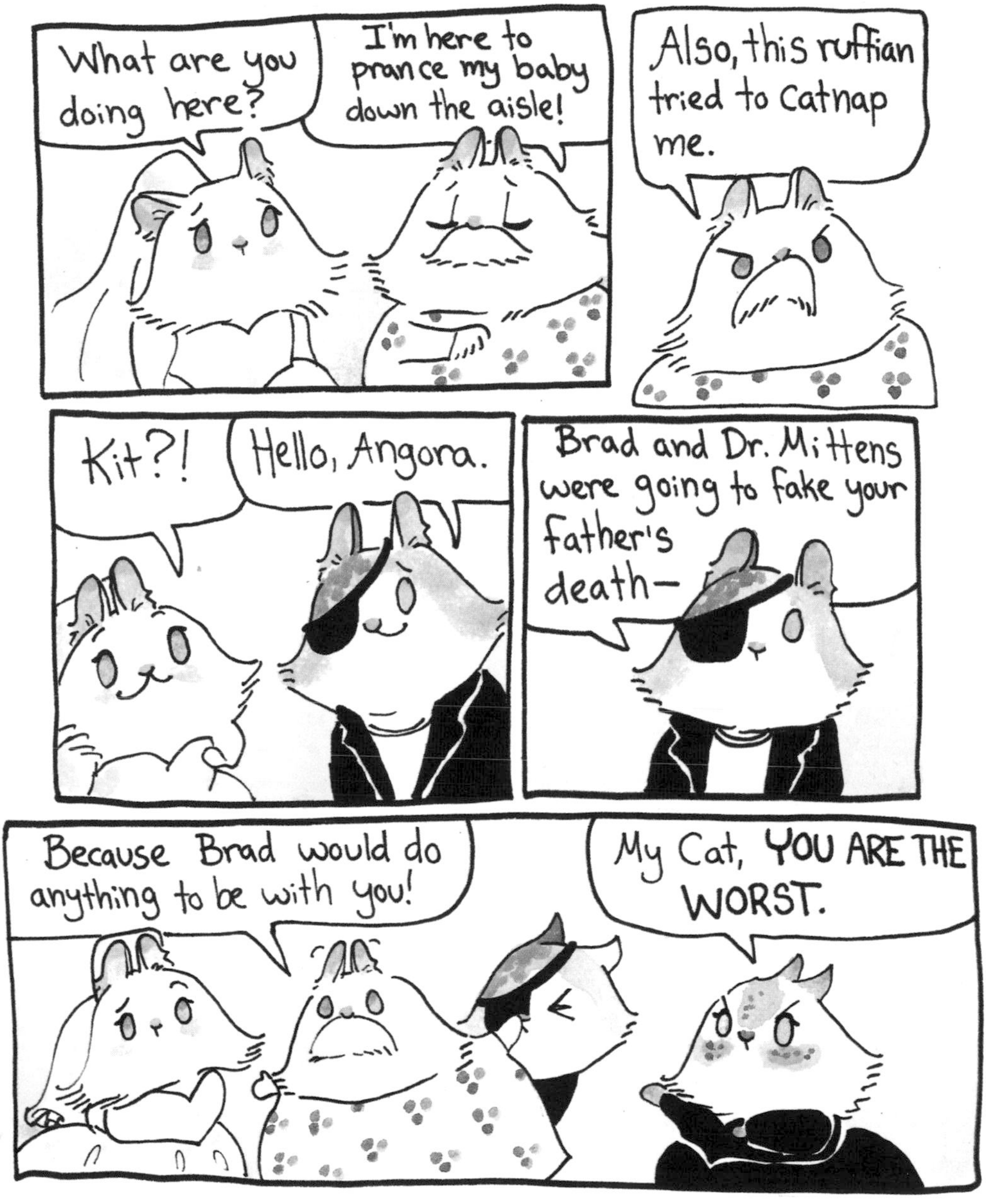
What are you doing here?
I'm here to prance my baby down the aisle!
Also, this ruffian tried to catnap me.
Kit?!
Hello, Angora.
Brad and Dr. Mittens were going to fake your father's death–
Because Brad would do anything to be with you!
My Cat, YOU ARE THE WORST.

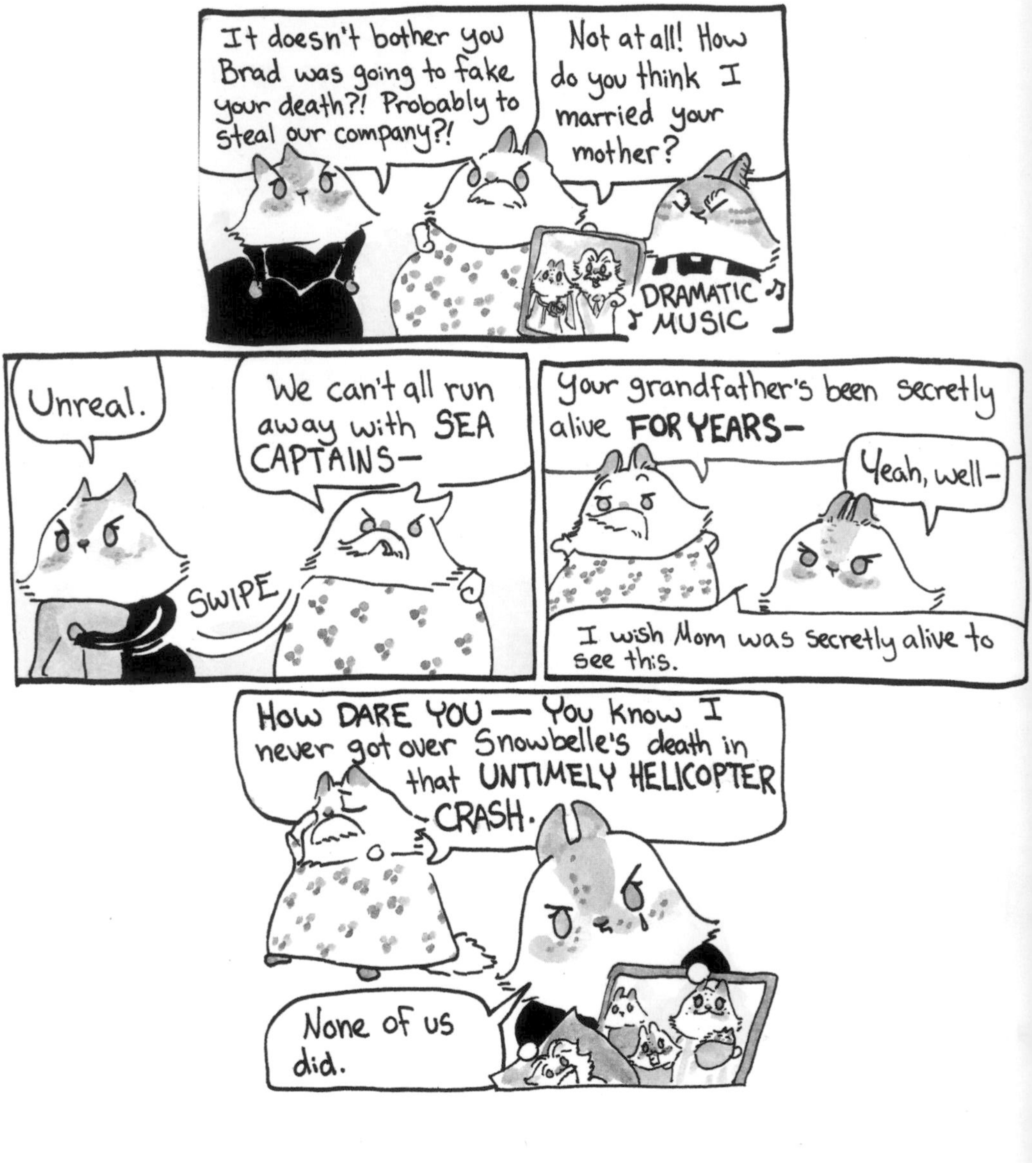
It doesn't bother you Brad was going to fake your death?! Probably to steal our company?!
Not at all! How do you think I married your mother?
DRAMATIC MUSIC
Unreal.
We can't all run away with SEA CAPTAINS—
SWIPE
Your grandfather's been secretly alive FOR YEARS—
Yeah, well—
I wish Mom was secretly alive to see this.
HOW DARE YOU— You know I never got over Snowbelle's death in that UNTIMELY HELICOPTER CRASH.
None of us did.

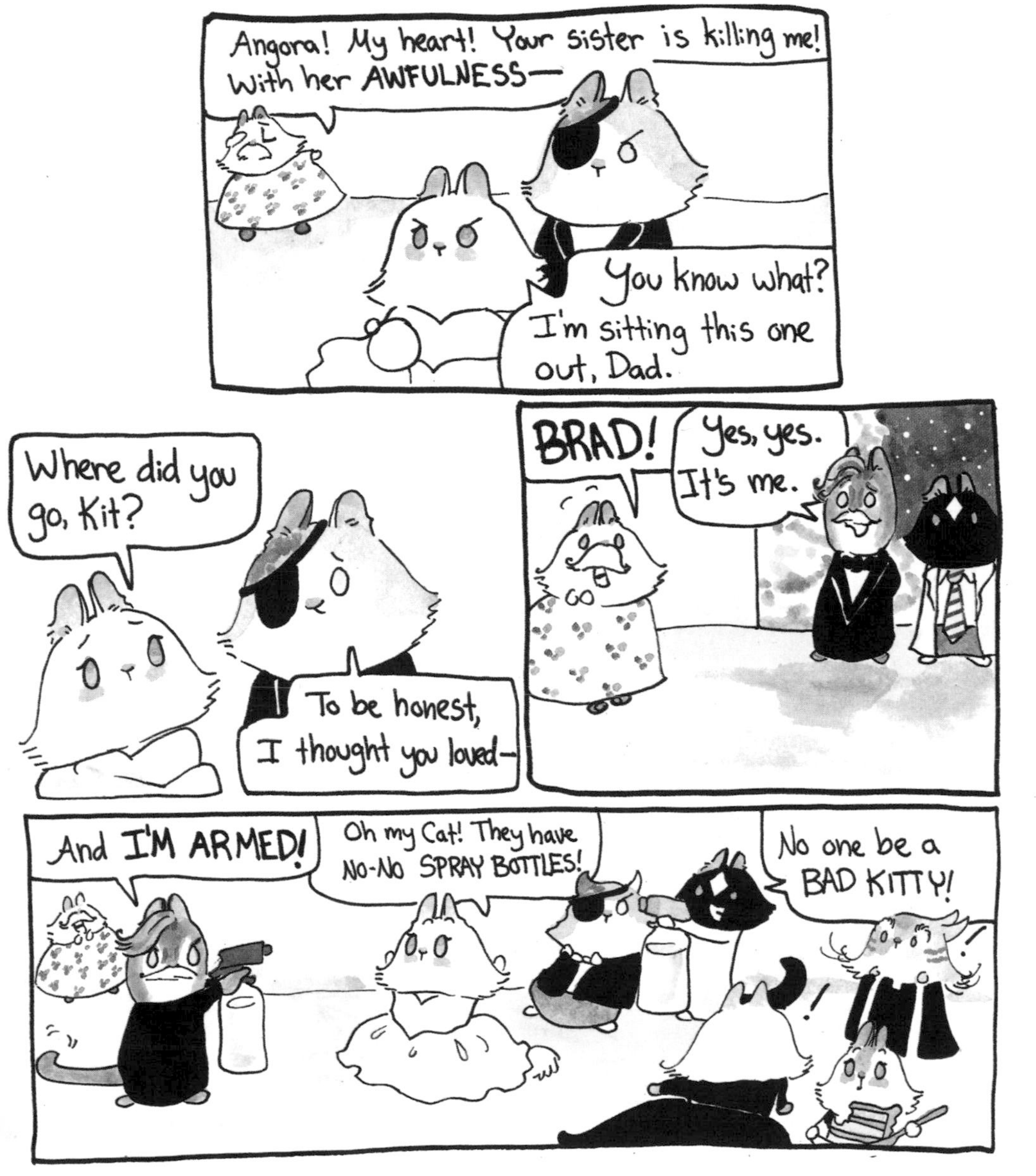
Angora! My heart! Your sister is killing me! With her AWFULNESS—
You know what? I'm sitting this one out, Dad.
Where did you go, Kit?
To be honest, I thought you loved—
BRAD!
Yes, yes. It's me.
And I'M ARMED!
Oh my Cat! They have NO-NO SPRAY BOTTLES!
No one be a BAD KITTY!

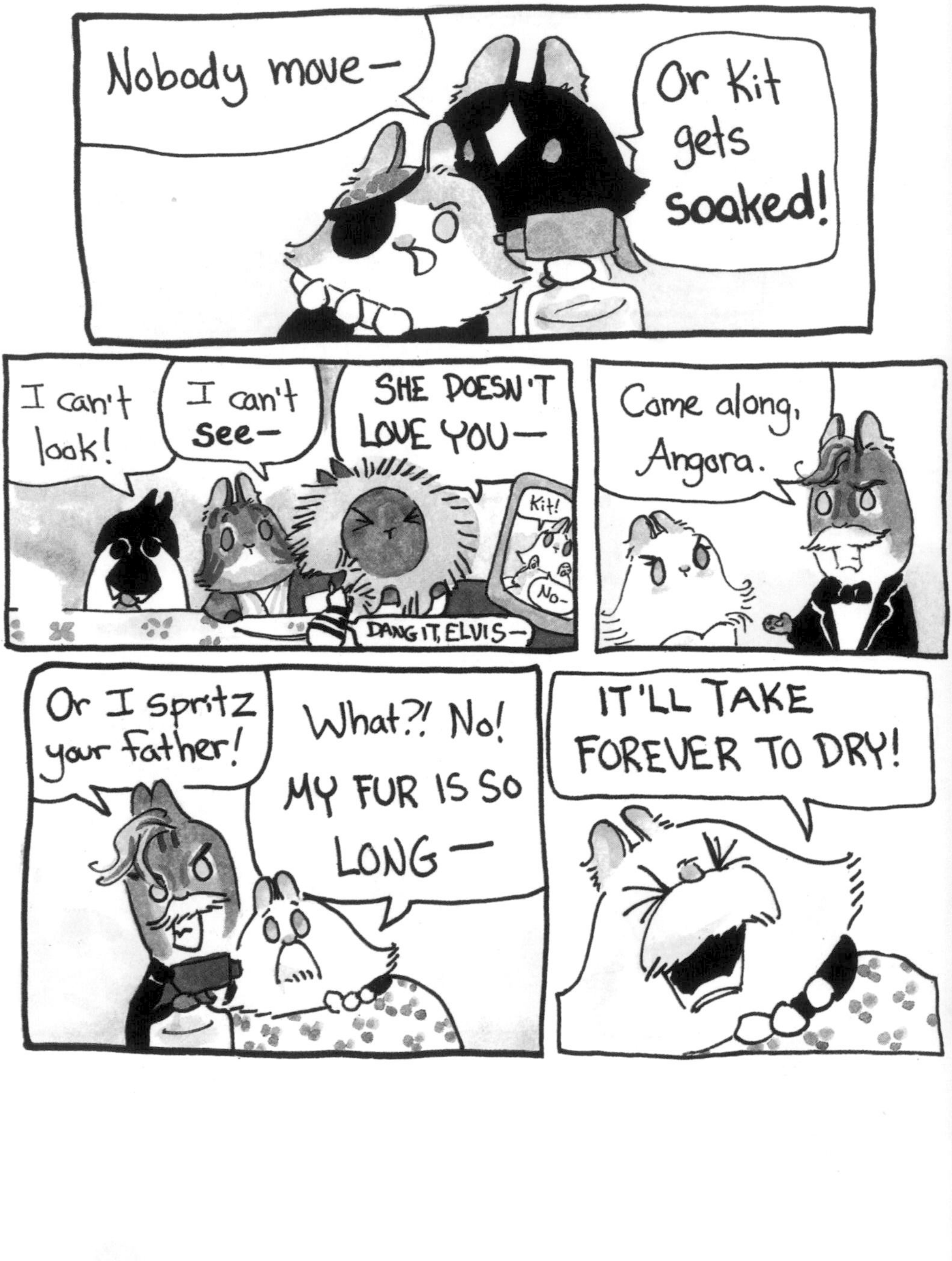
Nobody move—
Or Kit gets soaked!
I can't look!
I can't see—
SHE DOESN'T LOVE YOU—
Kit!
No—
DANG IT, ELVIS—
Come along, Angora.
Or I spritz your father!
What?! No! MY FUR IS SO LONG—
IT'LL TAKE FOREVER TO DRY!

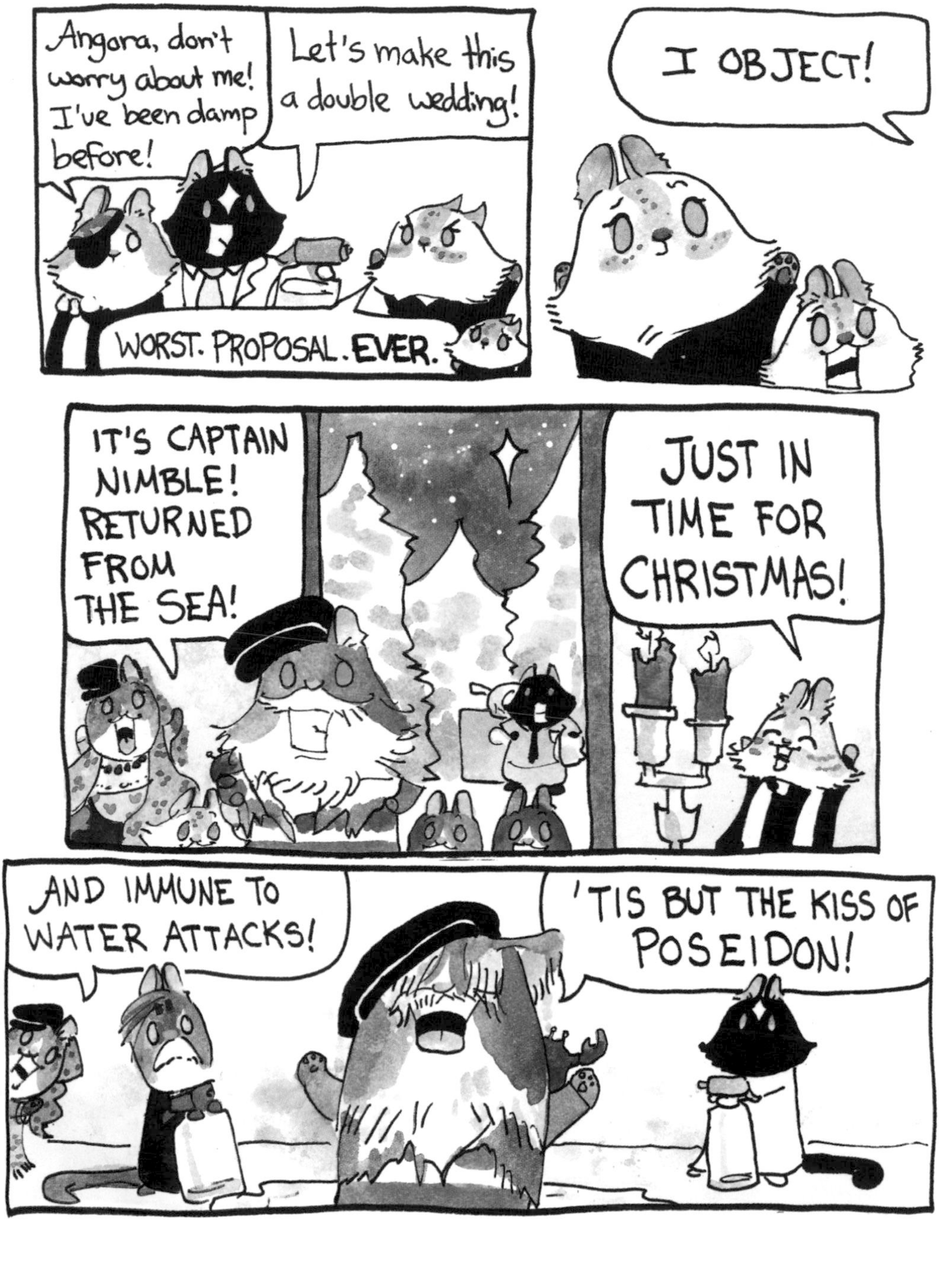
Angora, don't worry about me! I've been damp before!
Let's make this a double wedding!
WORST. PROPOSAL. EVER.
I OBJECT!
IT'S CAPTAIN NIMBLE! RETURNED FROM THE SEA!
JUST IN TIME FOR CHRISTMAS!
AND IMMUNE TO WATER ATTACKS!
'TIS BUT THE KISS OF POSEIDON!

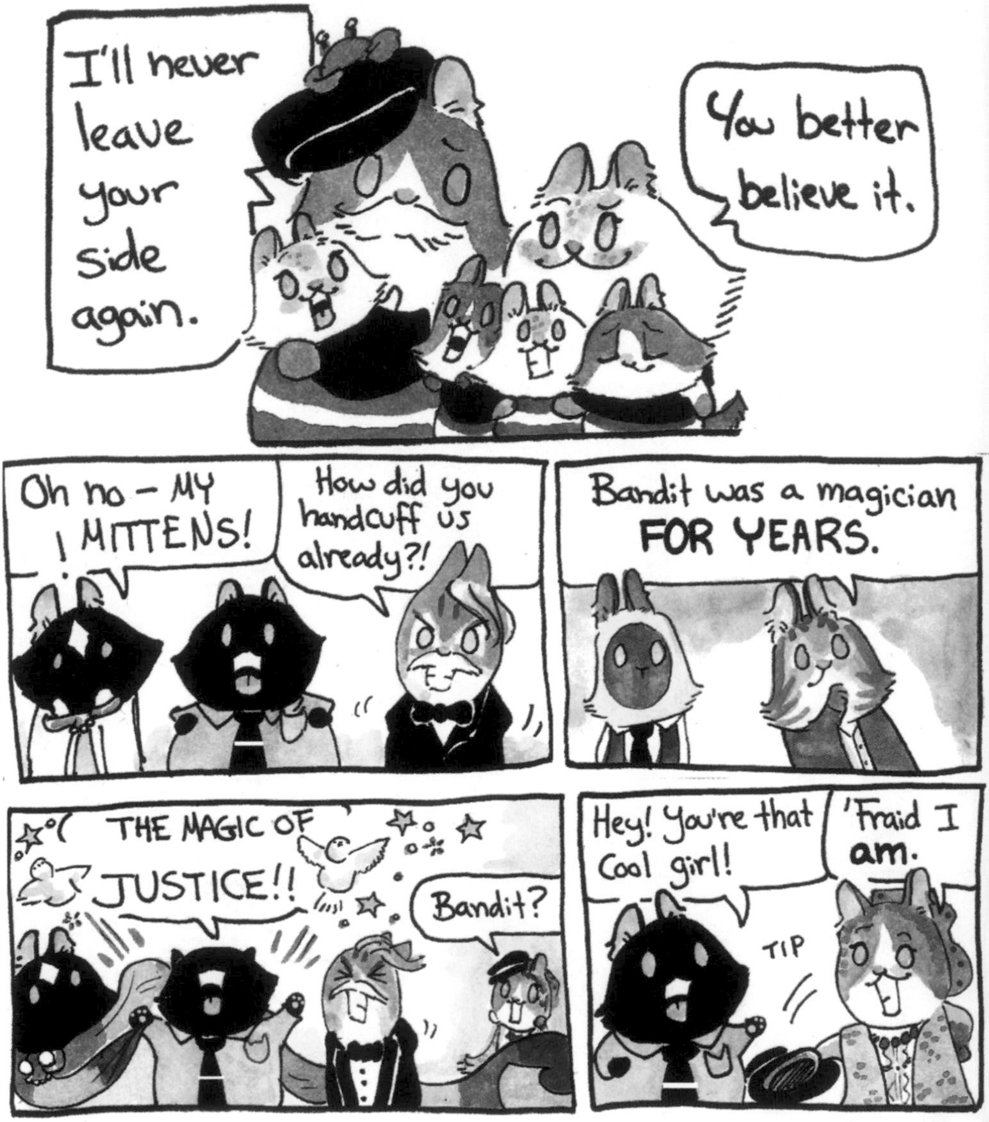
I'll never leave your side again.
You better believe it.
Oh no - MY MITTENS!
How did you handcuff us already?!
Bandit was a magician FOR YEARS.
THE MAGIC OF JUSTICE!!
Bandit?
Hey! You're that Cool girl!
'Fraid I am.
TIP

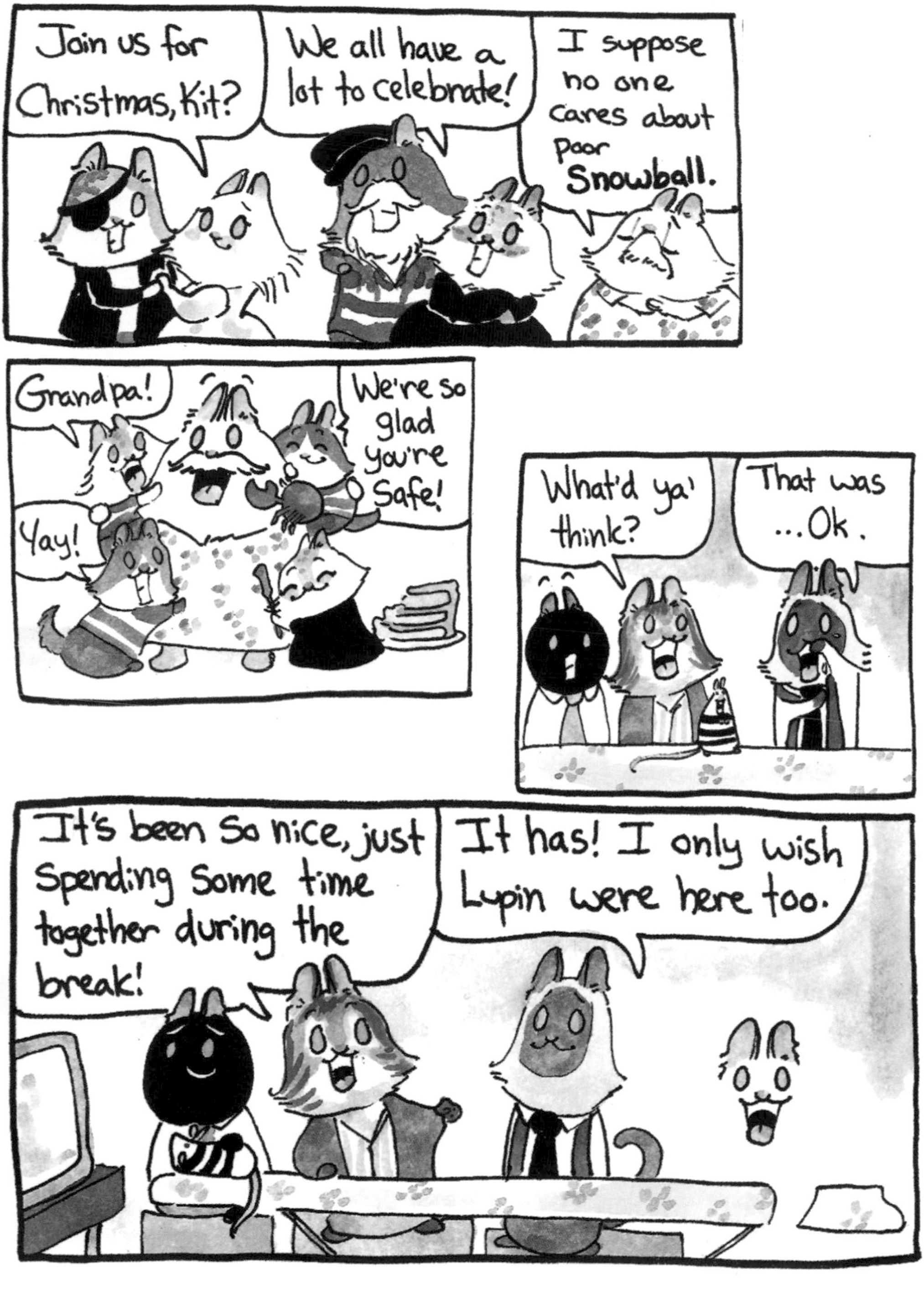
Join us for Christmas, Kit?
We all have a lot to celebrate!
I suppose no one cares about poor Snowball.
Grandpa!
We're so glad you're safe!
Yay!
What'd ya' think?
That was ...Ok.
It's been so nice, just spending some time together during the break!
It has! I only wish Lupin were here too.

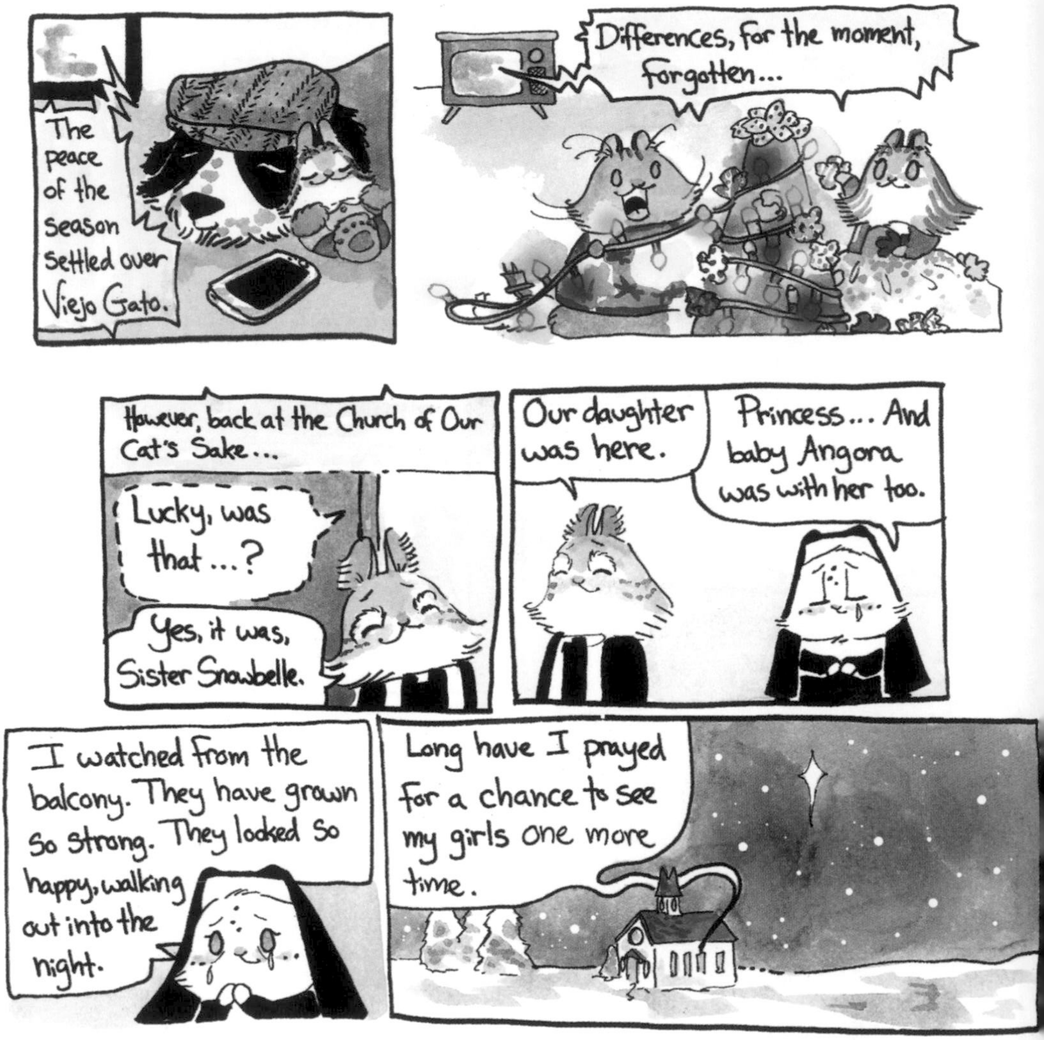
The peace of the season settled over Viejo Gato.
Differences, for the moment, forgotten...
However, back at the Church of Our Cat's Sake...
Lucky, was that...?
Yes, it was, Sister Snowbelle.
Our daughter was here.
Princess... And baby Angora was with her too.
I watched from the balcony. They have grown so strong. They looked so happy, walking out into the night.
Long have I prayed for a chance to see my girls one more time.

As you know, I've been remastering the old broadcasts.

Here's what the original footage looked like.

Ma'am

And here's the remastered, high resolution, 3200 feline-define version.

But what will happen to our old broadcasts?!

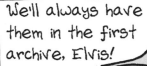

We'll always have them in the first archive, Elvis!

And, like, our hearts dude!

Elvis, this was your idea.

I know, but now I'm scared of something I love changing!

We'll finally see all our favorite moments remastered! When Tommy joined BCN, when the kids were born. Meeting Tabitha and Figaro, Sophie, me. When Beatrix was rescued—all of it!

I'll get to watch so much of it for the first time!

It'll be just like you remember it, Elvis... Beautiful!

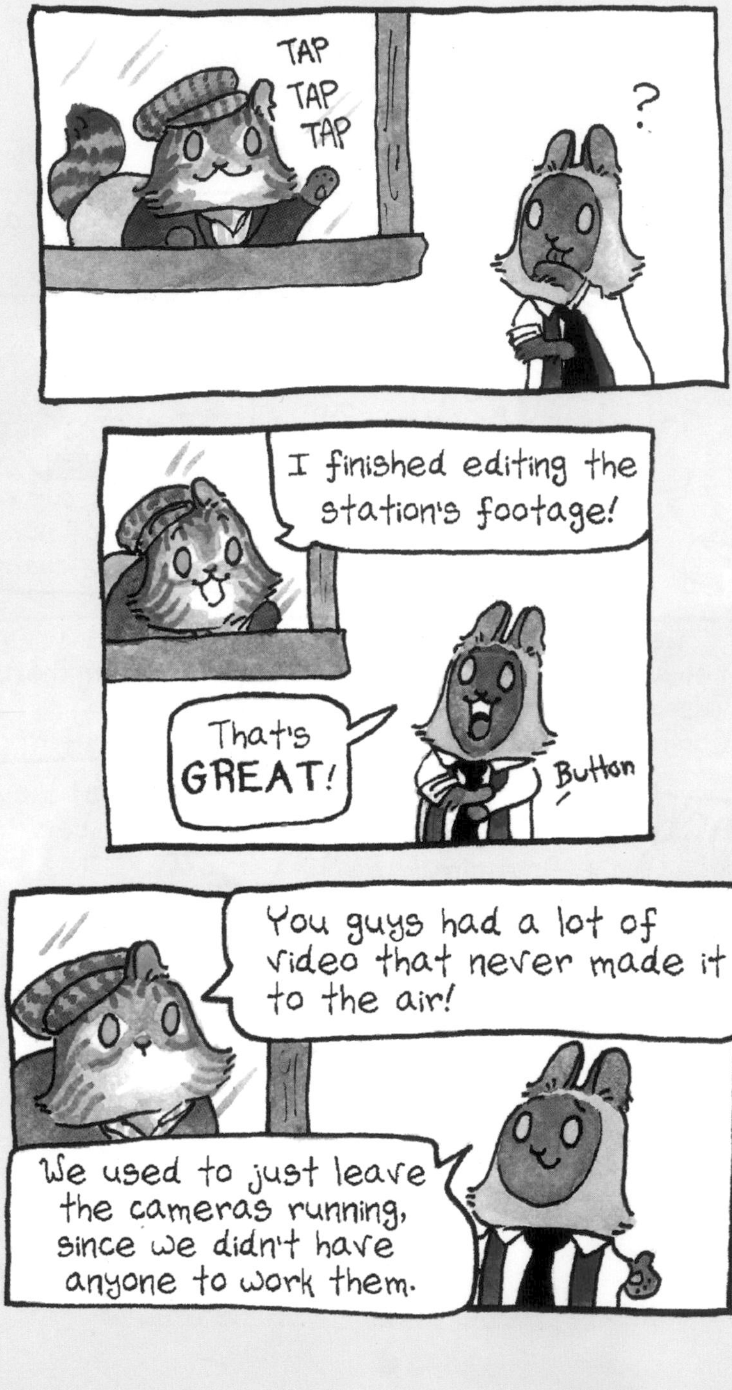
TAP
TAP
TAP
?
I finished editing the station's footage!
That's GREAT!
Button
You guys had a lot of video that never made it to the air!
We used to just leave the cameras running, since we didn't have anyone to work them.

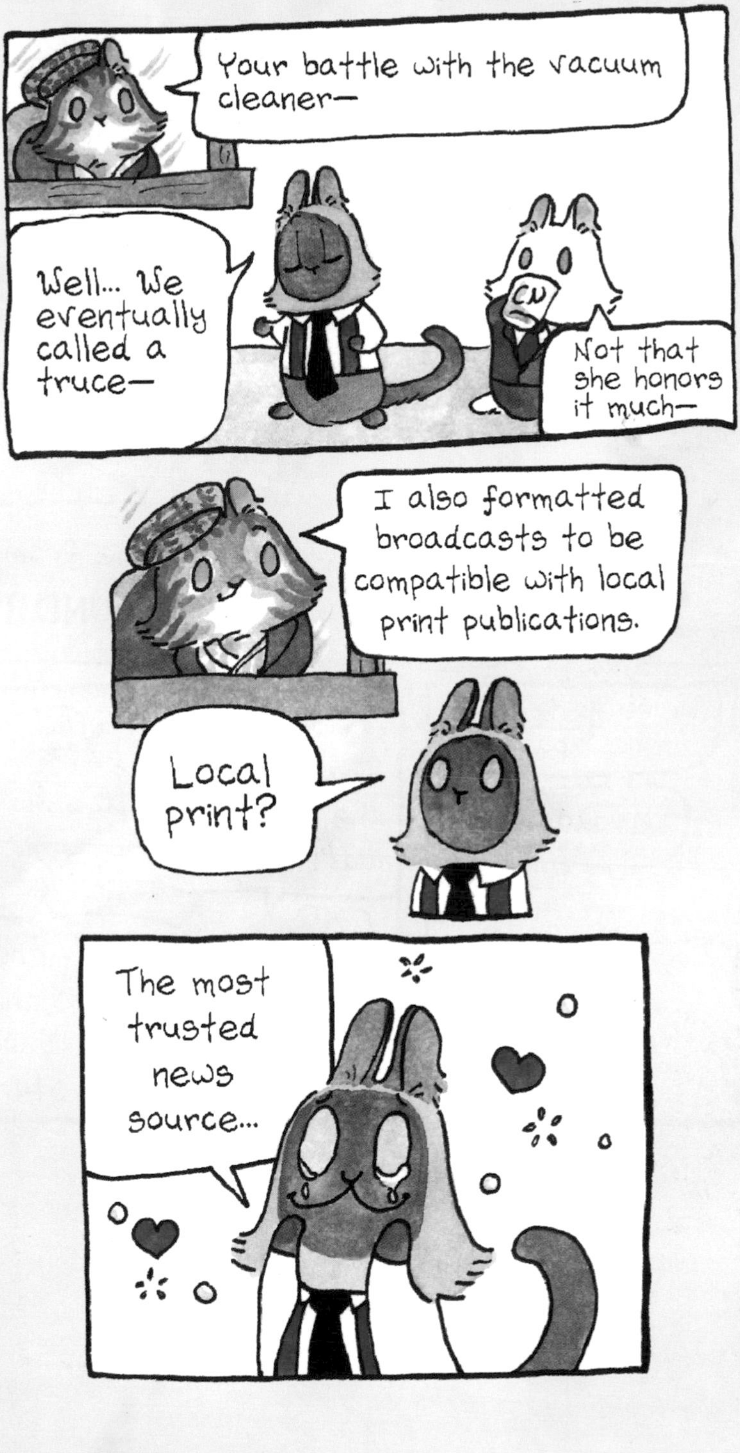
Your battle with the vacuum cleaner—
Well... We eventually called a truce—
CN
Not that she honors it much—
I also formatted broadcasts to be compatible with local print publications.
Local print?
The most trusted news source...

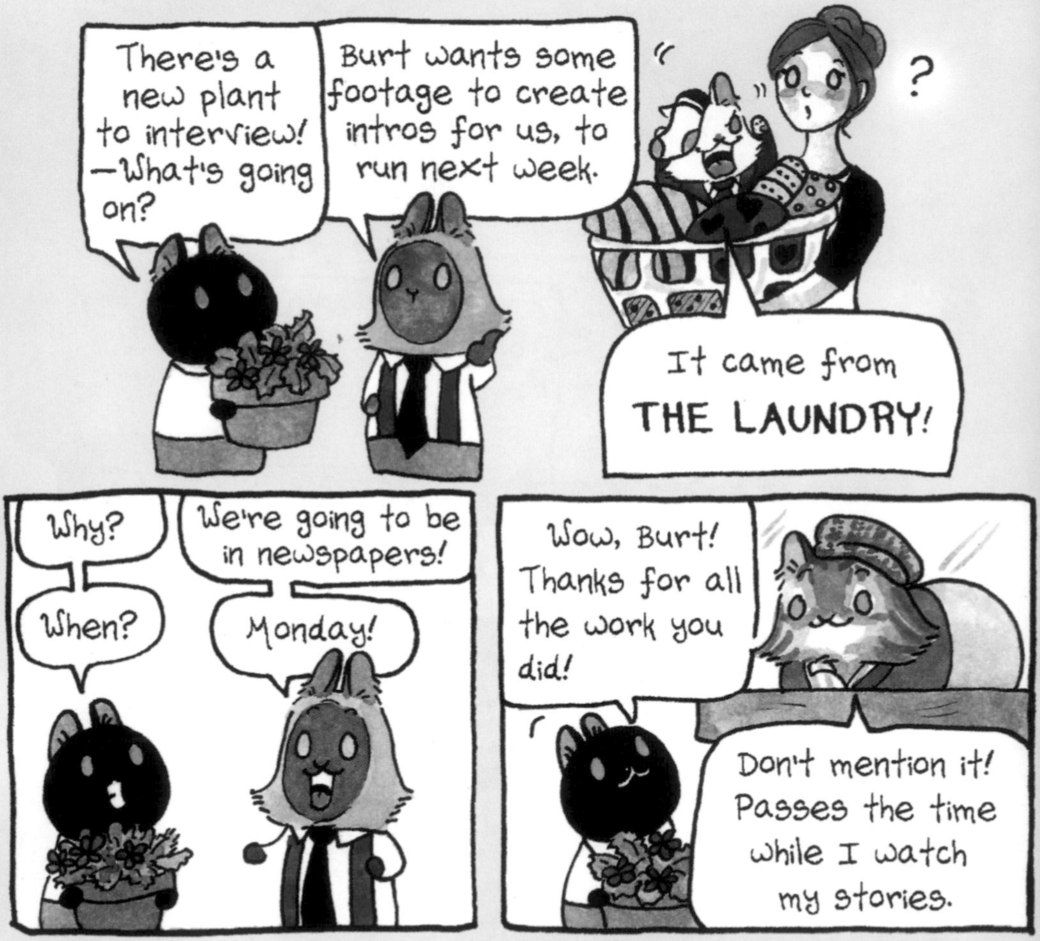
There's a new plant to interview! —What's going on?
Burt wants some footage to create intros for us, to run next week.
?
It came from THE LAUNDRY!
Why?
When?
We're going to be in newspapers!
Monday!
Wow, Burt! Thanks for all the work you did!
Don't mention it! Passes the time while I watch my stories.

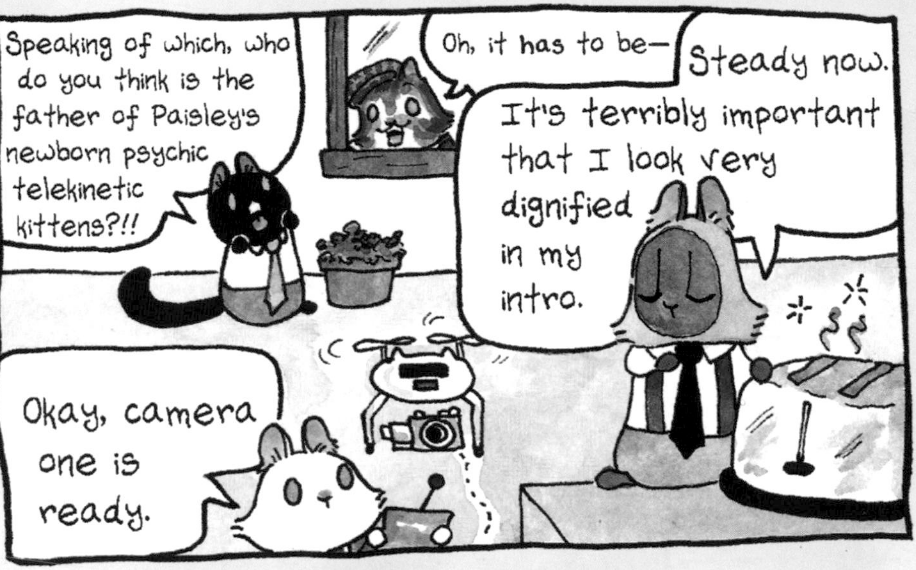
Speaking of which, who do you think is the father of Paisley's newborn psychic telekinetic kittens?!!
Oh, it has to be—
Steady now.
It's terribly important that I look very dignified in my intro.
Okay, camera one is ready.

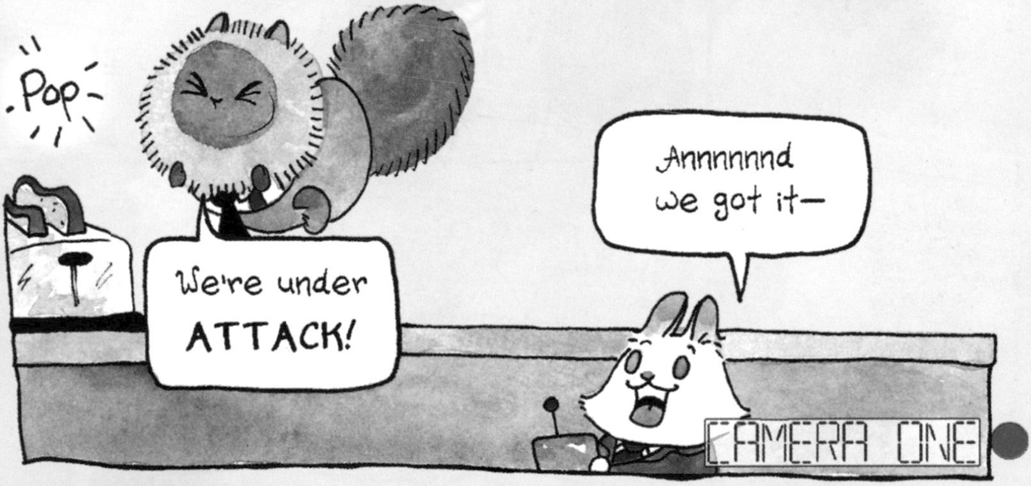
Pop
We're under ATTACK!
Annnnnd we got it—
CAMERA ONE

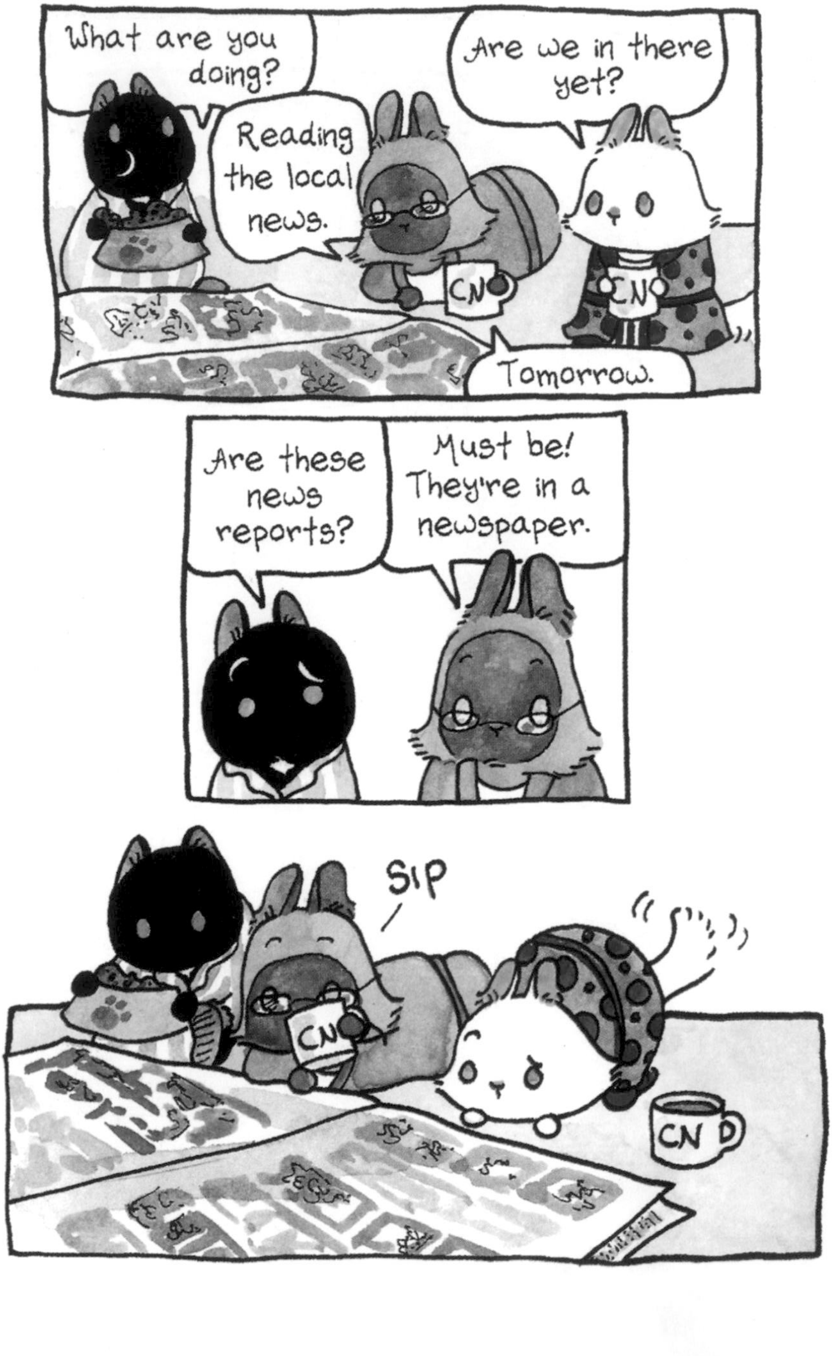
What are you doing?
Reading the local news.
Are we in there yet?
Tomorrow.
Are these news reports?
Must be! They're in a newspaper.
SIP

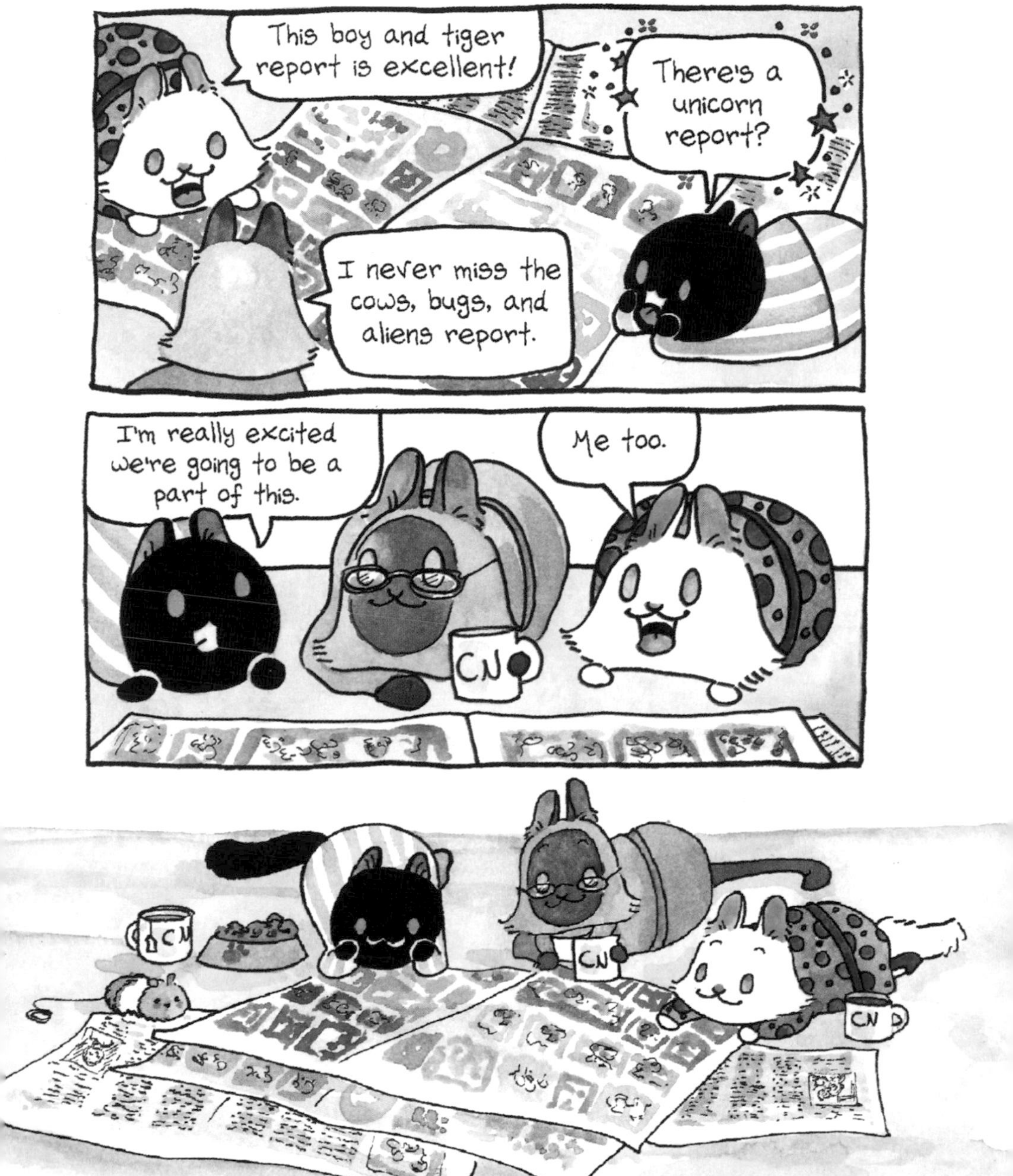
This boy and tiger report is excellent!
There's a unicorn report?
I never miss the cows, bugs, and aliens report.
I'm really excited we're going to be a part of this.
Me too.

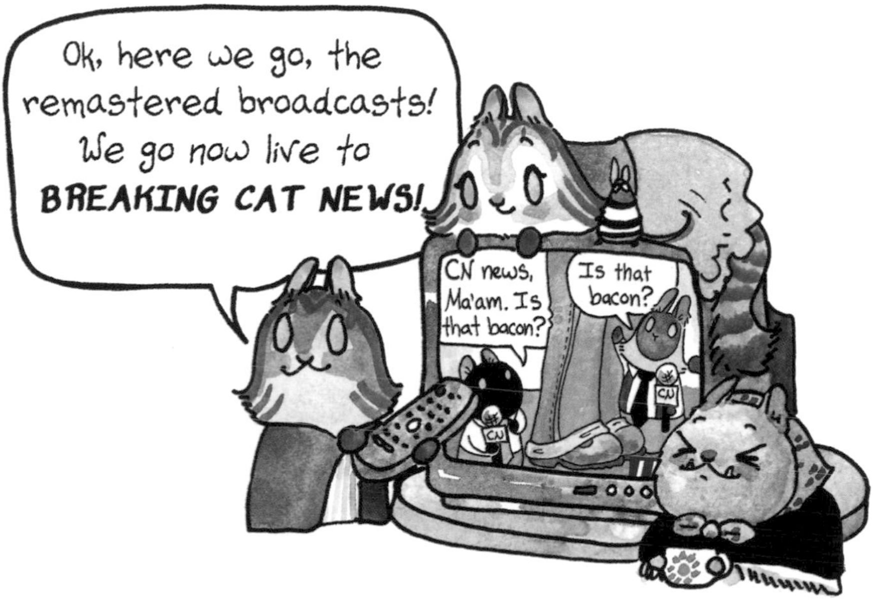
Ok, here we go, the remastered broadcasts! We go now live to BREAKING CAT NEWS!
CN news, Ma'am. Is that bacon?
Is that bacon?
CN
CN

On March 27, 2017, 'Breaking Cat News' debuted in newspapers across the country. The web strips were completely redrawn for newspapers, with new broadcasts regularly woven in.

For the BCN crew a dream had come true: Their news was finally in People papers. Cat news was being printed and delivered hot off the presses.

(It was a dream come true for me too.)

Thank you, Burt.

— Georgia Dunn

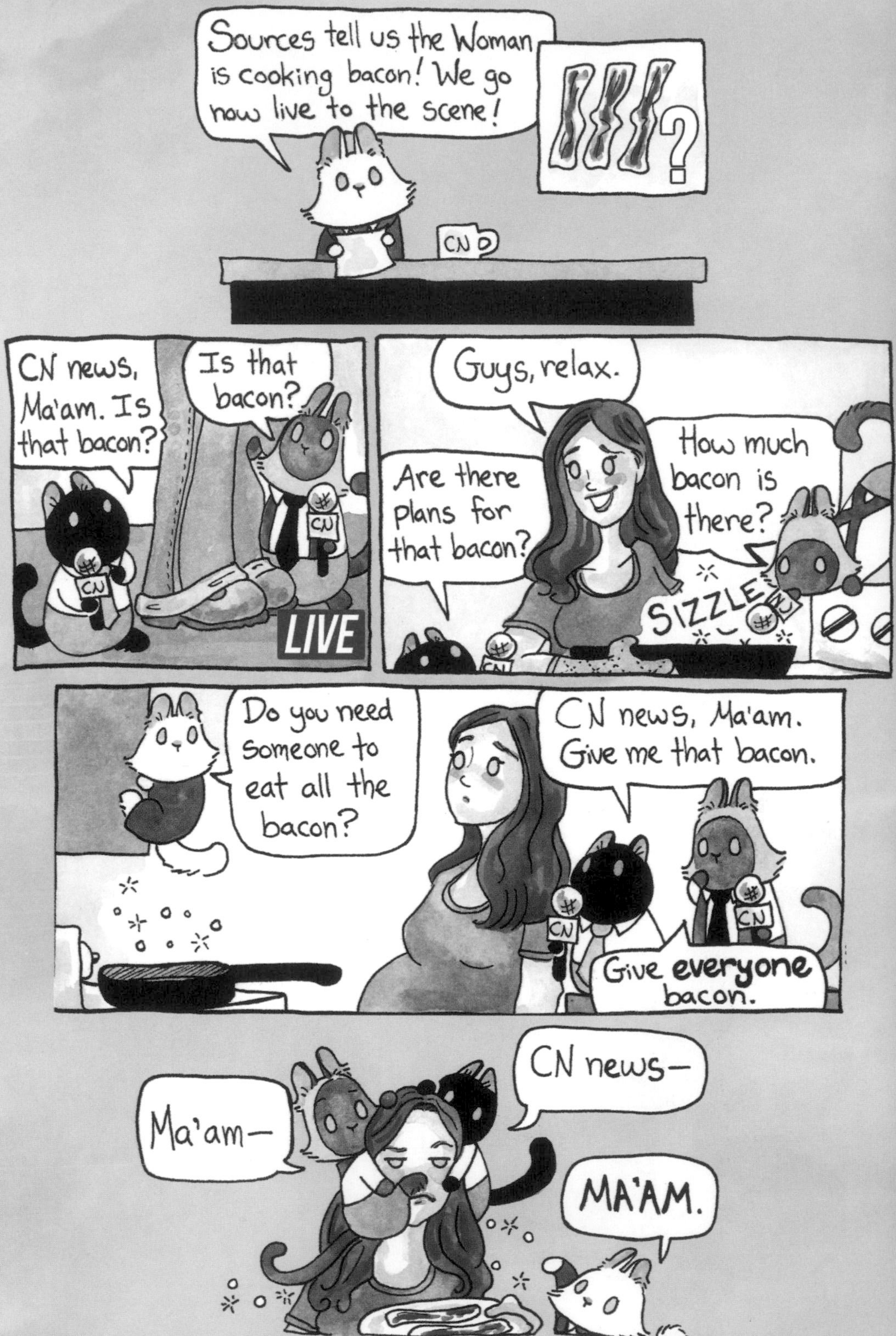
Sources tell us the Woman is cooking bacon! We go now live to the scene!
?
CN
CN news, Ma'am. Is that bacon?
Is that bacon?
CN
CN
LIVE
Guys, relax.
Are there plans for that bacon?
How much bacon is there?
SIZZLE
Do you need someone to eat all the bacon?
CN news, Ma'am. Give me that bacon.
CN
CN
Give **everyone** bacon.
CN news—
Ma'am—
MA'AM.

The Woman is in a room we can't get into.
We go now live to Puck.
CN
CN
CN news, Ma'am. What are you doing in there?
CN
LIVE
Ma'am?
CN news.
Pucky, I'll be out soon.
Ma'am?
Puck, Stop.
Ma'am?
Ma'am?
Sigh.
Ma'am?
CN

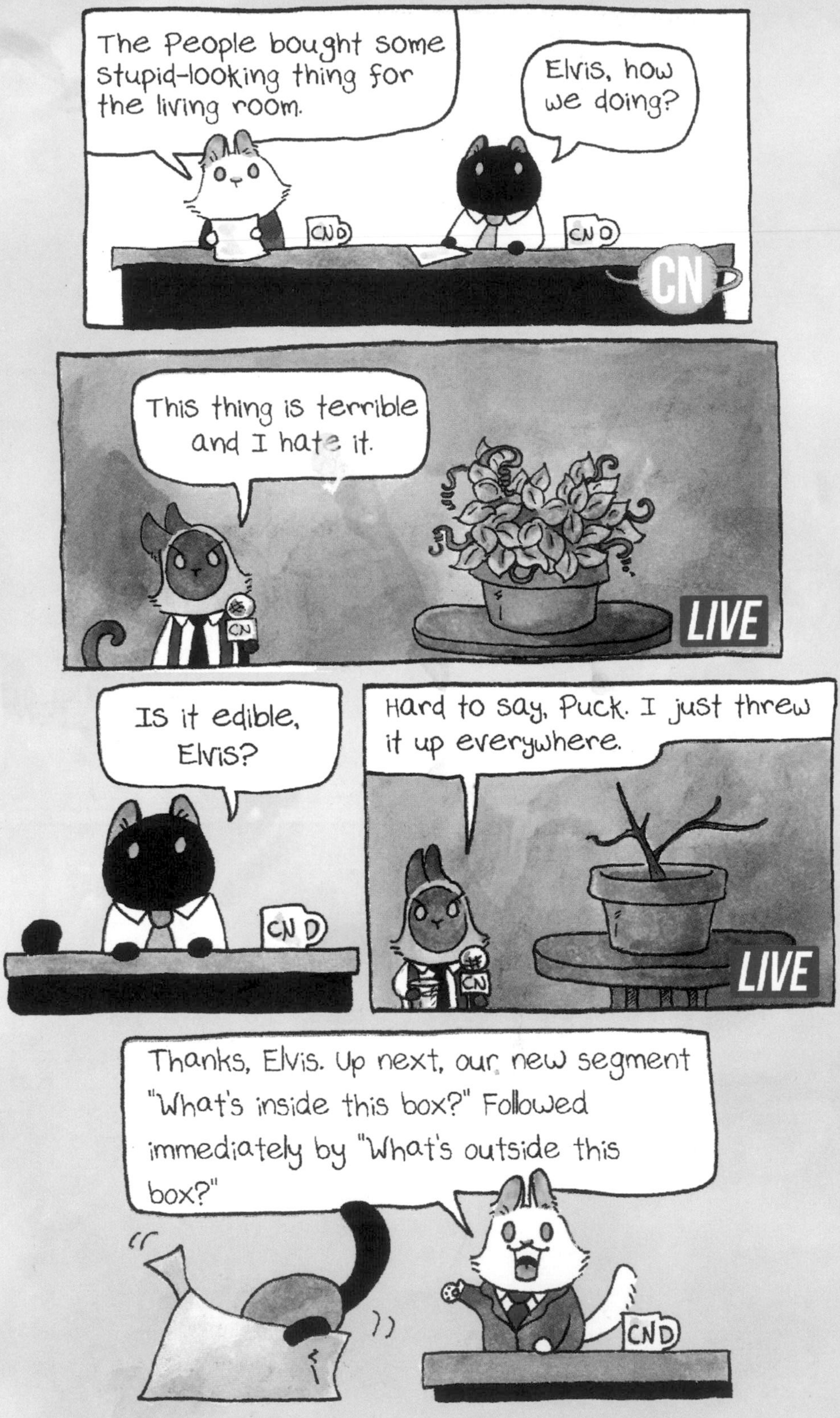

The People bought some stupid-looking thing for the living room.
Elvis, how we doing?
CN
This thing is terrible and I hate it.
LIVE
Is it edible, Elvis?
Hard to say, Puck. I just threw it up everywhere.
LIVE
Thanks, Elvis. Up next, our new segment "What's inside this box?" Followed immediately by "What's outside this box?"

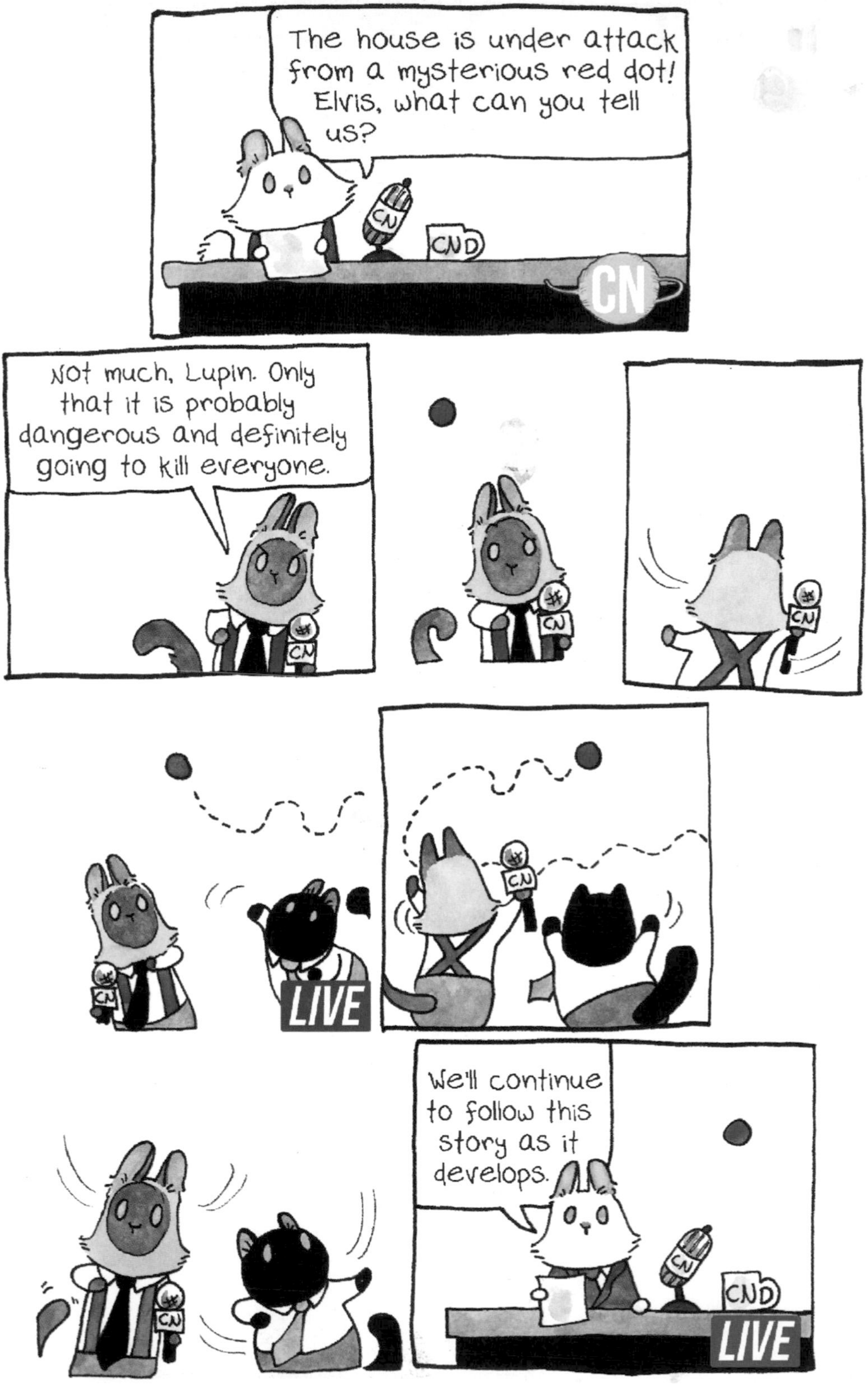
The house is under attack from a mysterious red dot! Elvis, what can you tell us?
CN
CND
CN
Not much, Lupin. Only that it is probably dangerous and definitely going to kill everyone.
CN
CN
CN
CN
LIVE
CN
CN
We'll continue to follow this story as it develops.
CN
CND
LIVE

Ma'am? ↖
Ma'am ...|

The woman is trying to use a laptop.

Elvis, what can you tell us?

The laptop is roasty on my toesies.

Elvis, c'mon—

LIVE

Ooh, that sounds nice!

It sure does, Lupin.

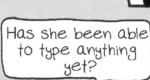

Has she been able to type anything yet?

Sip

Not a word. I locked the keyboard the moment I sat down.

How did you even DO this?!

LIVE

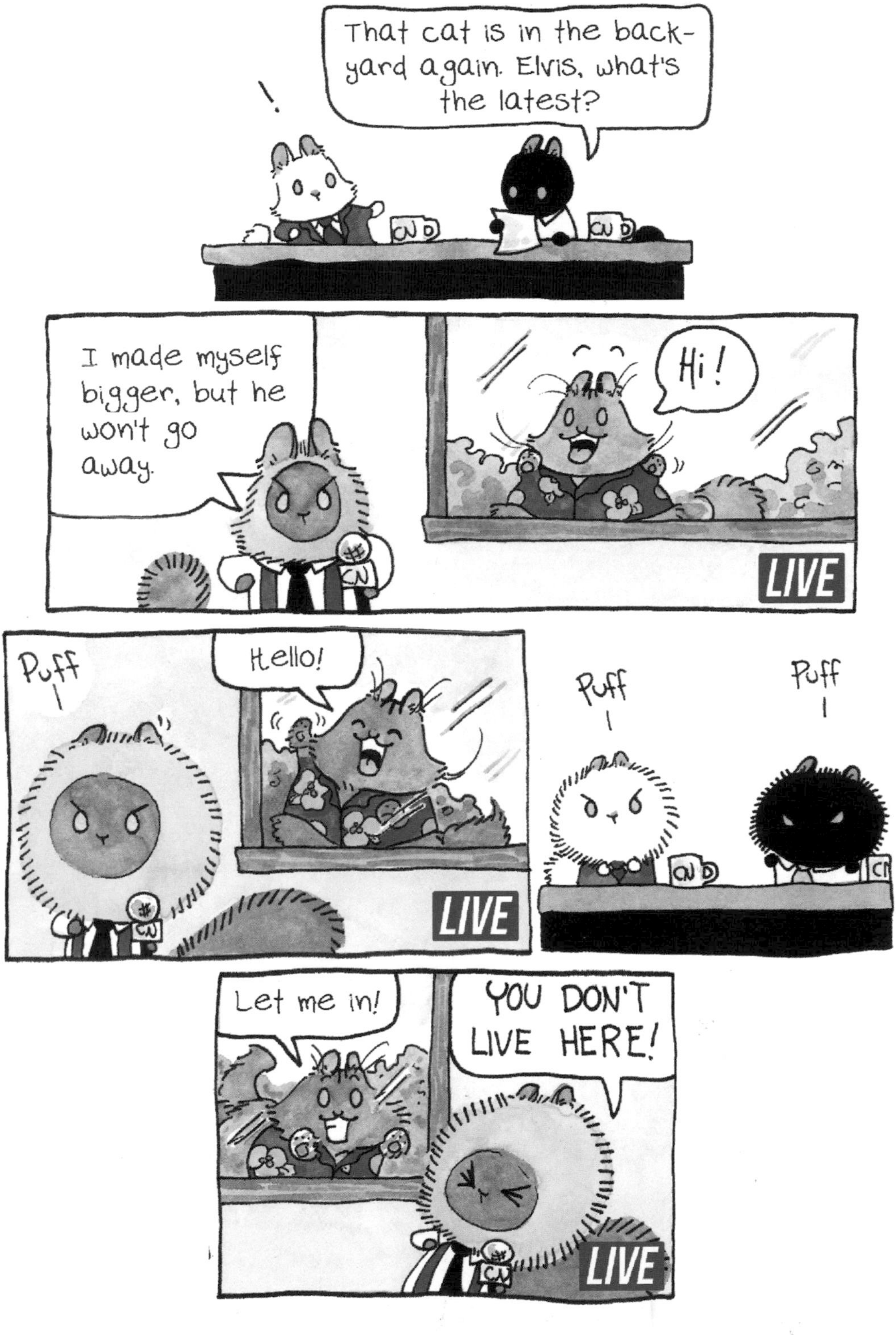
!
That cat is in the back-yard again. Elvis, what's the latest?
I made myself bigger, but he won't go away.
Hi!
LIVE
Puff
Hello!
LIVE
Puff
Puff
Let me in!
YOU DON'T LIVE HERE!
LIVE

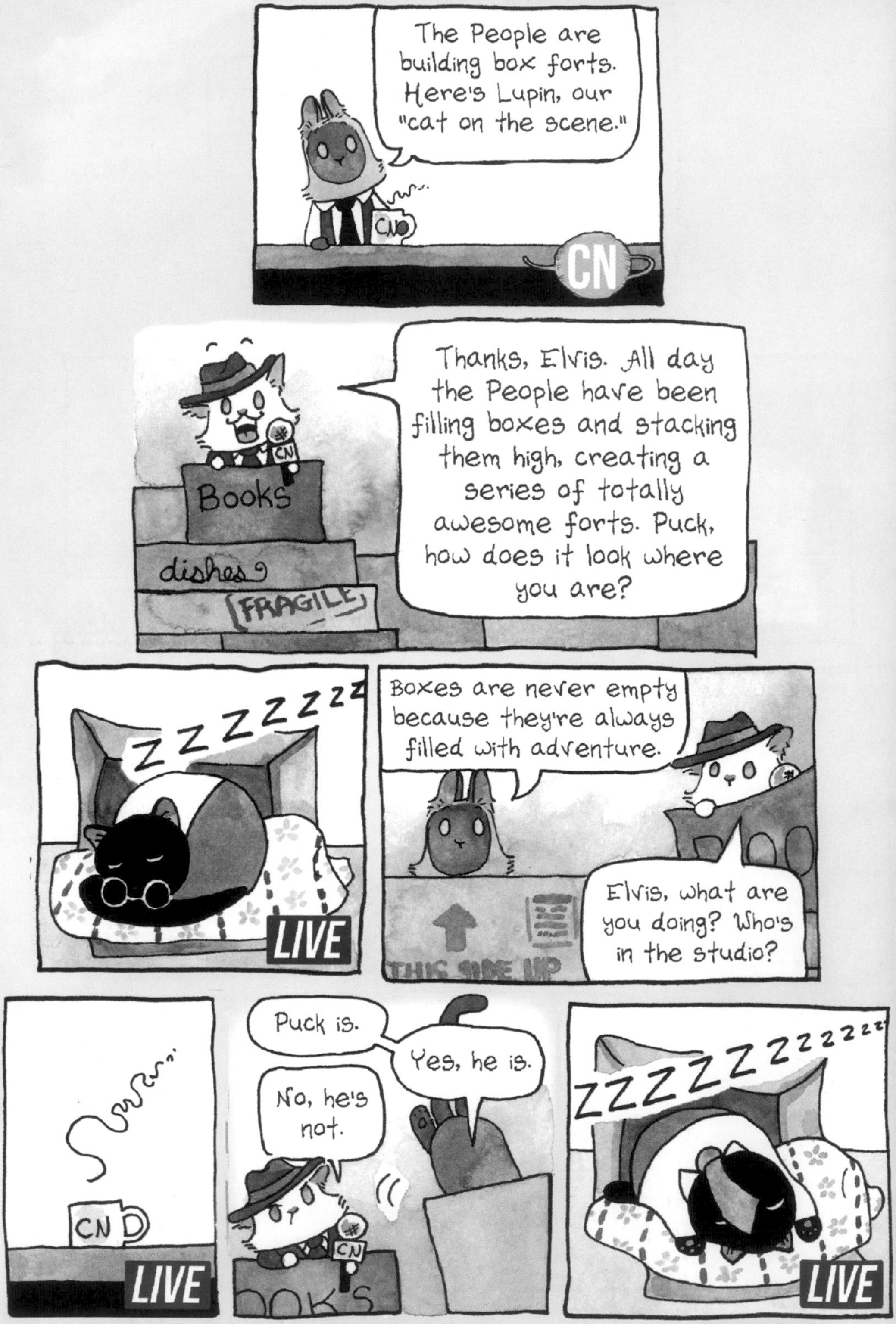
The People are building box forts. Here's Lupin, our "cat on the scene."
CN
CN
Thanks, Elvis. All day the People have been filling boxes and stacking them high, creating a series of totally awesome forts. Puck, how does it look where you are?
Books
dishes
FRAGILE
CN
ZZZZZZZ
LIVE
Boxes are never empty because they're always filled with adventure.
Elvis, what are you doing? Who's in the studio?
THIS SIDE UP
CN
LIVE
Puck is.
Yes, he is.
No, he's not.
CN
ZZZZZZZZZZZ
LIVE

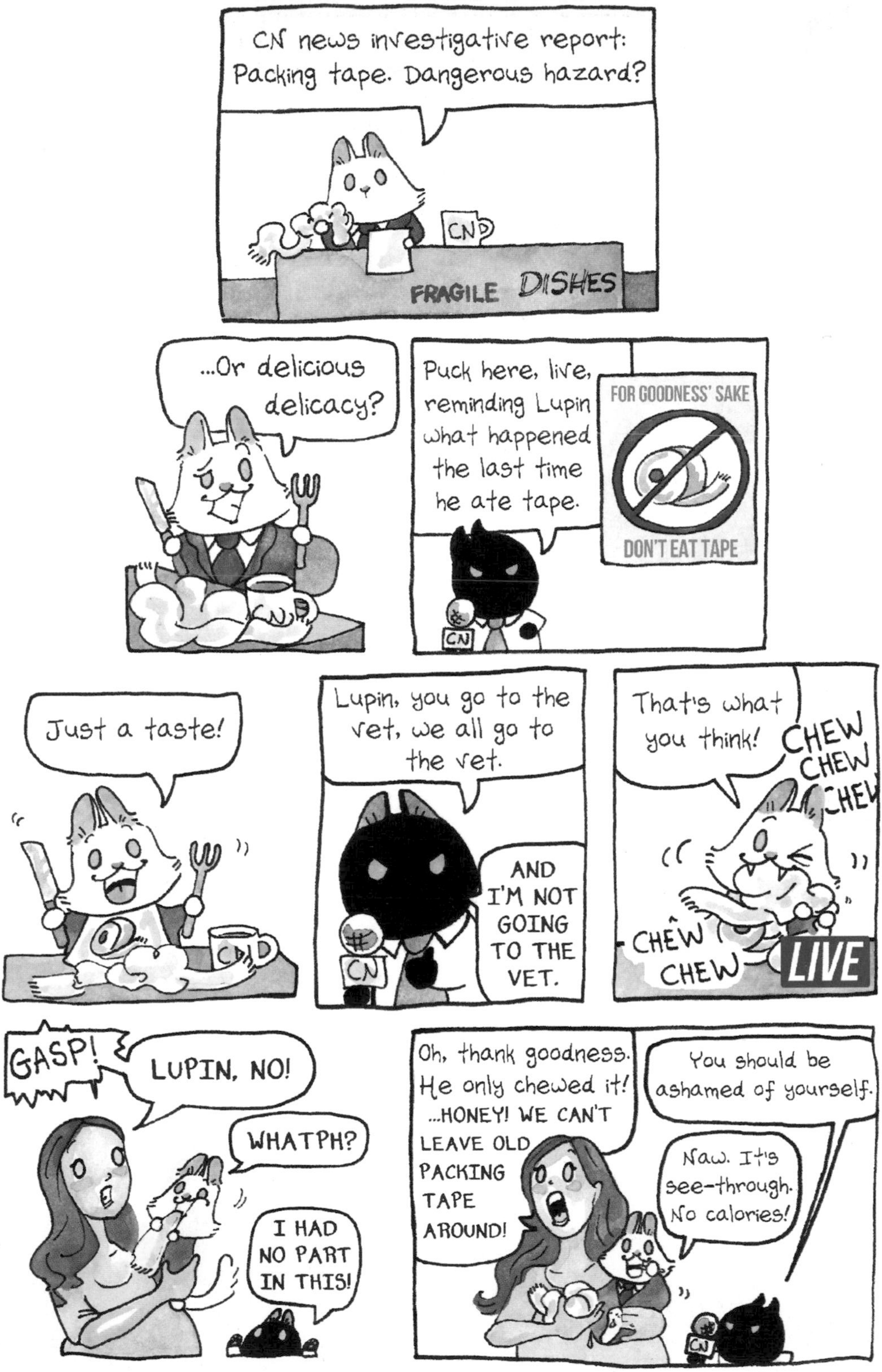

CN news investigative report: Packing tape. Dangerous hazard?
CN
FRAGILE DISHES
...Or delicious delicacy?
CN
Puck here, live, reminding Lupin what happened the last time he ate tape.
FOR GOODNESS' SAKE
DON'T EAT TAPE
CN
Just a taste!
Lupin, you go to the vet, we all go to the vet.
AND I'M NOT GOING TO THE VET.
CN
That's what you think!
CHEW CHEW CHEW
CHEW CHEW
LIVE
GASP!
LUPIN, NO!
WHATPH?
I HAD NO PART IN THIS!
Oh, thank goodness. He only chewed it! ...HONEY! WE CAN'T LEAVE OLD PACKING TAPE AROUND!
You should be ashamed of yourself.
Naw. It's see-through. No calories!
CN

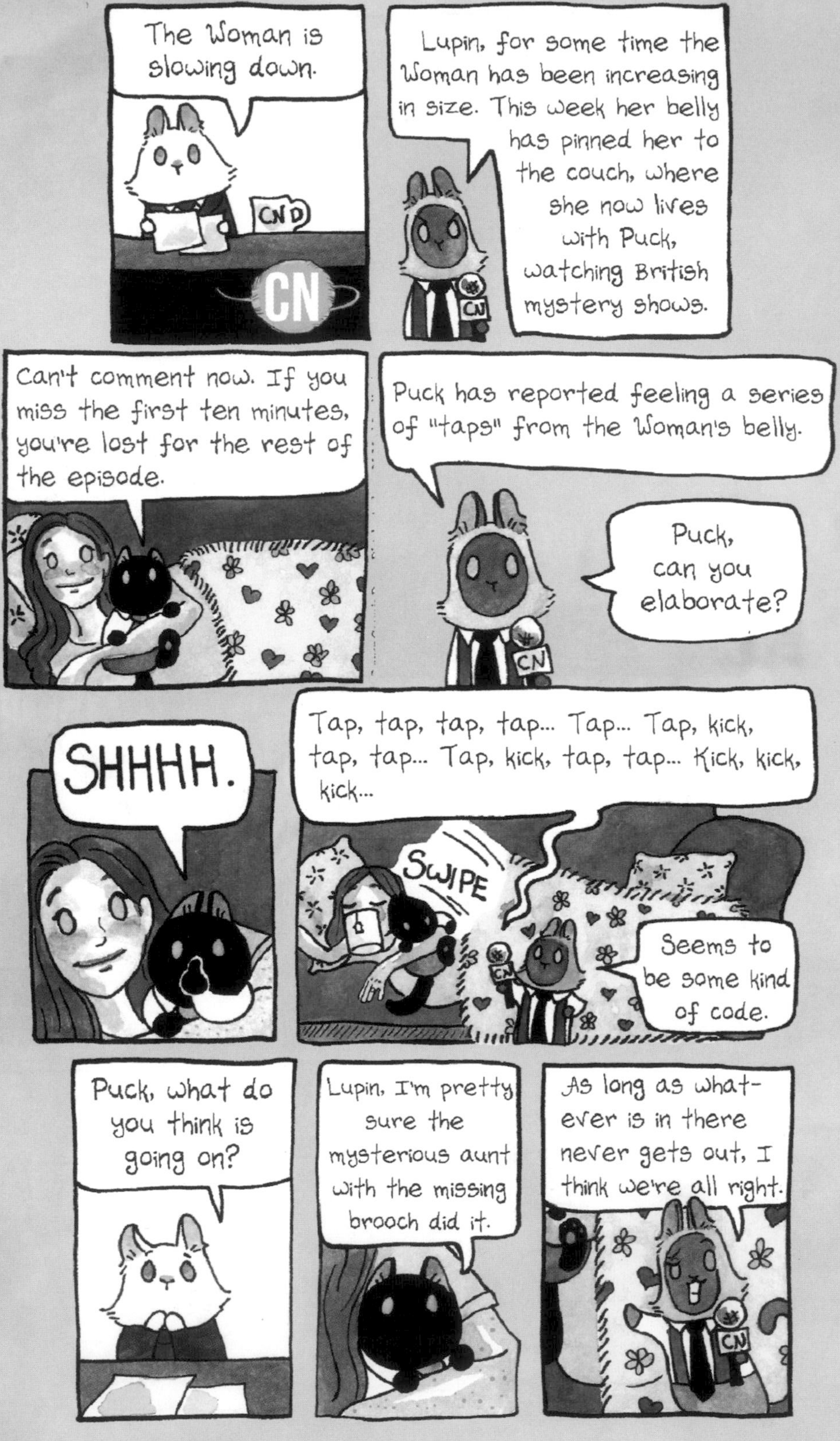

The Woman is slowing down.
CND
CN
Lupin, for some time the Woman has been increasing in size. This week her belly has pinned her to the couch, where she now lives with Puck, watching British mystery shows.
CN
Can't comment now. If you miss the first ten minutes, you're lost for the rest of the episode.
Puck has reported feeling a series of "taps" from the Woman's belly.
Puck, can you elaborate?
CN
SHHHH.
Tap, tap, tap, tap... Tap... Tap, kick, tap, tap... Tap, kick, tap, tap... Kick, kick, kick...
SWIPE
CN
Seems to be some kind of code.
Puck, what do you think is going on?
Lupin, I'm pretty sure the mysterious aunt with the missing brooch did it.
As long as whatever is in there never gets out, I think we're all right.
CN

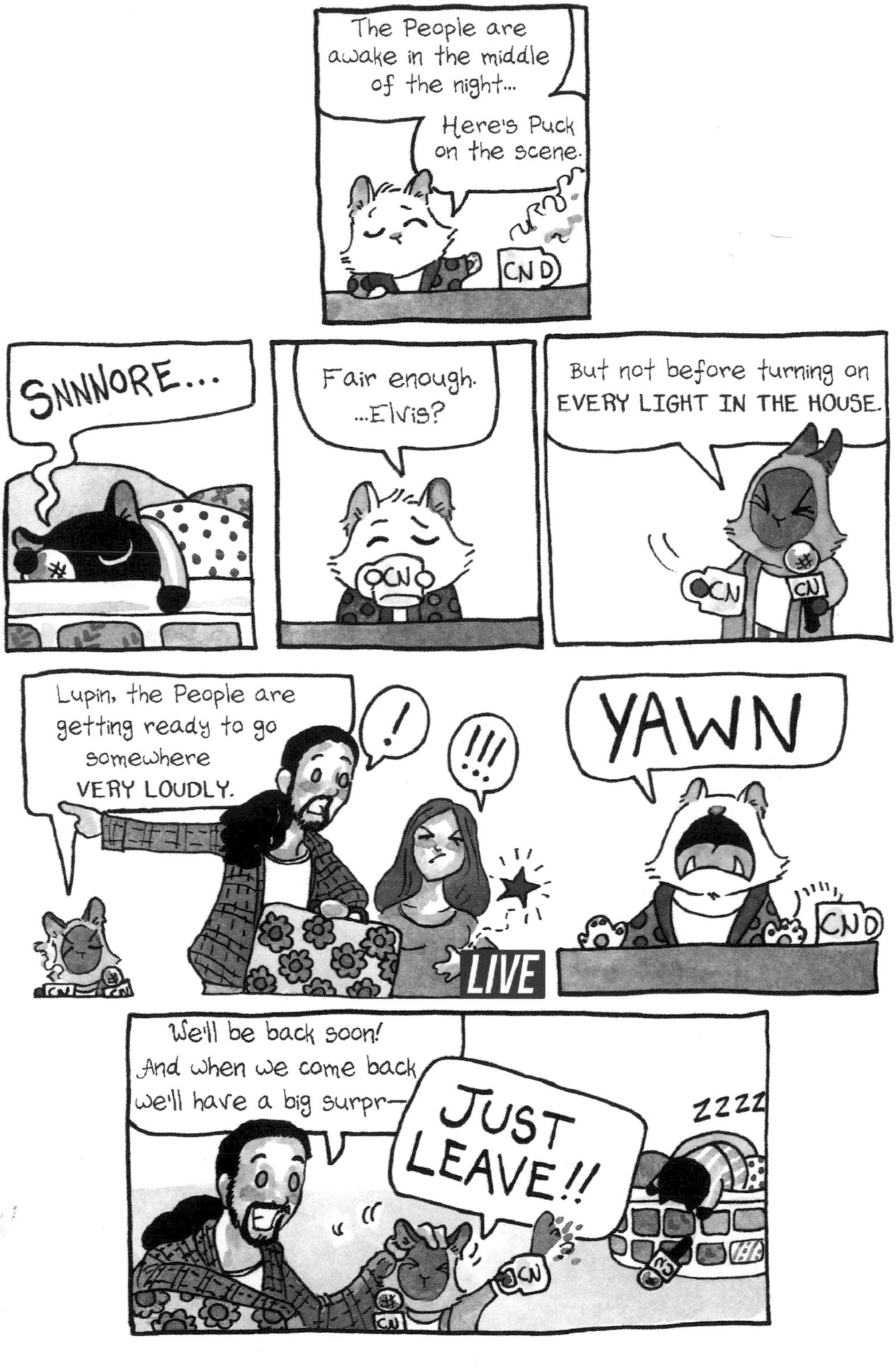
The People are awake in the middle of the night...
Here's Puck on the scene.
CND
SNNNORE...
Fair enough. ...Elvis?
CN
But not before turning on EVERY LIGHT IN THE HOUSE.
CN
CN
Lupin, the People are getting ready to go somewhere VERY LOUDLY.
!
!!!
LIVE
YAWN
CND
We'll be back soon! And when we come back we'll have a big surpr—
JUST LEAVE!!
ZZZZ
CN

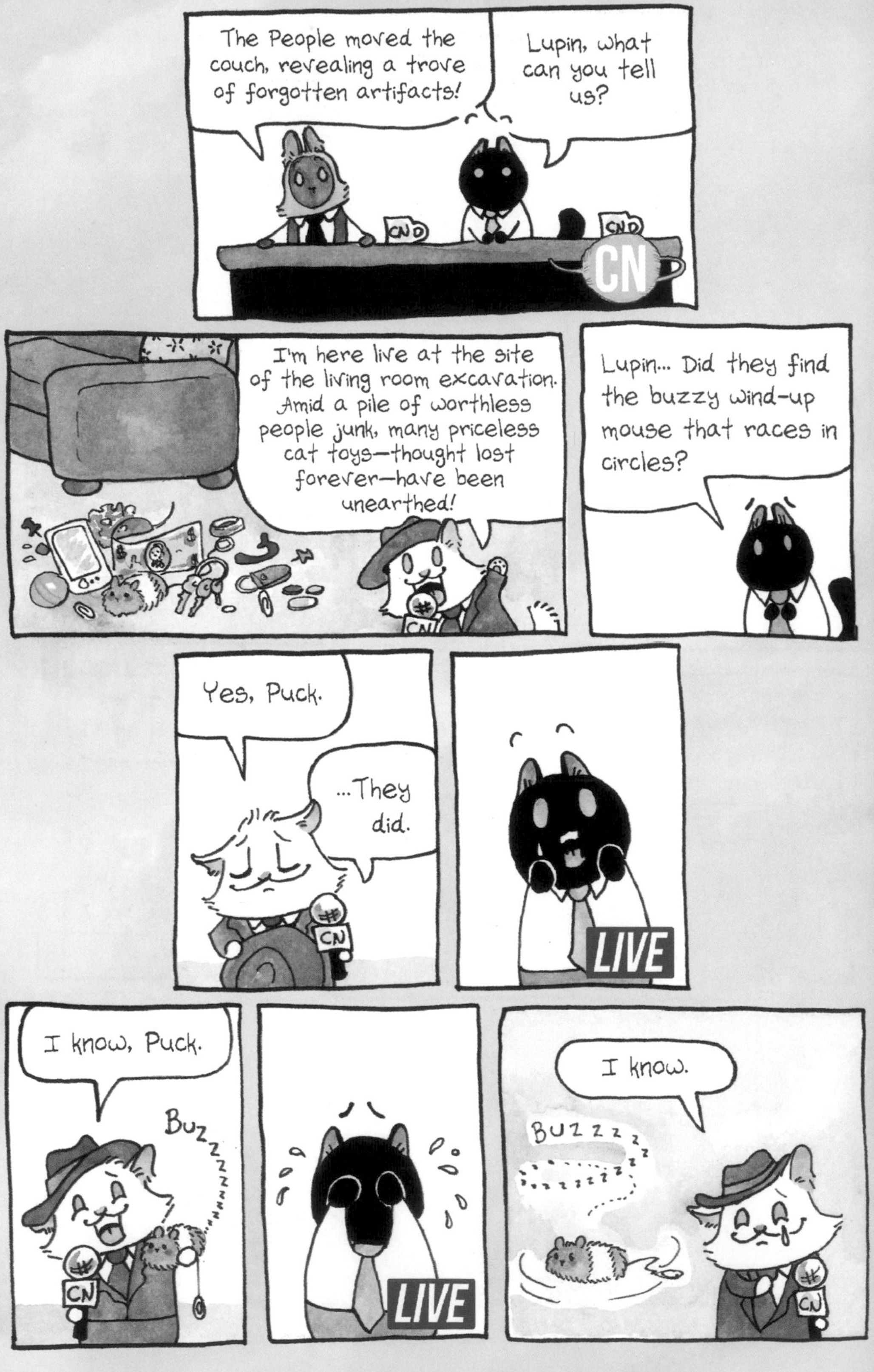
The People moved the couch, revealing a trove of forgotten artifacts!
Lupin, what can you tell us?
CND
CND
CN
I'm here live at the site of the living room excavation. Amid a pile of worthless people junk, many priceless cat toys—thought lost forever—have been unearthed!
Lupin... Did they find the buzzy wind-up mouse that races in circles?
Yes, Puck.
...They did.
LIVE
I know, Puck.
Buzzzzzzz
LIVE
I know.
BUZZZZZ

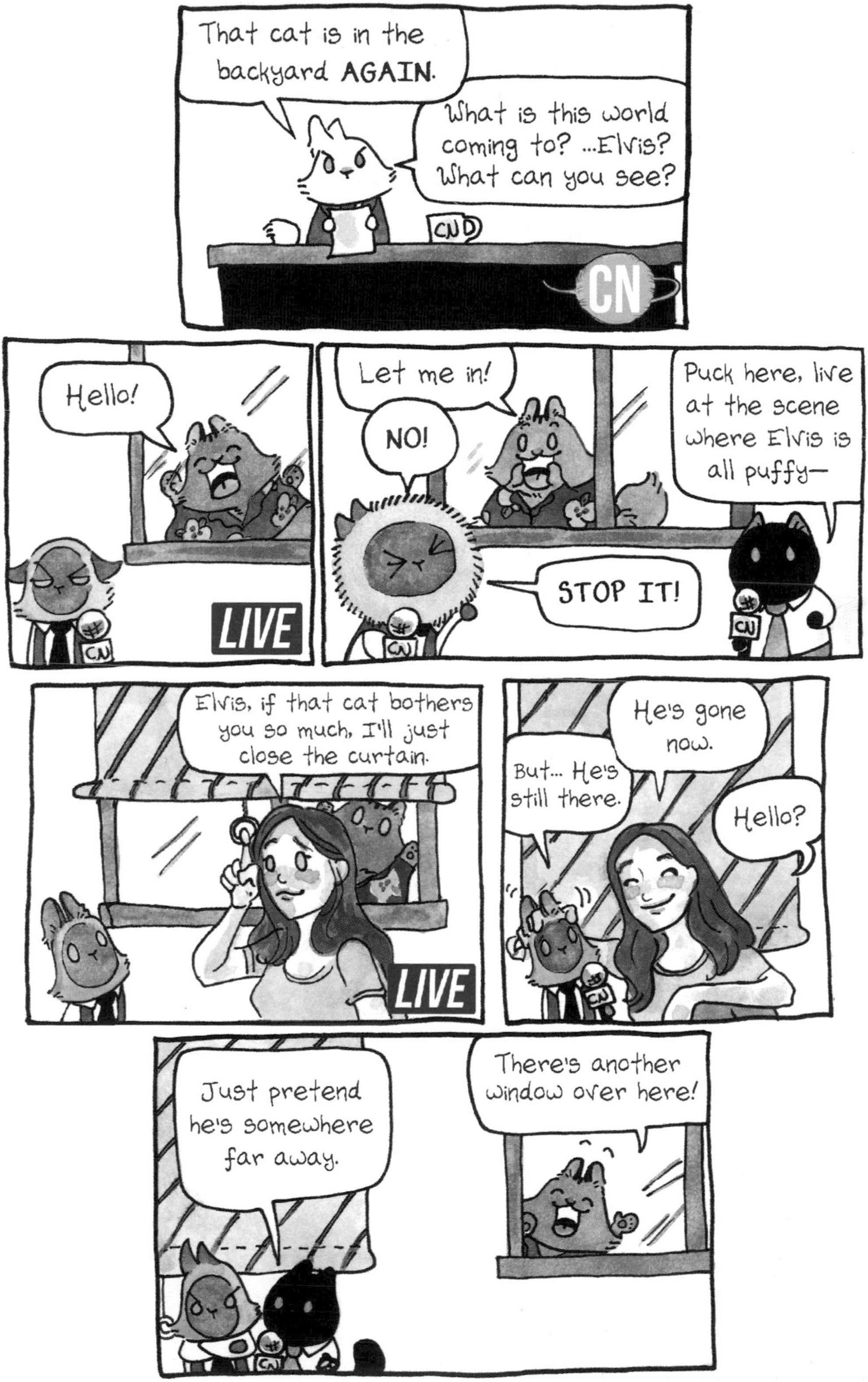

That cat is in the backyard AGAIN.
What is this world coming to? ...Elvis? What can you see?
CN
Hello!
LIVE
Let me in!
NO!
Puck here, live at the scene where Elvis is all puffy—
STOP IT!
Elvis, if that cat bothers you so much, I'll just close the curtain.
LIVE
He's gone now.
But... He's still there.
Hello?
Just pretend he's somewhere far away.
There's another window over here!

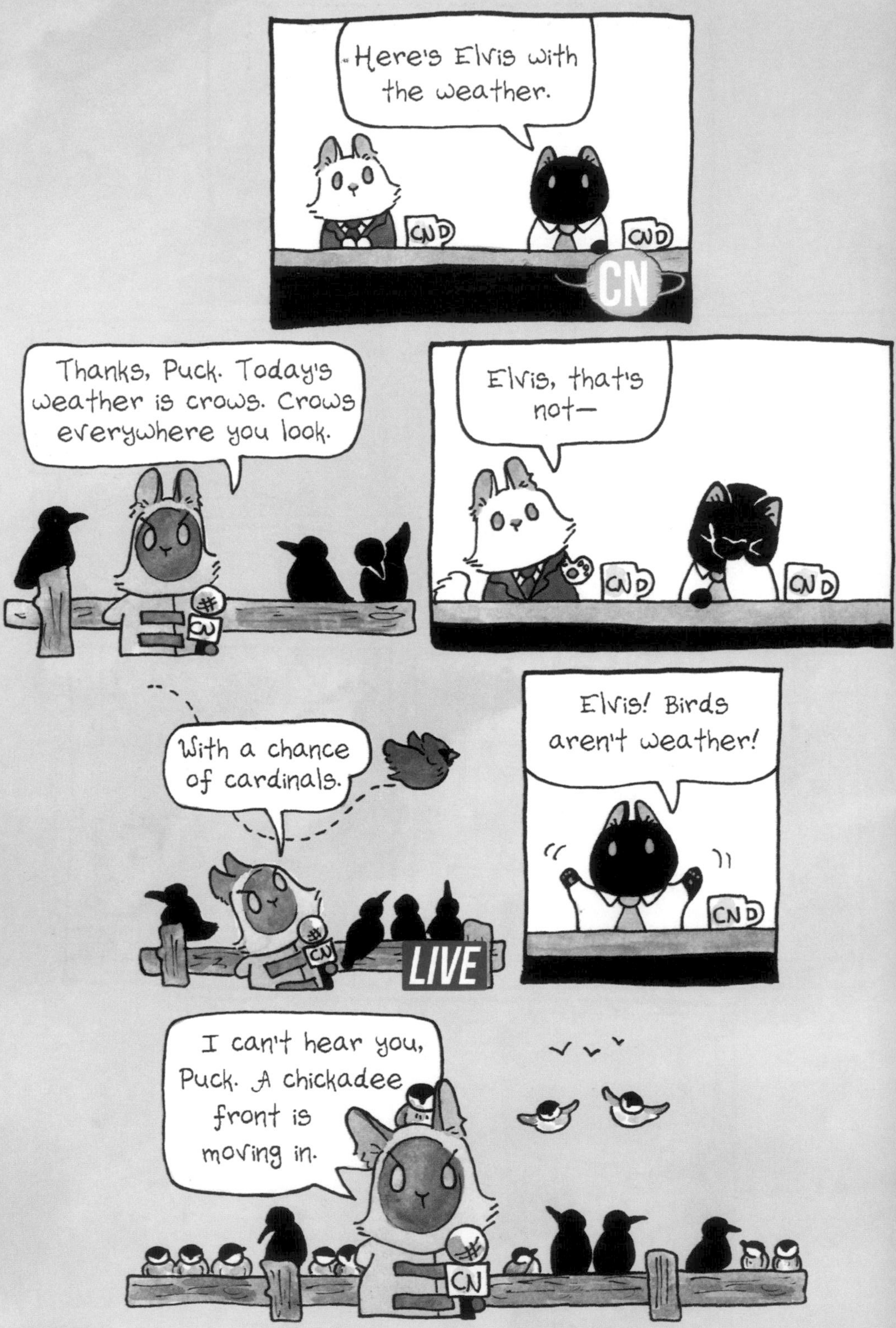
Here's Elvis with the weather.
CND
CND
CN
Thanks, Puck. Today's weather is crows. Crows everywhere you look.
CN
Elvis, that's not—
CND
CND
With a chance of cardinals.
CN
LIVE
Elvis! Birds aren't weather!
CND
I can't hear you, Puck. A chickadee front is moving in.
CN

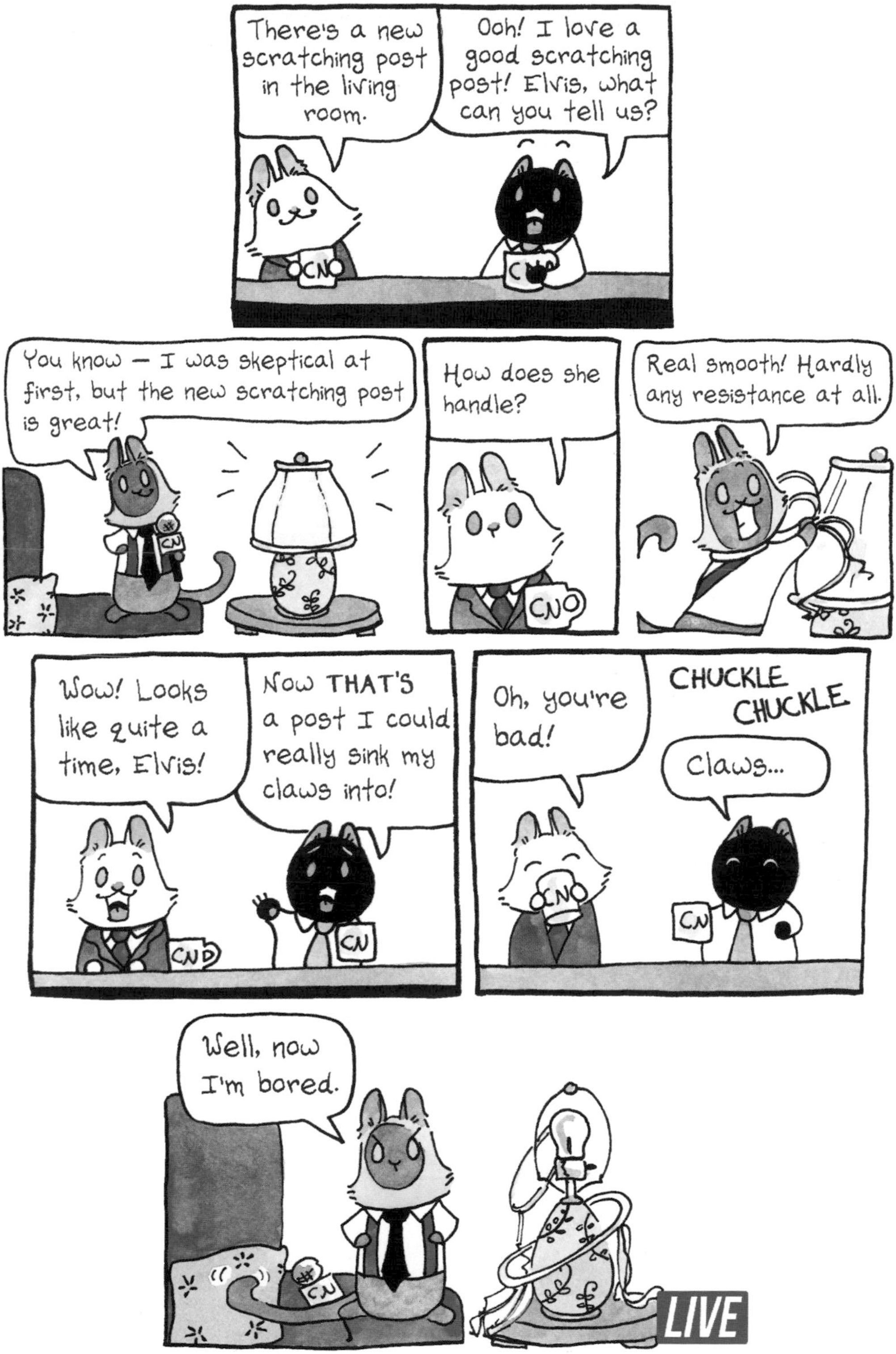
There's a new scratching post in the living room.
Ooh! I love a good scratching post! Elvis, what can you tell us?
You know — I was skeptical at first, but the new scratching post is great!
How does she handle?
Real smooth! Hardly any resistance at all.
Wow! Looks like quite a time, Elvis!
Now THAT'S a post I could really sink my claws into!
Oh, you're bad!
CHUCKLE CHUCKLE
Claws...
Well, now I'm bored.
LIVE

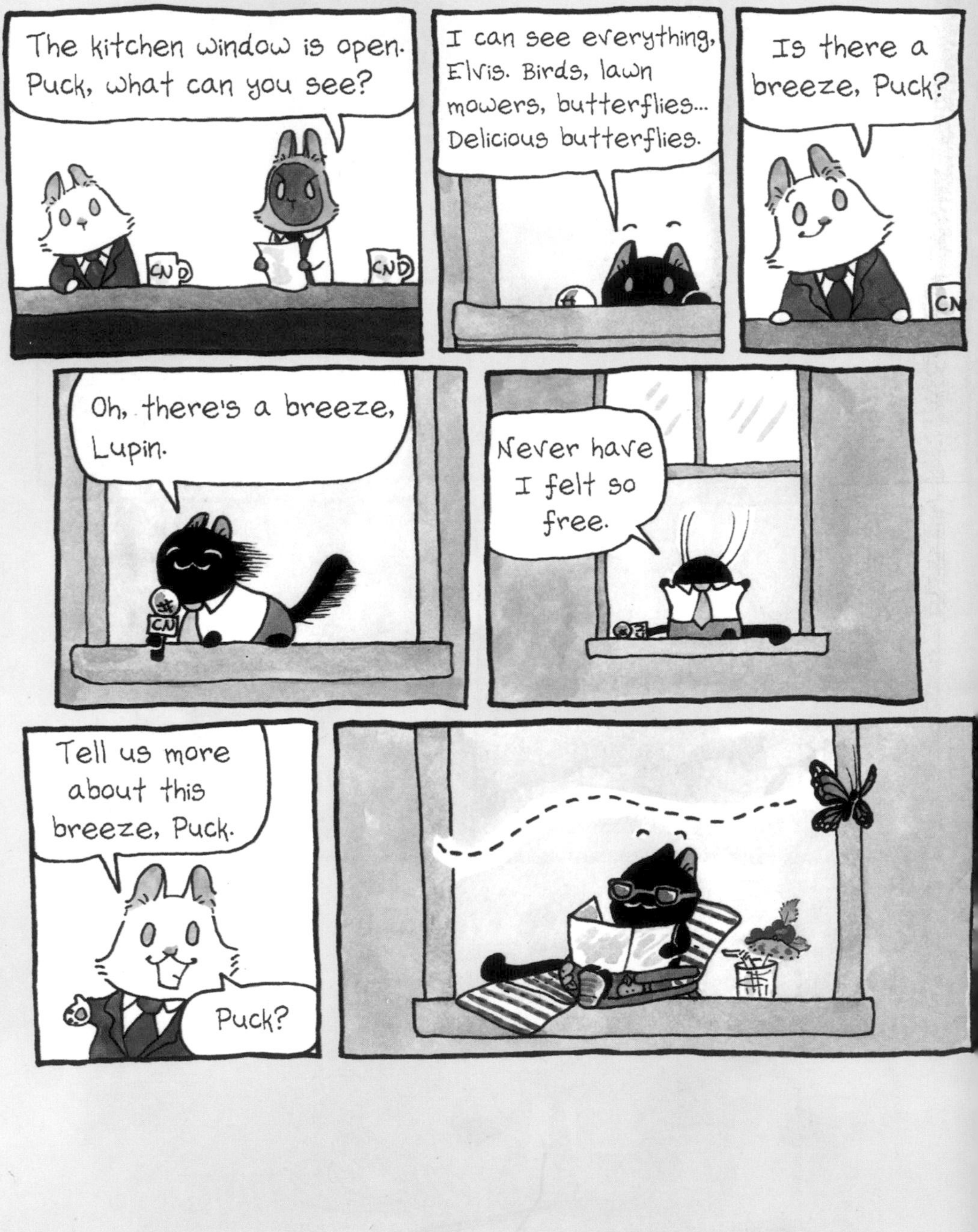
The kitchen window is open. Puck, what can you see?
I can see everything, Elvis. Birds, lawn mowers, butterflies... Delicious butterflies.
Is there a breeze, Puck?
Oh, there's a breeze, Lupin.
Never have I felt so free.
Tell us more about this breeze, Puck.
Puck?

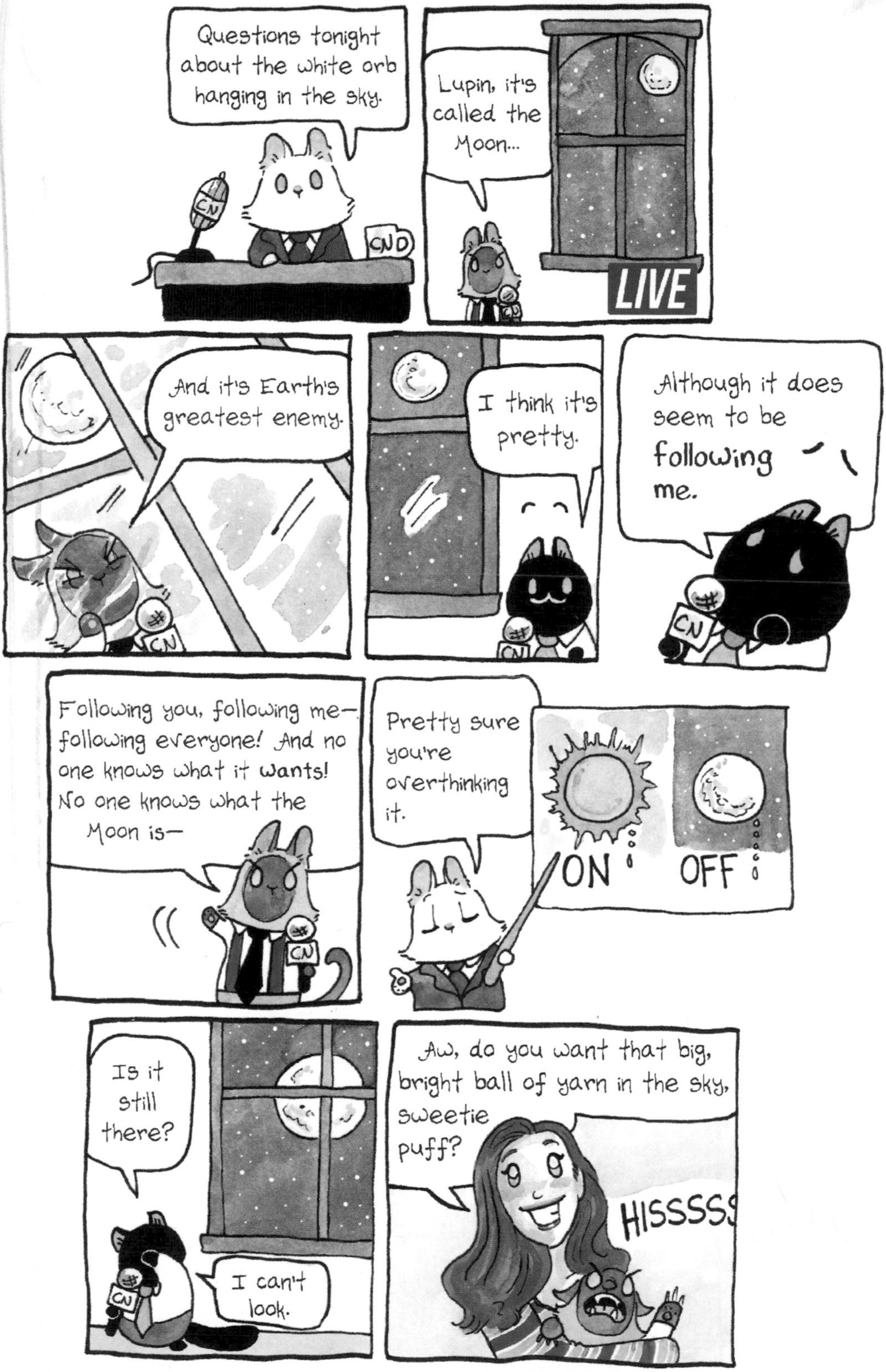
Questions tonight about the white orb hanging in the sky.
CN
CND
Lupin, it's called the Moon...
LIVE
And it's Earth's greatest enemy.
CN
I think it's pretty.
CN
Although it does seem to be following me.
CN
Following you, following me— following everyone! And no one knows what it wants! No one knows what the Moon is—
CN
Pretty sure you're overthinking it.
ON
OFF
Is it still there?
CN
I can't look.
Aw, do you want that big, bright ball of yarn in the sky, sweetie puff?
HISSSSS

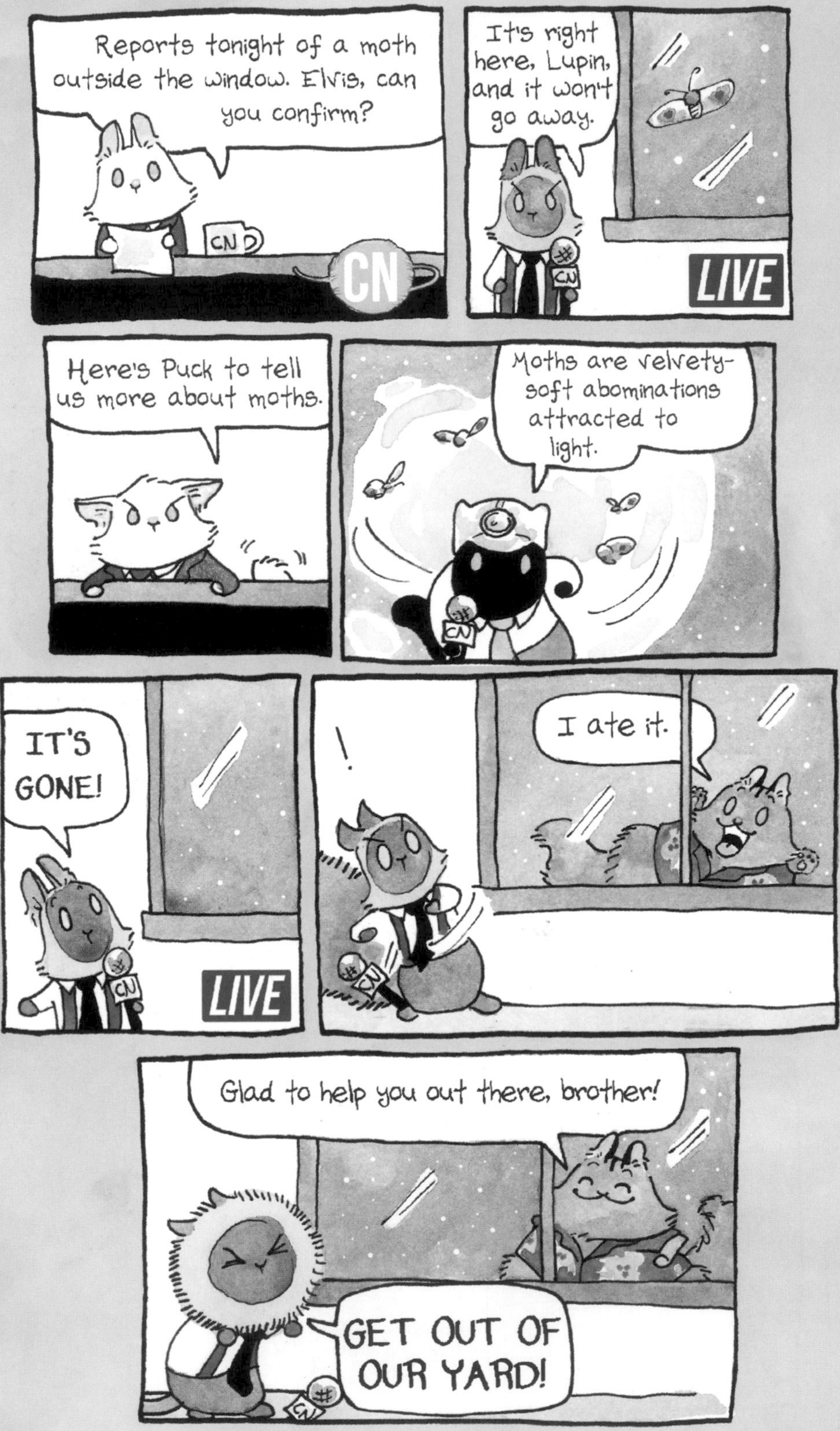

Reports tonight of a moth outside the window. Elvis, can you confirm?
CN
CN
It's right here, Lupin, and it won't go away.
CN
LIVE
Here's Puck to tell us more about moths.
Moths are velvety-soft abominations attracted to light.
CN
IT'S GONE!
CN
LIVE
!
I ate it.
Glad to help you out there, brother!
GET OUT OF OUR YARD!

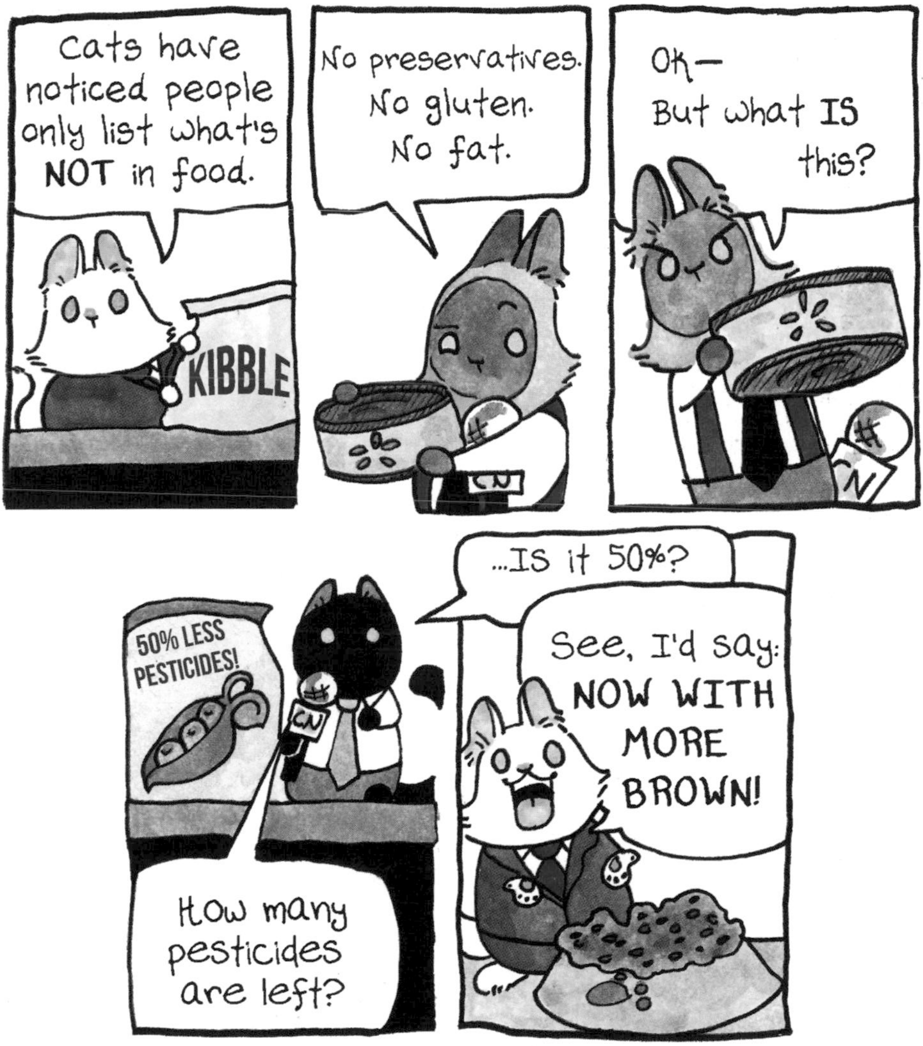
Cats have noticed people only list what's NOT in food.
KIBBLE
No preservatives. No gluten. No fat.
Ok— But what IS this?
50% LESS PESTICIDES!
How many pesticides are left?
...IS it 50%?
See, I'd say: NOW WITH MORE BROWN!

This just in: Elvis is holding onto the couch for dear life.
CN
Elvis, let go.
YOU LET GO.
ELVIS–
I'M. ALL. COMFY.
LIVE
Really got to admire the tenacity, Lupin.
CN
SO COZY.

A June bug got into the house—
CND
BRRRRRZzzzzzzz
GAH!
LIVE
Where'd it go?
Where'd it go?!
ZZZZZZZ
The June bug has been dive-bombing us for 20 minutes and seems—
GET IT AWAY!
BRRRRZZZ
EEEEEEEK!

A June bug is a Mediterranean date with a hard candy shell.
BUZZ TRUMPET
TOO MANY LEGS
IMPOSSIBLY FAST WINGS
MORE LEGS
CENTRAL BUZZING SYSTEM
CN
BRRRRR
They're battery-operated and remote-controlled by SATAN.
Hee Hee Hee!
Zzzzzz
There's no telling where it will strike next—

BRRRRRRZZZ
Hee Hee Hee
BRRRRRZZZZZZ
Is...
Is he gone?
ZZZ
BOINK
BOINK
BOINK
HA HA HA
BBBRRRRRZZZZZZZ
C'mon, dude—

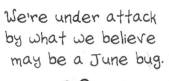

We're under attack by what we believe may be a June bug.

BB-BB-BRRRR

ZZZZZ Zzzz

UGH IT FEELS GROSS!

LIVE

SLAM

BBRRRZzzz

NOPE.

THAT'S ENOUGH.

PATH OF LEAST RESISTANCE.

Till next we make battle, noble adversary.

Guys, it's JULY!

JULY

The vacuum cleaner appeared suddenly in the hallway!

It was panic in the sheets, Lupin, as cats scattered to safety.

Leaving two reporters under the bed—

And stranding one abandoned, betrayed Siamese under the couch **TO DIE ALONE.**

We're live where the vacuum has divided cats under the couch and bed—

Wait— Where did you get a safety helmet?

Not important, Elvis.

Yes, it is! If there are helmets, I want one!

Elvis, the helmets are neither here nor there—

THEN GIVE ME **YOURS!**

This reporter cannot see the vacuum from his excellent vantage point under the couch...

...with **NO FRIENDS** to obscure his view.

We here under the bed would like once again to extend our sincerest apologies—

And once again, my anger shield is deflecting them back into your faces.

THIS JUST IN: THE VACUUM HAS COME FOR ME. GOODBYE FOREVER.

GUILT TRIP EXTENDED

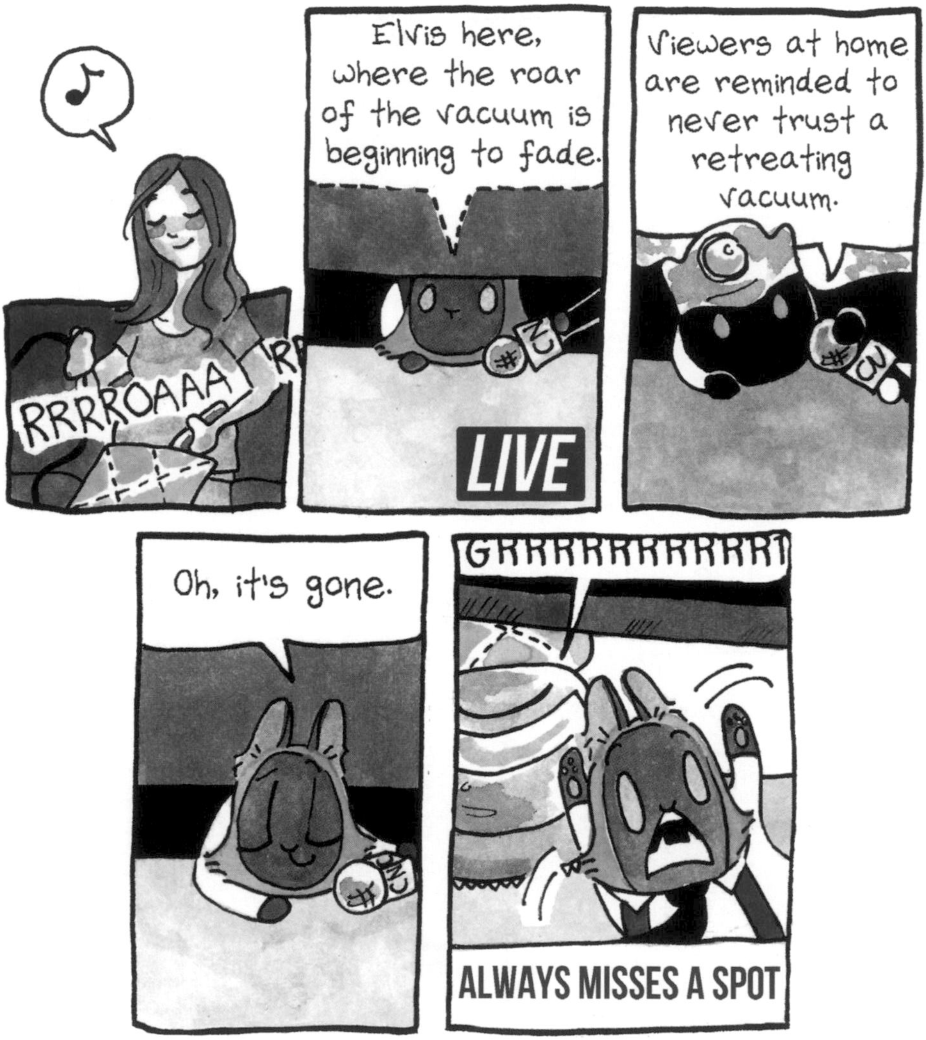

RRRROAAA
RR
Elvis here, where the roar of the vacuum is beginning to fade.
LIVE
Viewers at home are reminded to never trust a retreating vacuum.
Oh, it's gone.
GRRRRRRRRRRRT
ALWAYS MISSES A SPOT

The vacuum appears ready to strike right where Elvis is hiding!

Elvis! Are you ok?!

SILENT SCREAMING

Pucky, NO!

I can't just let this happen!

A HERO EMERGES!

Puck!

LEAVE HIM ALONE, HE'S HYSTERICAL!

BAT

BAT

BAT

BAT

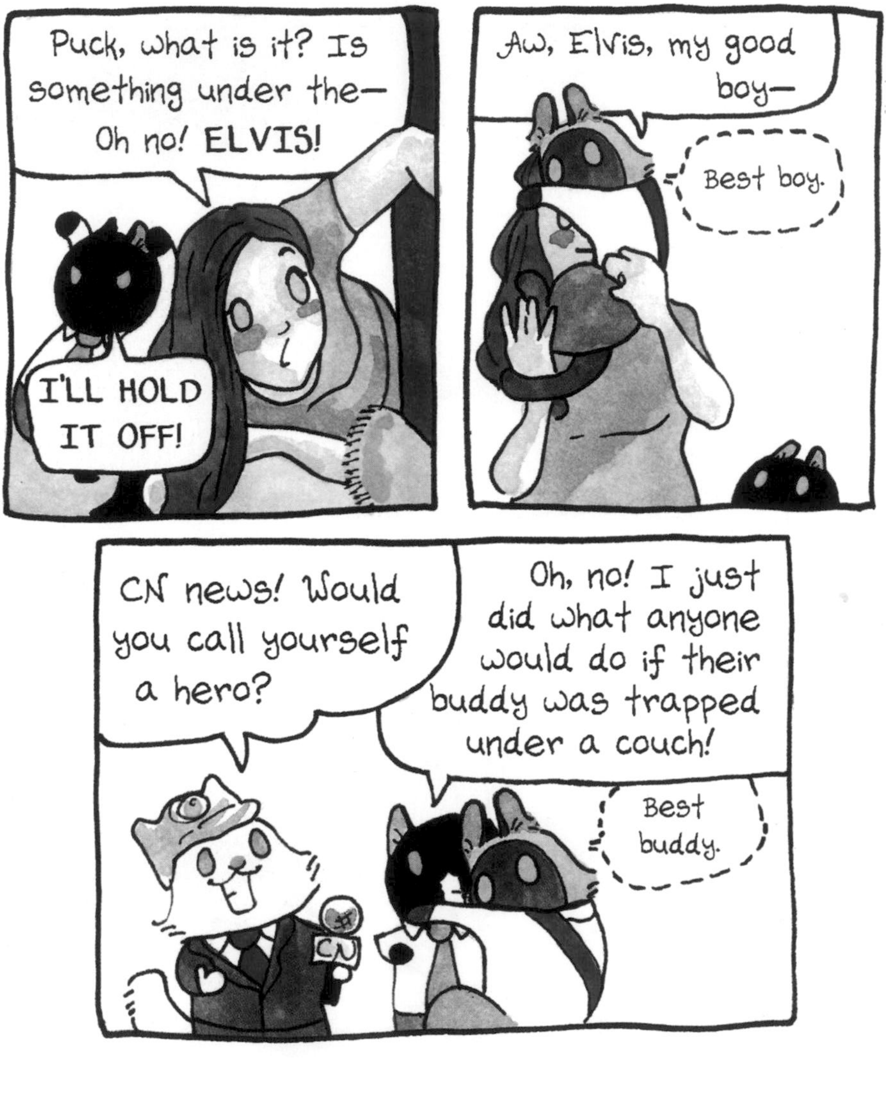
Puck, what is it? Is something under the— Oh no! ELVIS!
I'LL HOLD IT OFF!
Aw, Elvis, my good boy—
Best boy.
CN news! Would you call yourself a hero?
Oh, no! I just did what anyone would do if their buddy was trapped under a couch!
Best buddy.
CN

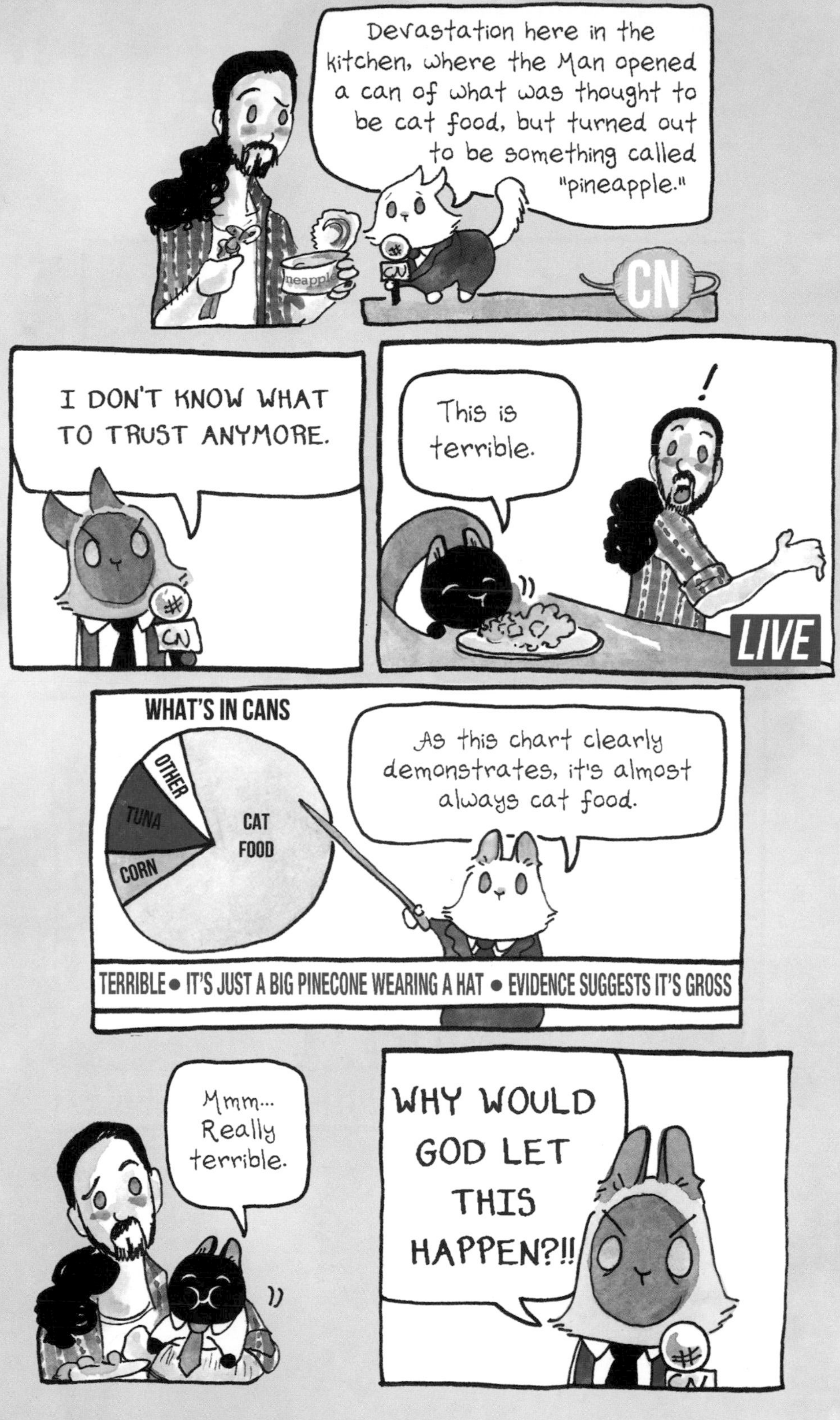
Devastation here in the kitchen, where the Man opened a can of what was thought to be cat food, but turned out to be something called "pineapple."
neapple
CN
I DON'T KNOW WHAT TO TRUST ANYMORE.
CN
This is terrible.
LIVE
WHAT'S IN CANS
OTHER
TUNA
CORN
CAT FOOD
As this chart clearly demonstrates, it's almost always cat food.
TERRIBLE • IT'S JUST A BIG PINECONE WEARING A HAT • EVIDENCE SUGGESTS IT'S GROSS
Mmm... Really terrible.
WHY WOULD GOD LET THIS HAPPEN?!!

Sounds of pouring kibble have been reported from the kitchen!

Oh, Elvis, no buddy—

Lupin, it's the biggest bag of kibble I've ever seen.

Rice

25 lbs

Lupin, Puck here with a conflicting report that it may not actually be kibble.

Rice

I know what I heard, Puck.

definitely Rice

More kibble for me.

NOTHING LIKE KIBBLE

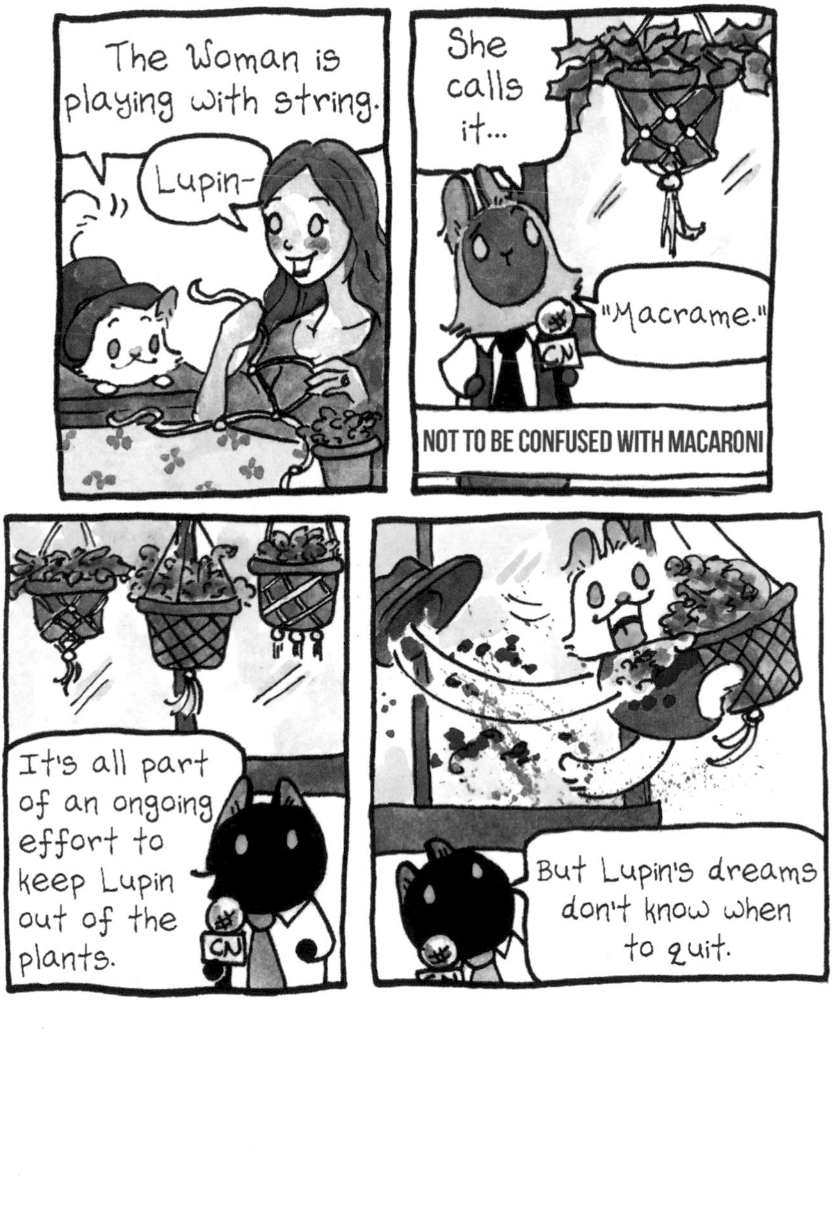
The Woman is playing with string.
Lupin-
She calls it...
"Macrame."
NOT TO BE CONFUSED WITH MACARONI
It's all part of an ongoing effort to keep Lupin out of the plants.
But Lupin's dreams don't know when to quit.

The People are yelling about something. Elvis, any idea what all the commotion is about?

ELVIS! OFF THE TABLE!

No idea, Puck.

GET DOWN, ELVIS!

NOW, ELVIS.

But it's really got them worked up.

ELVIS!

RIGHT NOW!

They're getting hysterical.

ELVIS!

SERIOUSLY, GET DOWN!

LIVE

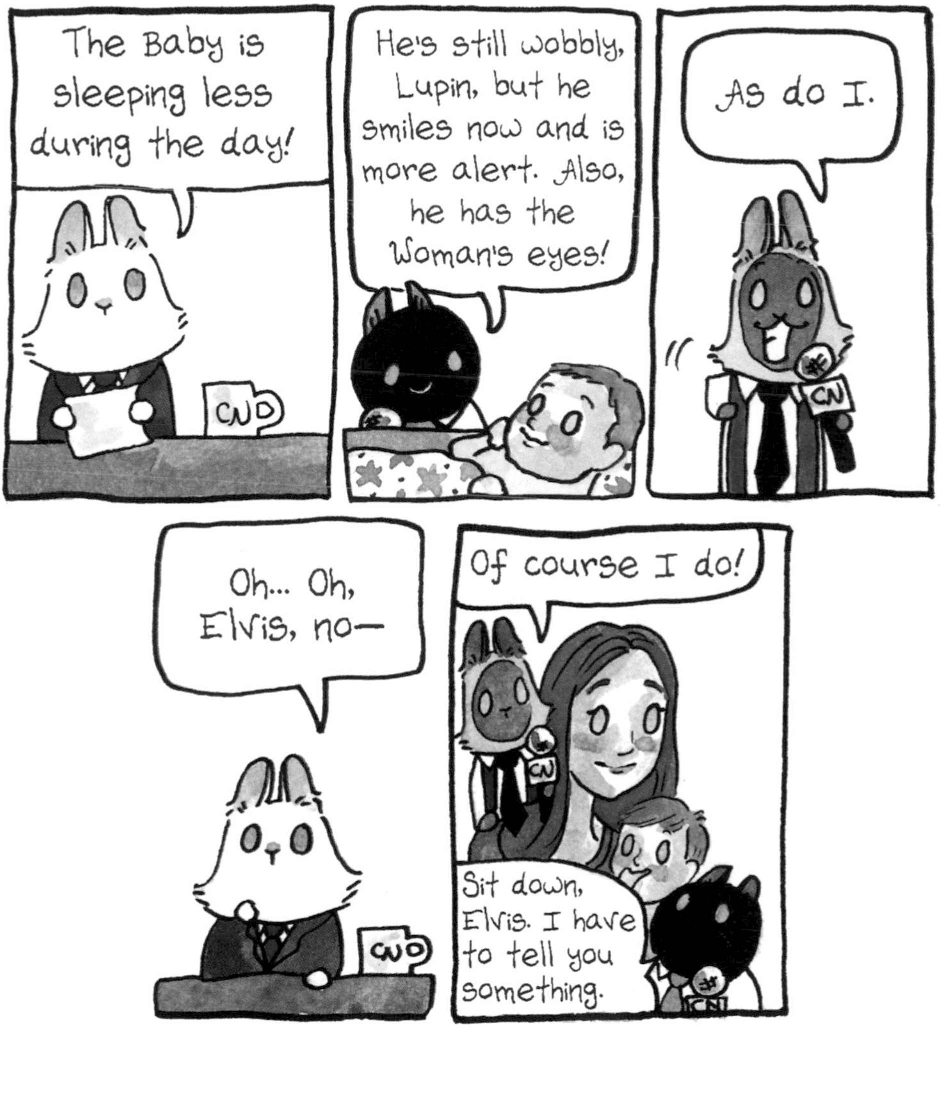
The Baby is sleeping less during the day!
He's still wobbly, Lupin, but he smiles now and is more alert. Also, he has the Woman's eyes!
As do I.
CN
Oh... Oh, Elvis, no—
Of course I do!
CN
Sit down, Elvis. I have to tell you something.

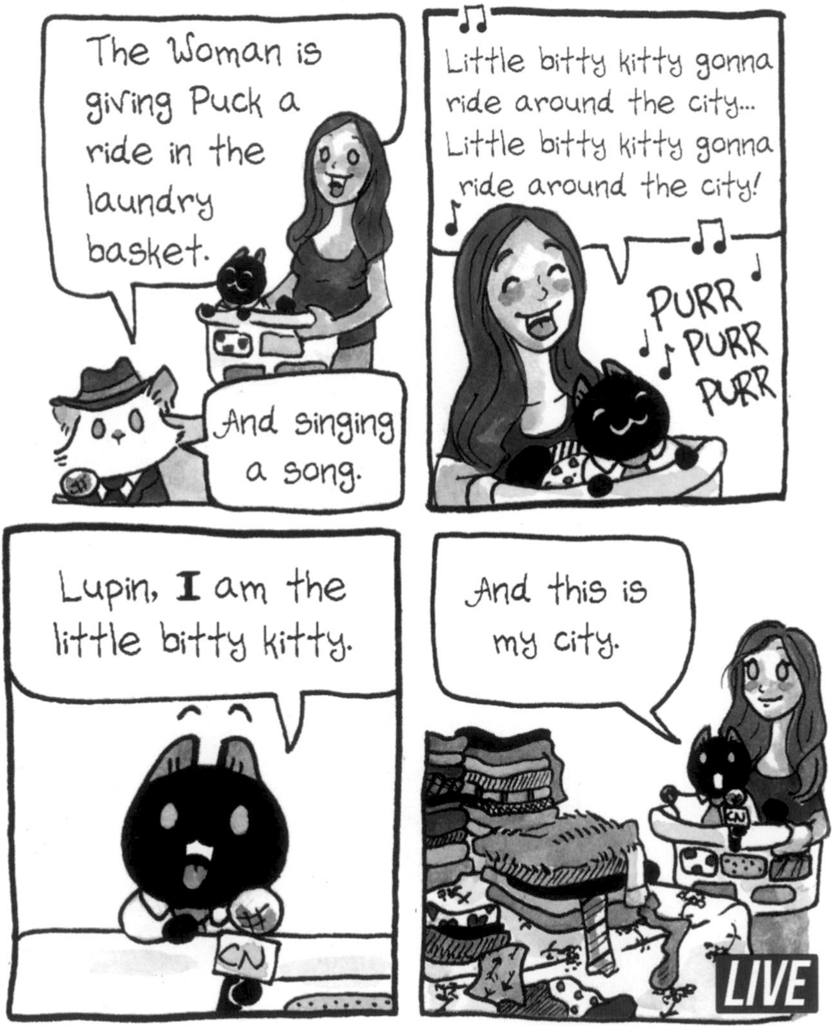
The Woman is giving Puck a ride in the laundry basket.
And singing a song.
Little bitty kitty gonna ride around the city... Little bitty kitty gonna ride around the city!
PURR PURR PURR
Lupin, I am the little bitty kitty.
CN
And this is my city.
CN
LIVE

Afternoon sunspot won't stay still!

TIMELAPSE FOOTAGE

1PM

2PM

3PM

I'M EXHAUSTED.

4PM

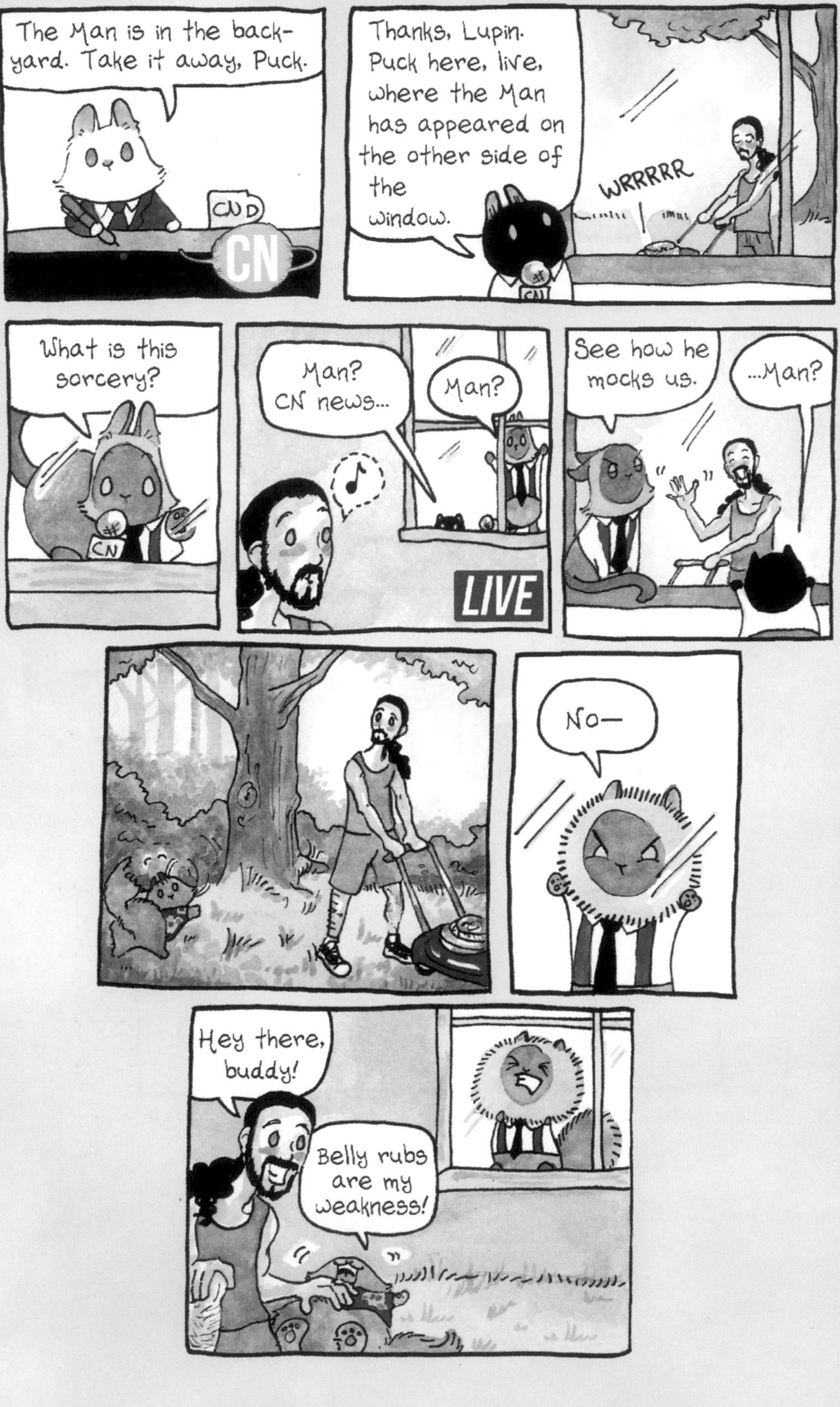

The Man is in the backyard. Take it away, Puck.
CND
CN
Thanks, Lupin. Puck here, live, where the Man has appeared on the other side of the window.
WRRRRR
CN
What is this sorcery?
CN
Man? CN news...
Man?
LIVE
See how he mocks us.
...Man?
No—
Hey there, buddy!
Belly rubs are my weakness!

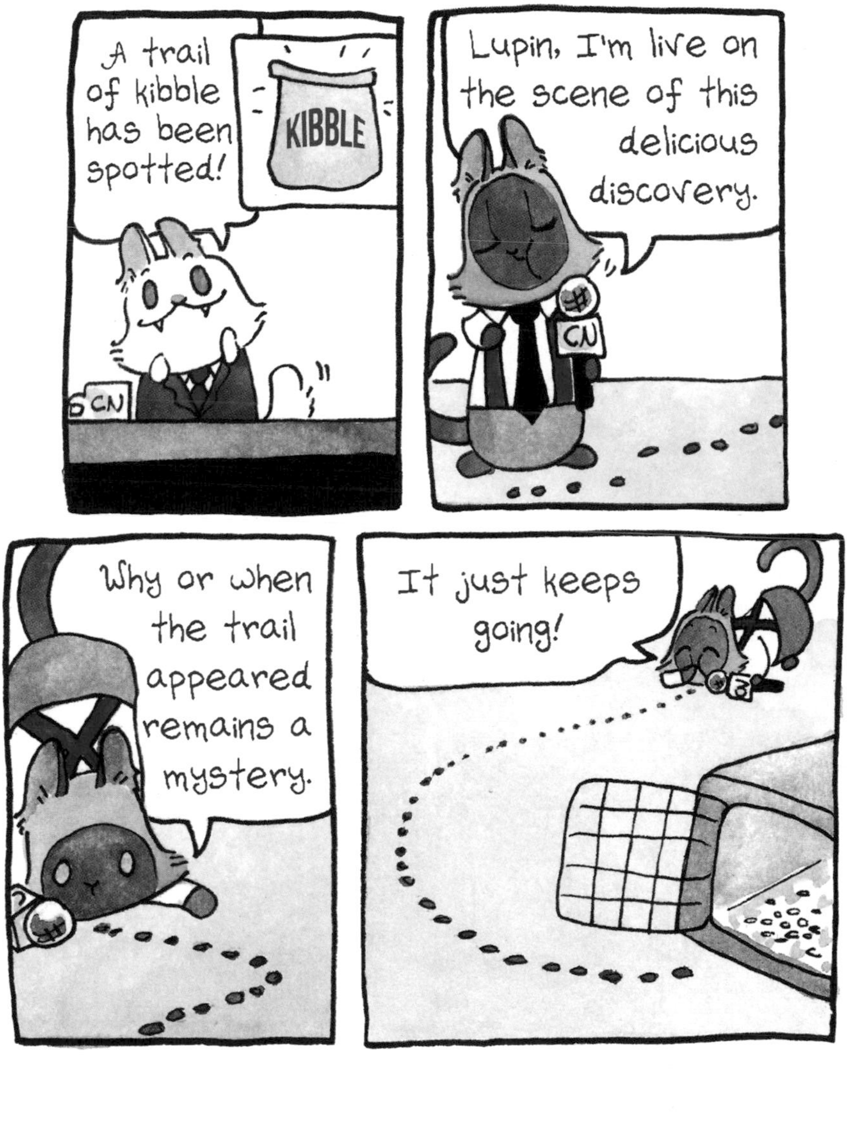
A trail of kibble has been spotted!
KIBBLE
CN
Lupin, I'm live on the scene of this delicious discovery.
CN
Why or when the trail appeared remains a mystery.
It just keeps going!

Trails of kibble have been—

OH, HELLO.

THIS JUST IN: THE KIBBLE IS BAIT! DO NOT FOLLOW!

LIVE

I'm not following the kibble.

...We both just happen to be here...

This whole thing smacks of TREACHERY!

We are being trapped in cages! THE KIBBLE WAS A TRAP!

KIBBLE QUIBBLE

Now that the kibble is gone...

...all this reporter tastes is regret.

Puck is our last remaining hope. Puck, wherever you are, don't leave! Stay where you are!

Will do, Elvis.

It'll be OK, Elvis!
—I won't stand for this! It's an OUT-RAGE!
LOCAL CATS OUTRAGED
You're just going to the vet!
WHAT?!
No, thank you.
I'm good.
Georgia Dunn
BCN-14
8-17

You'll pay for this!
CAT VOWS REVENGE

Aw, the boys are so upset.
Ma'am!
MA'AM!
It'll be ok.
CN news, Ma'am? ... Ma'am?
MA'AM
They're yelling at me.
They're yelling at both of us.
MA'AM!
CN news,
Thanks, honey.

I'm reporting to you live from the VET'S OFFICE, where we have been BETRAYED.
LIVE
The word "VET" is an acronym for "very evil tyrant."
Or is it "very eager tickler..."
Everything the vet does kinda tickles...
I had a chart, but it's at home.
VORACIOUS EAGLE TAMER

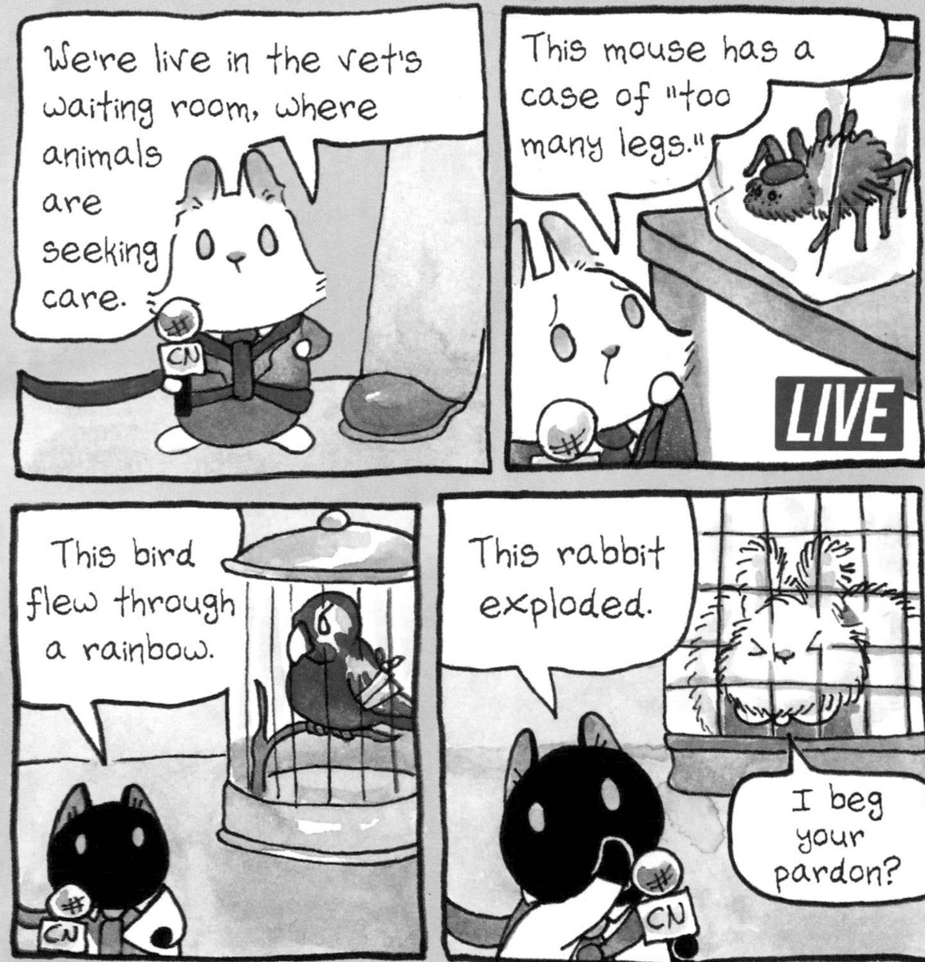
We're live in the vet's waiting room, where animals are seeking care.
CN
This mouse has a case of "too many legs."
LIVE
This bird flew through a rainbow.
CN
This rabbit exploded.
I beg your pardon?
CN

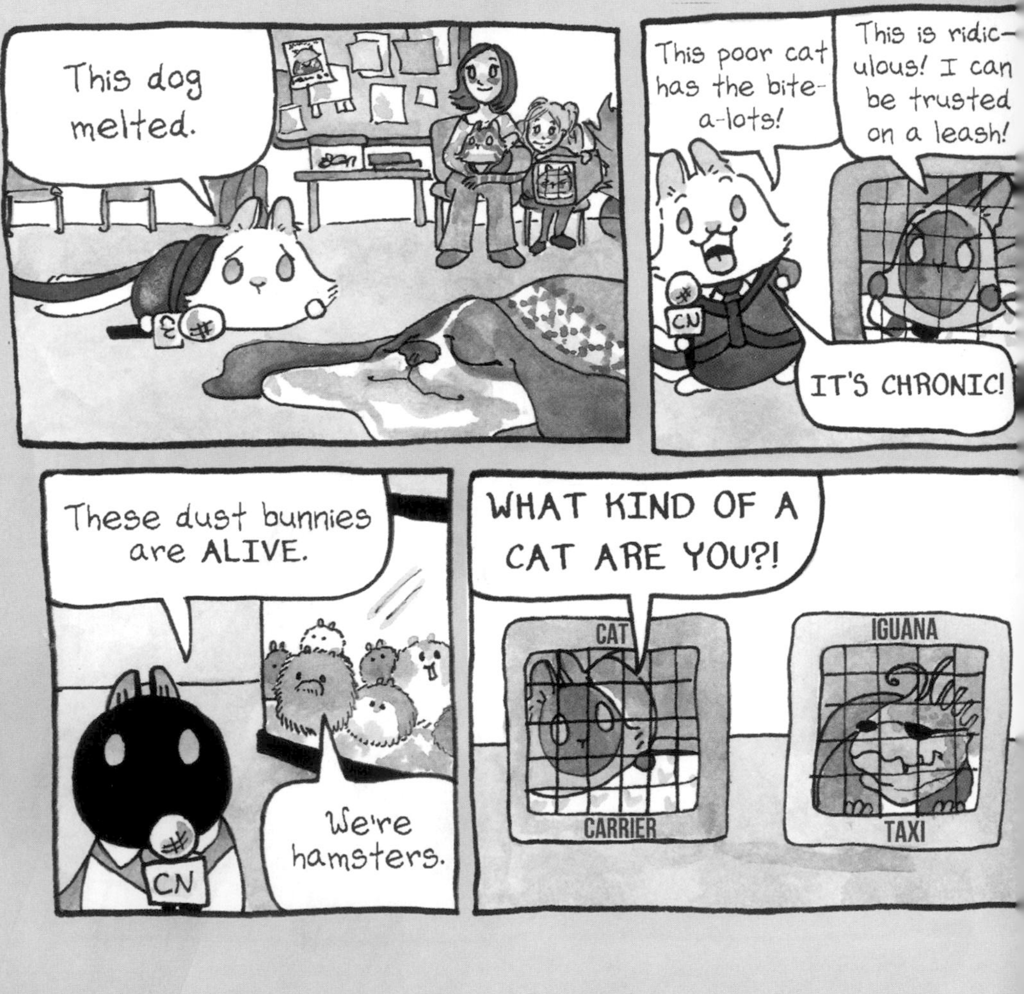
This dog melted.
This poor cat has the bite-a-lots!
This is ridiculous! I can be trusted on a leash!
IT'S CHRONIC!
These dust bunnies are ALIVE.
We're hamsters.
WHAT KIND OF A CAT ARE YOU?!
CAT CARRIER
IGUANA TAXI

And what's this little guy's name?
Elvis.
CAT CARRIER
Whew, he is angry!
Oh—I wouldn't—
CAT CARRIER
And STRONG.
RRIER
Probably shouldn't look directly into the carrier—

Good weight, good reflexes.
Hi!
Hey there, fella!
I'm overly friendly when I'm nervous!
I ate a butterfly once, should I be worried?
Looking good, boys!
The vet will be in shortly to see you!
WHAT DO YOU MEAN "THE VET"? WHO THE HECK ARE YOU?!
I told her my butterfly secret...

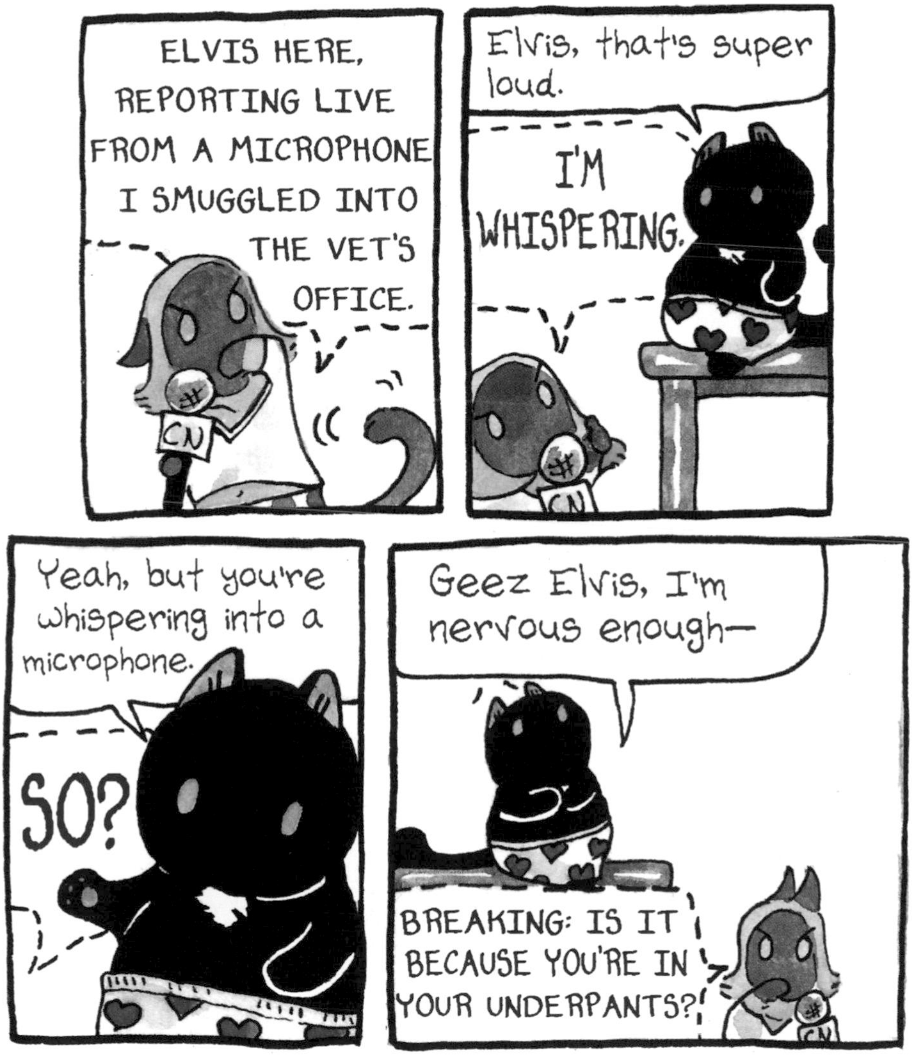
ELVIS HERE, REPORTING LIVE FROM A MICROPHONE I SMUGGLED INTO THE VET'S OFFICE.
Elvis, that's super loud.
I'M WHISPERING.
Yeah, but you're whispering into a microphone.
SO?
Geez Elvis, I'm nervous enough—
BREAKING: IS IT BECAUSE YOU'RE IN YOUR UNDERPANTS?

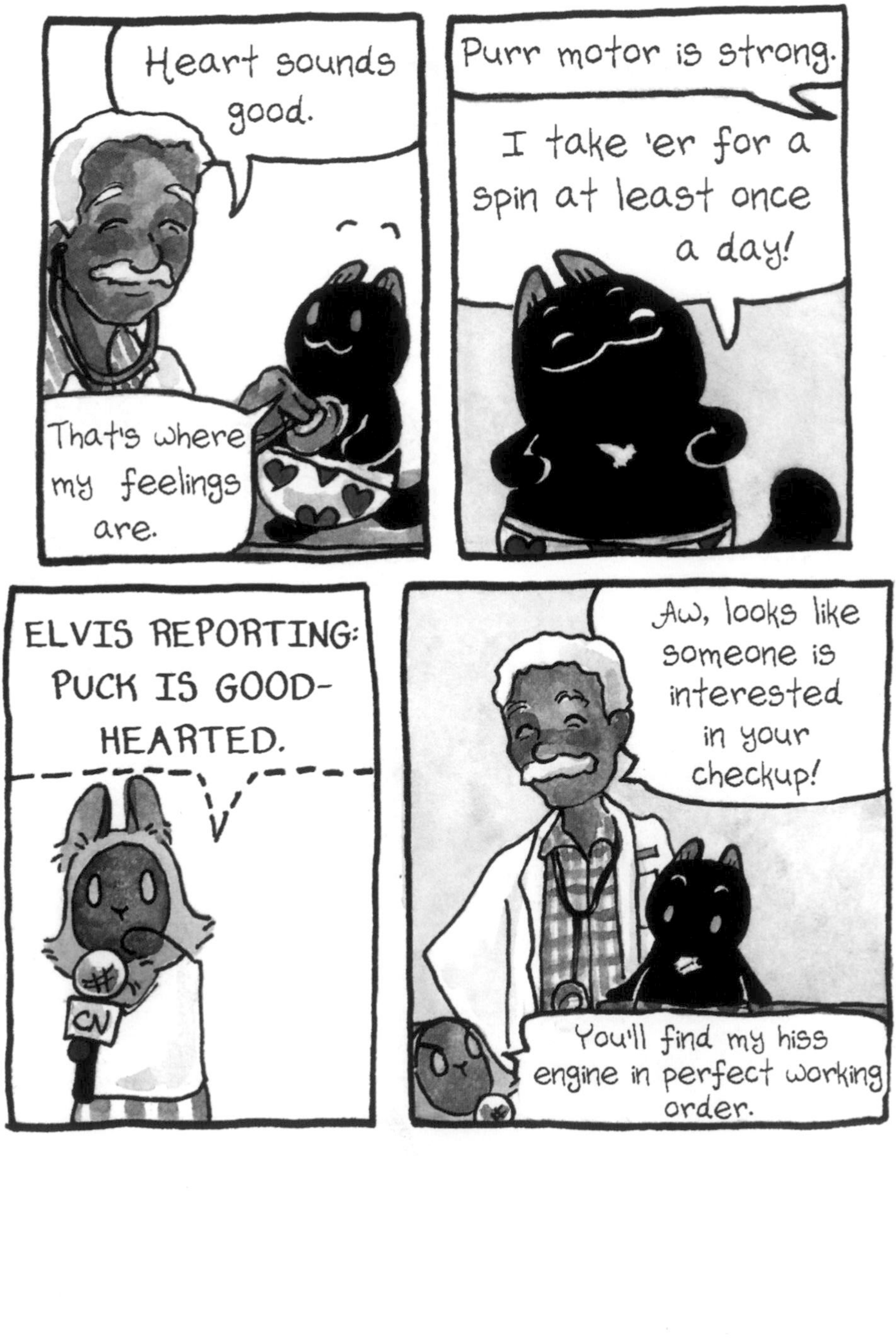
Heart sounds good.
That's where my feelings are.
Purr motor is strong.
I take 'er for a spin at least once a day!
ELVIS REPORTING: PUCK IS GOOD-HEARTED.
CN
Aw, looks like someone is interested in your checkup!
You'll find my hiss engine in perfect working order.

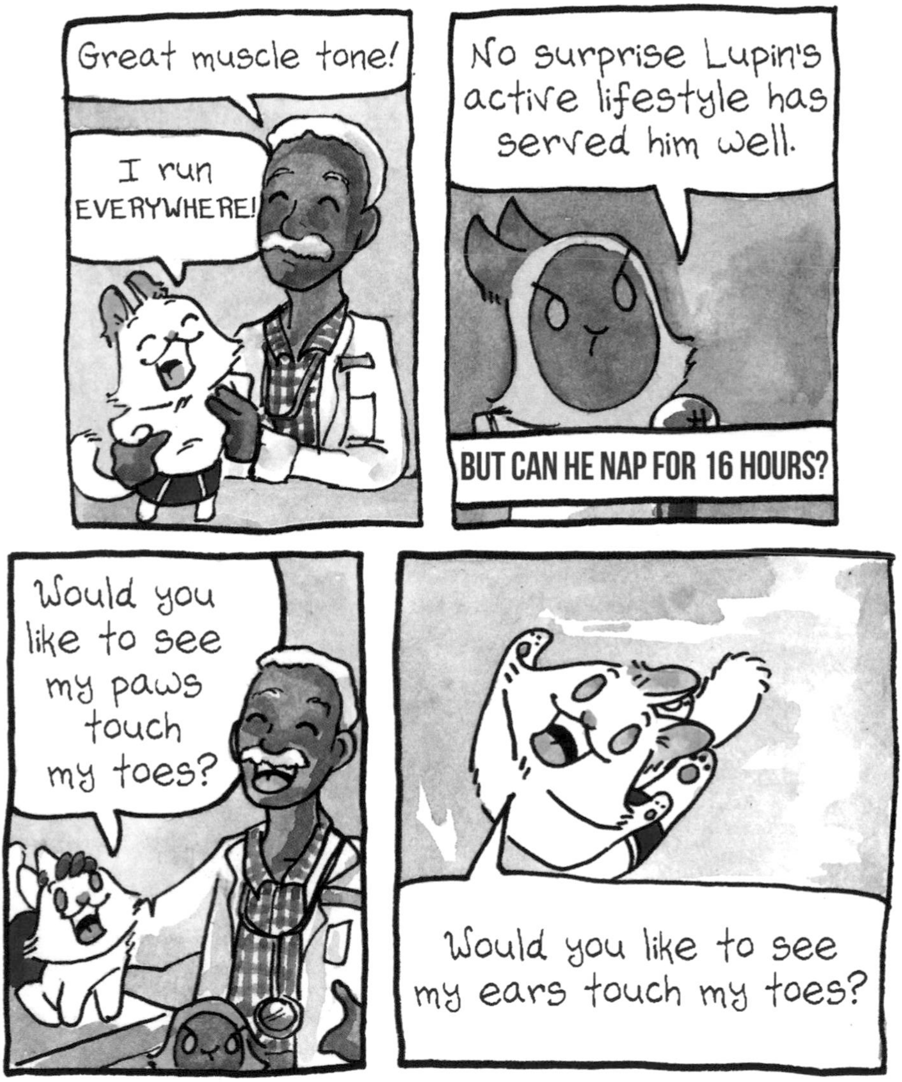
Great muscle tone!
I run EVERYWHERE!
No surprise Lupin's active lifestyle has served him well.
BUT CAN HE NAP FOR 16 HOURS?
Would you like to see my paws touch my toes?
Would you like to see my ears touch my toes?

Any questions or concerns today?

Sometimes I feel like doubling my food is the right choice for me.

Not really. Well—One of our cats seems a little nervous around new people.

Hmm.

Oh. Were you talking to her?

I'M NOT ANXIOUS, I'M CAUTIOUS. DON'T TELL STRANGERS MY BUSINESS!

I see.

So, can I have a prescription for extra food, or...?

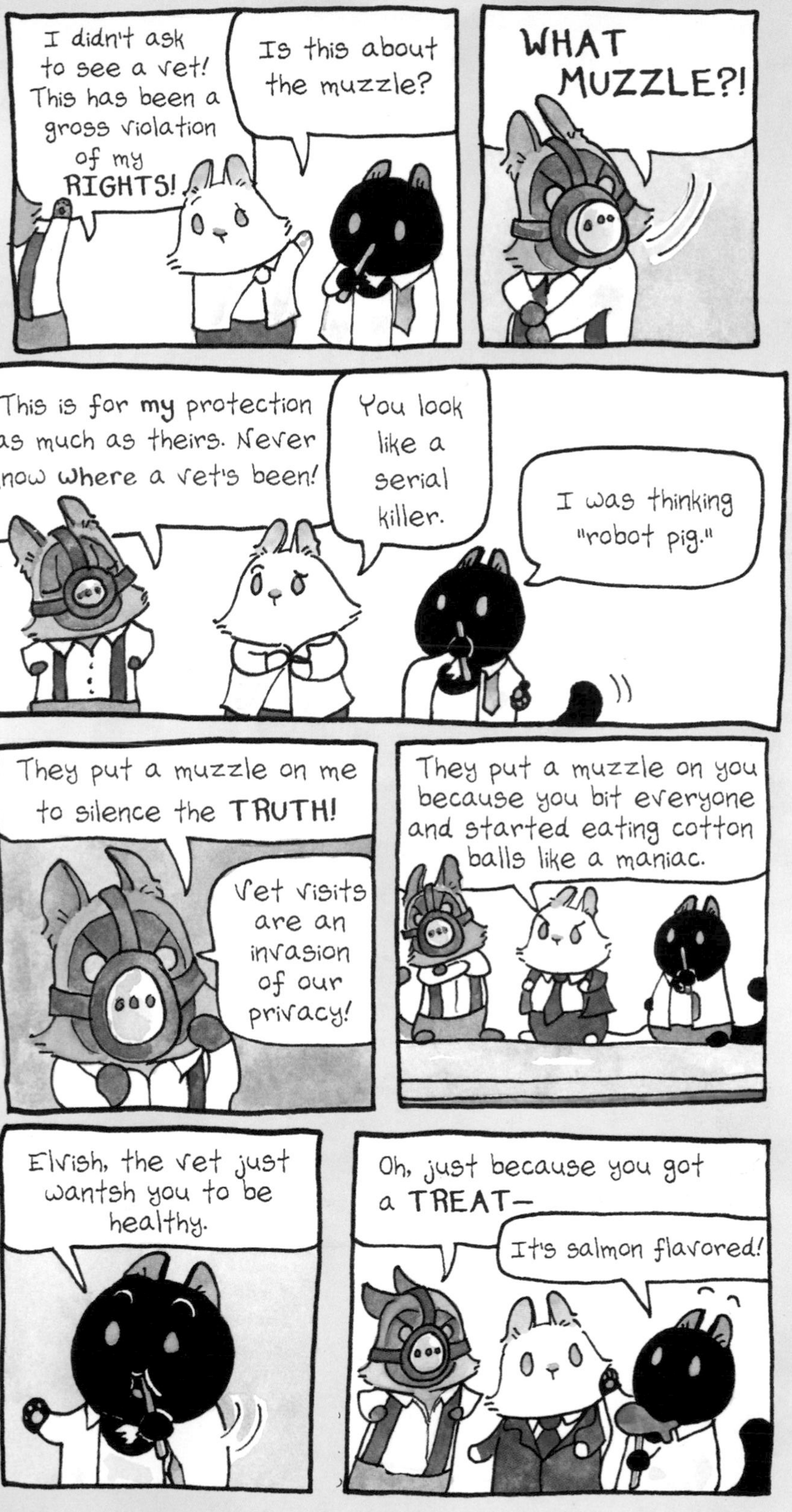
I didn't ask to see a vet! This has been a gross violation of my RIGHTS!
Is this about the muzzle?
WHAT MUZZLE?!
This is for my protection as much as theirs. Never know where a vet's been!
You look like a serial killer.
I was thinking "robot pig."
They put a muzzle on me to silence the TRUTH!
Vet visits are an invasion of our privacy!
They put a muzzle on you because you bit everyone and started eating cotton balls like a maniac.
Elvish, the vet just wantsh you to be healthy.
Oh, just because you got a TREAT—
It's salmon flavored!

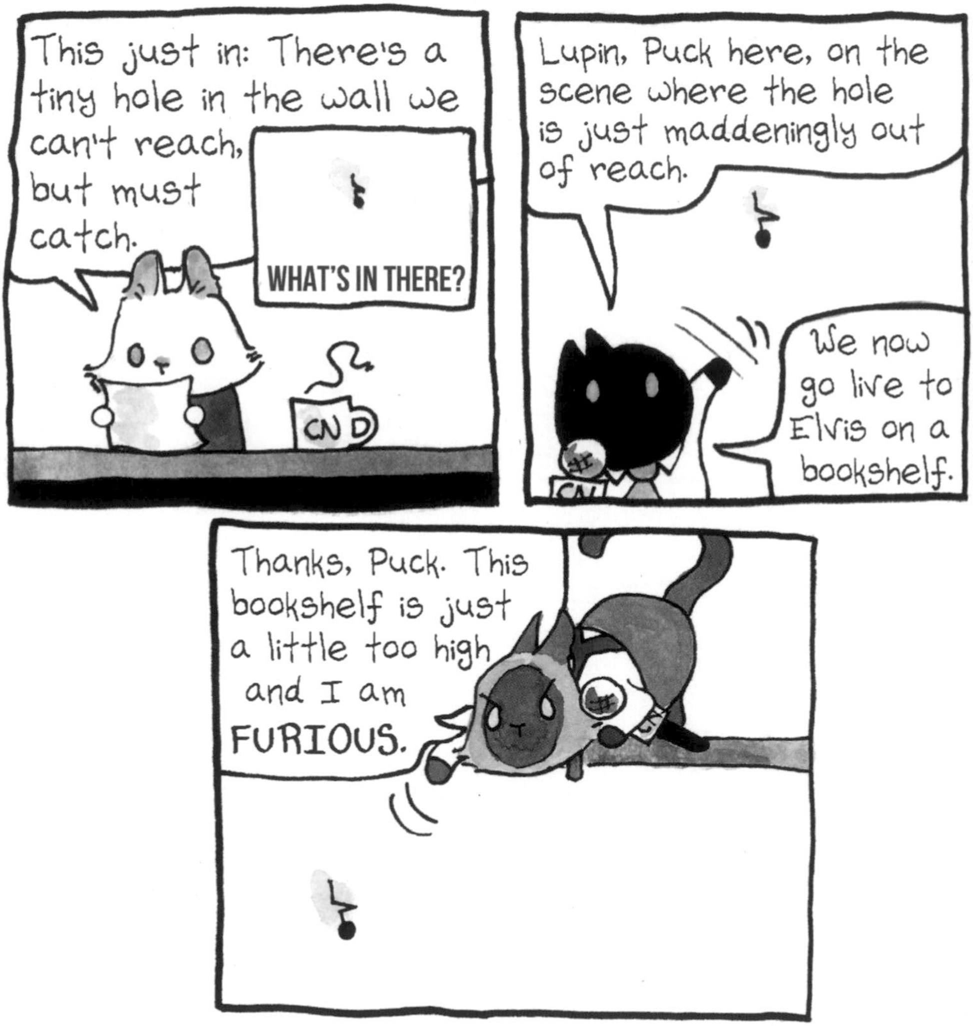

This just in: There's a tiny hole in the wall we can't reach, but must catch.
WHAT'S IN THERE?
CND
Lupin, Puck here, on the scene where the hole is just maddeningly out of reach.
We now go live to Elvis on a bookshelf.
Thanks, Puck. This bookshelf is just a little too high and I am FURIOUS.

Puck, any word on what made the tiny hole?

Based on its size, we assume a nail. However, there's no way to be certain until we can pry the hole off the wall, bite it several times, and examine it further.

Yes, of course.

Are volunteers needed?

"HOLE WATCH" • **WAS IT A NAIL?** • **IS IT DELICIOUS?**

TINY HOLE REMAINS ELUSIVE

Have you tried yelling at it?

PANT PANT OF COURSE!

Elvis here, where one fed-up cat is climbing the lamp.

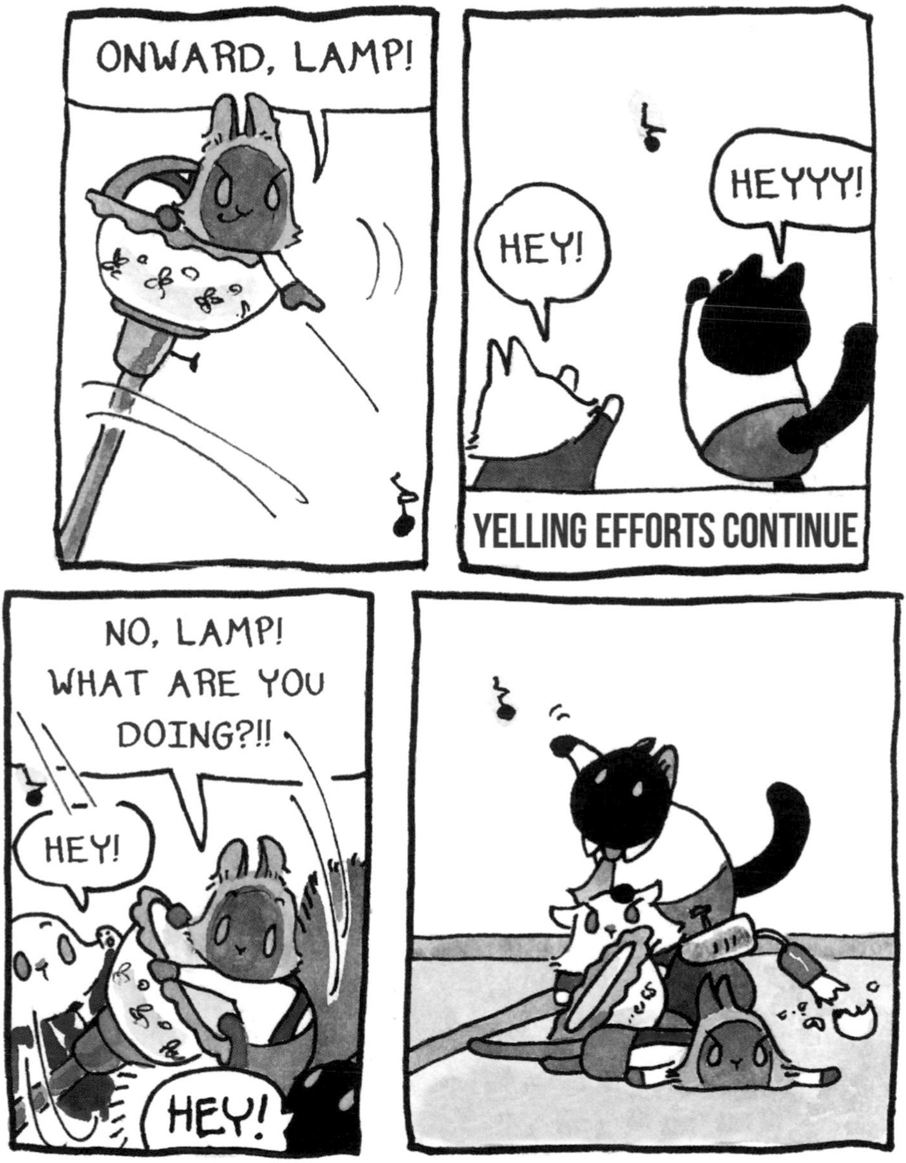
ONWARD, LAMP!
HEY!
HEYYY!
YELLING EFFORTS CONTINUE
NO, LAMP! WHAT ARE YOU DOING?!!
HEY!
HEY!

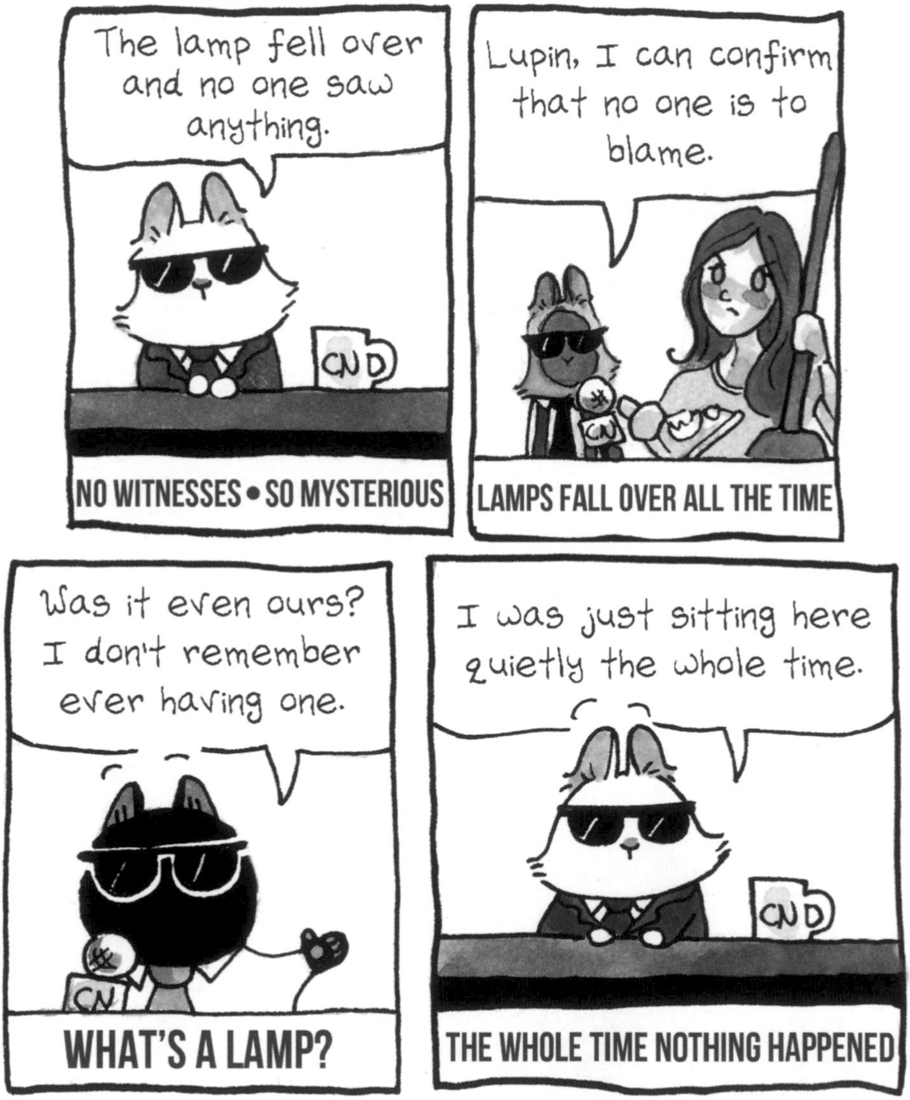
The lamp fell over and no one saw anything.
NO WITNESSES • SO MYSTERIOUS
Lupin, I can confirm that no one is to blame.
LAMPS FALL OVER ALL THE TIME
Was it even ours? I don't remember ever having one.
WHAT'S A LAMP?
I was just sitting here quietly the whole time.
THE WHOLE TIME NOTHING HAPPENED

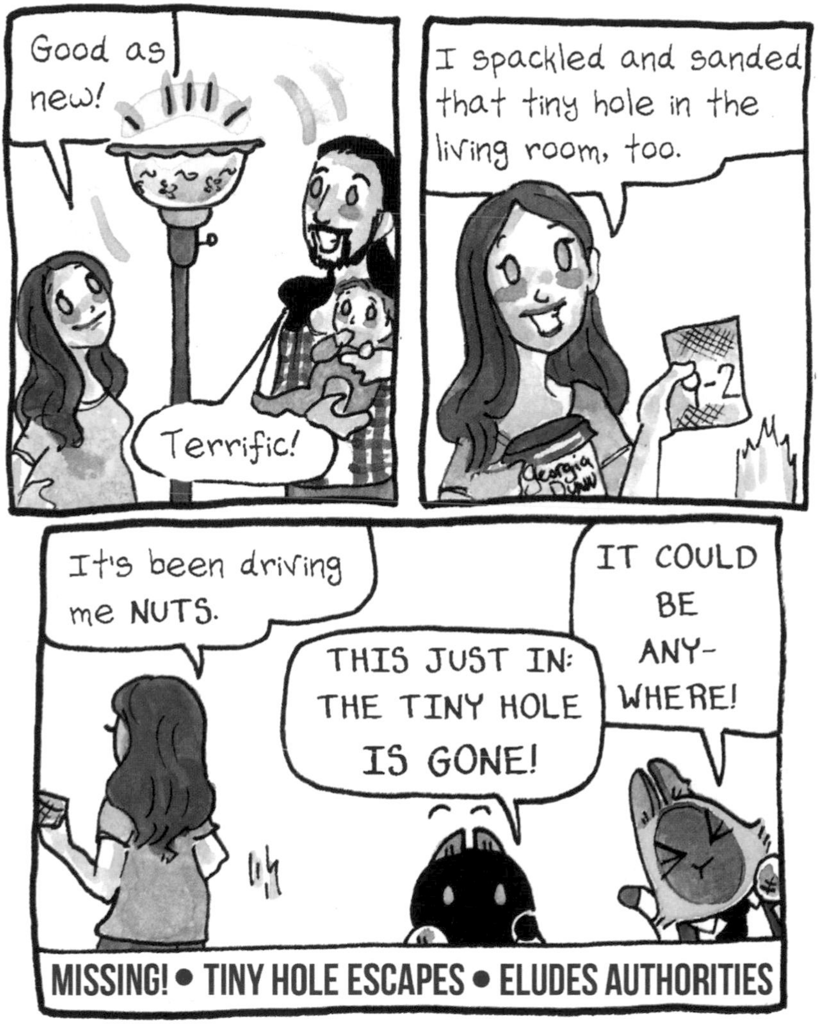
Good as new!
Terrific!
I spackled and sanded that tiny hole in the living room, too.
Georgia Dunn
It's been driving me NUTS.
THIS JUST IN: THE TINY HOLE IS GONE!
IT COULD BE ANY-WHERE!
MISSING! • TINY HOLE ESCAPES • ELUDES AUTHORITIES

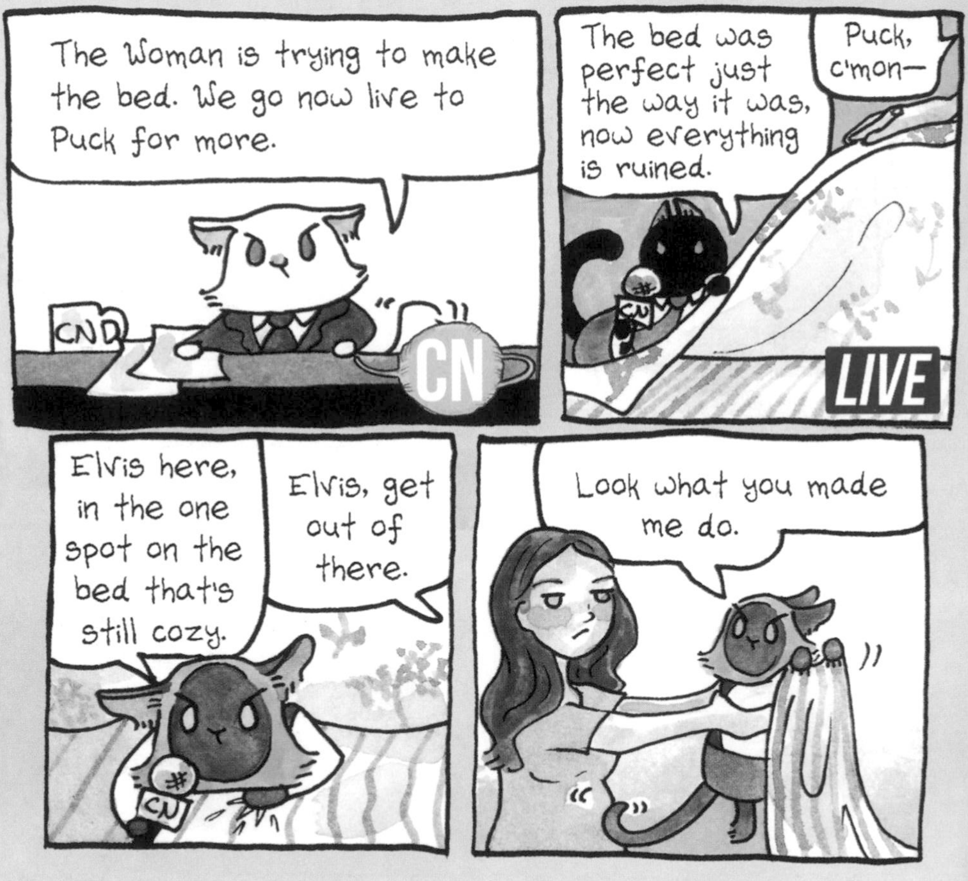
The Woman is trying to make the bed. We go now live to Puck for more.
CND
CN
The bed was perfect just the way it was, now everything is ruined.
Puck, c'mon—
LIVE
Elvis here, in the one spot on the bed that's still cozy.
Elvis, get out of there.
Look what you made me do.

POUNCE
JUMP
?
?
?
CN news, ma'am, why can't you just leave the bed alone?
Puck?
CN news, ma'am.

Elvis here, live on the scene, where Lupin is stuck in a drawer.
CN
CN
Lupin? What's it like in there?
CN
Elvis, I'm in a mystical cavern deep in the kitchen.
LIVE
...A drawer?
CN

Puck here, live with a witness to Lupin's disappearance. Sir, what did you see?

Stop it.

LUPIN STUCK IN A DRAWER

Elvis, the drawer was just a way in.

CRACKERS

Pasta

Pasta

Pasta

Georgia Dunn

ineapp

pineapp

I've discovered an interconnected series of cupboards stretching the entire expanse of the kitchen!

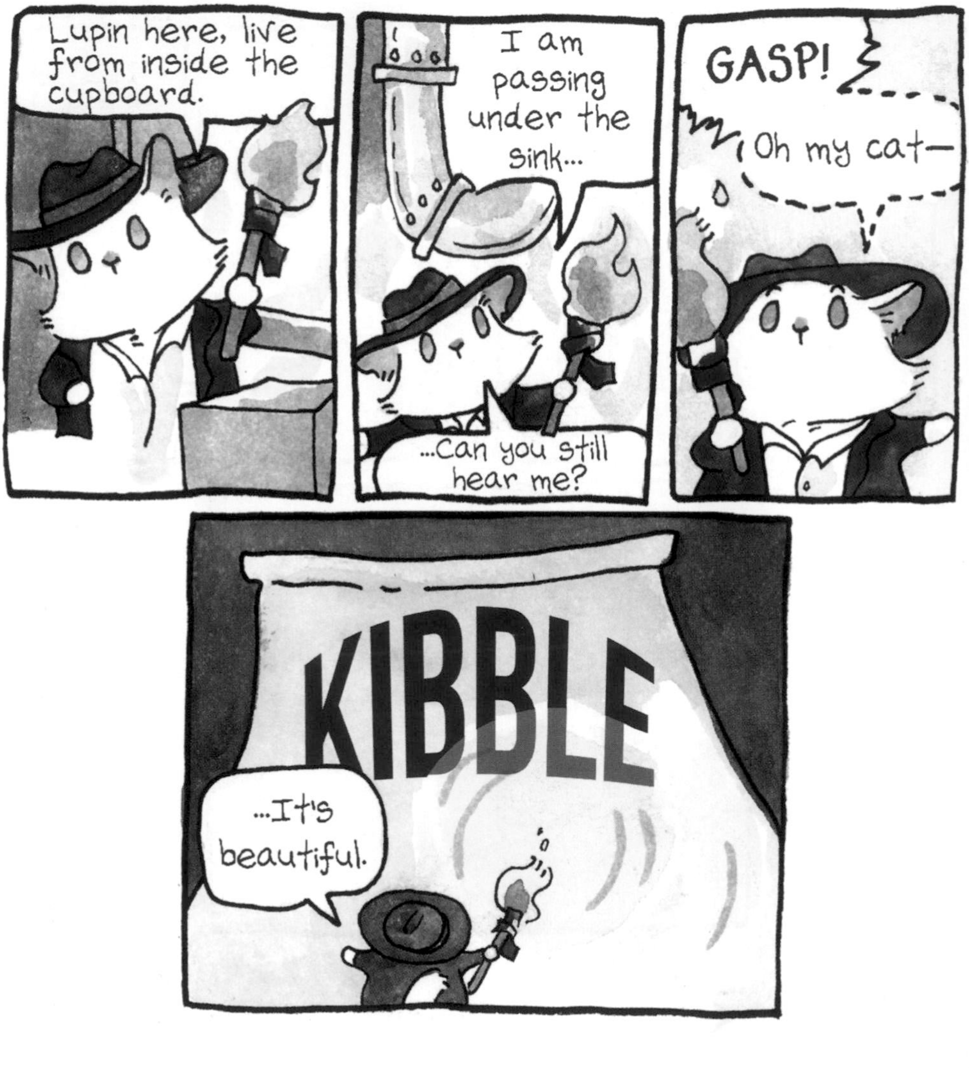
Lupin here, live from inside the cupboard.
I am passing under the sink...
...Can you still hear me?
GASP!
Oh my cat—
KIBBLE
...It's beautiful.

Lupin here, live under a KIBBLE FOUNTAIN!
LIVING THE DREAM.
Huh?
SO BRIGHT-
Oh, dangit.
What?
Lupin chewed a hole in the kibble bag.
Put me back!
I'm here with a witness to Lupin's reappearance. Sir, what did you see?

CN news, what are you doing?

You'd think it's silly.

I spent the morning attacking a doorstop. I'm not here to judge.

Ok... I'm trying to spot a Mailman. And I have a camera.

For evidence.

Not silly at all.

Also, I made signs.

WELCOME MAILMEN!

♥WE♥ BELIEVE

♪

Georgia Dunn

Ok, that's a little silly...

Welcome back to CN news. We've been waiting most of the afternoon, and still no sign of a Mailman.

Maybe if we leave out milk and cookies for the Mailman...

Actually, that's not a bad thought! Do we know if Mailmen eat People food?

It makes more sense that they eat paper.

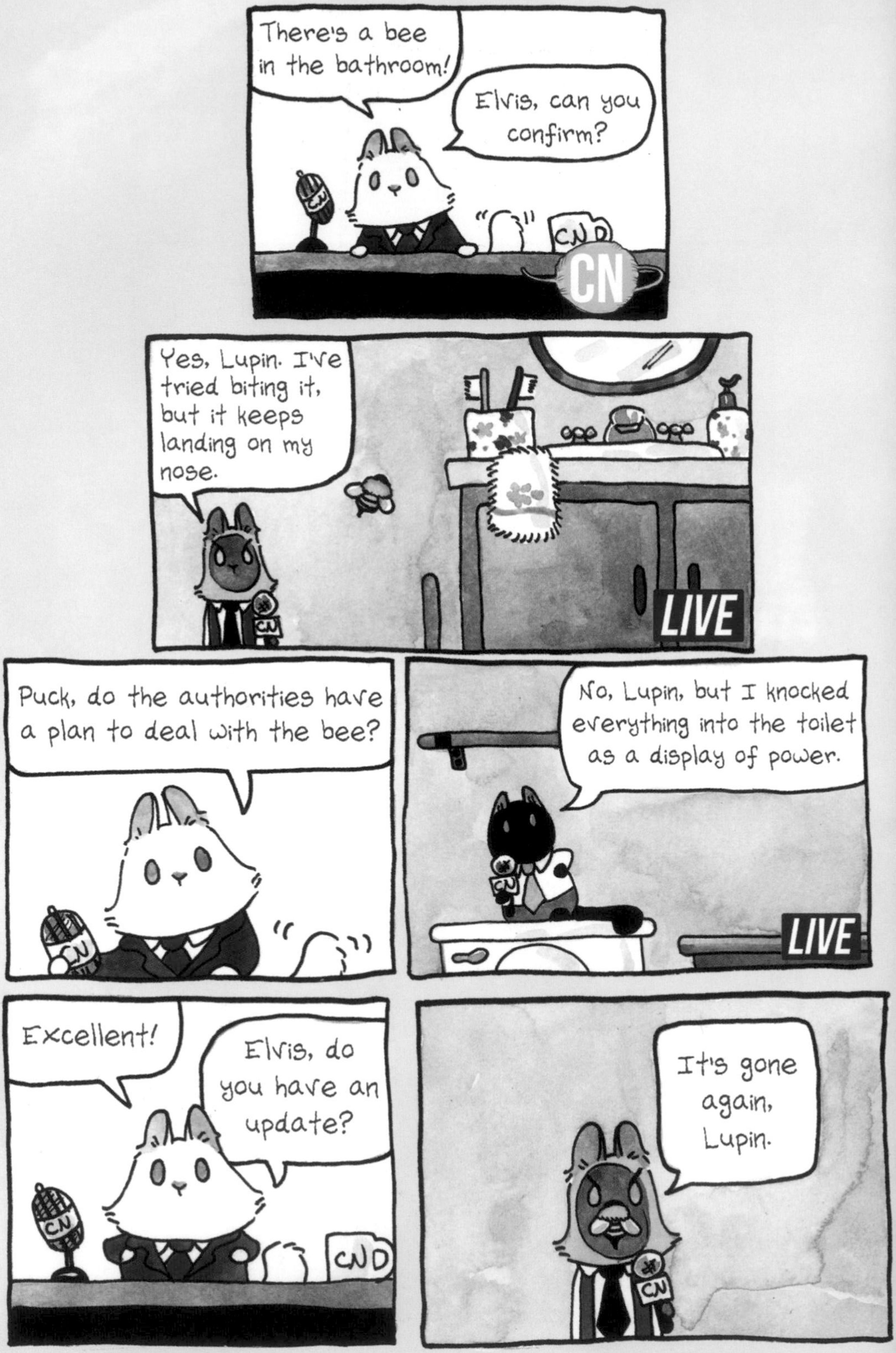
There's a bee in the bathroom!
Elvis, can you confirm?
CN
Yes, Lupin. I've tried biting it, but it keeps landing on my nose.
LIVE
Puck, do the authorities have a plan to deal with the bee?
No, Lupin, but I knocked everything into the toilet as a display of power.
LIVE
Excellent!
Elvis, do you have an update?
It's gone again, Lupin.

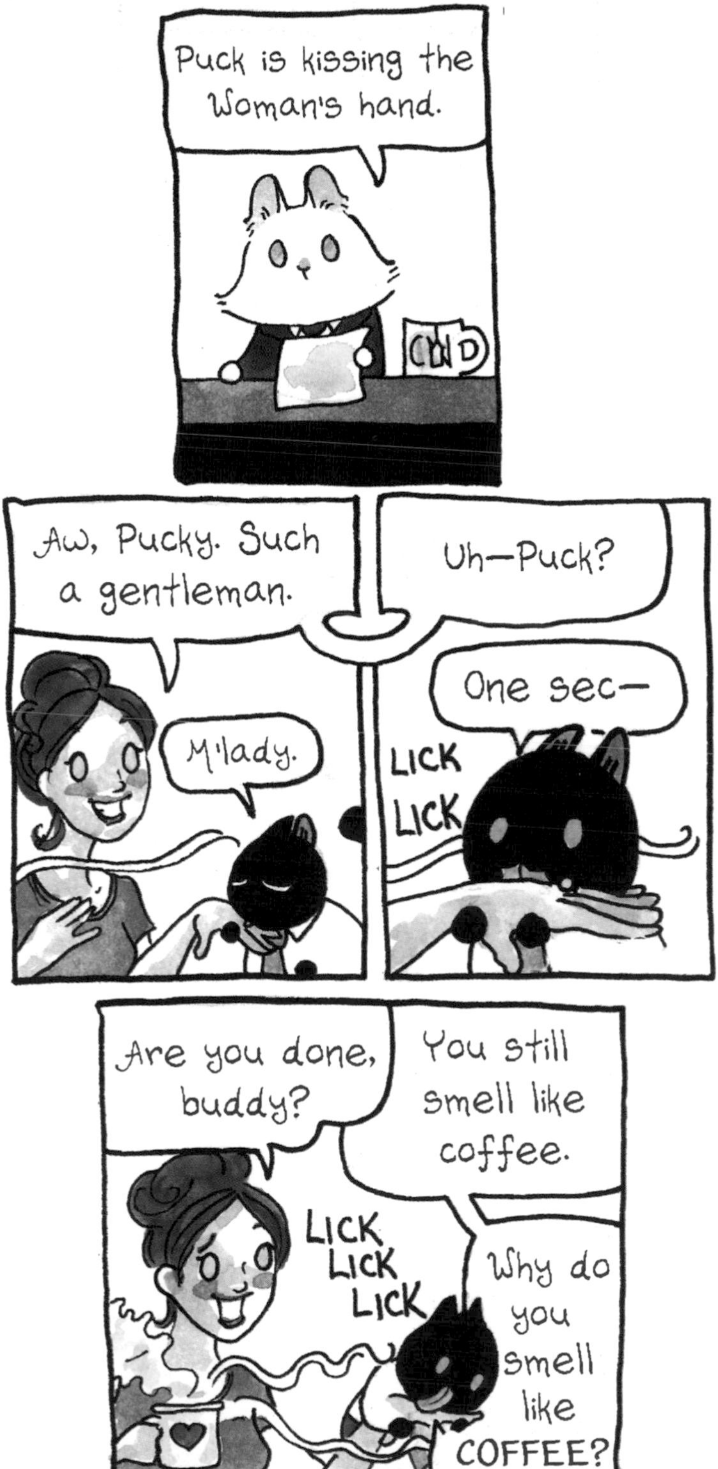
Puck is kissing the Woman's hand.
CND
Aw, Pucky. Such a gentleman.
M'lady.
Uh—Puck?
One sec—
LICK
LICK
Are you done, buddy?
You still smell like coffee.
LICK
LICK
LICK
Why do you smell like COFFEE?

The Baby is sitting up.
It's a little shaky here on the scene.
CN
LIVE
Annnnd he's down.
CN
Horrific live images, folks, TURN AWAY!

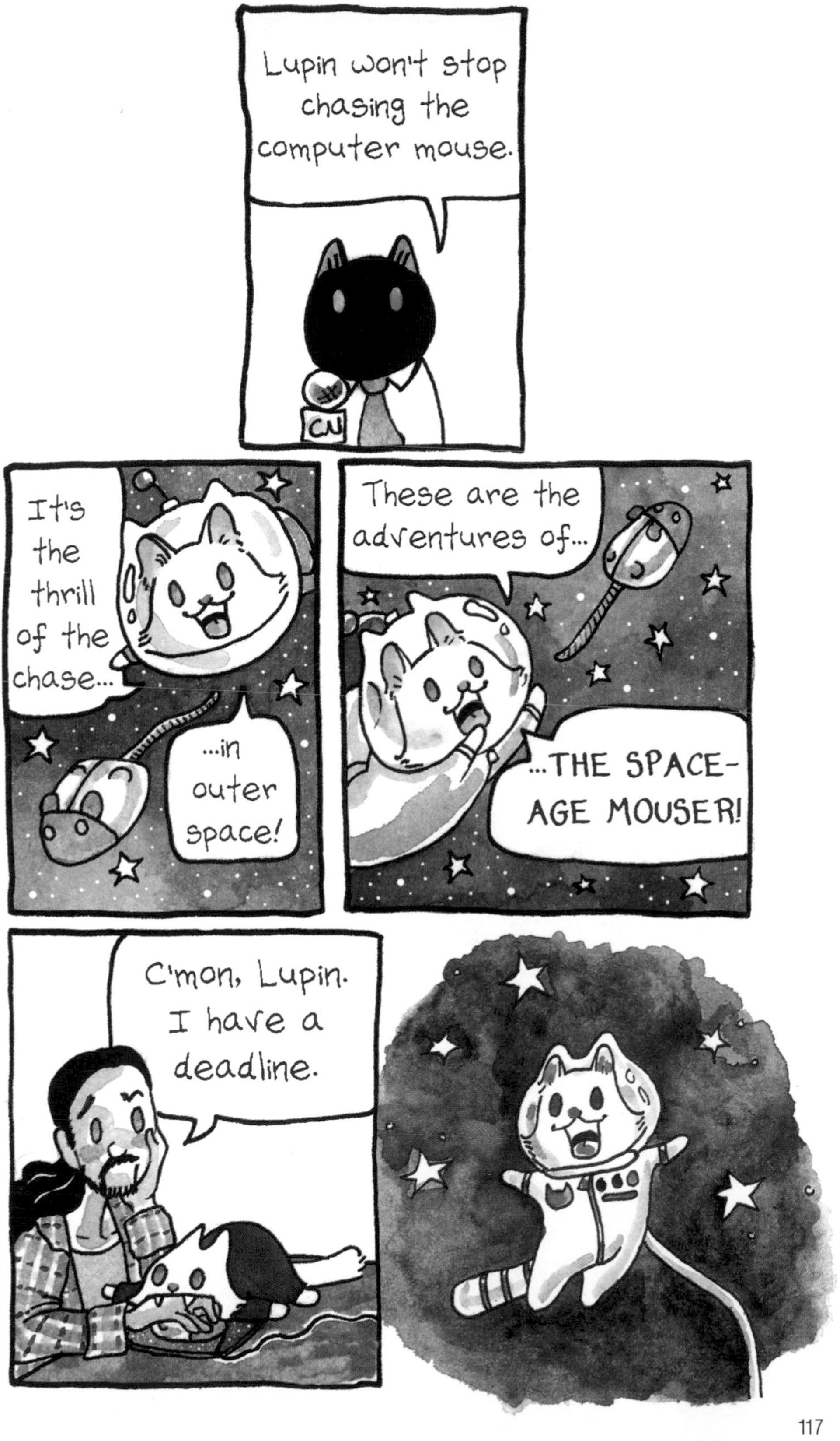
Lupin won't stop chasing the computer mouse.
CN
It's the thrill of the chase...
...in outer space!
These are the adventures of...
...THE SPACE-AGE MOUSER!
C'mon, Lupin. I have a deadline.

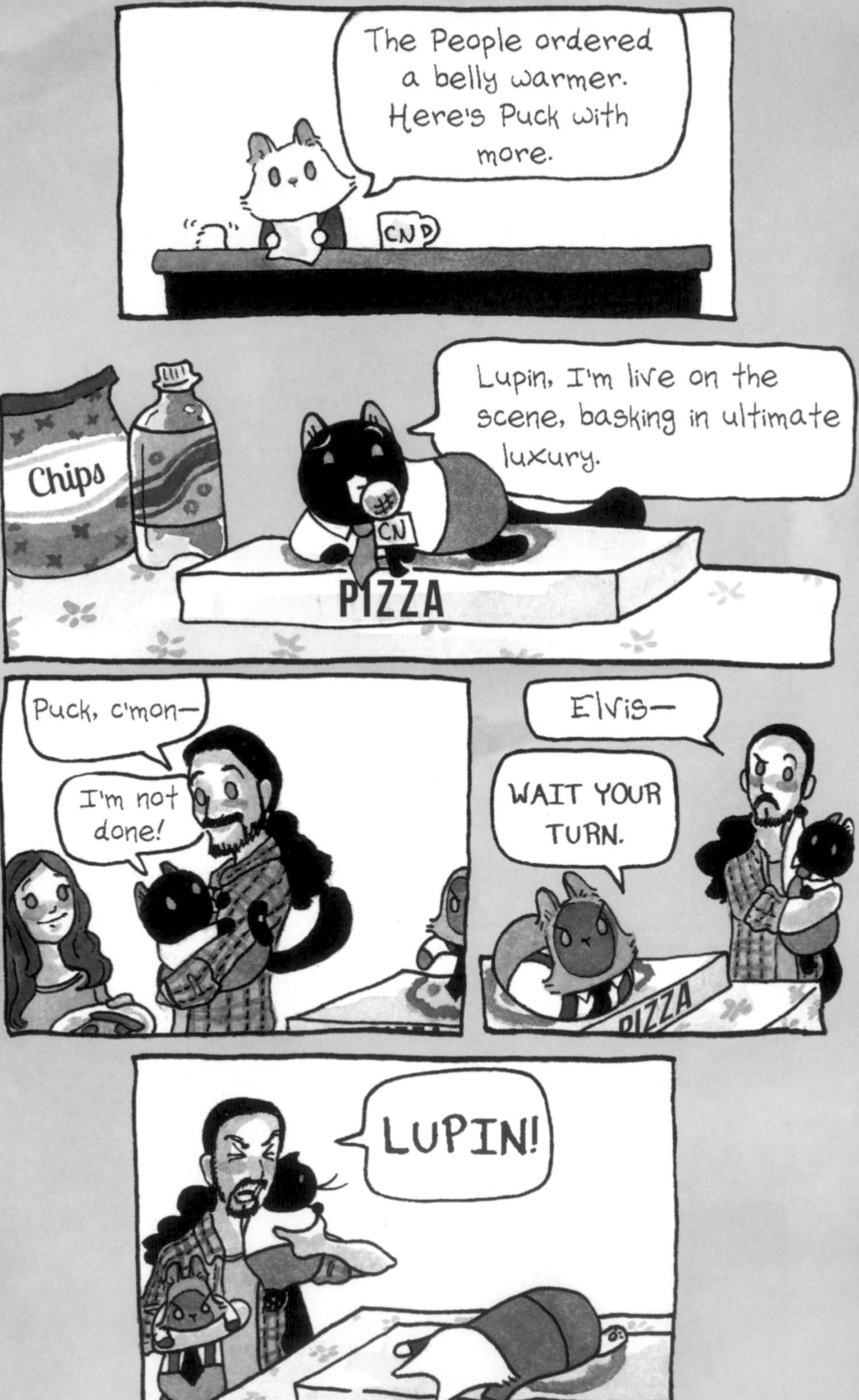
The People ordered a belly warmer. Here's Puck with more.
CND
Chips
Lupin, I'm live on the scene, basking in ultimate luxury.
CN
PIZZA
Puck, c'mon—
I'm not done!
Elvis—
WAIT YOUR TURN.
PIZZA
LUPIN!

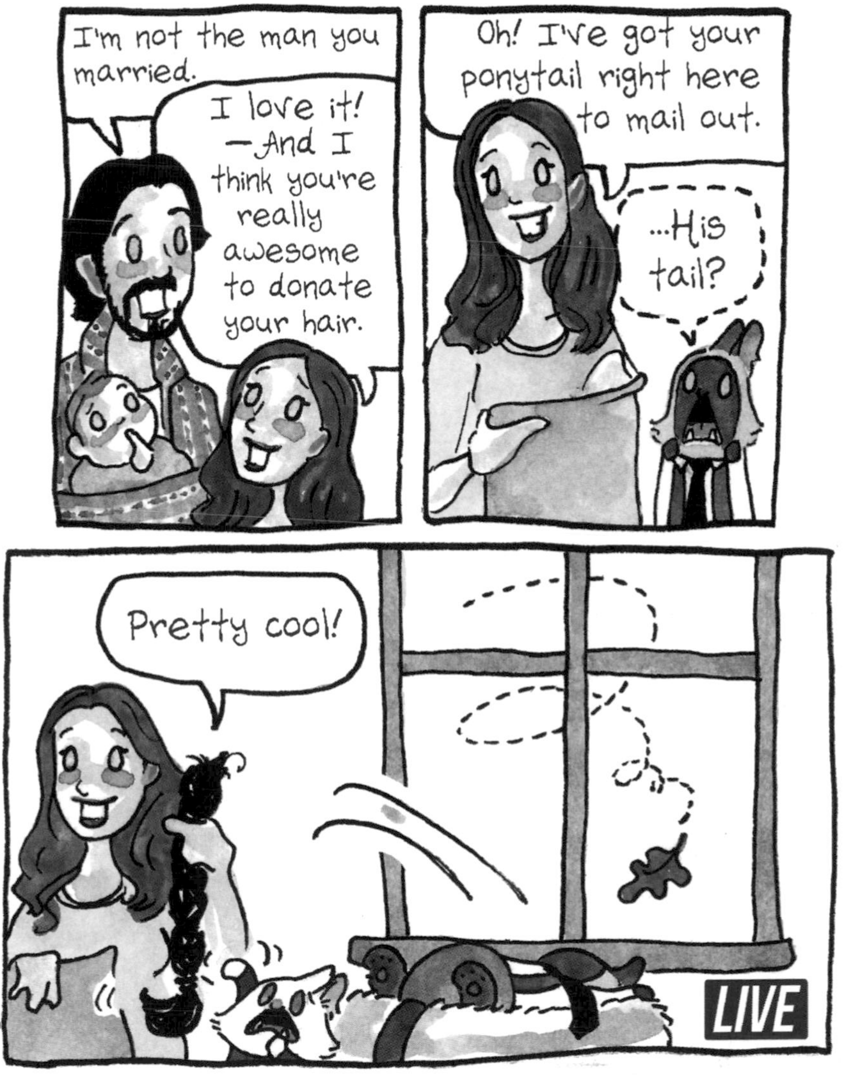
I'm not the man you married.
I love it! —And I think you're really awesome to donate your hair.
Oh! I've got your ponytail right here to mail out.
...His tail?
Pretty cool!
LIVE

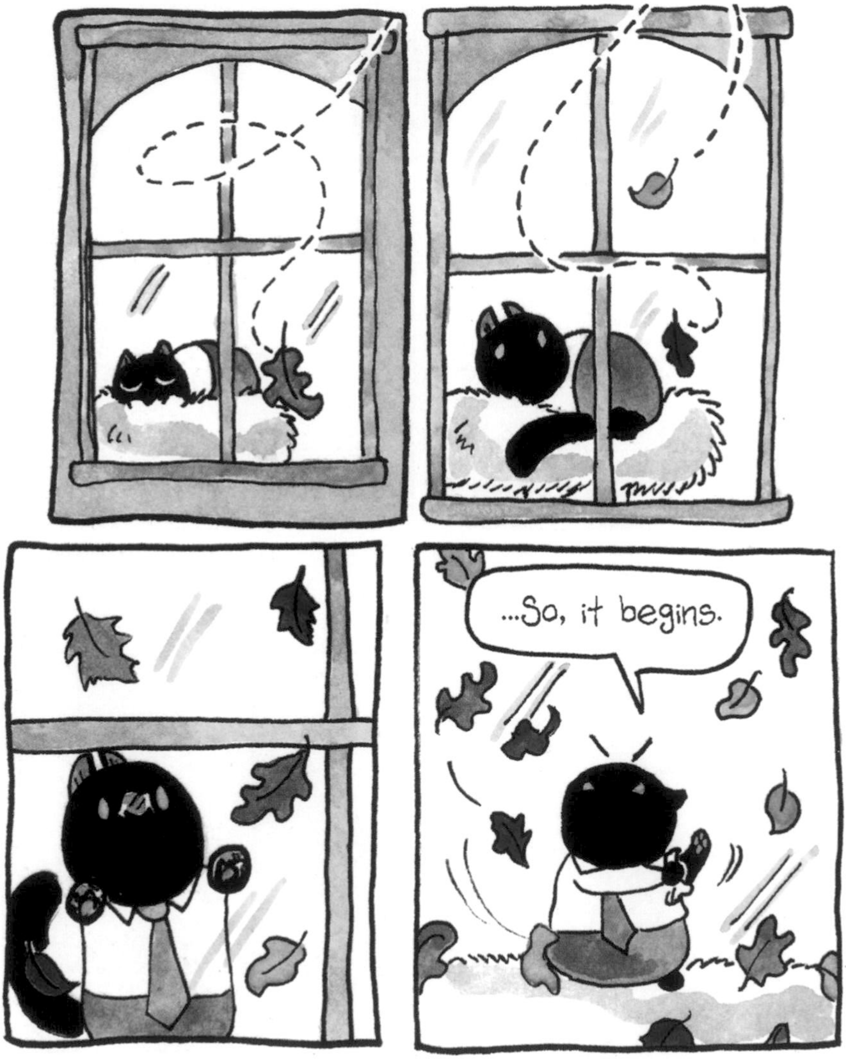
...So, it begins.

The trees are falling apart! Here's Elvis with an exclusive.

Thanks, Lupin. As you can see, the world is coming to an end right outside our window.

Shoo!

Git!

One cat's brave efforts stand between us and certain doom!

Smells like a woodstove.

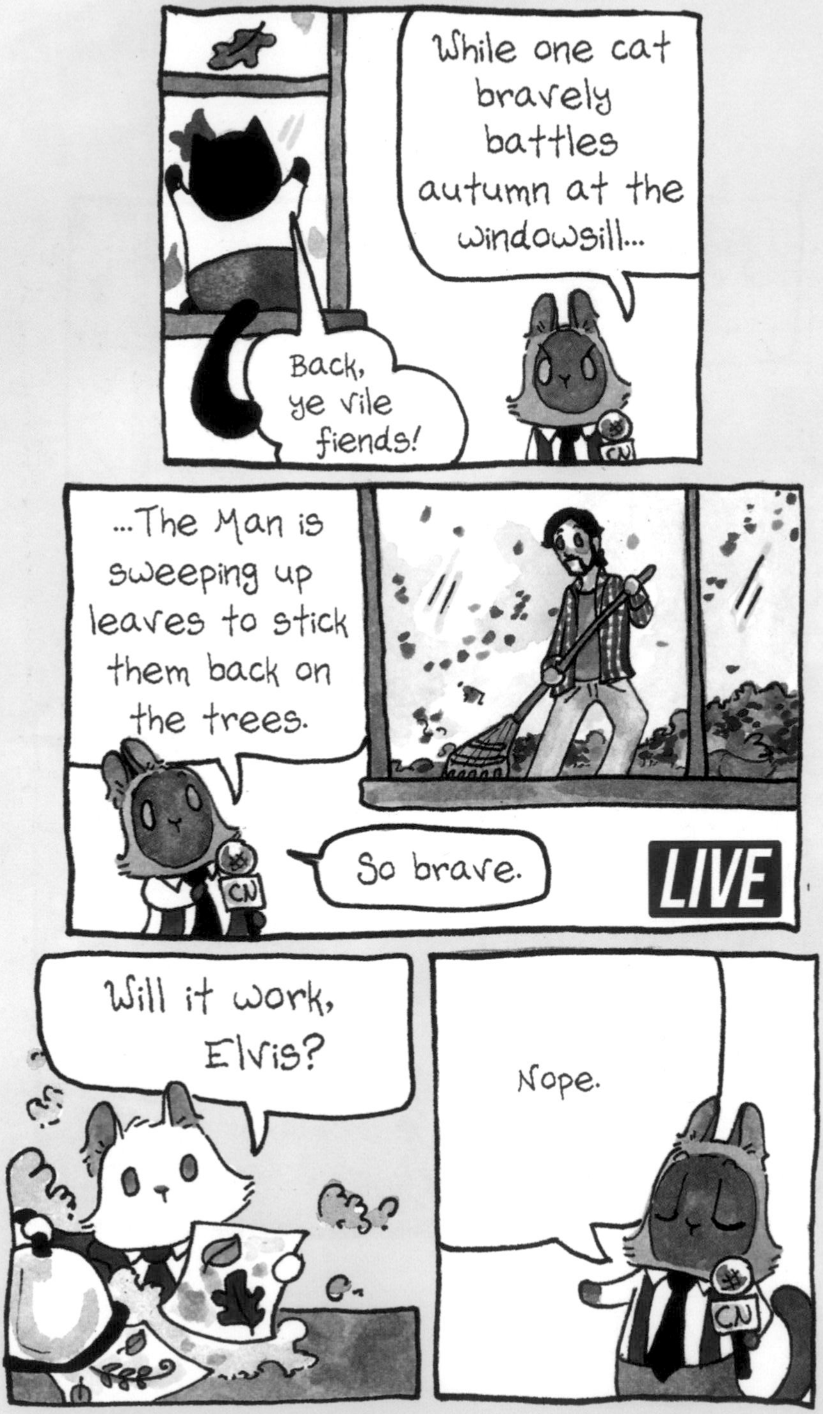
While one cat bravely battles autumn at the windowsill...
Back, ye vile fiends!
...The Man is sweeping up leaves to stick them back on the trees.
So brave.
LIVE
Will it work, Elvis?
Nope.

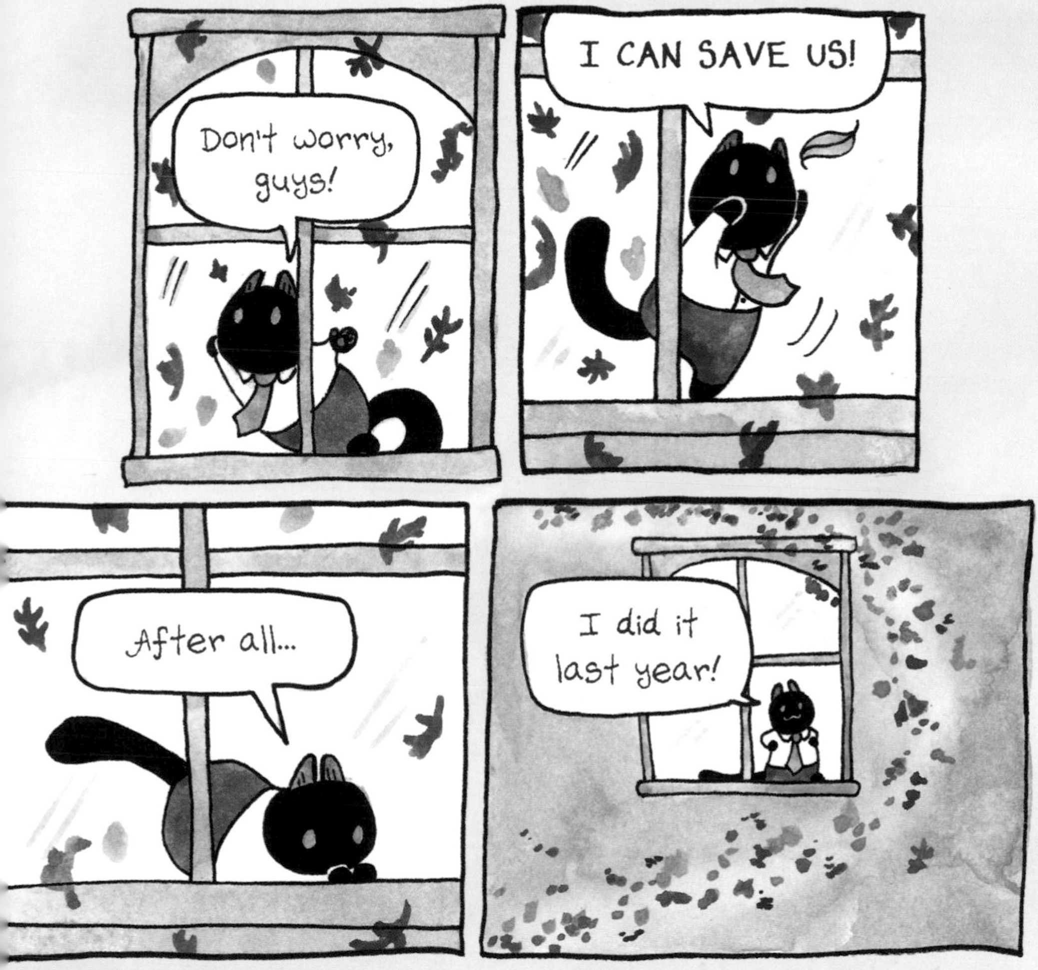
Don't worry, guys!
I CAN SAVE US!
After all...
I did it last year!

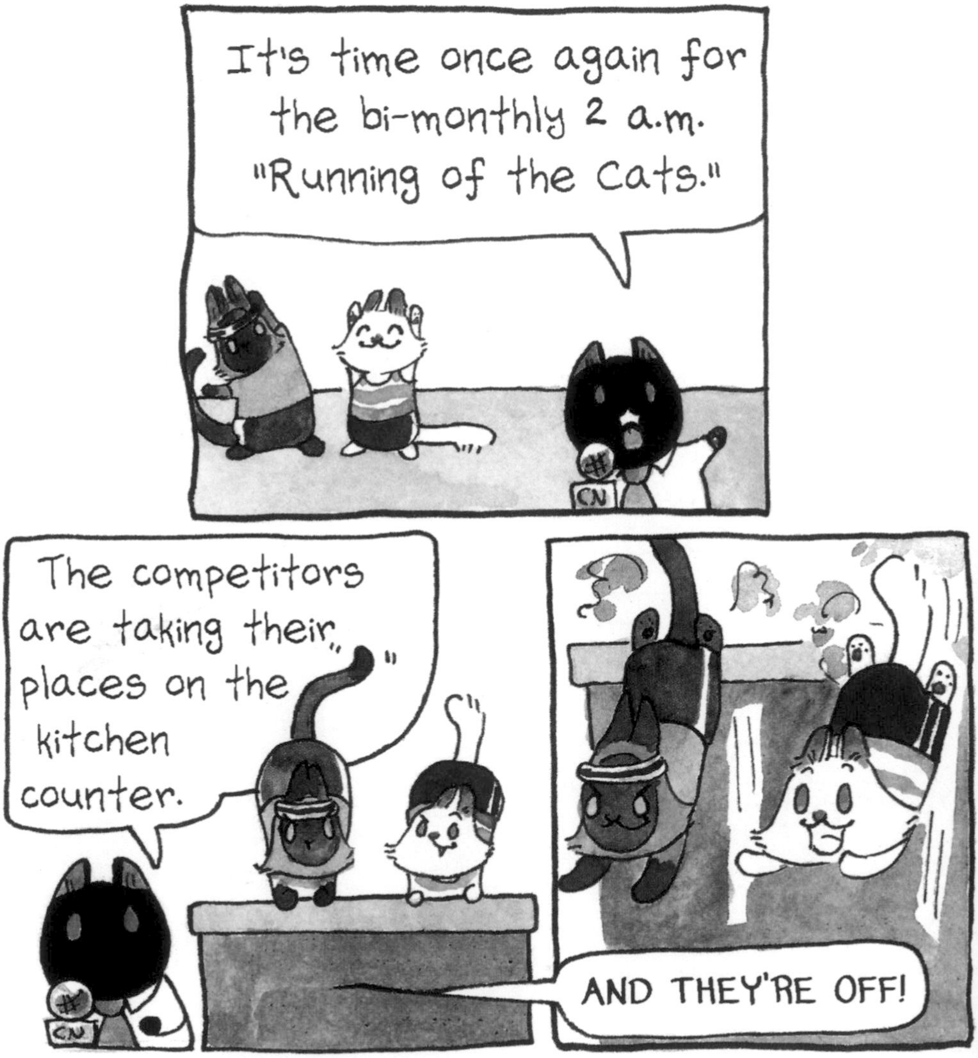
It's time once again for the bi-monthly 2 a.m. "Running of the Cats."
CN
The competitors are taking their places on the kitchen counter.
CN
AND THEY'RE OFF!

It's 2:01 a.m., and the "Running of the Cats" is underway!

Here's a look at the race route for viewers at home.

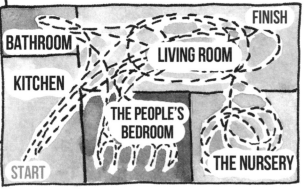

BATHROOM

FINISH

LIVING ROOM

KITCHEN

THE PEOPLE'S BEDROOM

THE NURSERY

START

A great deal of the track IS vertical—

A reminder to folks at home: In order to qualify, each competitor must knock over a lamp.
#1
Elvis is well on his way.
Did you hear something break?
TO GLORY!
Mmmph?

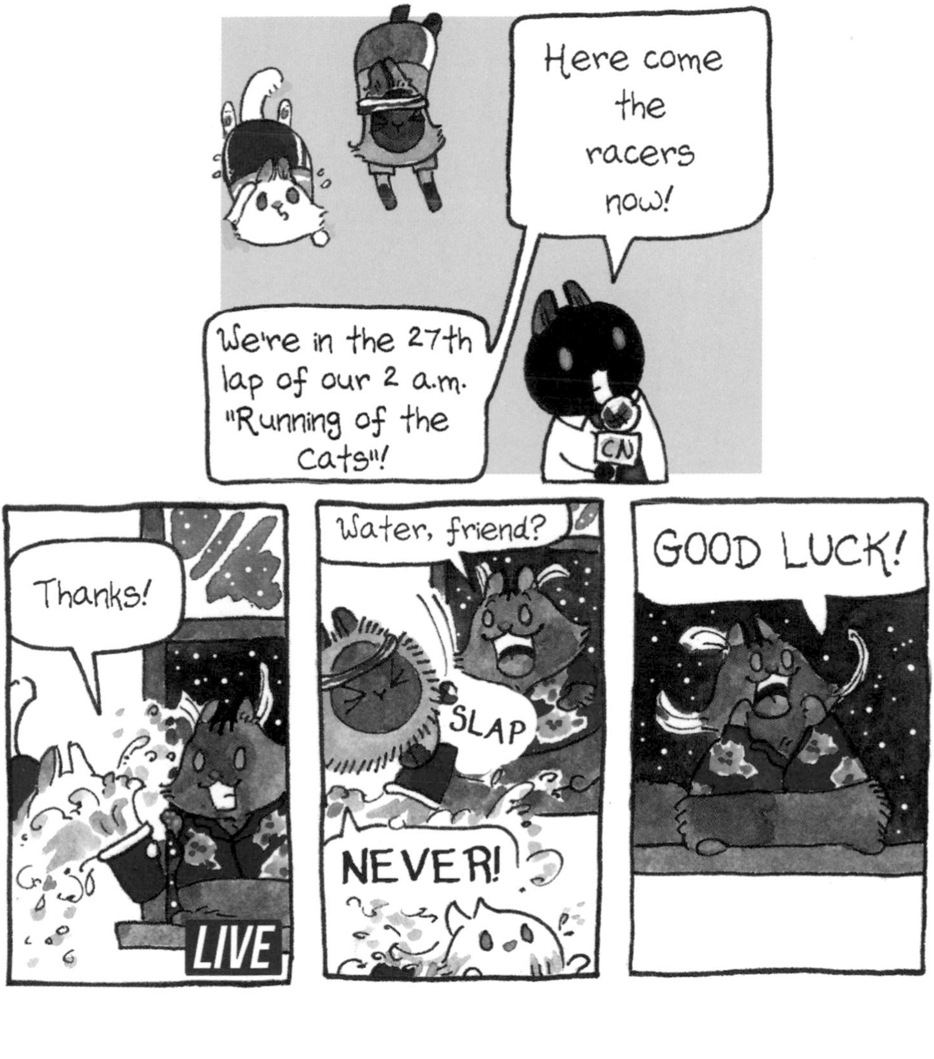
Here come the racers now!
We're in the 27th lap of our 2 a.m. "Running of the Cats"!
CN
Thanks!
LIVE
Water, friend?
SLAP
NEVER!
GOOD LUCK!

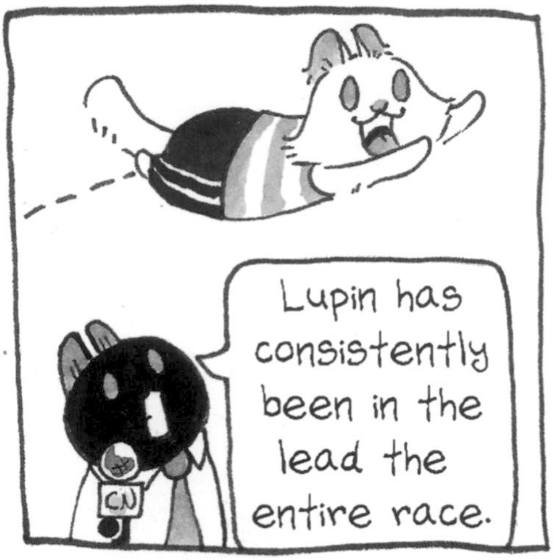
Lupin has consistently been in the lead the entire race.
CN

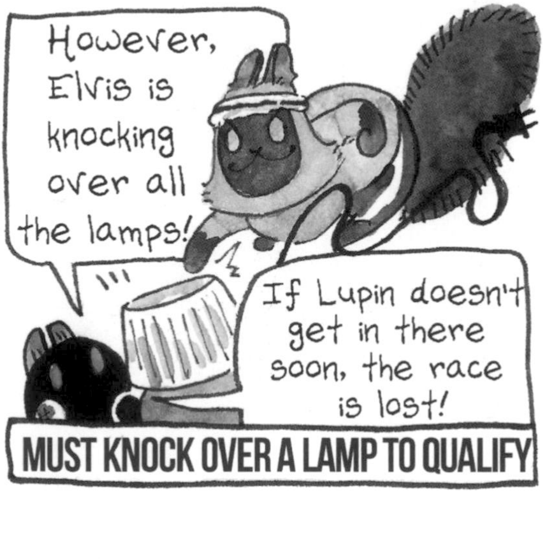
However, Elvis is knocking over all the lamps!
If Lupin doesn't get in there soon, the race is lost!
MUST KNOCK OVER A LAMP TO QUALIFY

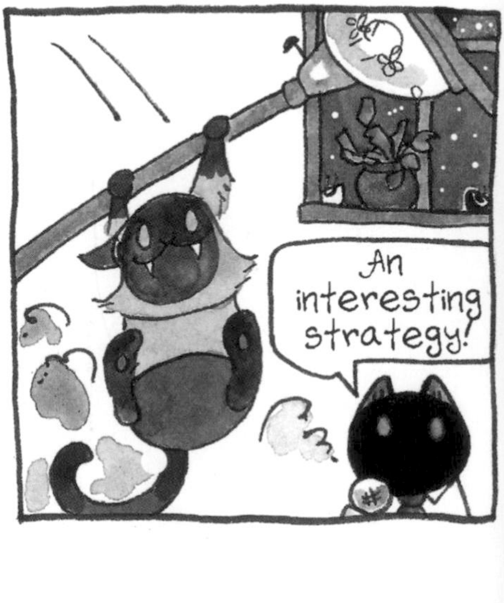
An interesting strategy!

Puck here, beside the last remaining lamp-
MOTHER OF CAT!
CN
This concludes our race! Until next time, folks!
Why is Lupin all wet?
10.0

Local cat demands pets, well past midnight.
TAP
TAP
TAP
TAP
LIVE
SHAKE
SHAKE
SHAKE
!

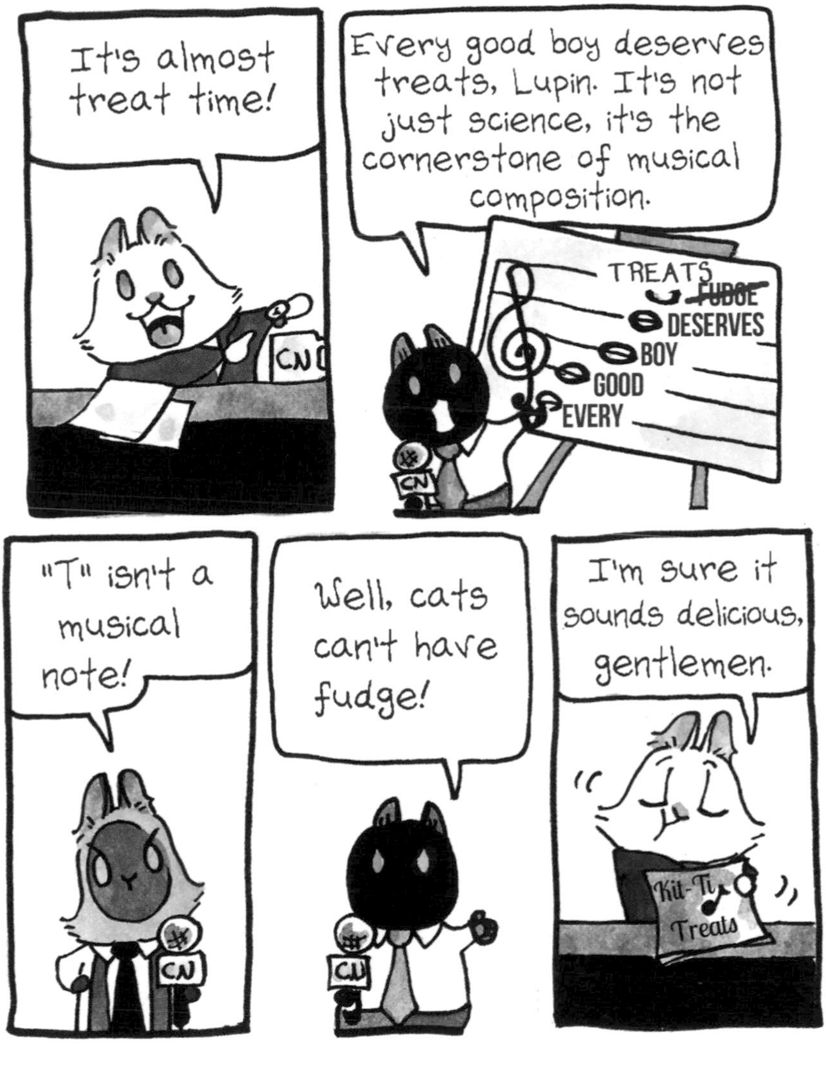
It's almost treat time!
Every good boy deserves treats, Lupin. It's not just science, it's the cornerstone of musical composition.
TREATS
FUDGE
DESERVES
BOY
GOOD
EVERY
CN
"T" isn't a musical note!
Well, cats can't have fudge!
I'm sure it sounds delicious, gentlemen.
Kit-Ti Treats

A spot on the kitchen floor smells odd.

It's a real weird smell, Lupin.

...Coconut? ...Old ham?

SNIFF SNIFF

Lemme try smelling through my mouth—

SNIFF SNIFF SNIFF SNERK

SNERK SNERK

SNERK SNERK SNERK SNERK SNERK

SNERK SNERK

Puck is attempting to break the world record for how many times a cat can jump on the table during dinner.

Puck!

Down!

He's trained all his life, Lupin.

FOR... HAM!

See the determination!

He has the heart of a champion!

Puck!

Boxes have been spotted outside.
CN
I'm not moving again!
ELVIS, RELAX!
CN
But I do LOVE BOXES.
I'm so torn!
Looks like we're getting neighbors!
CRASH! BANG! BOOM!
Neighbors... on the ceiling?
Flying boxes...
What are we looking at?

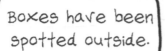

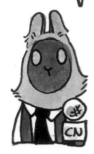

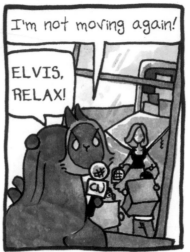

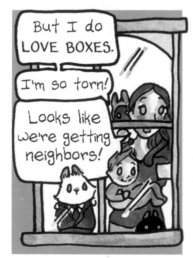

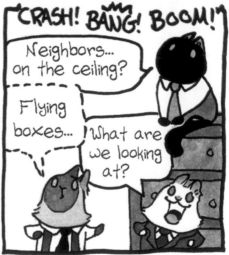

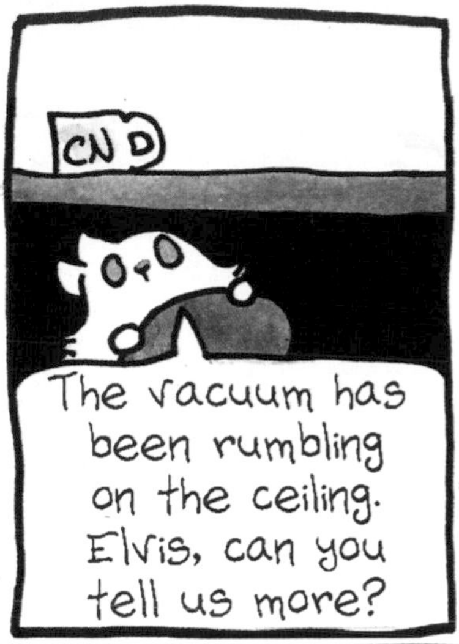
CNN
The vacuum has been rumbling on the ceiling. Elvis, can you tell us more?

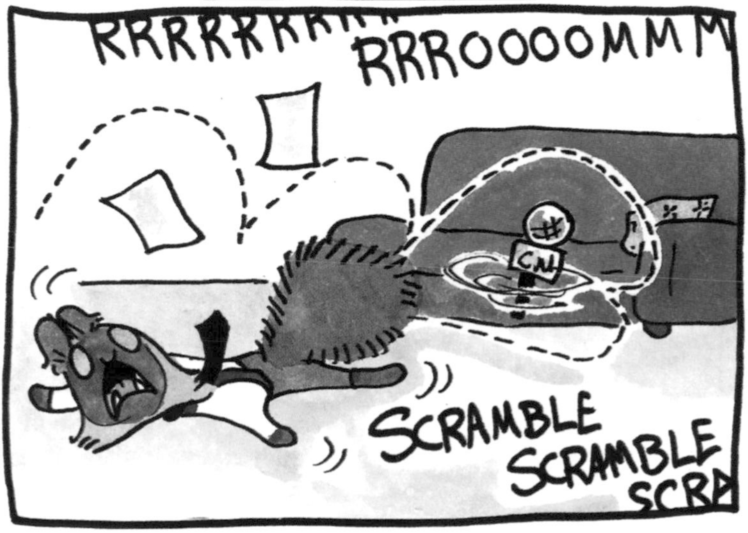
RRRRRRRR
RRROOOOMMM
CNN
SCRAMBLE
SCRAMBLE
SCRA

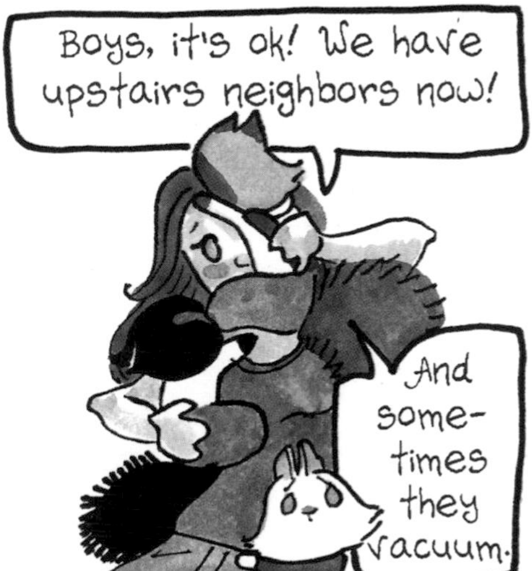
Boys, it's ok! We have upstairs neighbors now!
And some-times they vacuum.

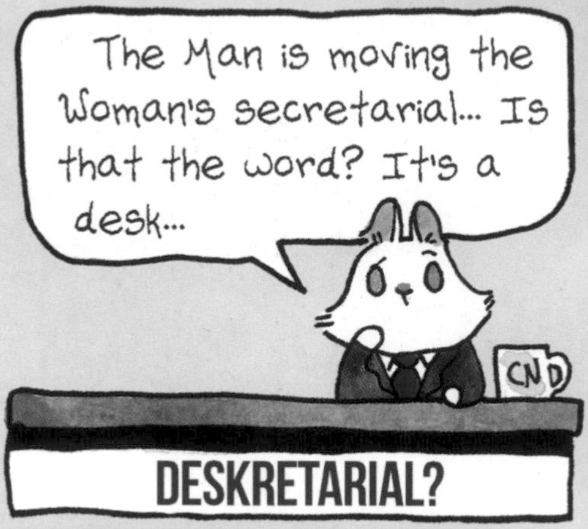
The Man is moving the Woman's secretarial... Is that the word? It's a desk...
CND
DESKRETARIAL?

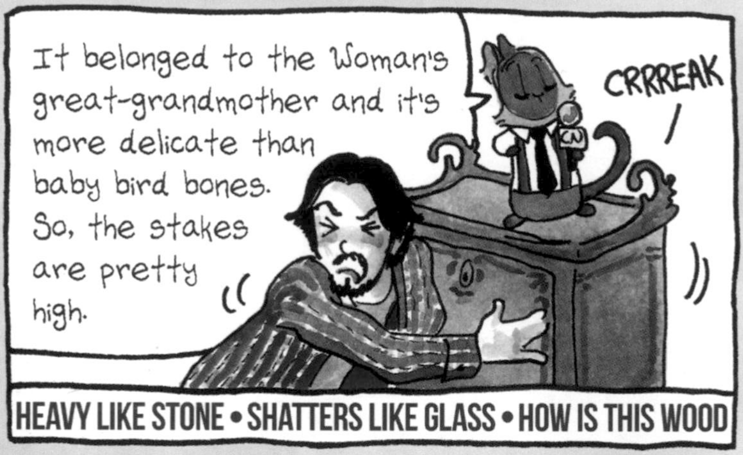
It belonged to the Woman's great-grandmother and it's more delicate than baby bird bones. So, the stakes are pretty high.
CRRREAK
HEAVY LIKE STONE • SHATTERS LIKE GLASS • HOW IS THIS WOOD

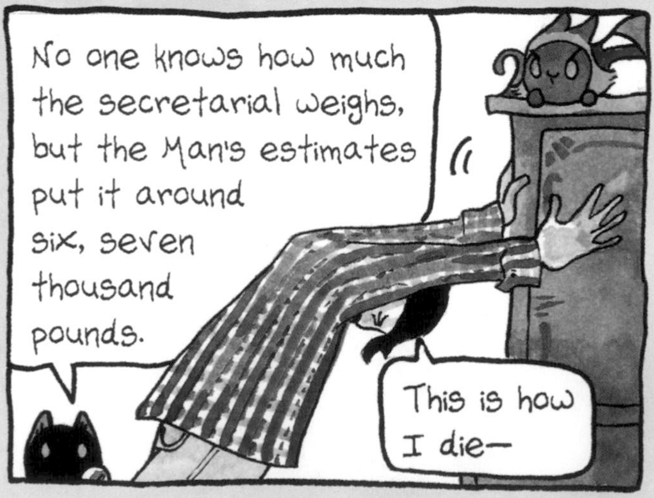
No one knows how much the secretarial weighs, but the Man's estimates put it around six, seven thousand pounds.
This is how I die—

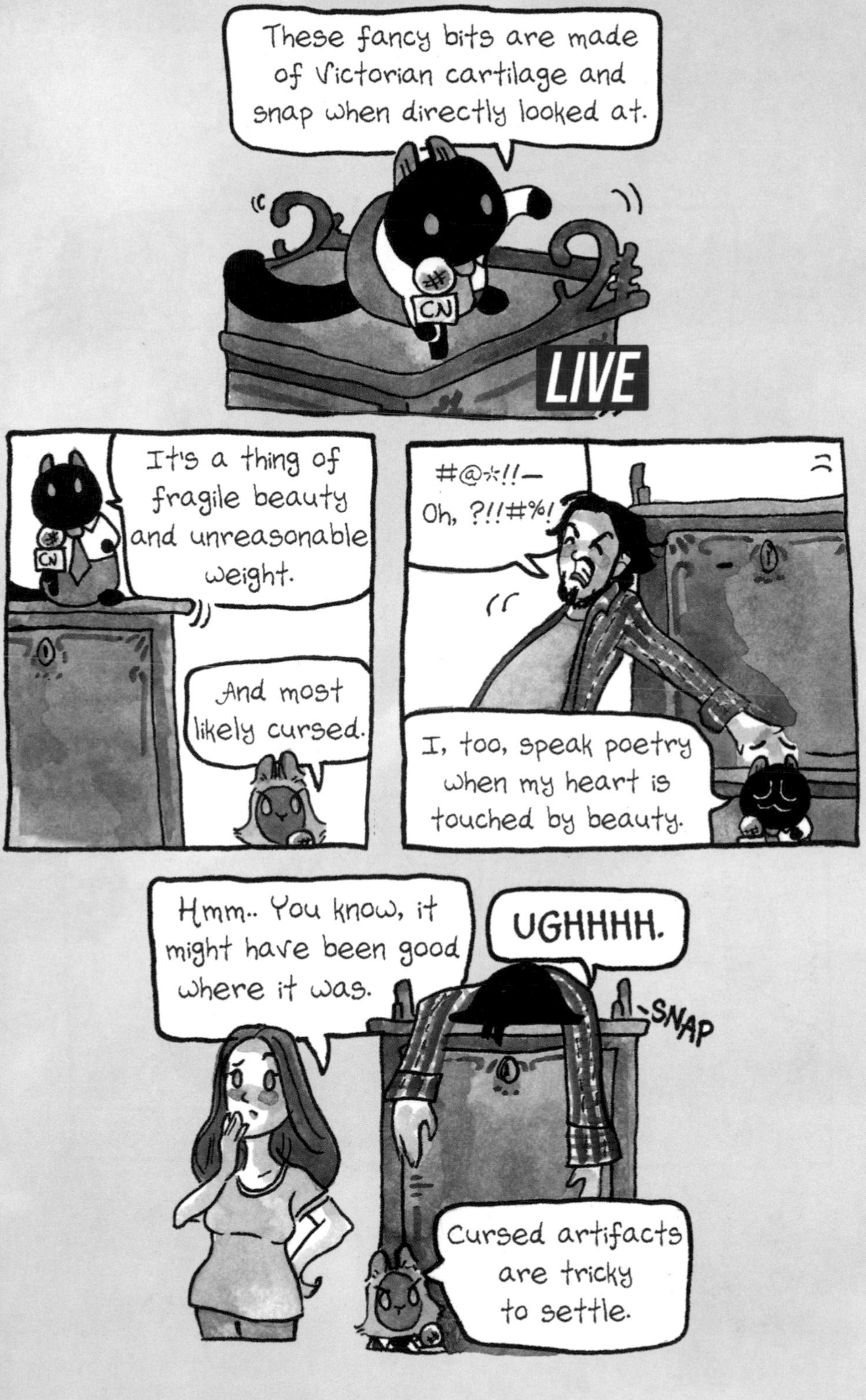
These fancy bits are made of Victorian cartilage and snap when directly looked at.
CN
LIVE
It's a thing of fragile beauty and unreasonable weight.
CN
And most likely cursed.
#@☆!!—
Oh, ?!!#%!
I, too, speak poetry when my heart is touched by beauty.
Hmm.. You know, it might have been good where it was.
UGHHHH.
SNAP
Cursed artifacts are tricky to settle.

Elvis got into a spider web.
No, I didn't.
Elvis, you look like an old chandelier—
I'm FINE.
Let me just groom your nose!

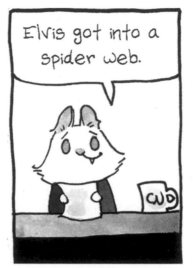

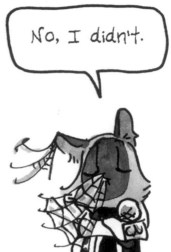

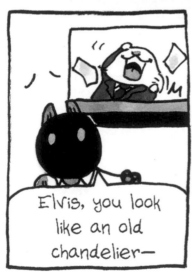

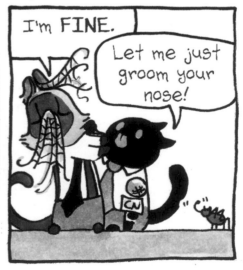

The Baby has been given a SPIRIT BOARD.

Puck, I don't approve of these dark arts.

The cow says "moooooooo—"

Summoning the disembodied voices of animal spirits is in poor taste.

The frog says "CROAK! CROAK! CROAK!"

But to expose a child to such EVIL—

The rooster says "cock-a-doodle-doo,-I-love-you!"

CLAP

CLAP CLAP

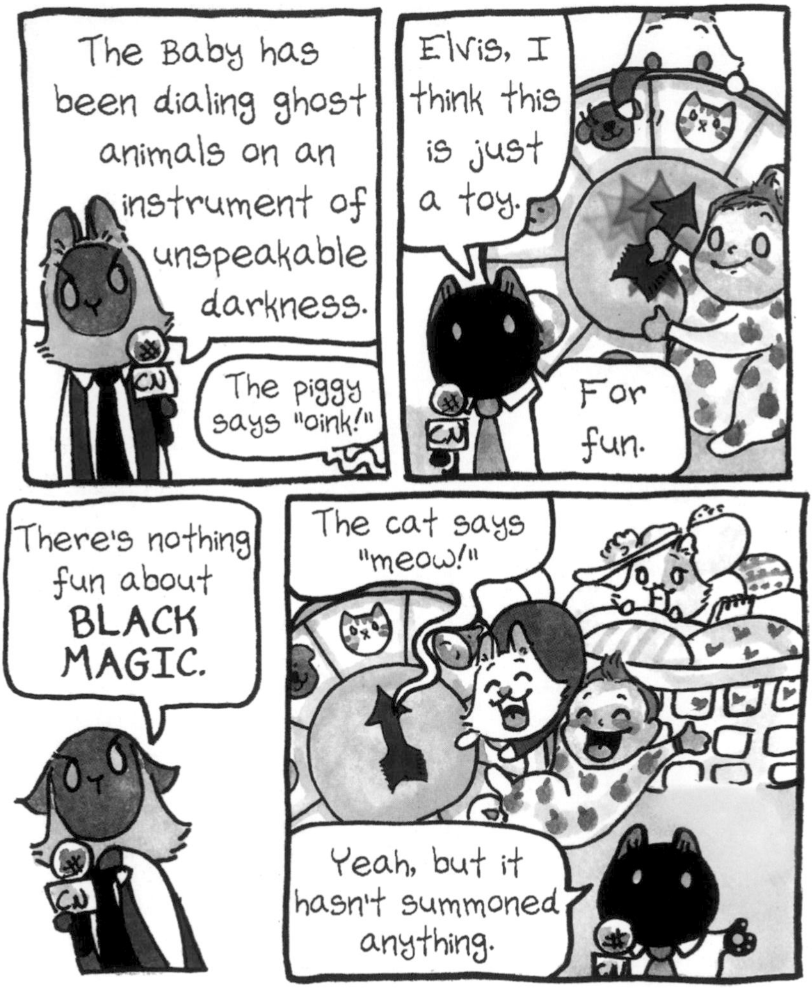
The Baby has been dialing ghost animals on an instrument of unspeakable darkness.
CN
The piggy says "oink!"
Elvis, I think this is just a toy.
CN
For fun.
There's nothing fun about BLACK MAGIC.
CN
The cat says "meow!"
Yeah, but it hasn't summoned anything.
CN

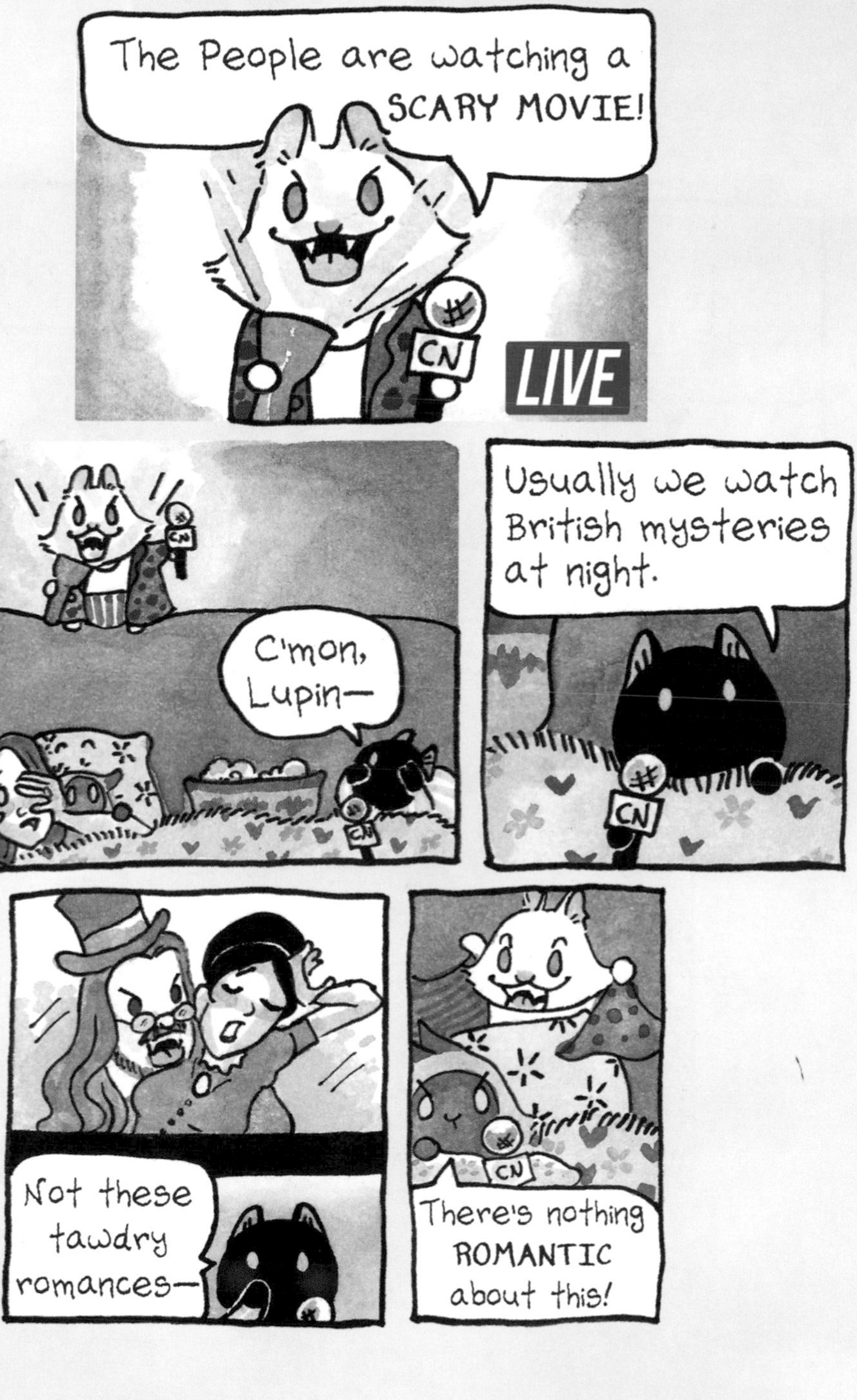
The People are watching a SCARY MOVIE!
CN
LIVE
C'mon, Lupin—
Usually we watch British mysteries at night.
Not these tawdry romances—
There's nothing ROMANTIC about this!

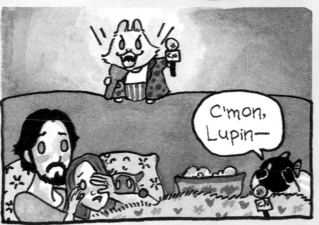

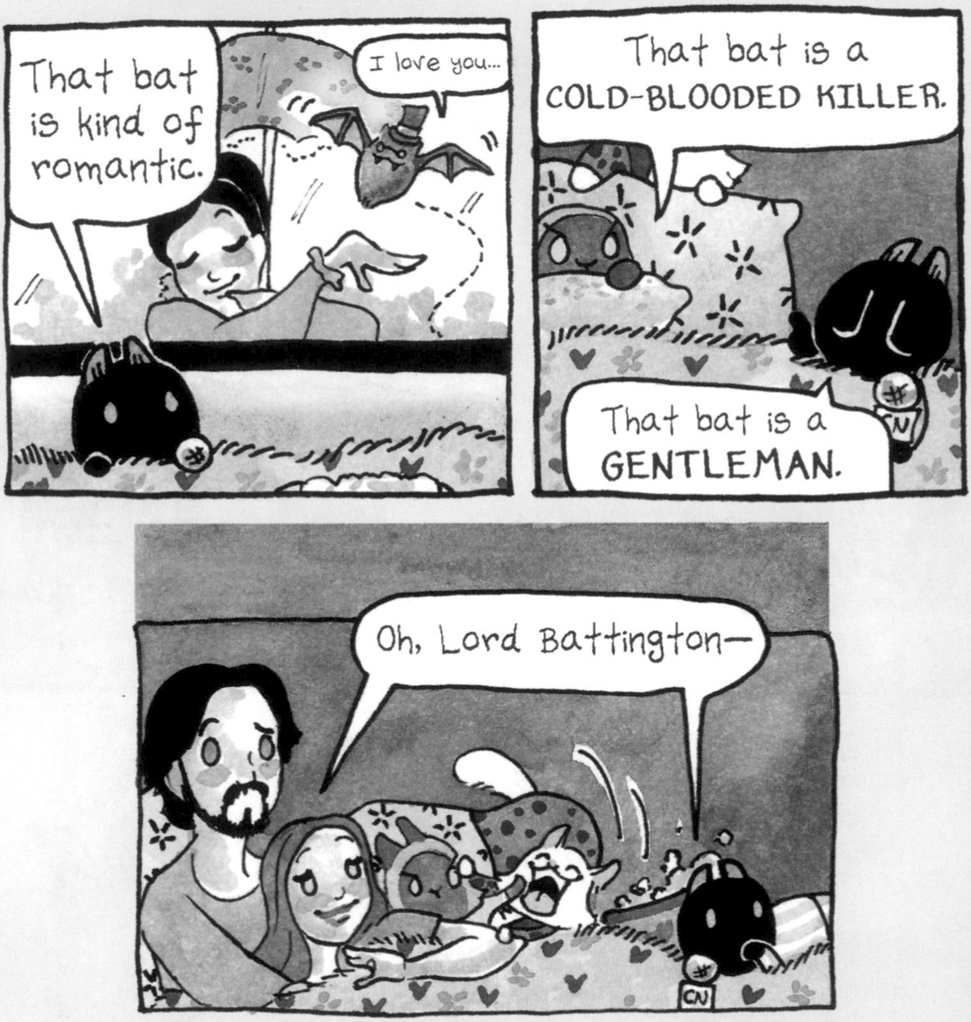
That bat is kind of romantic.
I love you...
That bat is a COLD-BLOODED KILLER.
That bat is a GENTLEMAN.
Oh, Lord Battington—

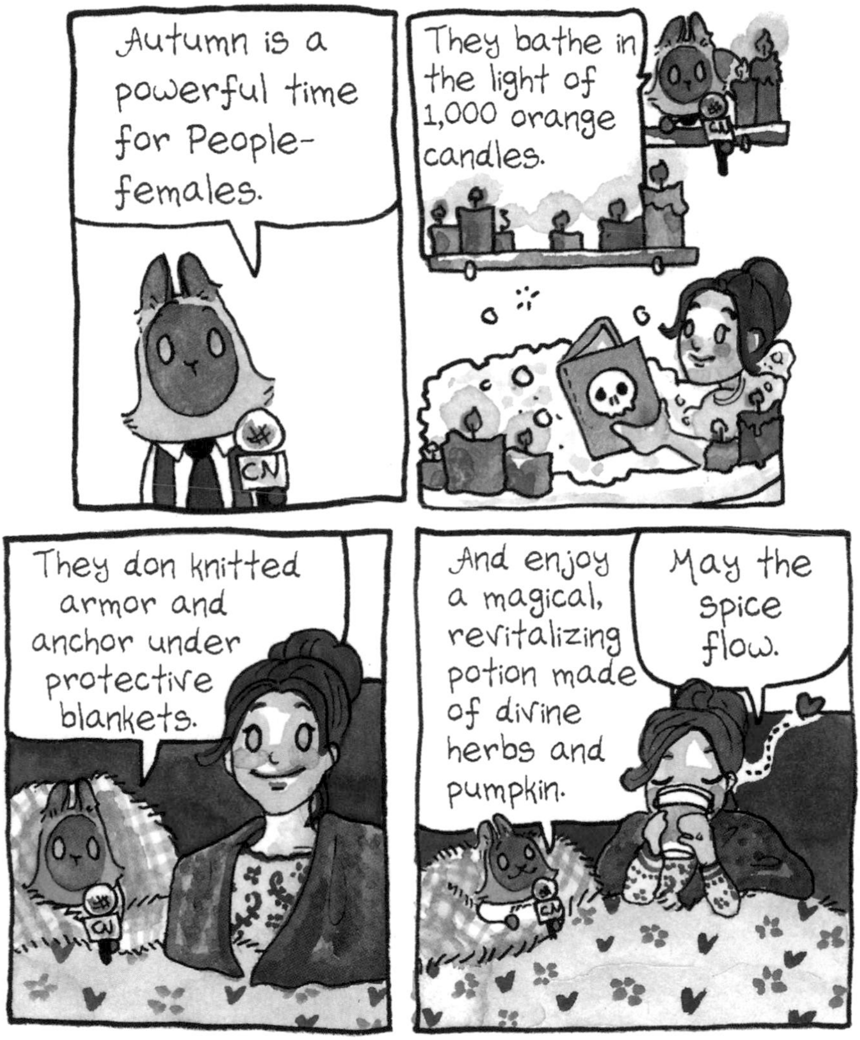
Autumn is a powerful time for People-females.
They bathe in the light of 1,000 orange candles.
CN
They don knitted armor and anchor under protective blankets.
And enjoy a magical, revitalizing potion made of divine herbs and pumpkin.
May the spice flow.

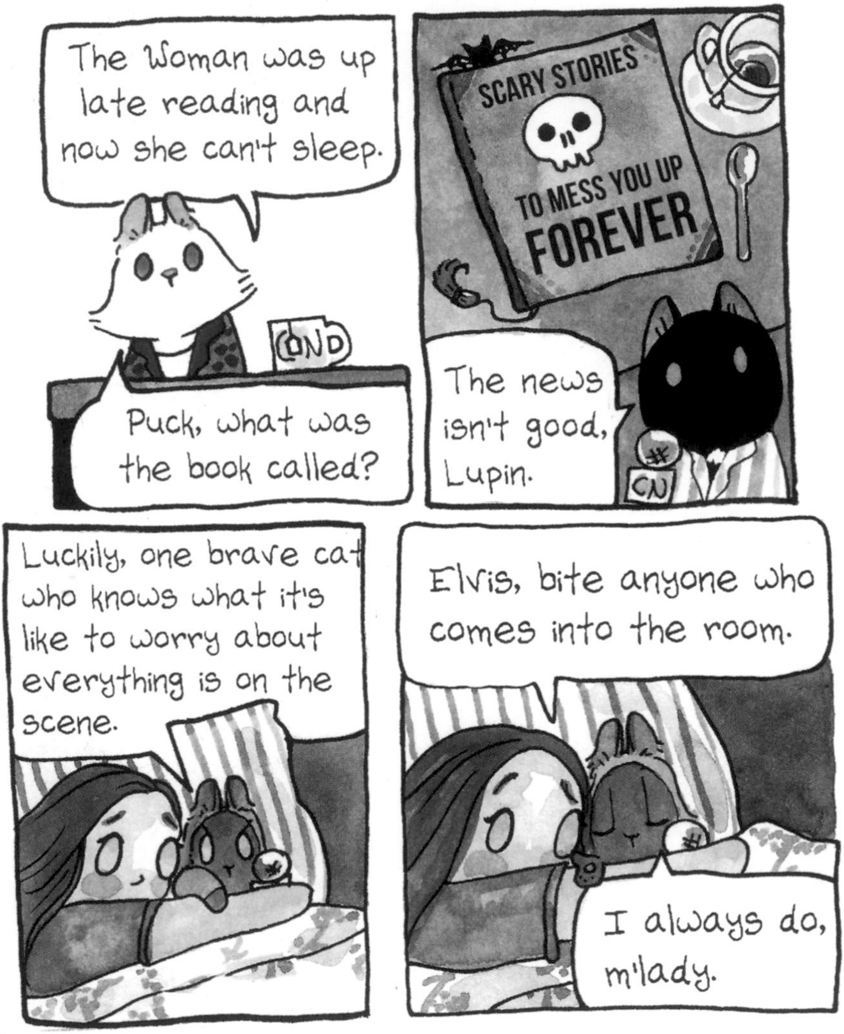
The Woman was up late reading and now she can't sleep.
Puck, what was the book called?
SCARY STORIES TO MESS YOU UP FOREVER
The news isn't good, Lupin.
Luckily, one brave cat who knows what it's like to worry about everything is on the scene.
Elvis, bite anyone who comes into the room.
I always do, m'lady.

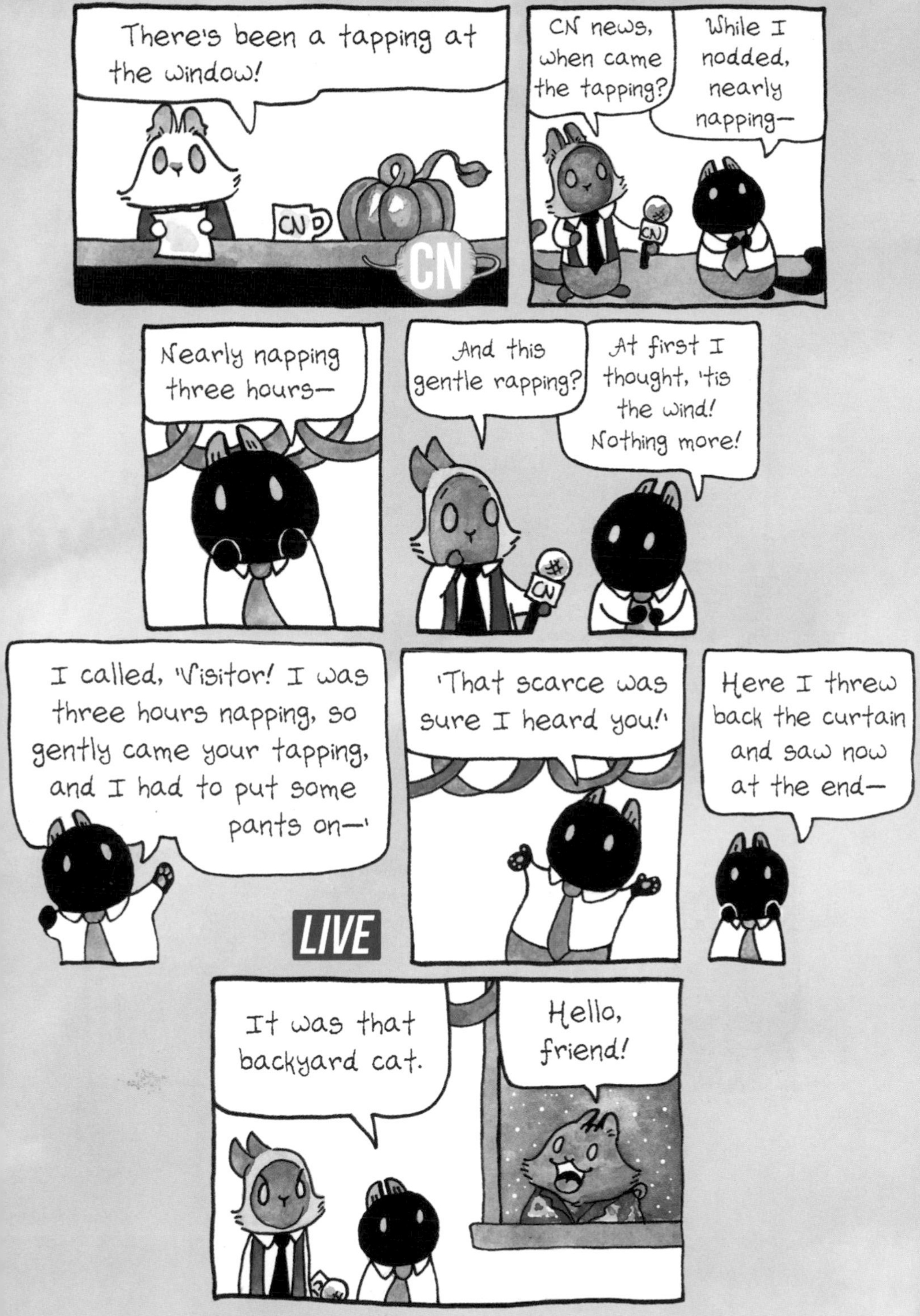
There's been a tapping at the window!
CN
CN
CN news, when came the tapping?
While I nodded, nearly napping—
CN
Nearly napping three hours—
And this gentle rapping?
At first I thought, 'tis the wind! Nothing more!
CN
I called, 'Visitor! I was three hours napping, so gently came your tapping, and I had to put some pants on—'
LIVE
'That scarce was sure I heard you!'
Here I threw back the curtain and saw now at the end—
It was that backyard cat.
Hello, friend!

DING DONG!
AW!
TRICK OR TRE—
NO SOLICITORS!
AURGHHH!!

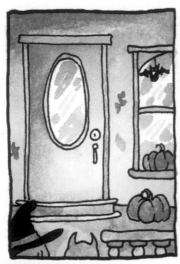

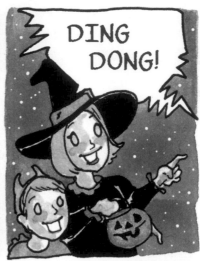

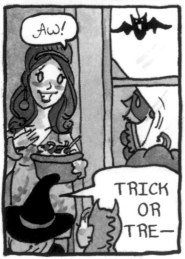

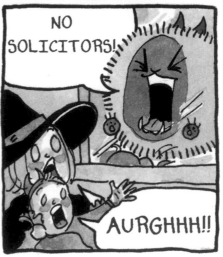

Elvis, it's Halloween. Kids are going to come to the door.

Those aren't kids. They're monsters and spooky ghosts.

We have to hand out candy! You can help!

I AM helping.

Just relax and be a taco!

But I'm not a taco... You're asking me to live a lie.

Our home is under attack and the People are hiding something.

LIVE

Elvis, I beg to differ. The People are giving children treats.

This could easily lead to cats getting treats.

"CHILDREN" ARE PEOPLE-KITTENS

Puck—

Please, Elvis. Tonight I'm "Pepperoni Pucky."

House under siege. Elvis here, live, where children have us surrounded—
AND CONTINUE TO DEMAND THEIR CANDY TRIBUTE.
CN
Elvis, take a break, will ya? You're going to have a fit.
CN
LIVE
IF YOU KEEP GIVING THEM CANDY, THEY WILL KEEP COMING BACK FOR CANDY!
Aw, a taco!

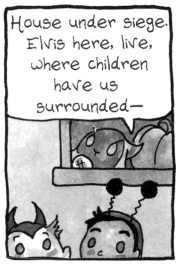

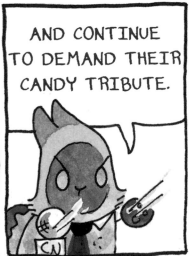

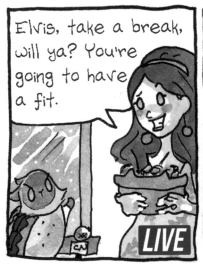

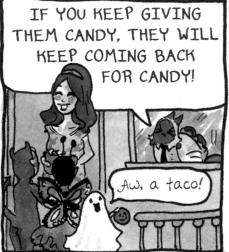

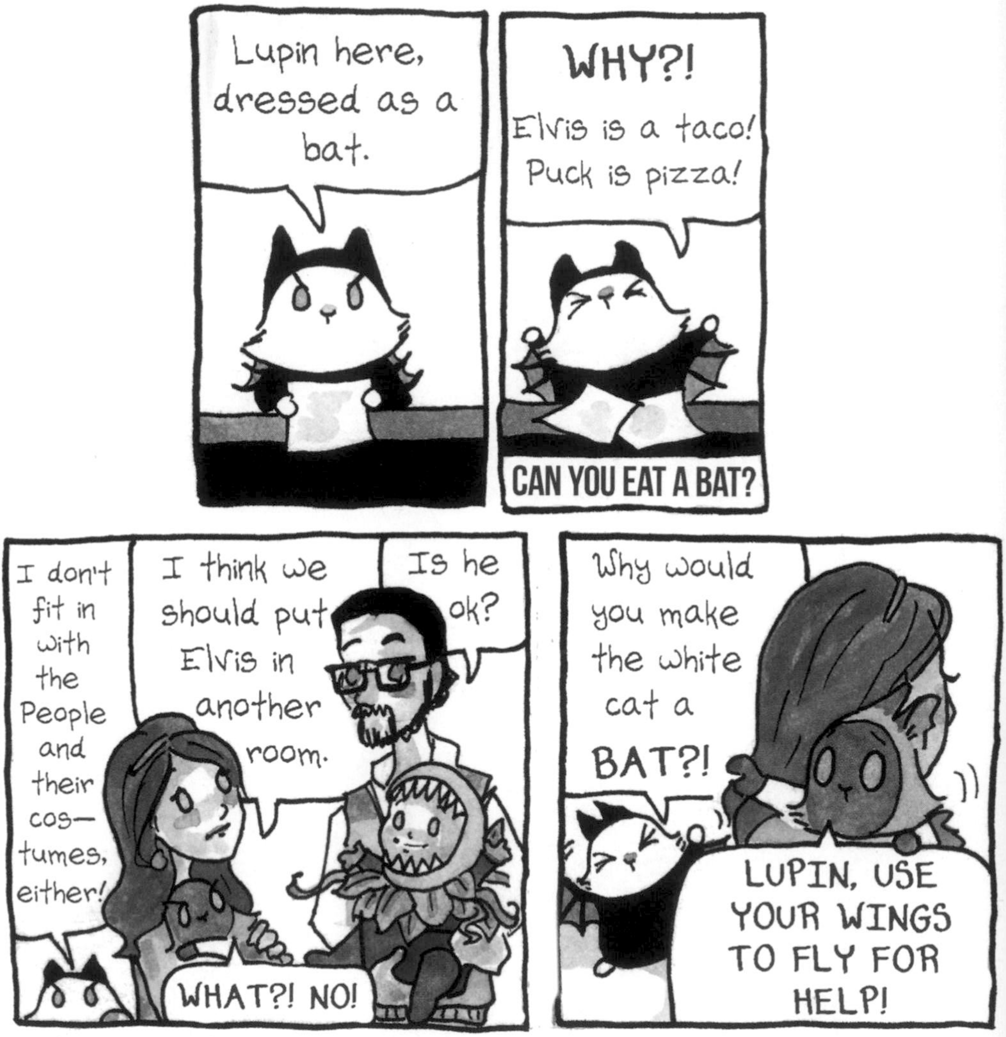
Lupin here, dressed as a bat.
WHY?!
Elvis is a taco! Puck is pizza!
CAN YOU EAT A BAT?
I don't fit in with the People and their cos- tumes, either!
I think we should put Elvis in another room.
Is he ok?
WHAT?! NO!
Why would you make the white cat a BAT?!
LUPIN, USE YOUR WINGS TO FLY FOR HELP!

Pepperoni Pucky, reporting live, where Elvis has been shut inside the bedroom.
Puck?
For his own safety and the safety of others.
Puck? ...Let me out, Puck.
...Pepperoni Pucky can't do that, Elvis...
Puck, I'm not going to hurt anyone. I just need to ATTACK THE CHILDREN-

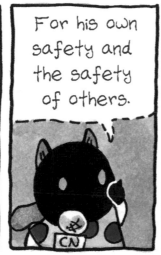

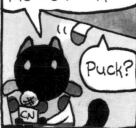

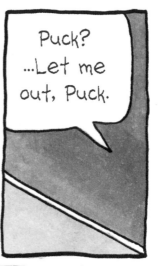

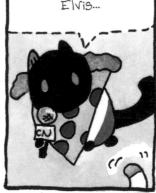

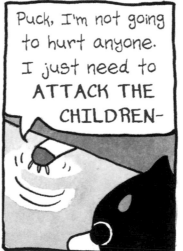

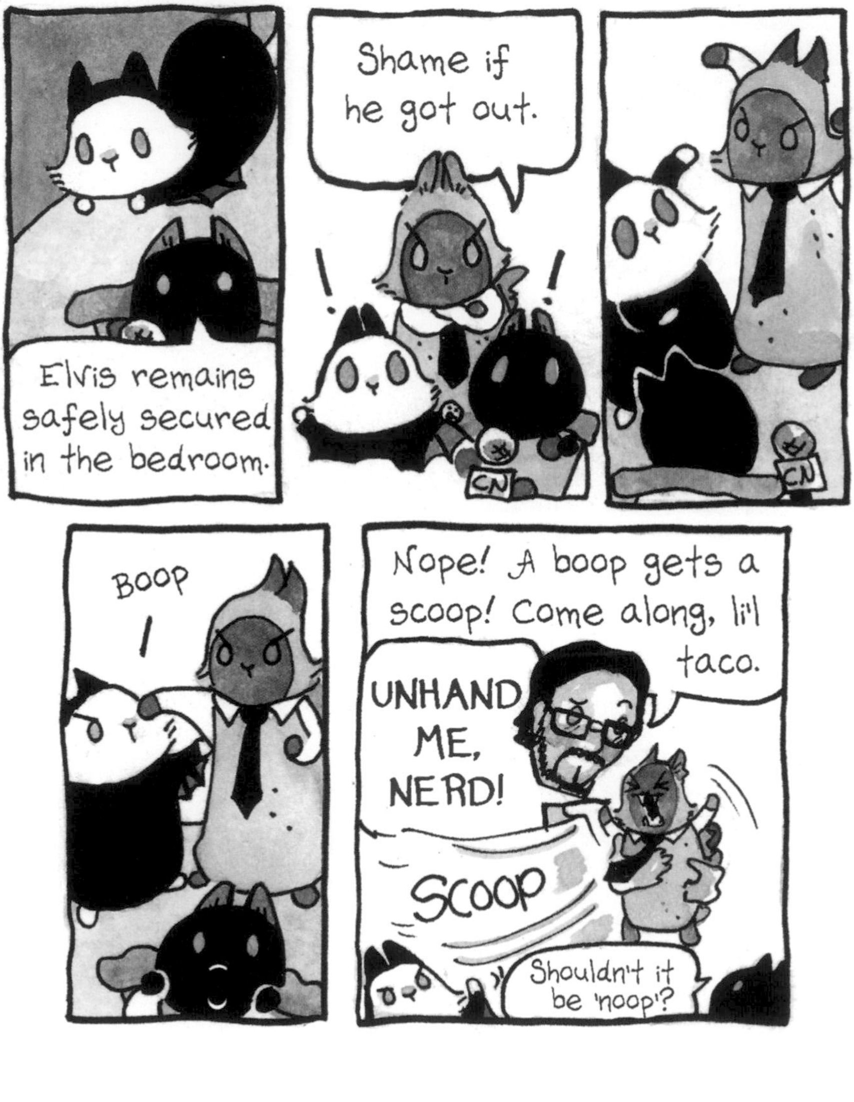
Elvis remains safely secured in the bedroom.
Shame if he got out.
!
!
CN
CN
BOOP
!
Nope! A boop gets a scoop! Come along, li'l taco.
UNHAND ME, NERD!
SCOOP
Shouldn't it be 'noop'?

Pepperoni Pucky,
Yum, yum, yum!
Yum, yum, yum!
What a great Halloween!
I'll say!
Don't be shy!
Pepperoni Lupin!
I WILL NOT REST UNTIL I HAVE RETRIEVED ALL OF OUR CANDY!
Happy Halloween!

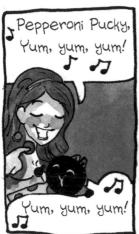

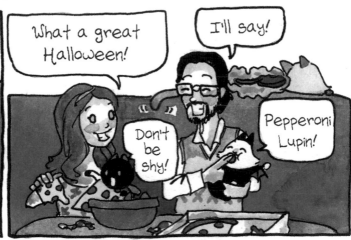

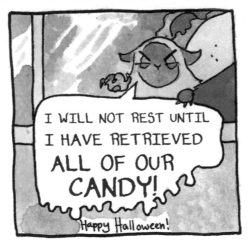

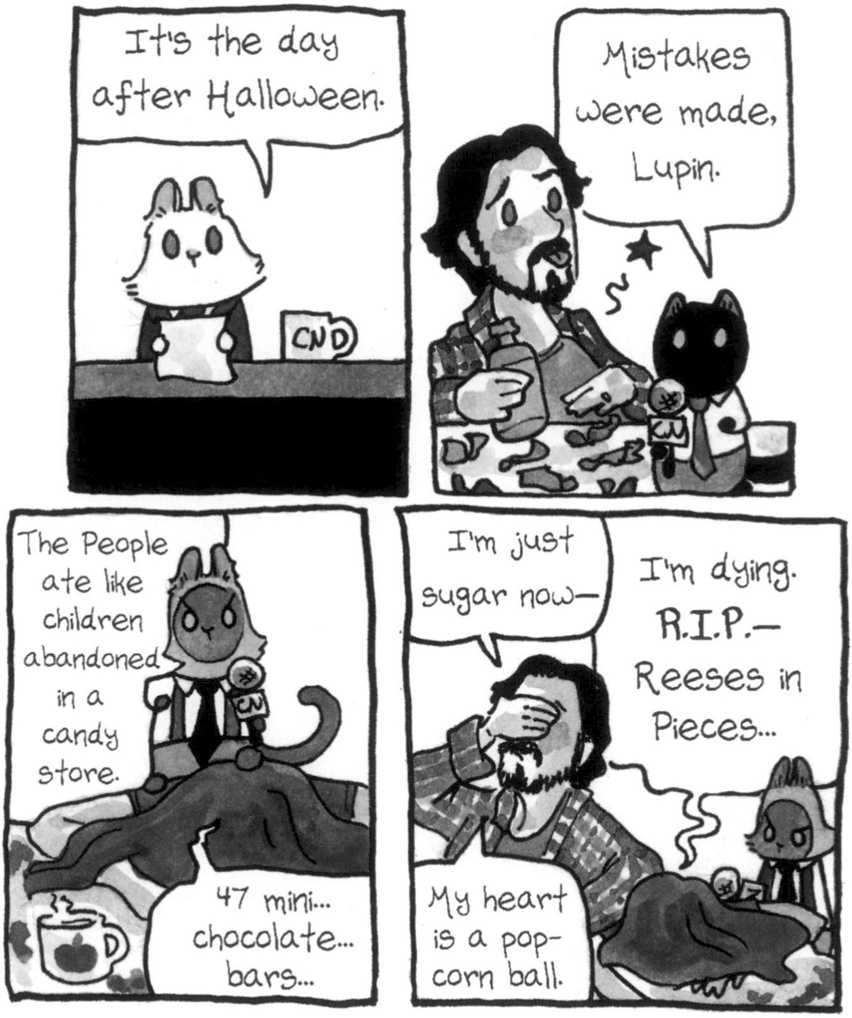
It's the day after Halloween.
Mistakes were made, Lupin.
CND
The People ate like children abandoned in a candy store.
47 mini... chocolate... bars...
I'm just sugar now—
I'm dying. R.I.P.— Reeses in Pieces...
My heart is a pop-corn ball.

The Man is attempting to put up a Christmas wreath...

...two days after Halloween.

It's a bold move, Lupin...

To try to hop over an entire month of the calendar year.

Pucky!

NO!

I WON'T LET YOU SKIP THE ONLY HOLIDAY ABOUT **TURKEY!**

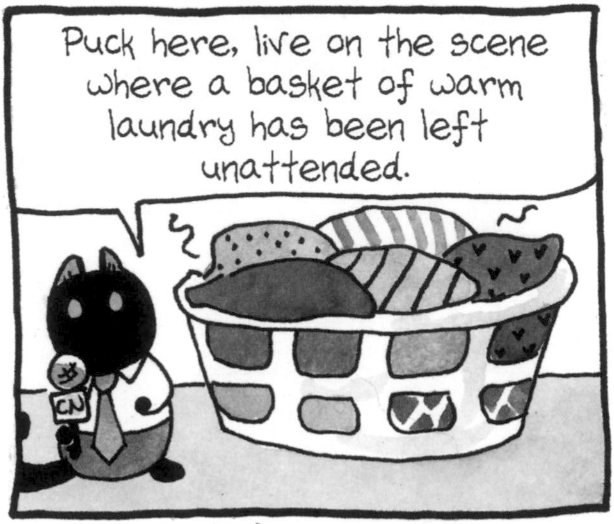
Puck here, live on the scene where a basket of warm laundry has been left unattended.
CN

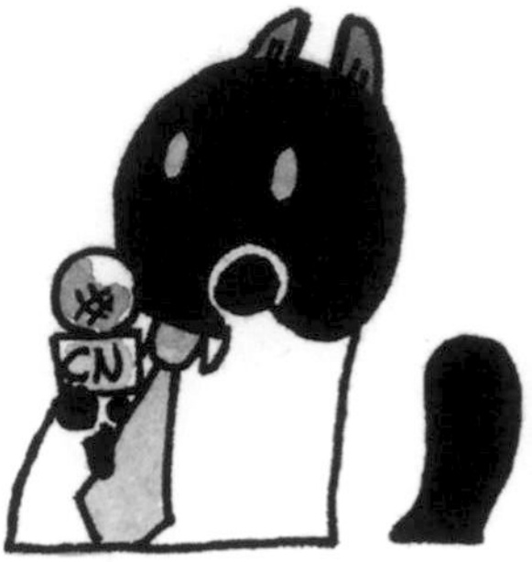
CN

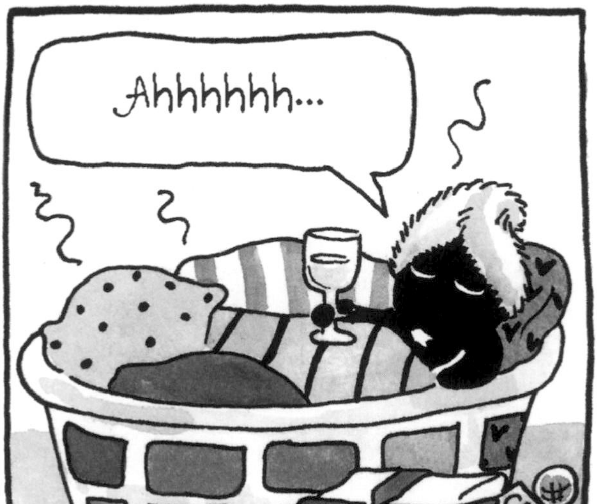
Ahhhhhh...

Local cat misses man.

This slipper smells like the Man and makes him feel close when he's gone.

He comes back **EVERY DAY.**

THERE'S ANOTHER ONE!

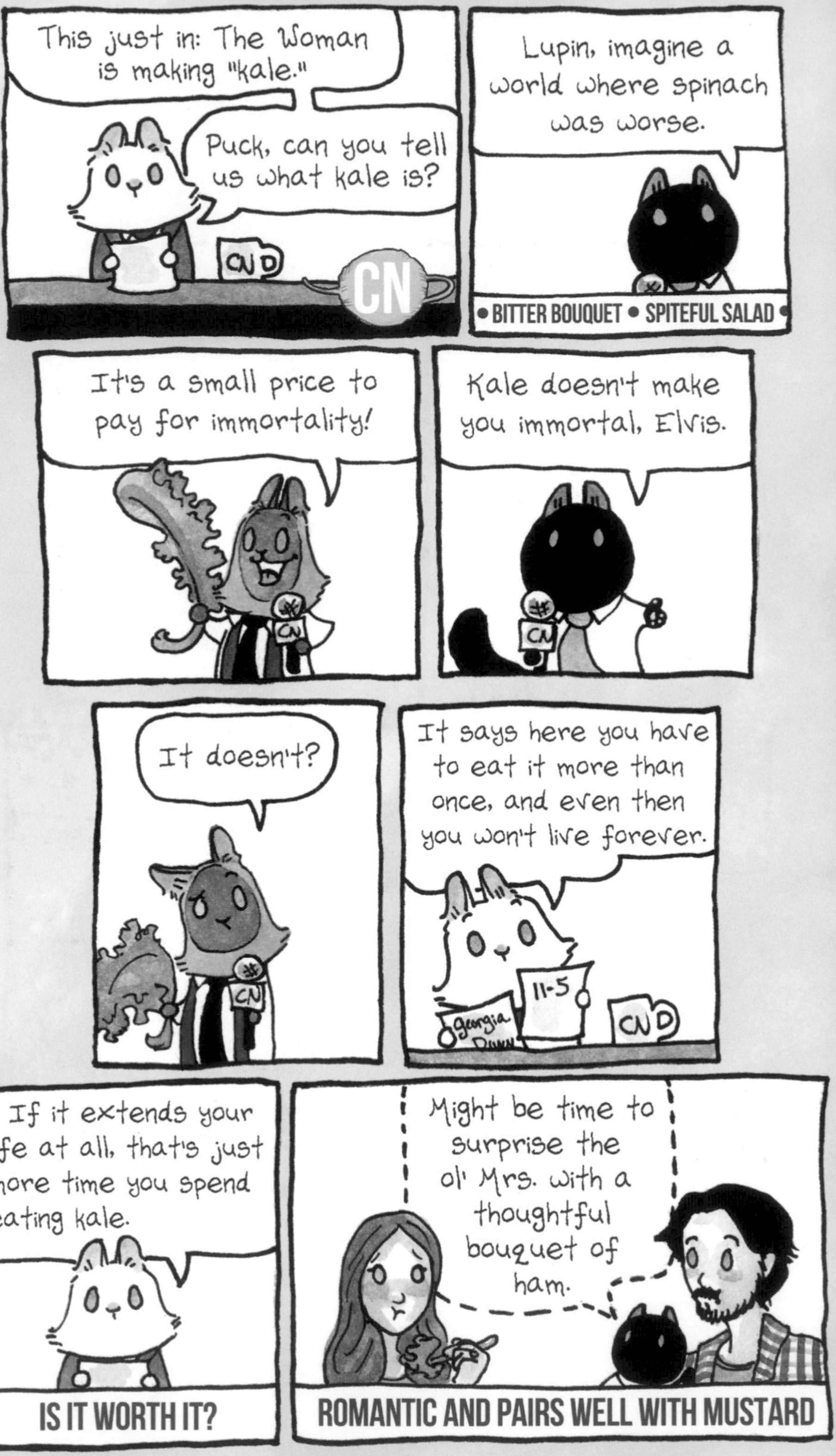

This just in: The Woman is making "kale."
Puck, can you tell us what kale is?
CN
Lupin, imagine a world where spinach was worse.
• BITTER BOUQUET • SPITEFUL SALAD •
It's a small price to pay for immortality!
Kale doesn't make you immortal, Elvis.
It doesn't?
It says here you have to eat it more than once, and even then you won't live forever.
11-5
If it extends your life at all, that's just more time you spend eating kale.
IS IT WORTH IT?
Might be time to surprise the ol' Mrs. with a thoughtful bouquet of ham.
ROMANTIC AND PAIRS WELL WITH MUSTARD

It's takeout night!

We go now live to Puck!

Thanks, Lupin. Puck here, live where the Man is expected to return with delicious People food...

TAKEOUT NIGHT!

Any minute now.

I think I speak for every cat when I say: Let it be fish n' chips.

WISH FOR FISH • WISH N' CHIPS

Let's have a rundown of tonight's possibilities, based on previous take-out nights.

If it's salad again, I'm puking in shoes.

WHAT IS THE POINT OF SALAD?

I wish this wheel could spin.

SIDE OF REGRET WITH VINAIGRETTE

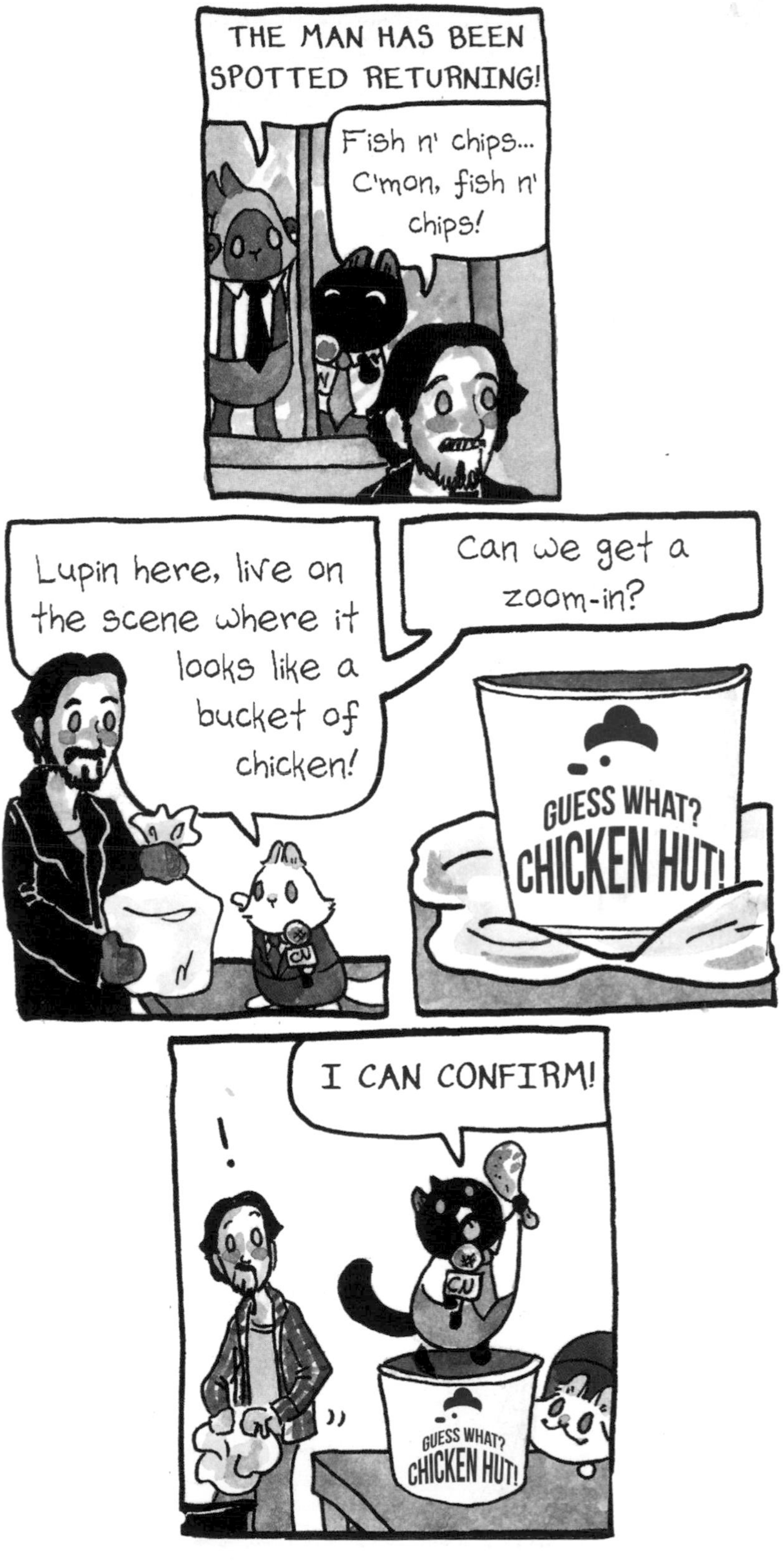
THE MAN HAS BEEN SPOTTED RETURNING!
Fish n' chips... C'mon, fish n' chips!
Lupin here, live on the scene where it looks like a bucket of chicken!
Can we get a zoom-in?
GUESS WHAT? CHICKEN HUT!
I CAN CONFIRM!
!
GUESS WHAT? CHICKEN HUT!

It's a great day in the kitchen, where a bucket of chicken has just arrived!
CN
Lupin, it's warm and smells like spicy breezes of peppered paradise.
CN
GUESS WHAT?
Guys!
YOU LEFT THE CHICKEN UNDEFENDED! STAY BACK OR FACE WHATEVER THIS THING IS!
CN
• TINY TRIDENT? • SPOON VAMPIRE? • ANGER SHOVEL? •

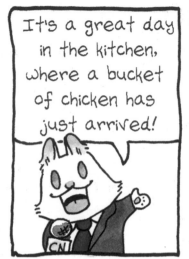

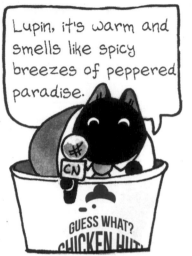

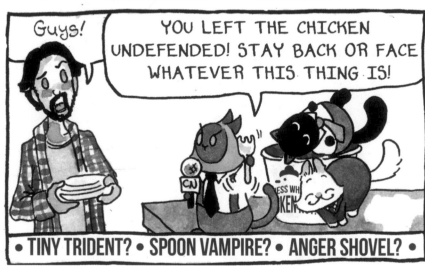

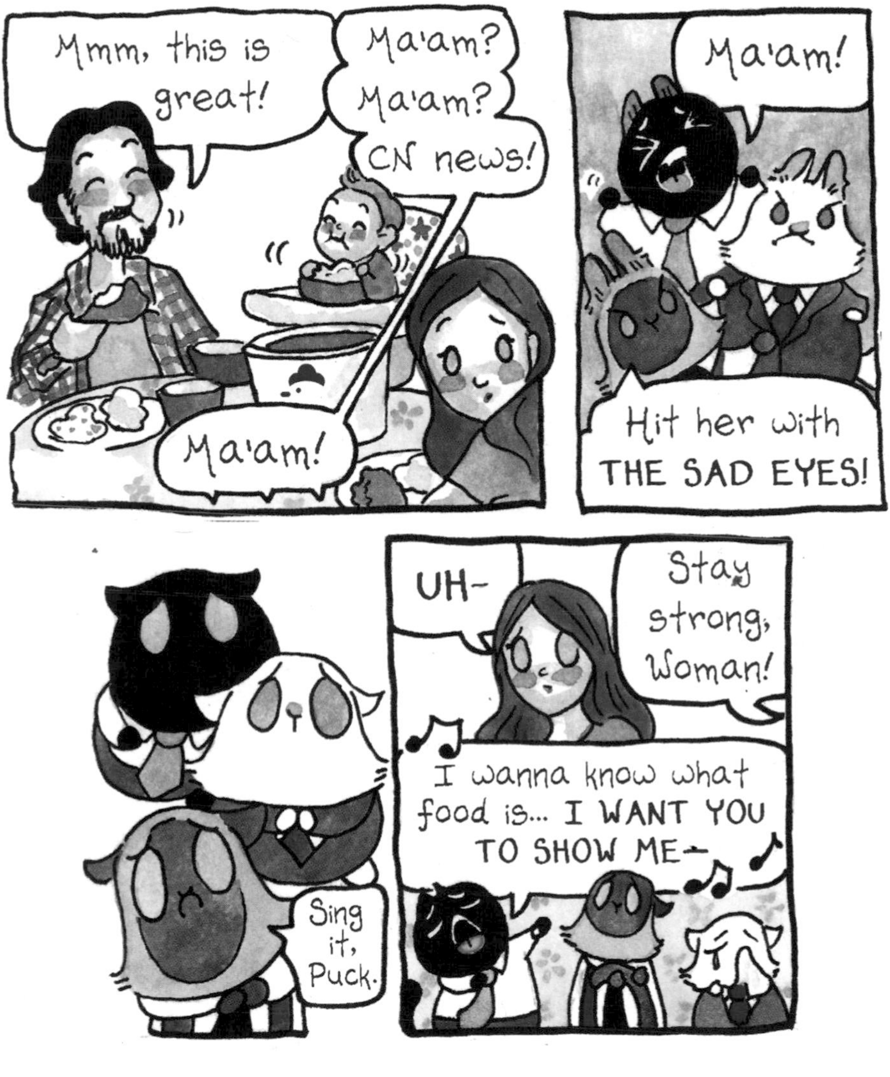
Mmm, this is great!
Ma'am? Ma'am? CN news!
Ma'am!
Ma'am!
Hit her with THE SAD EYES!
Sing it, Puck.
UH-
Stay strong, Woman!
I wanna know what food is... I WANT YOU TO SHOW ME-

I'm glad the boys stopped begging for food.
Mmm—hmm.
GUESS WHAT?
You're feeding them under the table, aren't you?
Who?
You know who.
Nothing to see here.
CN

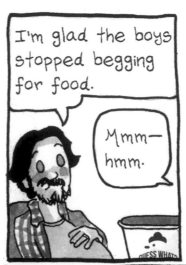

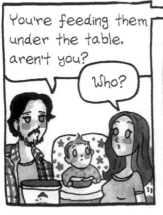

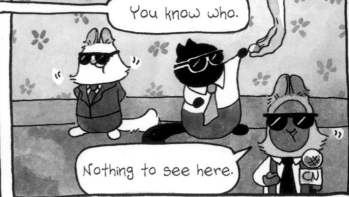

It's national leftovers day!

Lupin, tomorrow the Woman and I will be making soup and casseroles.

Today we're up to our whiskers in sandwiches and pie.

And itty bitty kitty bits of turkey.

I'll take a swipe of whipped cream, thank you.

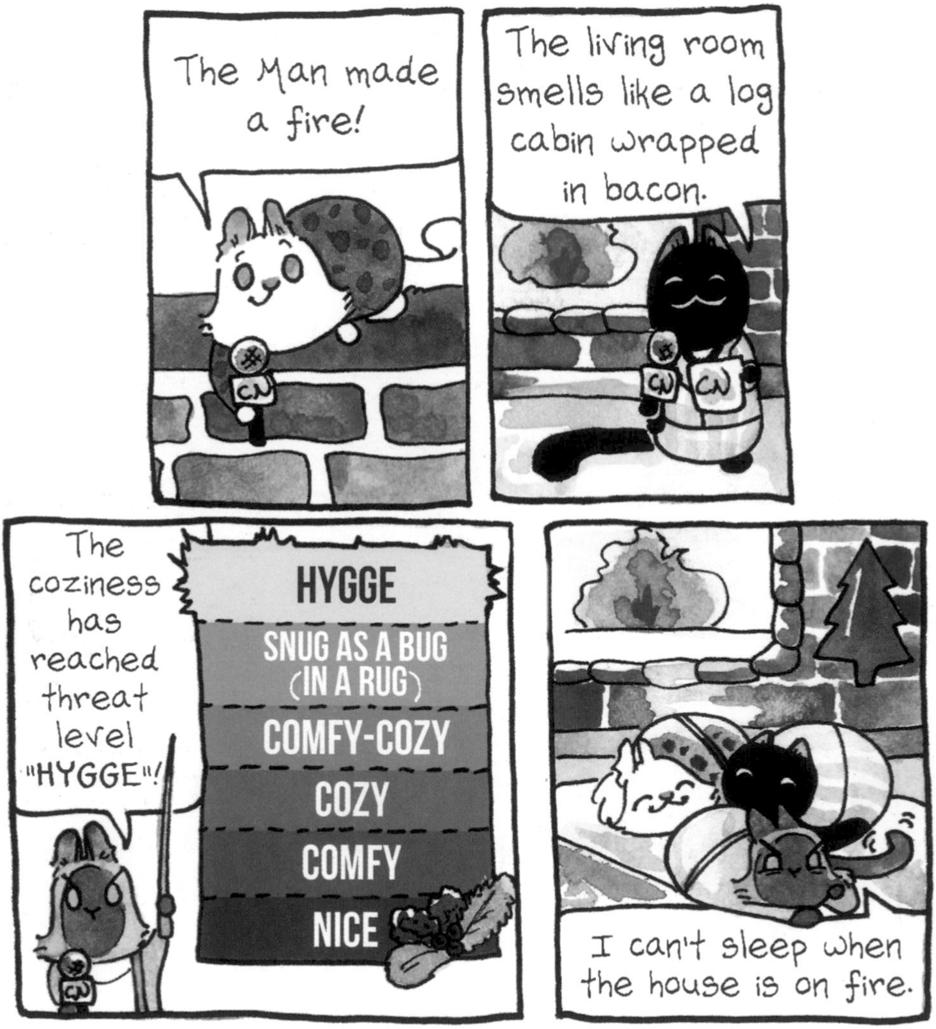
The Man made a fire!
The living room smells like a log cabin wrapped in bacon.
CN
The coziness has reached threat level "HYGGE"!
HYGGE
SNUG AS A BUG (IN A RUG)
COMFY-COZY
COZY
COMFY
NICE
I can't sleep when the house is on fire.

A package has arrived! Proof Mailmen exist!

Lupin, Mailmen are a myth. Like any of these made-up legends.

Make-Believe Impossible Creatures

Unicorns

Dragons

Phoenixes

Narwhals

Elvis, narwhals are real.

You mean, like, in your heart...?

Narwhals

...Where anything is possible?

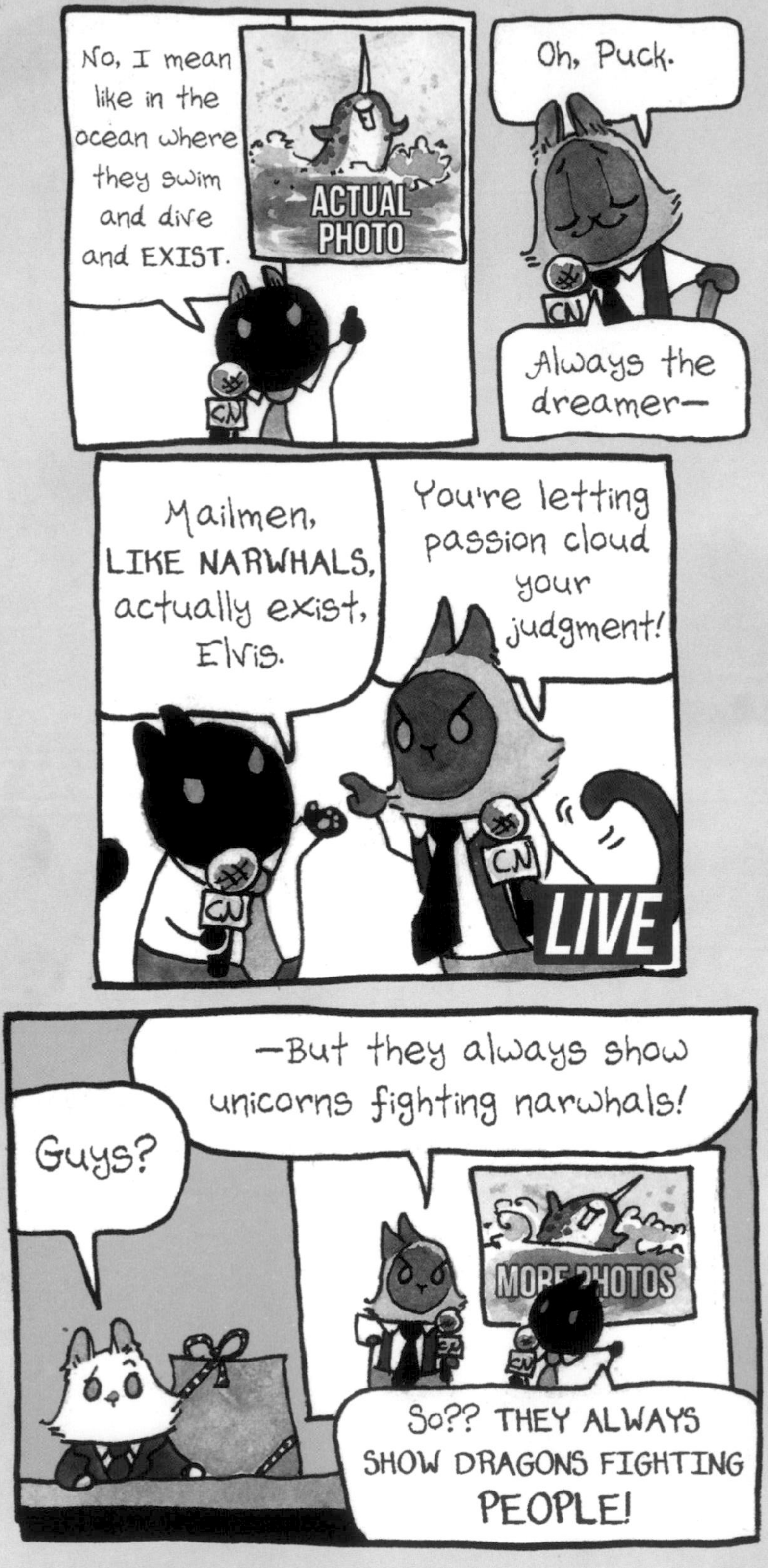
No, I mean like in the ocean where they swim and dive and EXIST.
ACTUAL PHOTO
CN
Oh, Puck.
CN
Always the dreamer—
Mailmen, LIKE NARWHALS, actually exist, Elvis.
You're letting passion cloud your judgment!
CN
CN
LIVE
—But they always show unicorns fighting narwhals!
Guys?
MORE PHOTOS
So?? THEY ALWAYS SHOW DRAGONS FIGHTING PEOPLE!

BREAKING CAT
NEWS
MORE TO EXPLORE

DIGITALLY COLORED BCN STRIPS

Most of the comics you see in the funny pages today are colored digitally. When BCN first came to newspapers, I initially tried working with a colorist. However, within a few weeks I missed painting the strips in watercolors myself very much. That's my favorite part of the process. And it turns out I need that quiet brain time to dream up new stories and gags for the comic—my ideas had all gone silent! Eek!

With apologies to the colorist, I began painting the comic in watercolors again and my writing gears sprang back to life. Sometimes you don't know quite how your process works until you try to change it.

It's fun to look back on these digitally colored BCN strips from the first three months the comic was in newspapers.

Welcome to Breaking Cat News! I'm your anchor cat, Lupin.

I'm Elvis, your cynical, trusted cat news reporter. TRUST NO ONE!

And I'm Puck, your feline-interest reporter.

Elvis again, reporting from inside a subtle raincoat that I'm also the weather cat.

LIVE

© 2017 Georgia Dunn/Dist. by Andrews McMeel Syndication

gocomics.com

3/27

How do you boys like the new apartment?

Wherever we go, wherever life takes us...

It's OK.

As long as we have this couch.

I would ride this couch into any sunset.

I would follow this couch to the ends of the Earth.

Lupin, there's a fire in the living room and the People ARE DOING NOTHING TO STOP IT!

TOASTINESS LEVELS RISING

Elvis, it's called a fireplace, and we've talked about this before.

TOTALLY NORMAL

gocomics.com

5/29

© 2017 Georgia Dunn/Dist. by Andrews McMeel Syndication

Isn't this nice?

Lupin, the fire rages on-

It's just nice to feel COZY.

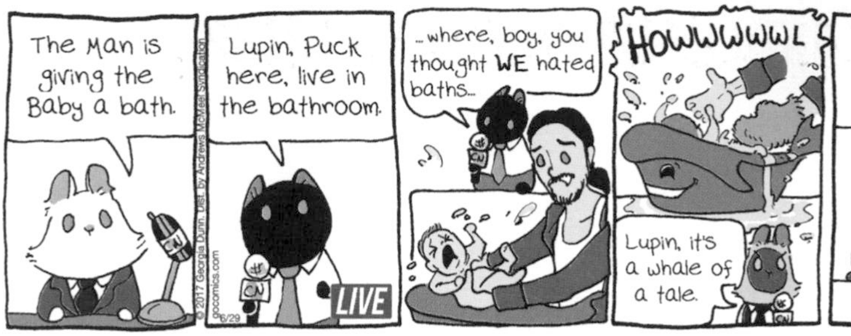
The Man is giving the Baby a bath.
Lupin, Puck here, live in the bathroom.
LIVE
© 2017 Georgia Dunn. Dist. by Andrews McMeel Syndication
gocomics.com
6/29
...where, boy, you thought WE hated baths...
HOWWWWWL
Lupin, it's a whale of a tale.
About one angry little bath-time bear.

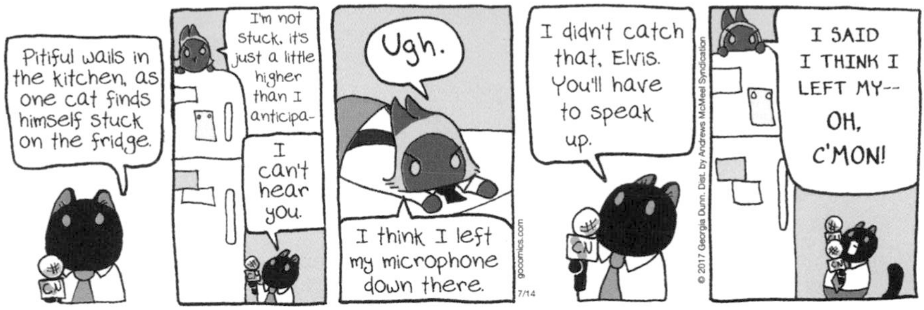
Pitiful wails in the kitchen, as one cat finds himself stuck on the fridge.
I'm not stuck, it's just a little higher than I anticipa-
I can't hear you.
Ugh.
I think I left my microphone down there.
gocomics.com
7/14
I didn't catch that, Elvis. You'll have to speak up.
I SAID I THINK I LEFT MY-- OH, C'MON!
© 2017 Georgia Dunn. Dist. by Andrews McMeel Syndication

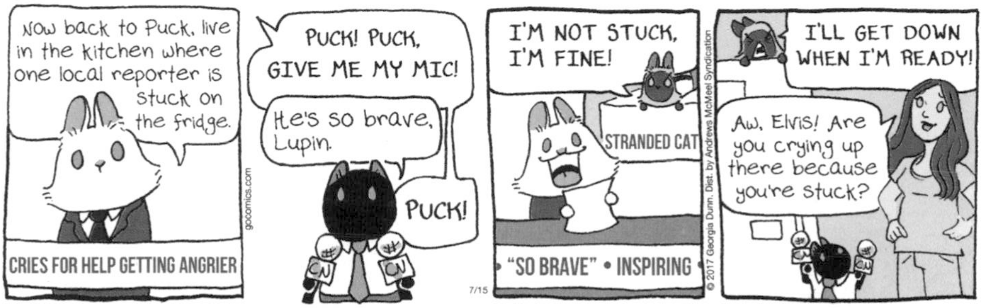
Now back to Puck, live in the kitchen where one local reporter is stuck on the fridge.
CRIES FOR HELP GETTING ANGRIER
gocomics.com
PUCK! PUCK, GIVE ME MY MIC!
He's so brave, Lupin.
PUCK!
7/15
I'M NOT STUCK, I'M FINE!
STRANDED CAT
• "SO BRAVE" • INSPIRING •
© 2017 Georgia Dunn. Dist. by Andrews McMeel Syndication
I'LL GET DOWN WHEN I'M READY!
Aw, Elvis! Are you crying up there because you're stuck?

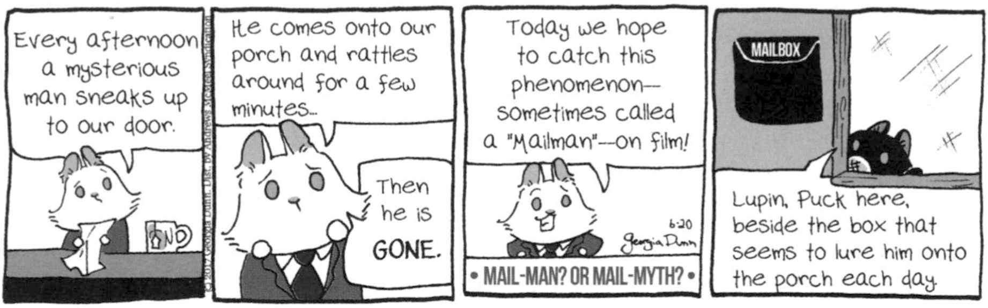
Every afternoon a mysterious man sneaks up to our door.
He comes onto our porch and rattles around for a few minutes...
Then he is GONE.
© 2017 Georgia Dunn. Dist. by Andrews McMeel Syndication
Today we hope to catch this phenomenon--sometimes called a "Mailman"--on film!
6-20
Georgia Dunn
• MAIL-MAN? OR MAIL-MYTH? •
MAILBOX
Lupin, Puck here, beside the box that seems to lure him onto the porch each day.

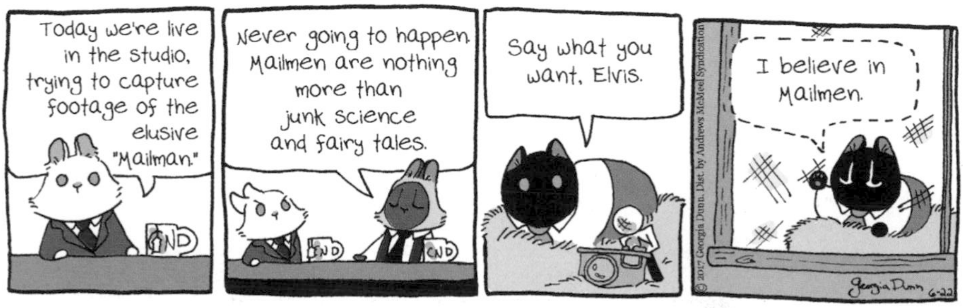
Today we're live in the studio, trying to capture footage of the elusive "Mailman."
Never going to happen. Mailmen are nothing more than junk science and fairy tales.
Say what you want, Elvis.
I believe in Mailmen.
© 2017 Georgia Dunn. Dist. by Andrews McMeel Syndication
Georgia Dunn 6-22

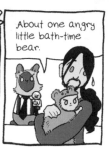

TIPS FOR PAPER DOLLS!

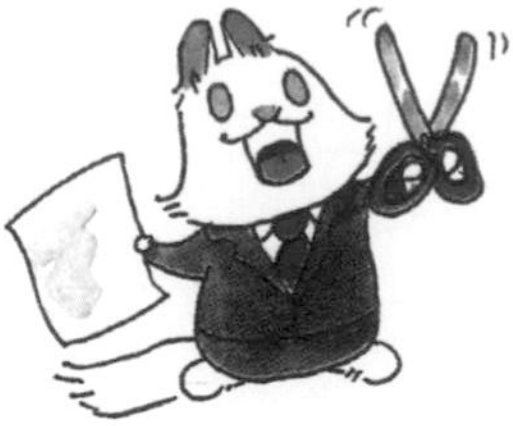

Scissors:
Safety first!
Be careful,
take your time.

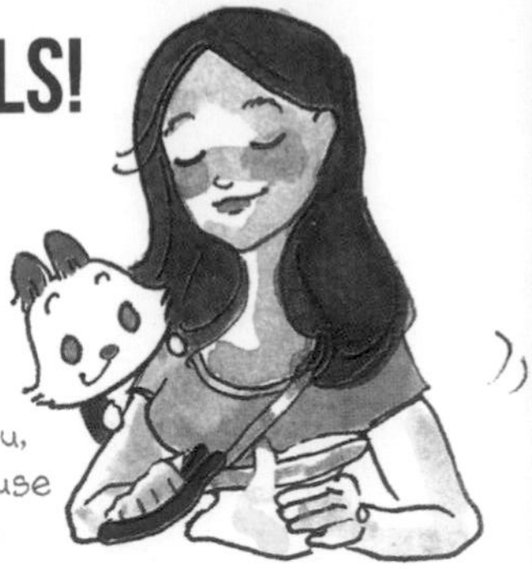

Ask someone to help you,
if you're not allowed to use
scissors. (...Like Lupin)

Make your own clothes:
Flip a patterned piece of paper over and trace an outfit face down. Cut it out and you've got pajamas or a fancy new suit! (Or draw and color an outfit on the tracing!)

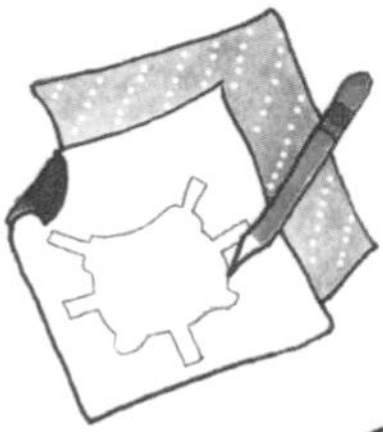

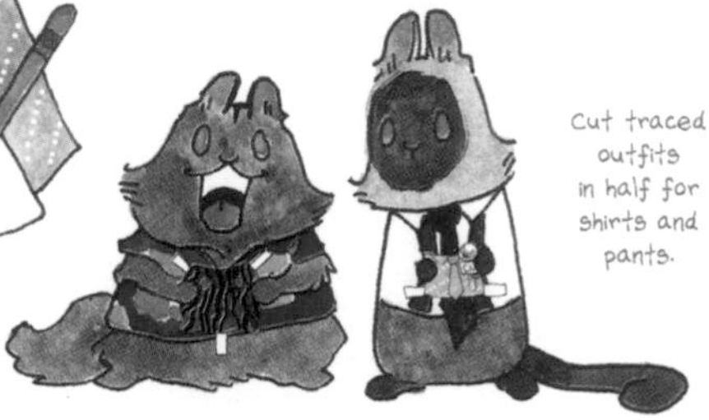

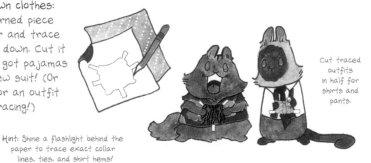

Cut traced outfits in half for shirts and pants.

Hint: Shine a flashlight behind the paper to trace exact collar lines, ties, and shirt hems!

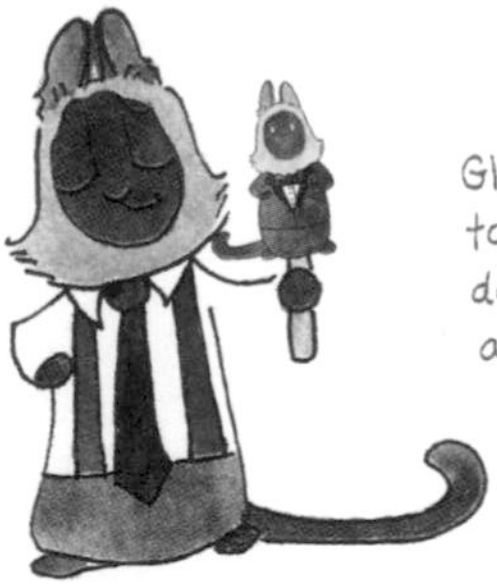

Puppets:
Glue a popsicle stick to the back of each doll, and you've got a little puppet to move around and voice!

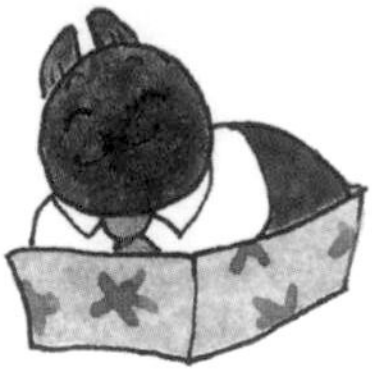

Boxes:
They're not just for naps anymore!
Turn any box into a puppet theater.

Puppet Theaters: By cutting a window into a box, you can create a puppet theater! You can even make your own cardboard television and act out broadcasts inside! Delivery boxes, shoe boxes, and oatmeal containers all make great little theaters.

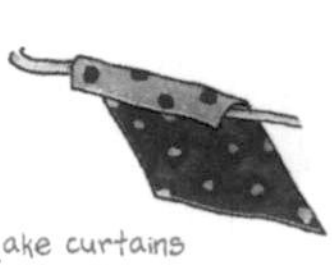

Make curtains for your theater by looping fabric over string and fastening it with glue, thread, or safety pins.

Decorate your theater with paint, crayons, craft paper, scraps of fabric, stickers—anything you have!

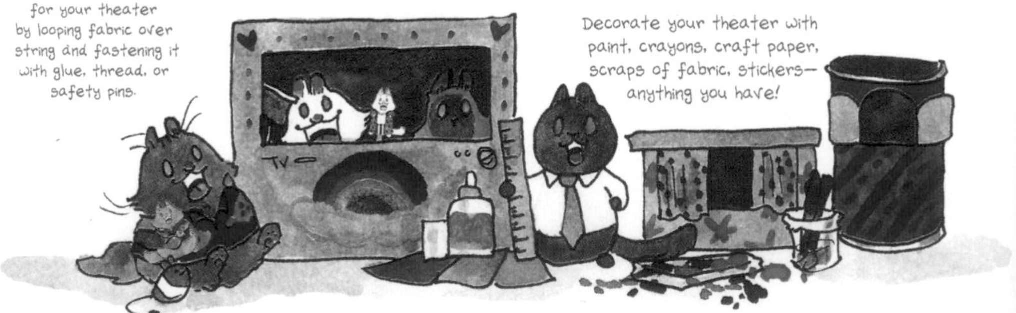
TV

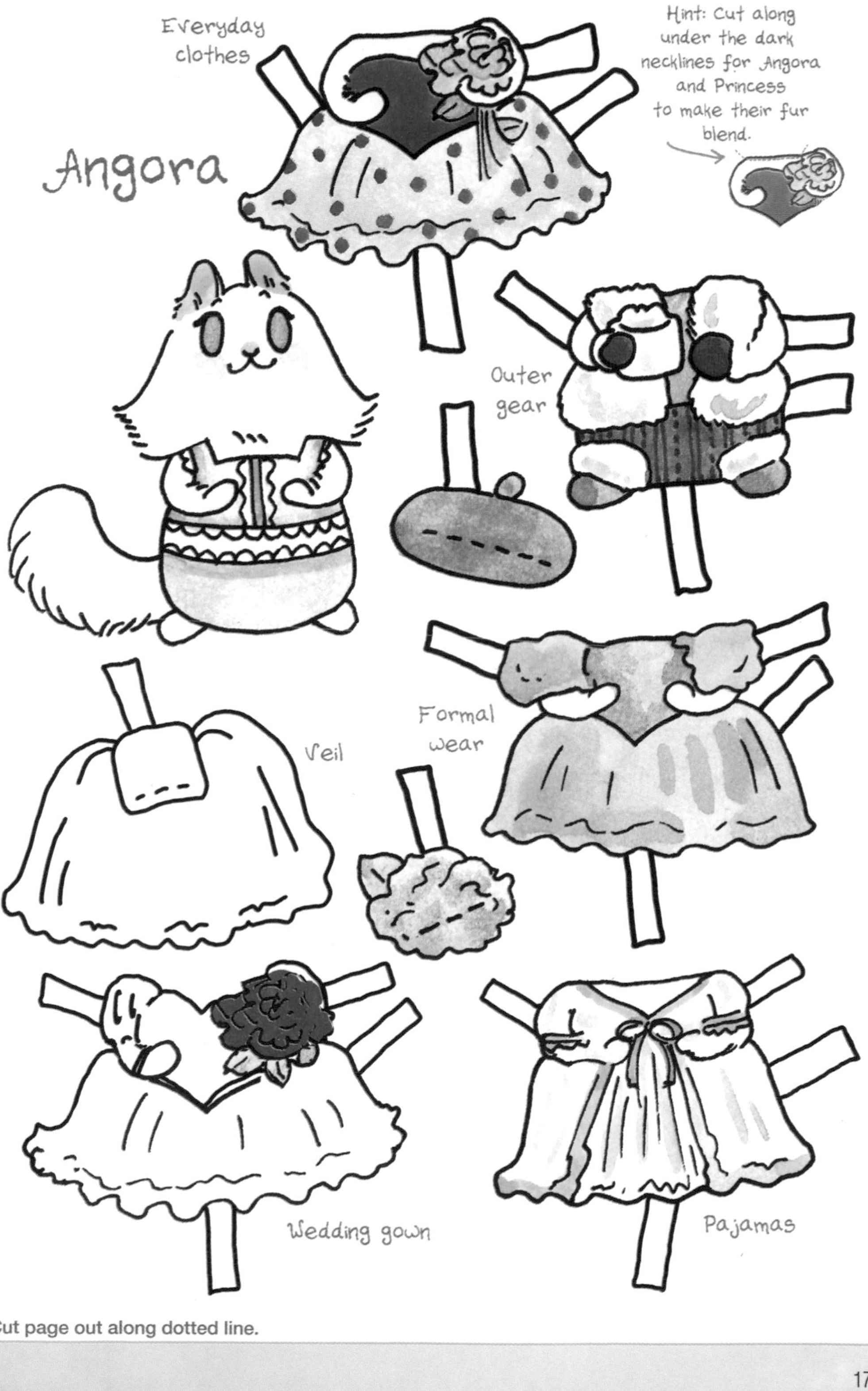

Everyday clothes
Hint: Cut along under the dark necklines for Angora and Princess to make their fur blend.
Angora
Outer gear
Veil
Formal wear
Wedding gown
Pajamas

Cut page out along dotted line.

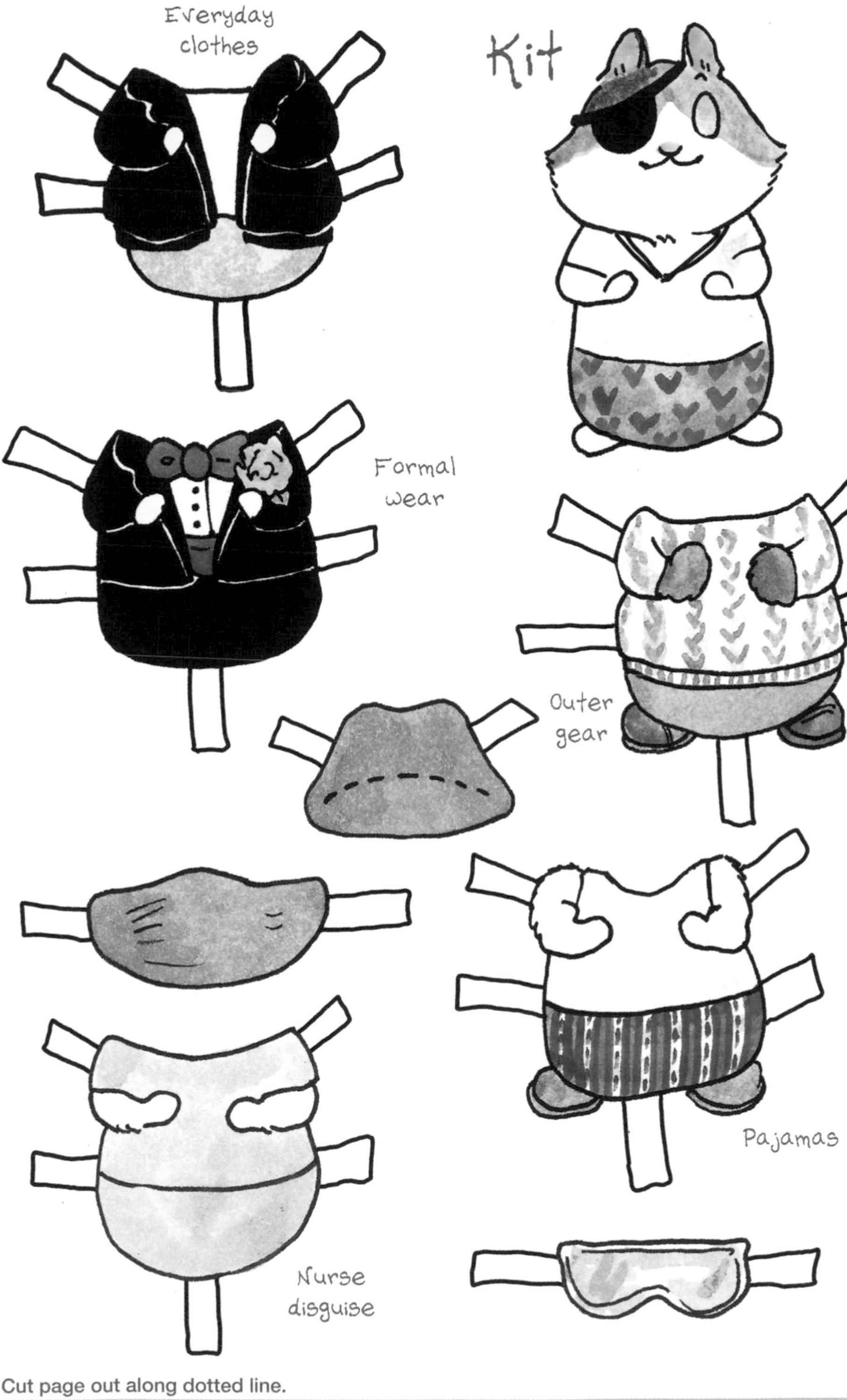
Kit
Everyday clothes
Formal wear
Outer gear
Nurse disguise
Pajamas

Cut page out along dotted line.

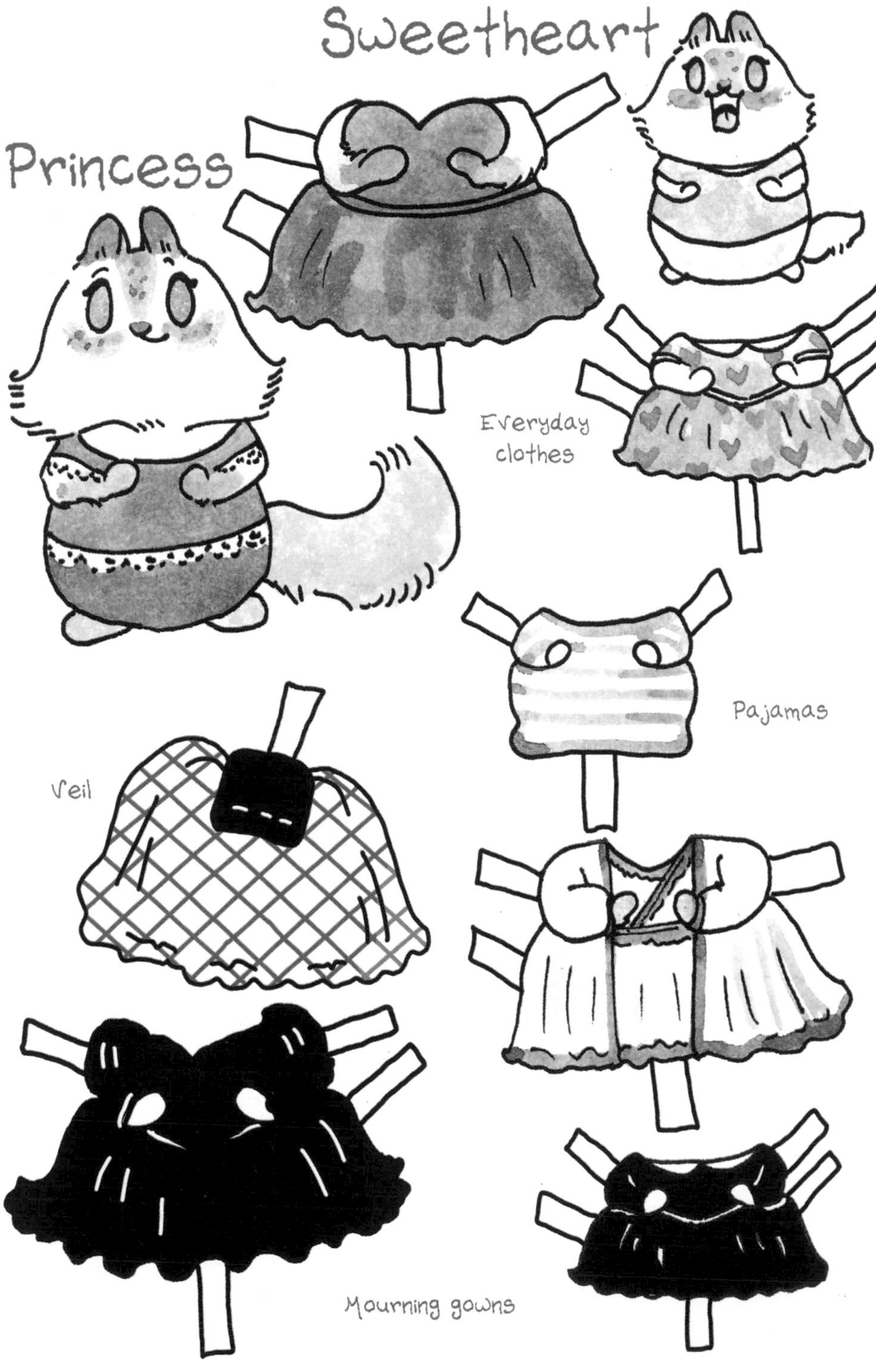
Sweetheart
Princess
Everyday clothes
Pajamas
Veil
Mourning gowns

Cut page out along dotted line.

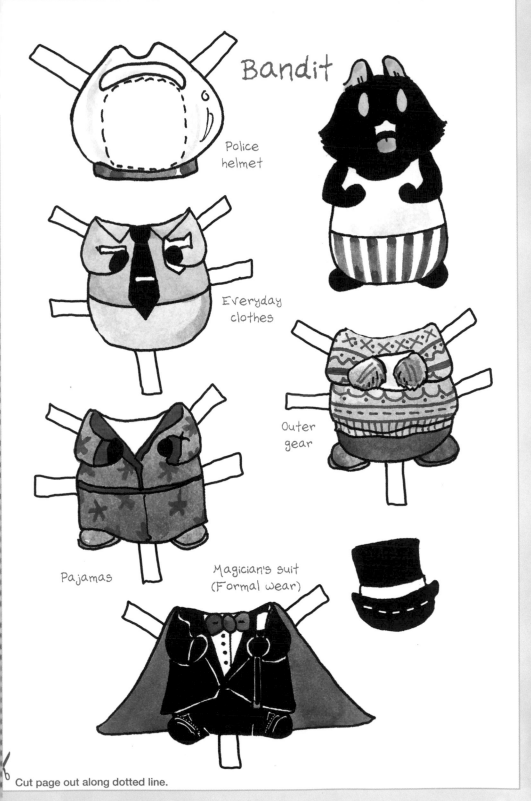

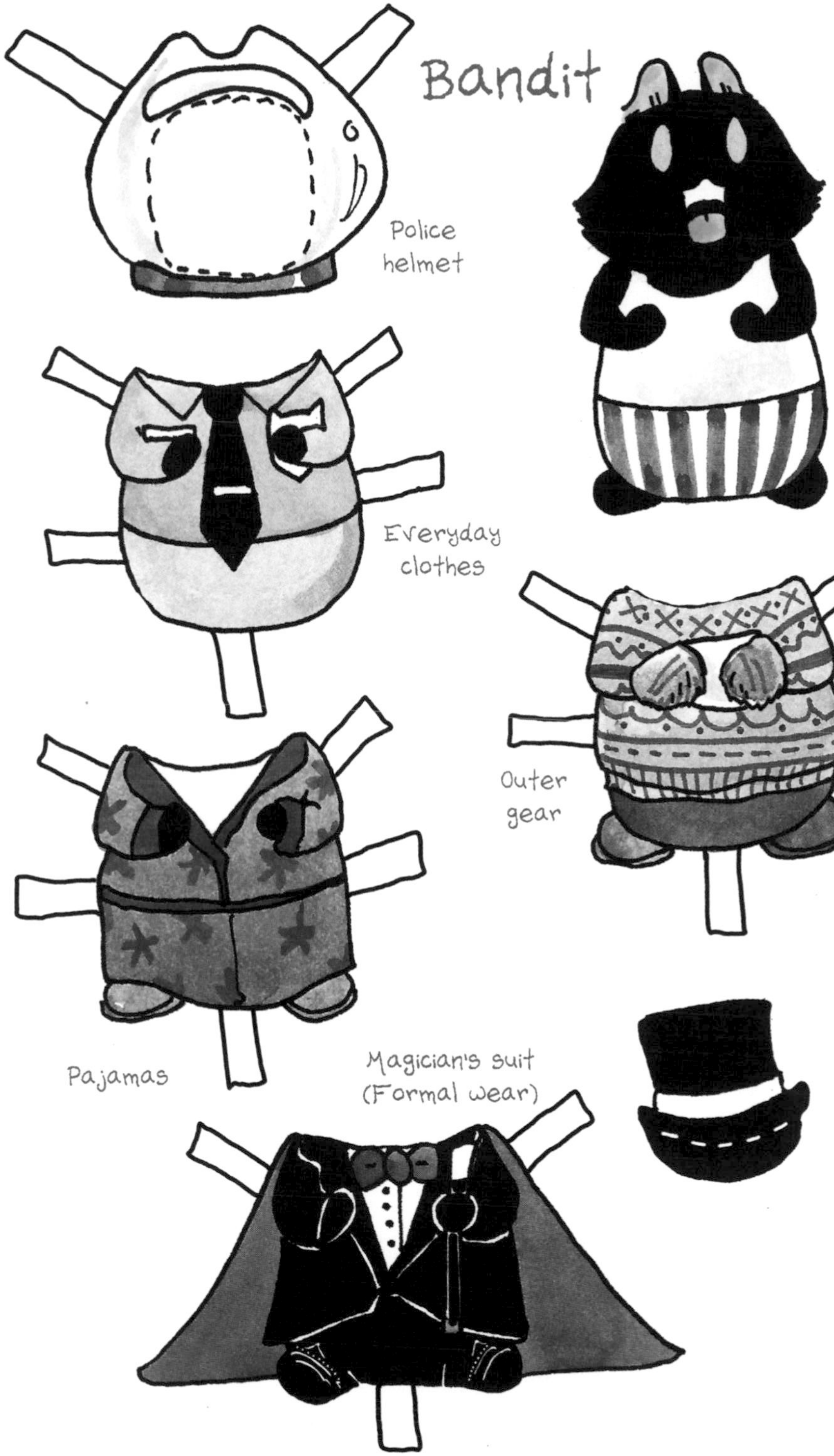
Bandit
Police helmet
Everyday clothes
Outer gear
Pajamas
Magician's suit (Formal wear)

Cut page out along dotted line.

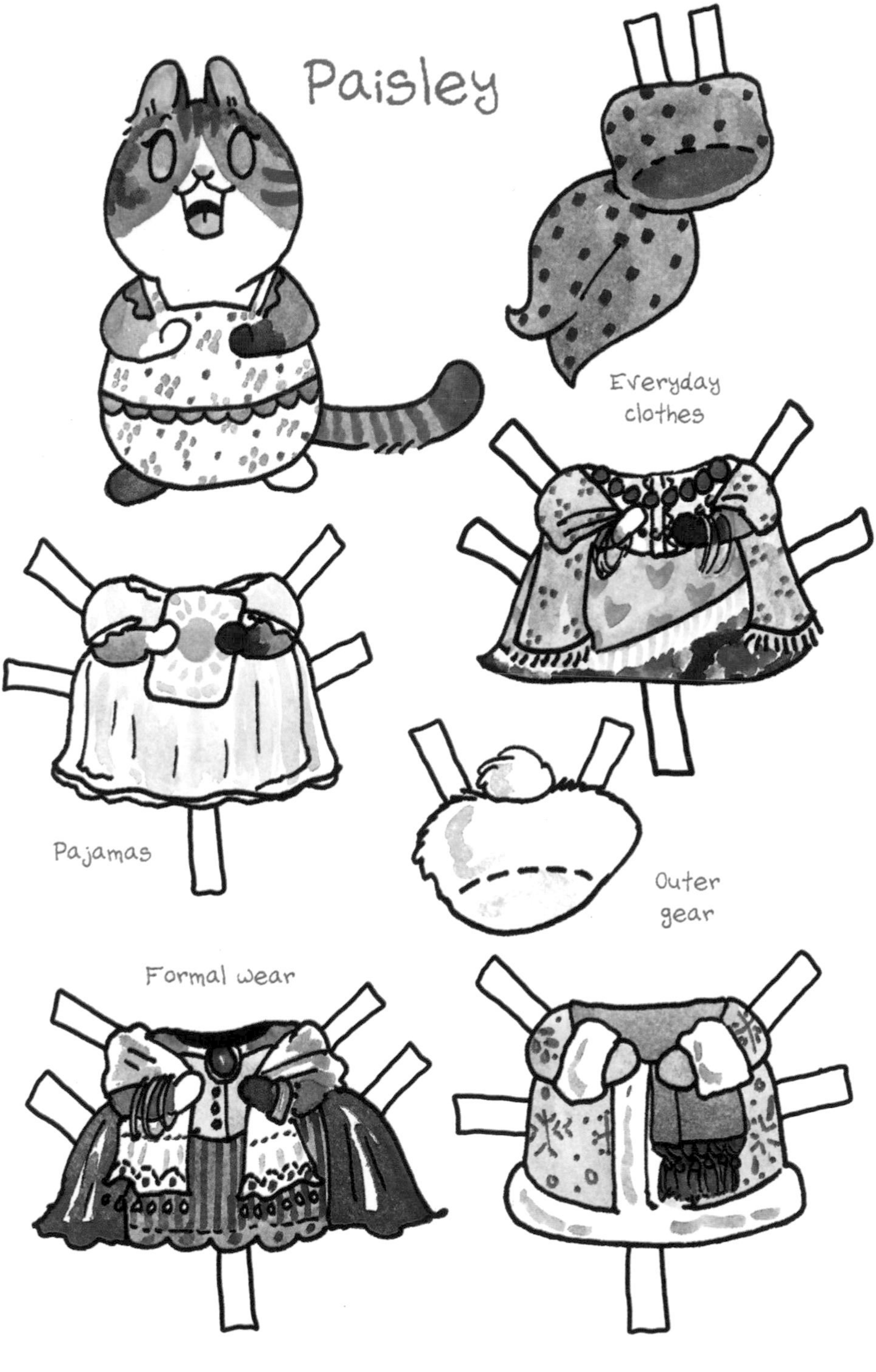
Paisley
Everyday clothes
Pajamas
Outer gear
Formal wear

Cut page out along dotted line.

Villains and Foes

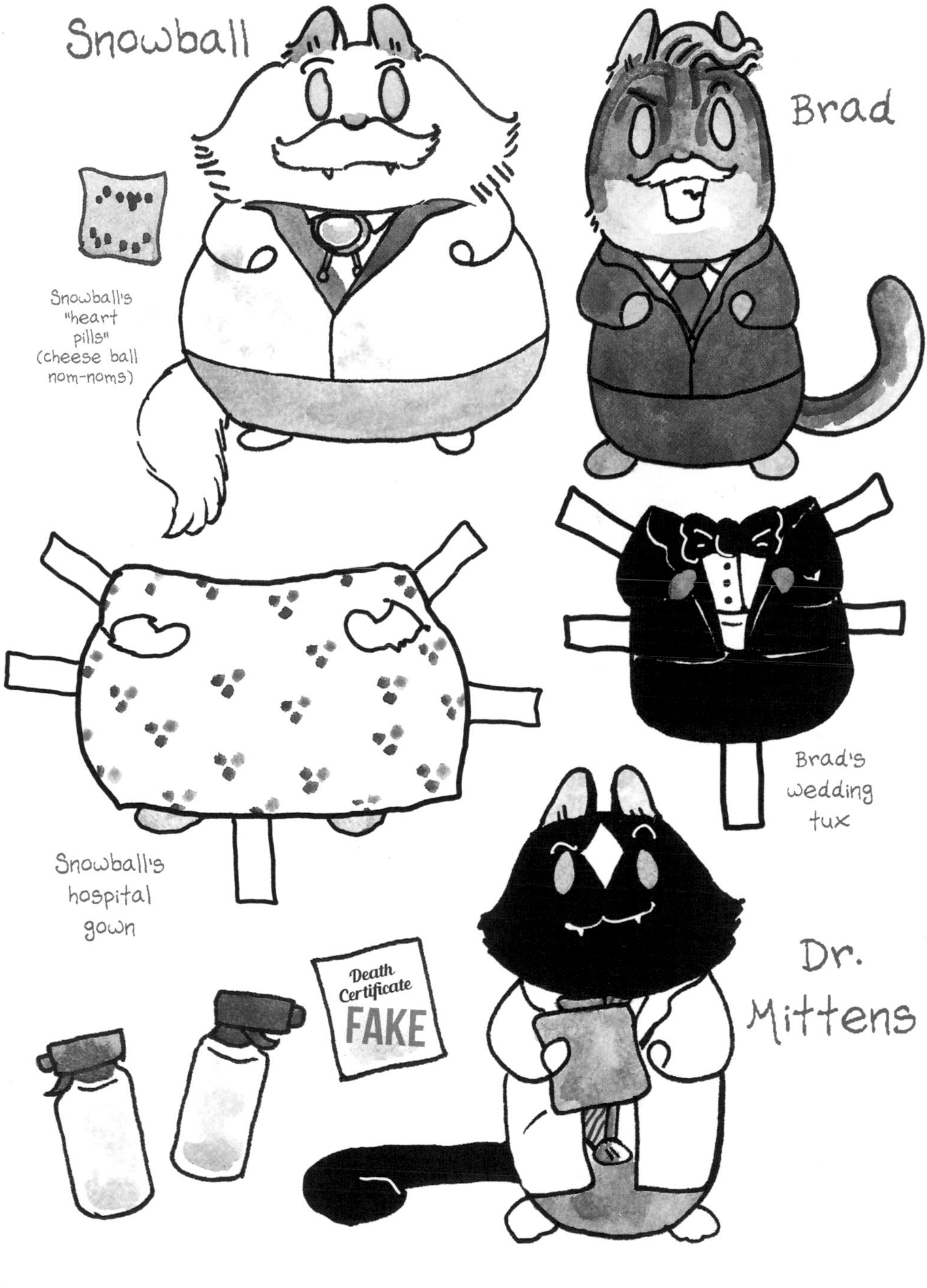
Snowball
Brad
Snowball's "heart pills" (cheese ball nom-noms)
Brad's wedding tux
Snowball's hospital gown
Dr. Mittens
Death Certificate
FAKE

Cut page out along dotted line.

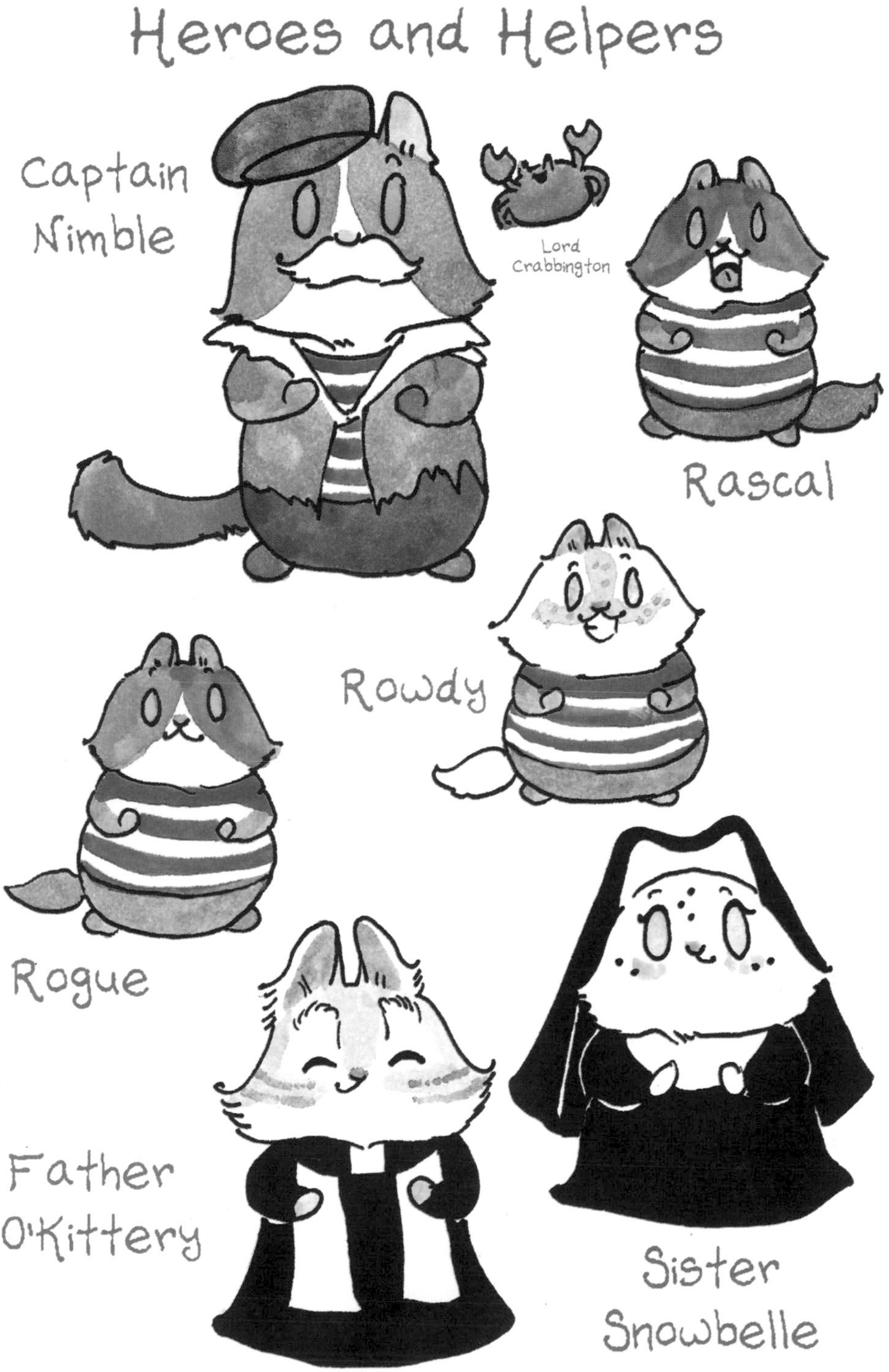
Heroes and Helpers
Captain Nimble
Lord Crabbington
Rascal
Rowdy
Rogue
Father O'Kittery
Sister Snowbelle

Cut page out along dotted line.

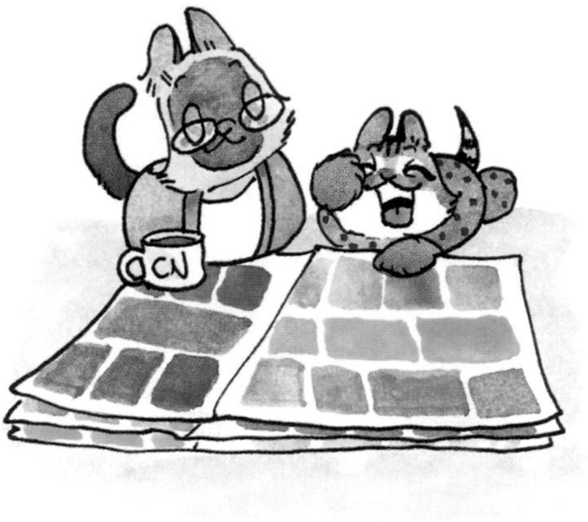
CN

Andrews McMeel Publishing
a division of Andrews McMeel Universal
1130 Walnut Street, Kansas City, Missouri 64106

www.andrewsmcmeel.com
www.breakingcatnews.com

22 23 24 25 26 SDB 10 9 8 7 6 5 4 3 2 1

ISBN: 978-1-5248-7127-7

Library of Congress Control Number: 2021947203

Published under license from Andrews McMeel Syndication
www.gocomics.com

Made by:
King Yip (Dongguan) Printing & Packaging Factory Ltd.
Address and location of production:
Daning Administrative District, Humen Town
Dongguan Guangdong, China 523930
1st Printing — 11/29/21

ATTENTION: SCHOOLS AND BUSINESSES

Andrews McMeel books are available at quantity discounts with bulk purchase for educational, business, or sales promotional use. For information, please e-mail the Andrews McMeel Publishing Special Sales Department: specialsales@amuniversal.com.

4/22

Check out these and other books from Andrews McMeel Publishing

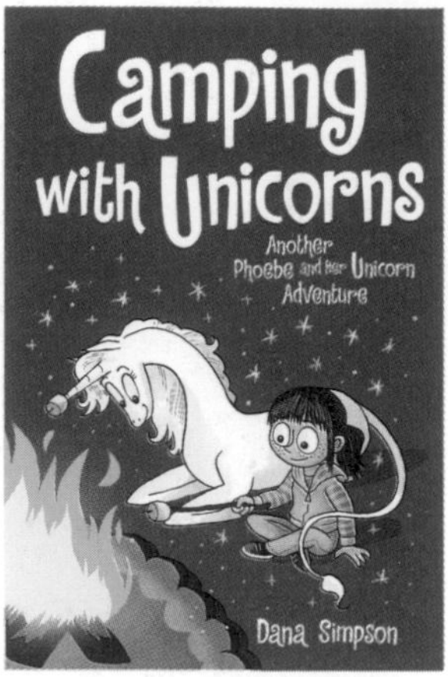
Camping with Unicorns
Another Phoebe and her Unicorn Adventure
Dana Simpson

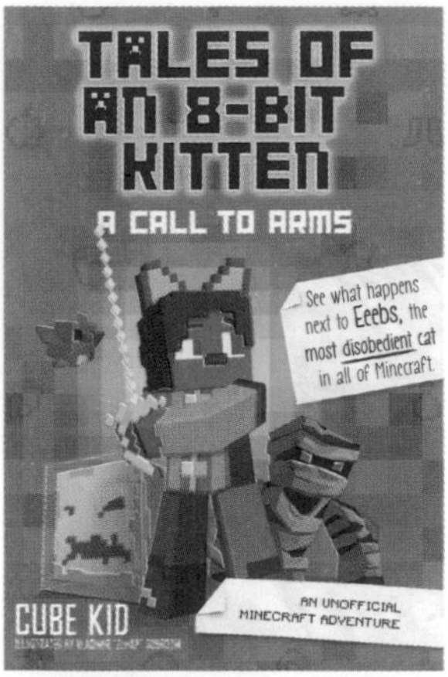
TALES OF AN 8-BIT KITTEN
A CALL TO ARMS
See what happens next to Eebs, the most disobedient cat in all of Minecraft.
CUBE KID
AN UNOFFICIAL MINECRAFT ADVENTURE

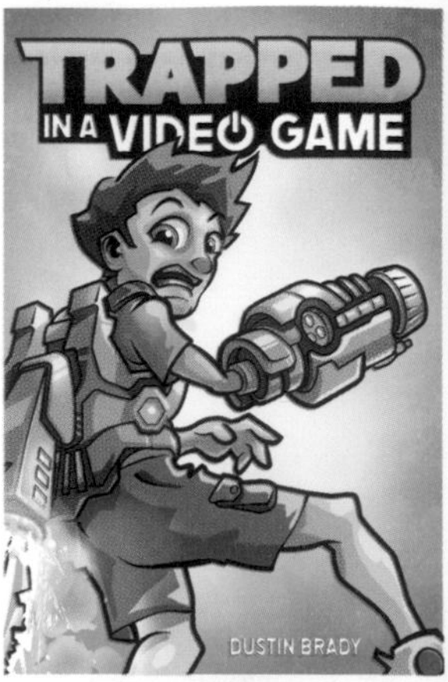
TRAPPED IN A VIDEO GAME
DUSTIN BRADY

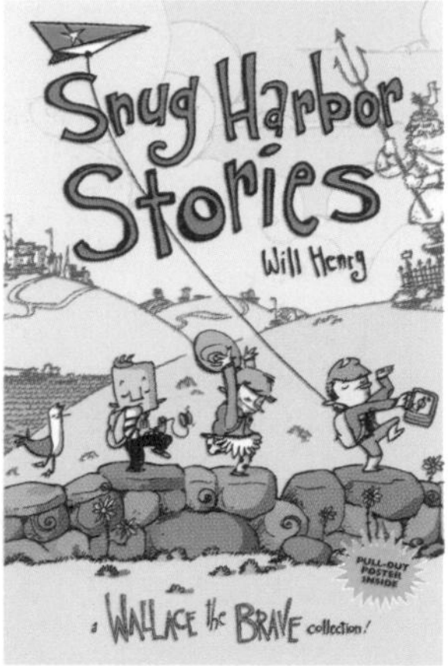
Snug Harbor Stories
Will Henry
PULL-OUT POSTER INSIDE
a WALLACE the BRAVE collection!

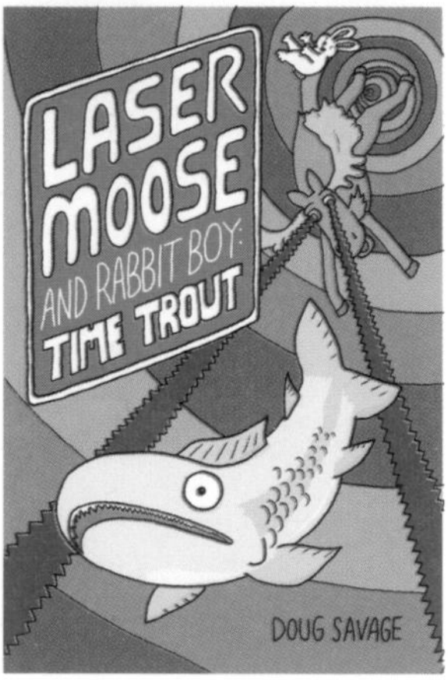
LASER MOOSE AND RABBIT BOY: TIME TROUT
DOUG SAVAGE

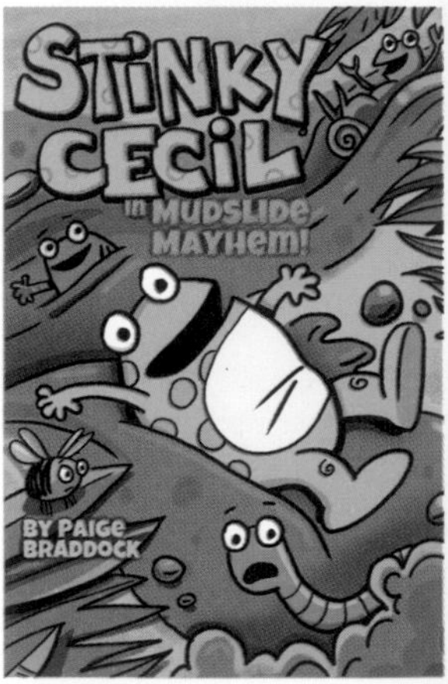
STINKY CECIL in MUDSLIDE MAYHEM!
BY PAIGE BRADDOCK

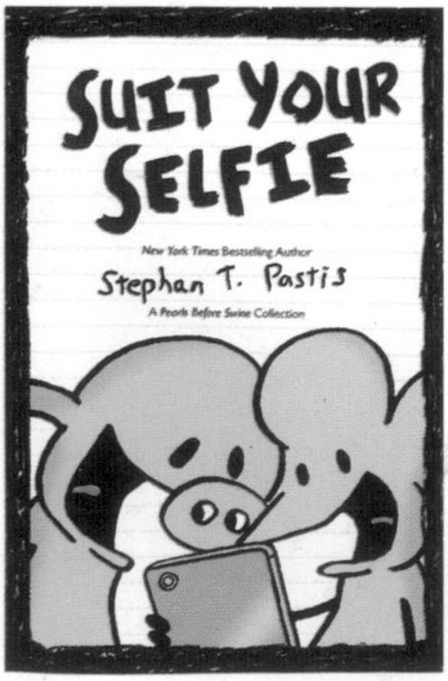
SUIT YOUR SELFIE
New York Times Bestselling Author
Stephan T. Pastis
A Pearls Before Swine Collection

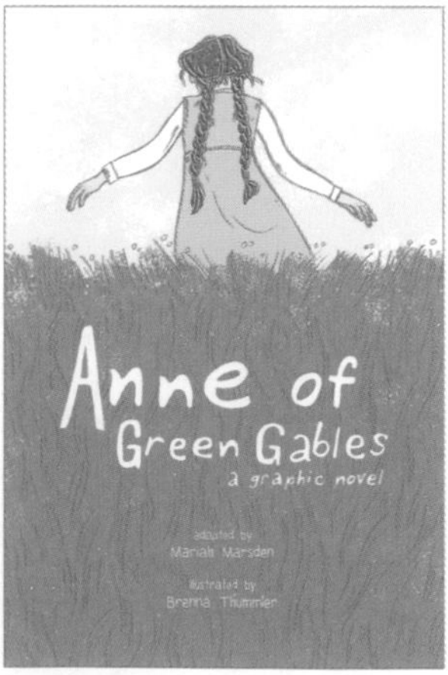
Anne of Green Gables
a graphic novel
adapted by
Mariah Marsden
illustrated by
Brenna Thummler

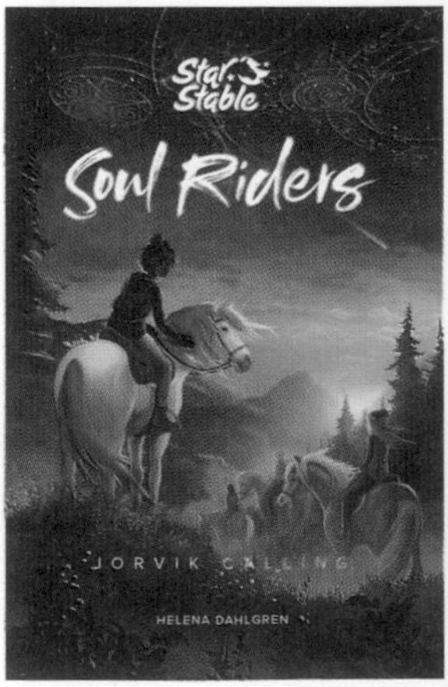
Star Stable
Soul Riders
JORVIK CALLING
HELENA DAHLGREN